The Chief of Staff

By Edgar Chae

New York, NY
2021

© Edgar Chae 2021

The moral right of the author has been asserted.

ISBN 978-1-7374985-0-6

Published by Edgar Chae 2021

About the Author

Edgar Chae is a first generation Korean American who works in corporate finance. He has worked in several Fortune 500 companies and has seen the inner workings of corporate America. His first passion is science fiction and fantasy, as he grew up reading Tolkien, and he hopes to write in those genres next. In his spare time, he loves to read, play board games, fish, and spend time with his family and friends. He spent much of his post graduate career in New York City, but now resides in the Bay area.

Acknowledgments

This is my first novel, but hopefully, not my last. I want to thank my wife for her support and thoughtful critiques. She keeps me grounded and pushes me to do better. Thank you so much for your love and support.

Dedication

To my crab, from honu.

1

Streets of Flushing

Laura was starving. Her stomach had twisted up in knots, and was now tightening, like a boa constrictor entwined around its prey, coiling ever tighter and tighter until she felt her stomach would collapse upon itself. For the umpteenth time, her stomach growled with anger, and she grimaced and tried her best to ignore it. She knew that there wouldn't be much food at home. Her parents were struggling to put food on the table for her, and she had no choice but to do what she was about to do now.

The streets were busy, as always, and teeming with people. Most of them were Chinese, although there were some Koreans, like her, as well as some Thai and Vietnamese folks. A few Caucasians, here to slum it in this part of Queens, or to get their Asian food fix and post it up on Instagram or Facebook. She dodged the people with ease, speed walking and at times running to leapfrog the slower pedestrian traffic until she got to the corner of Main street and Roosevelt. Taking a left turn, she slowed down as she navigated Roosevelt, passing by the noodle shops and dumpling houses, her mouth salivating at the aromas around her. Her stomach protested yet again.

"Hey, whattup chinky!" came a loud yell. She smiled and looked up to see Charlie grinning at her. Charlie was a tall, skinny, homeless man. His hair was streaked with gray, and his afro was thick and shaggy, definitely in much need of a haircut. He was sitting on the sidewalk, leaning back against the brick wall of a restaurant, one knee pulled up with his arm resting on it as he looked up at her.

"Aren't you supposed to be in school?" he chided her.

"School's done for the day. Anything good back there?" she asked hopefully, peering over to his right, where the alley opened up and then disappeared.

"Meh. A little bit. I found one bag that had some dumplings. You can try though. Maybe they dropped some more trash now. What grade are you in now, anyways?"

"Fourth. Where's Ansel? He back there?" she asked curiously. Charlie was never without Ansel, the other homeless guy who roamed this section of Roosevelt.

Charlie was quiet for a moment, and he frowned. "Nah. Dunno. Don't worry about Ansel. He'll turn up. Don't go to the end of the alley though. You know the Chans? They said they'd call the cops if they see you back by their door. So don't go there, promise?" He was staring intently at her. There was concern in his eyes, she could tell.

"Yeah," she replied slowly. "I'll stay to the right and just a few doors in."

"Good," he said, and he seemed relieved. "Don't go to the back."

She gave a thin smile and walked into the alley. It was still midafternoon, and the cold winter sun was still shining out on the street, but here, back in the alley, the tall roofs of either building to the sides were blocking off much of the light. The alley was shaded, but not dark. She walked confidently and hugged the right side of the alley, which was about eight feet wide. The first dumpster she came upon she knew would have hardly any food. The owners had trained the staff to empty out all the food into the garbage disposal, or to take it home. Almost every time she sifted through these trash bags, she hardly found anything edible at all. Sighing, she put down her backpack against the wall, and tried anyway. Her stomach demanded it. She carefully unzipped her jacket, and took it off, folding it neatly on top of her school bag. Though it was cold, and she felt goosebumps run up her arms even through her sweater, she knew better than to sift through the trash with her jacket. At least she could wash her sweater later

She pulled over one of the cinder blocks in the alley and used it to step up to the side of the dumpster, then undid the top of the first trash bag. As she suspected, it was just used paper plates, plastic utensils, some nasty napkins, and other useless garbage from the kitchen. The second, and third bags were the same, and she gave up and walked down to the next dumpster. She could tell that Charlie had already been through these bags, as they were opened, so she skipped the dumpster and moved on to the third one. By the time she reached the fourth dumpster, she had found a half carton of pork wontons, and a small portion of chow mein that looked edible, so she hungrily tucked into them. She didn't have any utensils, but hands make fairly good utensils she found.

She was nearing the end of the alley, but she remembered Charlie's advice and turned around, pausing only to wipe her hands on some somewhat clean napkins that she had found from dumpster two. Shivering, she hurriedly put on her jacket, and shrugged into her backpack, teeth chattering, but partially satiated by the leftovers.

At the entrance to the alley, she found Charlie, still in the same pose as before. He looked up at her and raised an eyebrow.

"So?"

"Found some wontons, and chow mein in the second to last dumpster," she said quietly. One white guy in his mid-twenties snapped his head up to stare at her as he walked by, and she felt her cheeks flush red with embarrassment.

"Alright, alright. There you go. Why don't you go see what those fools on Prince street are doing," he said roughly. "Don't be out too long though. You'll end up like me if you don't be studying and all."

"Alright, Charlie. See ya," she said, with a hint of sadness. Laura was old enough to know why certain people were homeless, but she still didn't understand why they couldn't be helped.

Walking down the street, Laura saw Mason, Randall, and Zeebats on their usual corner. They were hustling because it was Tuesday, and they hustled…well, they hustled every day she supposed.

"Come on! Easy money folks, easy money. Just find the queen, anyone can do it, and you can win some easy money. Anyone! I mean, even your grandma can find the queen," yelled Mason. The three black men were friends, but here, they were pretending that they didn't know each other as they hustled some three-card monte.

"Shit, man. There the queen right there. The middle one," Randall scoffed as he pointed to one of the three cards on the bucket.

"You sure 'bout that, brother? The middle one, you sure?"

"Yeah, man. The middle one, I said it."

With a flourish, Mason flipped the middle card and showed the queen.

""Aw, man. Cheatin' mo'fo. Aight, aight. You got it, here you go, here's your twenty," moaned Mason as he handed over the twenty. They had drawn a few passerby's now, Laura saw, and she smiled as she knew what was going to happen, and she crept closer to see.

"Aight, aight, who's next? My man. You think you can find the queen? That last dude got lucky. C'mon," said Mason as he pointed to a short white guy. He was dressed in a wool coat, and his girlfriend was tugging on his arm, whispering for them to leave, but he was undeterred.

"Ok. I'll play."

"Show me your twenty, brotha. No cash, no flash. Here's my twenty, where's yours? Pull it out. Show it to me. Aight. You ready now? Find the queen, boom, boom, boom, boom, where dat bitch yo?" Laura saw Mason move his hands deftly as he shuffled the three cards on the upturned bucket, but to her experienced eye, she knew that Mason had done some clever sleight of hand to displace the queen to a different spot.

"Right there."

"The middle one? You sure?" Mason flipped the middle card to show the ten of hearts. "BOOM! Wrong. Ay yo. Gimme that twenty. Give it to me!" The guy started to step away and pull the twenty back, but Zeebats gripped the man's other elbow tightly.

"Yo, you lost. Pay up," he said sternly.

The guy muttered something under his breath, but grudgingly handed over the bill.

"Double or nothing? C'mon man. You can do this," implored Mason, but the pair were already walking away.

"Ay, it's Laura. Whattup tiny?" said Randall with a grin. He was well over six feet tall, and had a deep, booming voice.

"I'm ok. Making a lot of money?" she asked.

"Man, we always making a lot of money. Like, all day, every day, tiny. What chu be up to?" Mason was short, maybe five foot five, but he was the ringleader of the three. He always had the quickest retort, and some trick up his sleeve. And he knew everyone on the streets. From drug dealers to undercover cops, to hookers. If they were on the streets of Flushing, Mason knew them.

"Finished school, just heading home before it gets dark."

"Aight, aight. Make sure you hit dem books, aight? Don't be flunking out 'yo school and then be hustlin' out here, ya feel me?"

"Aight. I feel you," she replied, as the three men roared into hoots of laughter.

"What! You see that! She a street thug, yo!" yelled Zeebats as he doubled over, cracking up.

"Catch you later," she yelled over her shoulder as she walked away. It was getting dark now, and her parents would be worried.

The apartment they lived in was several blocks away. It was an old, run down walk up, and damned if they didn't live at the top of the five floors. It was a two-bedroom flat, a thousand square feet, but three families lived there, eleven people altogether. The paint was peeling and cracking in the hallways, and the lightbulbs were out on every other floor, to conserve electricity, she was told, but it was home. Trudging up the five flights, she used her key and walked into the living room. The four other kids, ages three to ten, were huddled on the floor, watching cartoons. She didn't know them too well, despite their close living situation, as her parents limited their contact with the other folks in the apartment and instructed her to do so as well.

"Umma! I'm home!" she yelled, as she shrugged off her backpack and took off her shoes. She walked over to the left bedroom, where the door was closed, but paused just outside and leaned in. She could hear her parents in there, and they were arguing, as usual, in Korean.

"You can't even find any job to put food on the table! You're worthless. How can you let us live like this, huh? We're like dogs here, worse than dogs. And we have no money, no food, and nothing to get us out of here, huh? What do you have to say?" her mother screamed.

"Shut up! You're the worthless one! You don't have a job either and you can't even speak English! So what? What are you going to do to contribute, huh? I can't find any work in this fucking city, huh? So, fuck you!"

Laura heard them struggle as they grappled with one another, and then heard her mother sobbing and screaming incoherently.

"What! Huh? What can I do, huh? Nothing! There's nothing I can do! This is hopeless!" raged her father, and then the door opened suddenly, and she was staring up at him, his face contorted in anger. He was a young man, only twenty-seven, but he looked as if he had aged a decade overnight. His black hair was tussled, and unkempt, and dark circles were marking a permanent residence underneath his eyes. His eyes were red and bloodshot, and he slapped her hard across her cheek, causing her to stumble and fall to the floor. He often beat her, and her mother, and the hit didn't come as a surprise.

"You! You're worthless too, just like your fucking whore of a mother! You'll never amount to anything!" He walked to the couch and grabbed his coat from the top, pulling it on.

"Appa! Don't go!" she wailed. Despite the fact that he hurt her repeatedly, she still felt a need to try and please him, and a yearning for his love. Tears were welling up in her eyes and she crawled over to her father. He snarled at her and as she turned her face up to beg him to stay, he slapped her again, sending her sprawling to the ground. The other kids were watching her, mouths agape and she felt her face flush red with shame and embarrassment for the second time that day. Without saying another word, her father walked out the door, slamming it shut. She never saw him again.

2

The Interview

Thirty years later...

Laura was nervous, and she smoothed the hem of her black skirt yet again. She opened her portfolio and read through her resume for the millionth time. She could recite it by heart and had good examples and stories for each of the bullet points listed. On the left side, she had carefully written several thoughtful and probing questions to ask for the end of the interview, and she knew that they showed that she had done her homework.

"I'm going to kill this interview," she muttered to herself. *"I'm ready and qualified for this role."*

"Laura? Stacy is ready for you. Just go right in," said Geoff, the executive admin. He was tall and handsome, and dressed sharply in a white shirt and blue blazer.

"Thank you," she said, and inhaled deeply as she stood up and gathered her courage once more. *"You got this,"* she muttered. She pushed the wooden door open and walked into Stacy's office. The office was huge, maybe thirty feet square, or three times the size of a normal office. There was a black leather couch and single leather seat to the left, with a small glass coffee table. Fortune, National Geographic, and the Economist magazines were neatly fanned out on top, and a large flat screen TV was mounted above the leather sofa with CNBC news playing on mute. To the right was a small, round glass table, with four chairs around it, and straight ahead was Stacy's brown, oak desk, immaculately clean and barren except for her monitor, keyboard, and mouse. The back of the office was floor to ceiling windows that showed a sweeping view of Central Park. It was breathtaking, with the green leaves and grass, neatly cut into the rectangle bordered by cold concrete, steel and glass buildings. It was mother Nature, caged for man's pleasure.

"Laura, nice to meet you, have a seat," said Stacy without a hint of a smile. Stacy Atkins was the Chief of Staff to the Chief Executive Officer, John Lancet, at Abernathy Consumer Products. The company was close to a hundred years old, and sold everything from dish washing liquid, to detergents, diapers, and cereal. Almost anything you could think to find in a CVS or a Walmart, Abernathy most likely made a version of it. As Chief of Staff, Stacy was probably one of the fifteen most powerful people within the company. Laura knew that working in this team under Stacy would get her valuable exposure to the CEO and other Business Unit heads and could springboard her to a better role down the road as a result. She learned that when it came to the most senior positions, it wasn't so much what you knew, it was *who* you knew. Stacy didn't get up to shake her hand or even look up at her. She was focused on Laura's resume, which was on her desk with some pencil notes scribbled in the margins. She was older, maybe in her early to mid-fifties, with a few gray strands showing through her dark brown hair. The woman's hair was tied back into a severe bun, and her brown eyes were flickering quickly down her resume. She was dressed in an ivory white shirt, with ruffles at the wrists, and wore an expensive looking stainless-steel watch to match with her diamond earrings. Laura wouldn't exactly call her beautiful, per se, but handsome and proud would be how she would describe her.

"Thank you for applying for this role. We only have thirty minutes, so let's jump right into it. Do you know what this role entails?" Stacy asked, as she finally looked up and made eye contact with her.

"Yes. You are looking for an assistant Chief of Staff. Someone to help you organize and run your staff meetings, prepare for board meetings, handle any ad hocs from the Executive Leadership Team or CEO, and track down and keep tabs on projects and requests that are in progress," she said calmly.

"Yes, that's right. That's most of it. But there are other things as well, things that will be less glamorous. If I need you to run out to grab something from a store, or call to make a reservation, or pick up packages from the other side of the city, are you willing and able to do that?" Stacy raised an eyebrow as she looked intensely at her.

Laura was a little surprised to hear those tasks but hid it well. "Yes, whatever you require, I'm here to make your job easier. That, and to learn what it is that keeps the CEO and leadership team up at night."

Stacy seemed unconvinced. "Ok. And this job is twenty-four seven. I will almost certainly ring you on Friday night, Saturday morning, or even Sunday at one a.m. Any time of day, all year, even on Christmas. Can you handle that?"

Laura didn't bat an eyelash. "Yes. That won't be a problem."

Stacy's expression was blank and unreadable, but after a few uncomfortable seconds, she peered down at the resume in front of her.

"Senior Director of Finance. Later moved into Strategy. You've done stints across the company in marketing and finance, and even managed a brand. I like your breadth of experience and knowledge."

Laura gave a small smile, which was quickly dashed.

"But honestly, I've interviewed ten candidates, and everyone can say the same. Great breadth of experience in the company, with a strong knowledge base of how we operate. That's table stakes. Tell me something. I've handpicked the candidates, and most of them are Harvard undergrads or Harvard or Penn MBAs. You went to the University of Maryland. Four point oh GPA, perfect score on your SAT's, that part is good. But listen, I only took this interview as a favor to your manager, whom I know quite well. Tell me. Why should I hire you over everyone else? They have a much stronger pedigree."

Laura blinked once but recovered quickly. She wasn't expecting a question like this. *"What the hell?"* was what she was thinking, but instead, she said, "Well, to be fair, I did get into Harvard, but I opted for a state school. The reason you should hire me-"

"Wait. Why did you decide on Maryland over Harvard?"

"Maryland gave me a full ride, and at the time, my mom couldn't afford the tuition for a private college."

"Ah, ok. Continue."

"The reason you should hire me, is because I'm hungrier than anyone else you'll meet. I soak up knowledge like a sponge, and no one can outwork me. All of my experiences in my past roles-" but she was cut off again.

"No, I know what you've done in this company. I've spoken to all of your previous managers, so I understand what you bring to the table. I need to understand what motivates you and why you want this role. Where do you see yourself after this role?" Stacy was impatient and glanced at her watch.

"*This isn't going well,*" she thought. "Honestly, after this role, I want to be in your position, as the Chief of Staff to the CEO."

Stacy paused, and put her index finger to the side of her nose, slightly covering her mouth with the rest of her fingers and palm as she studied her. She felt naked and bare, as if she were on a slide underneath a microscope being studied for cancerous cells. Seconds went by, and the silence grew uncomfortable.

"And after that role, then what?"

Laura answered honestly. It didn't seem like she would get the role anyway, so might as well lay it out there.

"I want to be CEO someday. If not here, then somewhere else. And I need to know how CEOs operate, and what they think about, and how they got to where they are."

"Why? Why CEO? Why not Chief Operating Officer or Chief Strategy Officer?"

Laura squirmed slightly in her chair, and said out loud her ambitions, voiced aloud for the first time in anyone's hearing.

"Because I want to be in control and call the shots. I want the power to decide."

For the first time, Stacy gave a small smile as she placed her hands in her lap.

"Power. You're ambitious. You said you chose Maryland because of the full ride. You didn't want to take out loans and go to Harvard? Most folks would rather go that route." Stacy picked up her pencil and made a note on the resume.

"I would have loved to have gone there, sure. But my mom, well, we didn't really have a lot of money growing up. I knew that I needed to finish my education with as little debt as possible."

Stacy nodded her head and put her pencil down. She rested her elbows on the sides of her chair and steepled her hands in front of her.

"And there we have it. You are poor, smart, and hungry. And ambitious and seeking power. I was much like you, once." She paused, and looked over Laura's shoulder, staring off into the past. Her eyes narrowed, was it anger, determination, or regret? She couldn't tell. But Stacy quickly snapped back to the present and turned to lock eyes with her once again.

"I'm going to offer you the role of Assistant Chief of Staff. Do you accept?"

Laura was shocked and blinked her eyes several times. *"Who offers a job after a few minutes of an interview? She doesn't know me!"* was the thought running through her mind, and she was so dumbfounded, that she had nothing to say.

"Perhaps I made a mistake," Stacy started, but now it was Laura's turn to interrupt her.

"No! I accept. I was just surprised by the offer is all," she said, and she was impressed with herself, that her hands weren't shaking, and her voice was somewhat smooth.

Stacy pursed her lips in a tight line and studied her for several seconds before she spoke.

"Lesson one. You need to be decisive. A lot of this role is

working in ambiguity. You won't have all of the facts or all of the analysis to make your decision. But you have to learn that eighty percent of the information or analysis is enough to make the decision, otherwise you get stuck in paralysis by analysis, yes? Lesson two. Even when you are surprised, you must not show it. It shows that you were caught off guard. It shows that you were unprepared, and as Chief of Staff, you are *never* unprepared. Understand?"

Laura smoothed the hem of her skirt and nodded her head. "Yes, I understand."

"Good. Don't make me regret this, because I will not hesitate to fire you and pick my second choice, even if you last a week, a month, or three months. I don't care about the optics of such a move. Ok. Have a pen? Good. Then take some notes because your job starts today."

As Laura raised an eyebrow and took out her pen from her portfolio, Stacy opened her desk drawer and pulled out a small black notebook. She opened it to the middle of the notebook and read through some notes, then looked up at her and gave her a small smile.

"First of all, congratulations on your new role. Your title will be Vice President, and I'm going to be giving you a significant raise. But we'll talk compensation tomorrow. Second of all, I need you to take care of these items urgently. As in, today. You need to write your own intro, bio, and welcome aboard message, as if from me. I am swamped, and you know how those intro emails work. Send it to Geoff and he'll blast it out to the company tomorrow. Next, I'm going to be giving you access to my expense account. I have three million dollars set aside for me this year, as discretionary funds to see that everything I need to get done, gets done. Geoff is going to give you a credit card linked to that account, and you'll run all your business expenses through it, and he'll do the expense report. Needless to say, keep track of all your receipts. Now listen to this part carefully. That expense account is mine. I can do whatever I want with it, no questions asked. I can pay people to keep quiet. I can settle lawsuits off the books. If a board member is having an affair and the mistress is about to blow the whistle, I can pay that woman to shut up and get the hell out of town. Understand? Ninety nine percent of the problems we face, we can solve with our brains and ingenuity, or with money, and that money is to fix problems. You should handle it the same way, carte blanche. Any questions on this?" Stacy was leaning forward slightly, with a calm and blank expression on her face, but staring very intently at Laura's face, looking for…who knows what she was looking for, but something.

Laura was taking notes and was slow and measured with her response. "So, carte blanche? But if you handle certain…things… off the books, do I still get a receipt for that and have Geoff expense it?" She was confused and shocked at the same time. *"Bribes? Hush money? What the hell?"*

Stacy shook her head. "No. Any normal business expenses, get receipts for, give those to Geoff. Any…extraordinary expenses, shall we say? Those, you need to get someone to write you a fake receipt, or tell me, and I'll have Geoff generate an invoice from a vendor that we use. And I know what you're thinking. Just trust me on this. We won't be audited, and yes, this is a little below board, but the things we handle and the problems we fix, sometimes it requires getting our hands dirty. Still with me?"

This was an opportunity of a lifetime, and she was not going to blindly throw it away, despite her initial misgivings. Stacy Atkins was a rising star and had the CEO's ear. She needed to learn the ropes here, and she had higher ambitions than just Chief of Staff anyways.

"Yes, of course," she said as she managed to muster up a small smile. She hoped that it passed for confidence. "Stacy. You said that ninety nine percent of our problems we can fix with our brains and money. What about the other one percent?"

"Ah, yes. You were paying attention, I see. The other one percent, Laura, is when we face people who don't need money. They can't be influenced by what most folks would be persuaded by. Tickets to shows, exclusive events, money, sex, et cetera. These people are powerful, with means, and large egos. That's when we have to find alternate ways to influence them, be it power plays, political favors, or even promises of favors to be returned later. An, I.O.U., if you will. They are the hardest to move, the most difficult to deal with, but in the end, the most powerful piece on the chess board." Without waiting for Laura's nod of assent, Stacy continued. As she neatly folded her resume in half and put it away in her desk drawer, she quickly took a peek at her outlook calendar, typed up a quick email, and then gave Laura her last set of instructions.

"Ok. Next, I need you to get me a table for two, tomorrow night at Per Se, eight p.m. Don't mess this one up, it's especially important. As you leave, Geoff will give you my cell phone number, and the credit card for the expense account. Any questions?"

Laura didn't know whether the woman was joking, or insane. Per Se was a three-star Michelin restaurant, and eight p.m. was the most popular dinner time in New York City. To get a table for the next night would be impossible, even if it was only a Tuesday night. There was a short silence as Laura stared at Stacy, waiting for the punch line or joke. There was only silence, so she cleared her throat and did what any person in her shoes would do. *"Fake it til you make it,"* she thought.

"I'm on it. Um, do you need my personal information, cell phone, address…?"

"Already have it. Two steps ahead of you, but in about six months, I need you to be two steps ahead of *me*. Yes? Ok, out you go. I have a meeting with John at five." John Lancet was the CEO, and she hoped she would get to meet him soon.

Laura smoothly stood up and walked out towards the door, then closed it softly behind her. She turned to see a smiling Geoff seated at his cubicle.

"Congratulations, Laura! You're going to love working for Stacy. She is tough, but fair. Here is a welcome aboard folder for you. Inside, you will find the particulars of your compensation package, as well as specifics of how Stacy likes to operate. I've also noted down her personal information, including her cell phone and address. Lastly, there is an American Express account number there. I won't have your actual credit card until tomorrow afternoon, but you can use the details there to make any purchases that you may need for today. I also noted my office and cell phone number, in case you need to reach me at any time. I'm sure Stacy has told you, but this job is twenty-four seven, but don't let that scare you."

"Um, ok. Thank you! She's very smart, isn't she? Did you already have this material ready for me the whole time?!" she asked with curiosity. *"How the hell was this folder ready to go for me? It has my name neatly typed on the front for God's sakes!"*

Geoff beamed a grin and gave her a chuckle. "Oh, I can't give away all our secrets on the first day, Laura! Call me if you need anything. I'll have your new business cards ready for you in the morning." And with that, he turned away to answer the phone.

"*Fucking crazy,*" she muttered. "*I'm in la-la land now.*" But she didn't have time to waste, as it was almost five p.m., and she needed to get a reservation ASAP. She navigated the hallways and took the elevator down to her floor and double timed it to her office. Closing the door, she opened Chrome and did a search for Per Se's phone number. Taking a deep breath, she dialed it.

"Good evening, you've reached Per Se, this is Bailey speaking, how can I help you?" said a pleasant woman who was far too cheerful.

"Yes, hi. I need to make a reservation for two."

"Great, I can assist you with that. What day and time were you looking?"

"Tomorrow evening, eight p.m.?" She held her breath.

"Oh. I'm so sorry. We are completely booked up for the next several weeks. The earliest table I have is, April twentieth. Would that work?"

"No, unfortunately not. Are there any tables at all for tomorrow at eight? Any four tops available, or larger? I could book a larger table if that is available."

"No, I'm sorry. We are completely booked up tomorrow."

Laura paused. "This is impossible," she muttered.

"Excuse me?"

"Oh, nothing. Listen, is your manager available to speak with me?"

"He's making some rounds in the dining room now, but he should be back in ten minutes. Shall I have him call you?"

"Yes. Wait, no. I'll come to the restaurant directly, thank you."

"My pleasure. Have a good evening!"

Laura shook her head and mumbled to herself. "*There is no way*

I can get a table for tomorrow." But she couldn't accept failure this easily. Not on her first assignment. Scooping up her welcome aboard folder, her jacket, and her purse, she walked briskly down the carpeted hallway towards the elevator, nodding politely to some of her colleagues as she passed them. She was lost in thought as she exited the building and hailed a cab. She brainstormed and tried to think of how her conversation would go, but nothing came to mind. In a blink, she was standing in front of the Time Warner Center at Columbus circle, and she still had no solid plan, other than to beg.

Per Se was inside the shopping mall at the Time Warner center, and it was crowded as it always was, as she moved through the throng of businessmen and women, tourists, and moms with their kids. Finally, she made it to the third floor and found herself at the entrance to the elegant Thomas Keller restaurant. She had never been here before, but she knew she was out of her element. Whereas growing up, she had been lucky to once in a while eat at one of the dumpling houses in Flushing, this place was altogether different. White linen tablecloths adorned every table, and every man was required to wear a jacket, she could see. There was a smooth and synchronized interplay of the wait staff, as they filled water or wine glasses, cleared plates, and set down new utensils after each plate. She had been on nice dinners with her company, but this was another level.

"May I help you?" asked a tall, beautiful blonde-haired woman. She was in her late twenties and was dressed sharply in a black business suit and pants.

"Yes. Uh, I need to speak to the manager. I think he was making the rounds in the dining room? Is he free now?" Her tone sounded steady to her ears, but inside, she was nervous and antsy.

Stacy had said this was really important, and she didn't want to mess up her first assignment, no matter how trivial it seemed.

"He is. Is there something that perhaps I could help you with?"

"No. I need to speak with the manager, and it's very important."

"Of course. One moment please." The woman gave her a friendly smile and turned to address the man next to her. He listened for a moment and then nodded his head, turning to stride off in the direction of the kitchen.

She stood off to the side and admired the plates as they came out of the kitchen. Each dish was plated beautifully, artfully, and her stomach growled with envy at the smells. Eventually, a short man in a blue suit and matching blue tie came out and held out his hand. He was balding, and wore glasses that were thick and black, starkly contrasting with the paleness of his face. He was in his mid-forties, if she had to guess, and his grip was firm and strong.

"Hello, my name is Bernard, and I am the manager," he said with a slight smile.

"Hi, my name is Laura. Thank you for meeting with me. Could we speak in private?"

If the request bothered the manager, he didn't show it. Instead, he merely nodded his head once and gave another one of those small smiles. "Not a problem. Please follow me to my office." He turned and led her down a hallway past the kitchen, and opened a door into his office, which was small, but neat and orderly. There was just a small oaken desk, and a brown leather couch.

"Please, have a seat," he said as he walked around his desk and sat down. "How may I help you?" She sat down on the sofa and set her purse and folder off to her side.

"Yes, uh. I was hoping, well I tried calling before for a table for two, for tomorrow, but, uh, the hostess said the restaurant was

21

booked up? I wanted to see, just to check with you that is, if there was any way another table could be made?" She fumbled her words and cursed herself for sounding so flummoxed. She had hoped to sound calm and measured, but she knew that she sounded desperate, crazy, and yammering too fast, like a hummingbird on steroids.

"Ah, I see. Let me see our booking status." The short man opened up his laptop, and furiously typed onto the keyboard. He tilted his head back and peered down his nose at the screen, making a few noncommittal noises every so often. *Hmm. Ummm. Mmmm.*

He pursed his lips into a tight line and shook his head mournfully. "I'm so sorry, Laura. We are completely booked, and I just don't see a way that we can fit one more table. May I ask? Who is this reservation for?" He raised an eyebrow and peered at her.

"Oh! Uh, the reservation is for my boss, Stacy Atkins. We are at Abernathy-" but she was cut off before she could finish.

"Ahh, yes! Ms. Atkins of Abernathy Consumer Products. Wonderful, wonderful woman. She is a most valued and excellent client and friend of the restaurant," said Bernard, as his eyes lit up and a broad smile infused his face.

"You know her?" she said with surprise. "That is great! She would be delighted if you could find some way to squeeze her in," she started, but already, Bernard was shaking his head.

"I'm really, really sorry, Laura. Ms. Atkins *is* a dear friend of the restaurant. But there simply is nothing we can do. We are booked up." The man had the beginnings of a smile, or was it a smirk? He knew something but wasn't saying it. "There's nothing we can do...with the situation as it *stands.*" He emphasized the last word and there it was again, the smirk that he was trying to hide. He smoothed the desktop with one of his hands and then turned his hand towards him to inspect his nails. He was... waiting for something.

"Bernard, um, is there nothing you can do? I mentioned to the hostess, if there is a four top or larger table, I'll take it. Do you have a private dining room, or is there a chef's table you could set up in the kitchen? I mean, something, anything, there has to be a solution, right?" Her words were fast and frantic, not the way she wanted to sound. Small beads of sweat were starting to form on her forehead. Bernard looked up from his scrutiny of his nails and tilted his head to one side, as if considering her ideas.

"Well, you know. There is something, perhaps, that we could arrange. You know, anything can be had...for a price." Again, the beginnings of a smirk on the corners of his mouth appeared. *"What the...he's not suggesting, like a sexual favor? What?!"* was the first thought that jumped into her head.

She smoothed the hem of her skirt and realized that her palms were sweaty as well. There was no hiding it now, as her forehead was glistening with perspiration. She pulled a tissue from her purse and dabbed her forehead quickly. "I'm sorry," she managed to stammer. "I'm not following you. What price are you referring to?"

Bernard raised an eyebrow and cleared his throat. Apparently, Laura's thick headedness and asking him to repeat himself made him uncomfortable. "Well, you know, simply that, if the price is right, certain things can be had..." he trailed off, expecting Laura to finally understand. Instead, she just blankly stared at him, uncomprehending. She didn't know whether to stand up and walk out or tell him off and then walk out. Or plead ignorance and beg for a table out of the kindness of his heart if he had one. *"I'm not going to degrade myself like that, just for a table, even if Stacy will be disappointed,"* she thought angrily. But before she could decide on her next course of action, Bernard made the decision for her.

He sighed, and then nodded to the purse and folder by her side. "Don't you have an expense account? I'm sure you can expense…say, ten thousand dollars? Then I can get you the table you seek."

"Oh," said Laura softly. He didn't want a sexual favor. He wanted money. Her mind was racing a thousand miles a minute, and she was stunned inside. The fact that the tenor of the conversation shifted in her mind from sex over to money made it somewhat of a relief, but still shocking, nonetheless. He was asking for a bribe! *"What. The. Hell."* She wanted to get up and leave, but instead, she slowly reached for the folder to her right, and opened it up, her body numb with disbelief of the whole situation.

Bernard sighed a sigh of relief, and scribbled on a notepad, sliding it over. "Just wire the money to this account, and once the funds are confirmed, I'll have the hostess call you to confirm the reservation. Please write your phone number on the notepad." There was no smirk, no grin of 'victory' from the man. He seemed ready to be done with this whole business as well. She paused, considering her action at the moment, that she was bribing someone using company funds, and after a moment's hesitation, finally copied the account number in her folder, and then wrote her cell number on his notepad. She felt unclean and wanted to vomit.

"So very generous of you," he murmured as he pulled the notepad back. But the words hardly registered with her, as she sat quietly, her head spinning at what had just transpired.

The next morning, Laura had her first meeting with Stacy as her Assistant Chief of Staff. Laura was dressed in a sharp navy-blue blazer, white shirt underneath, and a matching blue skirt that went to just above her knees. She wore black heels, though not too tall, and had her hair pulled back into a ponytail. Stacy was sitting across from her, reading through an email on her monitor, and she had her small notebook open and was jotting some notes in it. As Laura waited, she peered over Stacy's shoulder to look at the gray Manhattan sky. *"Did it say it was going to rain today?"* she wondered. She hadn't brought her umbrella, which was annoying. She envied the view from this office and hoped to one day be sitting where Stacy was. It was just past eight a.m., and the first thing they had discussed was her new compensation package. It was quite generous, and more than she had ever thought she would make, when she was just a poor, starving daughter of immigrants in the streets of Flushing.

"Sorry about that. Just had to tackle this urgent response from John. So. Were you able to secure a table for tonight?" Stacy titled her head and looked at her askance as if to say, *"I'm doubtful, but let's see what you got."*

She nodded her head. "Yes, table for two, eight p.m."

Stacy nodded in reply. "Any difficulties? That's not an easy reservation to get."

"They were fully booked up. But I used the expense account…" Laura trailed off and waited to see what kind of reaction she would get.

"Good. How much did it cost you?" Stacy asked with just the hint of a smile.

"Ten thousand."

"Ok. When you head out, have Geoff make an invoice for Regency Services in that amount. For consulting services. Do you have dinner plans tonight?"

She shook her head no. "Not tonight, no. Is there anything you need?"

"Nope. But that table is for you. A congratulatory dinner if you will. Expense the meal and take whomever you want as your guest. You passed the first test."

"Oh! Uh, wow, thank you," she said with surprise. She blinked several times and felt a mix of joy, surprise, and confusion. *"She was testing me? What the…"*

"Alright. Got your notebook ready? We have a busy day."

"Wait. Did you tell Bernard that I was coming and set that all up?" she blurted out before she could stop herself. She knew that her face was an open book right now, and Stacy was reading it easily. Shock and disbelief. Stacy gave a small, coy smile, and Laura knew the answer then. She knew the truth.

3

Per Se

After an exhausting first day, which ended at seven forty-five for her, she quickly left the building to make her way to Per Se for dinner. She had called her mom earlier that morning and cajoled her into meeting her for dinner at the restaurant. Her mom didn't usually venture into Manhattan, especially on a weeknight, but when she explained that it was a free dinner provided by her company, her mom finally agreed.

Her office wasn't that far from the Time Warner Center, so she walked the handful of blocks to the shops, where she took the escalators to the third floor. Her mom was prompt, as always, and was standing outside the restaurant. She had asked her mom to dress nicely for the meal, as this place required jackets for men, and all the women she had seen yesterday were dressed very elegantly. But when she saw her mother dressed in a somewhat worn and aged brown dress, her spirits fell with disappointment. *"I shouldn't be disappointed, stop it. She's your mom,"* she chastised herself, but the feeling was there, nonetheless.

"Hi, umma. How was the train ride in?" she asked with a smile.

"So many people on the seven train! That's why I never come here on a weeknight. Are you eating a lot? You look so thin!" her mom exclaimed, all in Korean.

"I'm eating a lot, don't worry. The train is just crowded because it's rush hour. This is Manhattan. Millions of people work here. Are you hungry? This is going to be a great meal."

"You look thin, and you need to eat more. And why are you wearing your nice watch, huh? I told you to lock it up in the safe deposit box, and only wear it for weddings and funerals. You'll scratch it or lose it, and it cost so much money," scolded her mom. She sighed, but what can you say.

They made their way through the doors and up to the hostess. It was the same woman from yesterday, although she didn't recognize Laura. After they got seated, her mom became noticeably quieter, as they opened up their menus. It was a set menu. Either the tasting menu or the vegetarian tasting menu, both for $360.

"How can it be so expensive?" her mom whispered. "This is too expensive!"

"It's ok. The company is paying for dinner," she replied in Korean.

"Still…who can pay this much?" her mom shook her head in disbelief. "So did you get the new job you wanted?"

"Yes! I got the job I told you about, and it's a promotion to Vice President!" she beamed. Vice President was a role she had been trying to get for several years now, and she finally got it.

"Good, you did well. And it pays well?" her mom asked with a raised eyebrow. To her, money was one of the most important things in life. Ever since her dad had left, money had been an even bigger issue, and they had struggled together all through her high school and even college years, scratching out a meager living. Money, and the lack or surplus of it, ruled her mom's happiness, and to some extent, shaped Laura's feeling of self-worth. The more she made, the better she felt about her station in life and where she was heading.

"Yes. More than two hundred fifty thousand. Plus, bonus and options."

"Good job. Very good job. I'm so proud of you," her mom said quietly. Laura felt as if her heart had swelled to double in size, and she just smiled in return.

"You can do that job and keep it until you retire."

She blinked. "Well. I want more, umma. I want to be CEO someday, and after that, I want to be in politics."

"Politics? It's so public, and everyone knows too much about your life. Why bother?" her mom frowned.

"Because, I can get laws passed to help people, umma. People like us. And, you know when appa hurt us-" but she was interrupted quickly.

"Don't talk about him to me. You know that," her mom warned sternly.

"I know," she replied quietly. "But that's why I need to go higher. So that I can be in control, and make sure the people do what I say, and how I want it to be run." She wanted to be in control and call the shots, but even deeper than that, she wanted to create stronger laws around domestic violence, and the only way she could do that was if she pushed from the politics side of things. *"One thing at a time. Time to learn how to make it to CEO,"* she thought with determination.

The meal was the best meal she had ever had in her life. Everything was exquisite, from the halibut dish with morel mushrooms, to the smoked pigeon, and the braised rabbit, each more delicious that the previous. Her mom, however, found it just so-so.

"Too fancy. And why such small portions? For so much money!" complained her mom. Laura could only sigh, but this was pretty much how her mom felt about high-end dining establishments. Nevertheless, it was great seeing her mom, and spending time eating with her in the city. Although her mom insisted on taking the train home to Flushing, Laura refused to listen to her and hailed an UBER to make sure she got home directly and with less hassle.

"Call me when you get home, umma," she ordered.

"Aiyah. I know how to get home safely. I changed your diapers, remember that. I'll always be older and wiser than you," her mom chastised with the slightest of grins. "Do good at your job. And don't worry about CEO. Just keep it until you retire."

She rolled her eyes and hugged her mom, then she was off into the night, driving back east towards her home, leaving Laura alone in the busy sidewalk. She pulled her coat tighter around her and started the walk home. It would only take her ten, fifteen minutes, and she inhaled the crisp, cold air. She mulled over her mom's last words. It wasn't enough for her to just tread water and ride out a good job. Part of the reason she wanted to be CEO was that she was ambitious, ever since she was a child. Her competitive fire had always burned brightly. But the other part was that her father leaving them had made her feel helpless. Without power or control of her situation and life. Taking on a position of power like CEO would give her that sense of power and control that she now craved. Ultimately, it would also be a good steppingstone for when she made the move into politics, she mused. She hoped that learning under the Chief of Staff would help take her one step closer to her dreams.

4

King Maker

She was three weeks into her job when she witnessed her first mafia like mob hit. It was shocking, to say the least.

"Wait, wait. Stop. Go back one slide. You're telling me that you want to spend twenty million dollars of combined market research, advertising, and customer support, to generate twenty million of revenue, spread out over two years? And you said it yourself, the probability of success in reaching these new customers is only forty percent. It doesn't add up, Jacob."

"Stacy, it's not just about the numbers here. This is about tapping an unreached consumer base for us. We haven't had much traction in breaking in to the thirty to forty-five year old female demographic with our product. We're number three in market share and losing ground by the week. We have to do something drastic, or else we will slip to number four in share by year end.

This could be a game changer." Jacob was a forty something executive running their detergent business. He was wearing a light gray suit without a tie, and his black, horn rimmed glasses looked expensive. His hair was graying, but he was handsome, and tall. His team was lined around the table, and Laura even knew some of the folks from her time running the hair care business unit.

"I get that. But this doesn't sound like a game changer to me, Jacob. And recall, last year, you tried a supposed game changing tactic and it failed, miserably if I recall. I gave you the benefit of the doubt on that one, but you missed the mark. And now you want my green light to move ahead with this one? Show me how you'll win."

Jacob looked down at the table, then back up to stare at Stacy. He was not pleased.

"Guys, can I have the room for a minute?" He looked around the table at his team, and they slowly gathered up their laptops, notes, and pens, and shuffled out of the conference room. He looked at her, but Stacy noticed and jumped in.

"She stays with me." He grimaced but narrowed his eyes and focused his attention on her boss.

"Ok. Look. We've spent the last hour going around and around on this. You've beaten and battered this analysis to the ground. There's nothing more that I am going to have the team investigate for you. I'm going to make this recommendation to John, and I would greatly appreciate your support, or for you to just stay silent when I present this. Frankly, I don't need your blessing here. I run this business unit and I'm only presenting this to you as a courtesy."

"Wrong, Jacob. You *do* need my blessing," said Stacy with heat in her voice. Laura watched Stacy and Jacob carefully, flipping her eyes from one to the other as they argued back and forth. While watching Jacob defend himself was entertaining, as he sputtered and indignantly rebutted each point that Stacy brought up, it was Stacy whom Laura concentrated on the most. She watched her body language, how she sat upright with a slight lean forward, both hands resting comfortably on the table, with no nervous energy. Her voice was loud, strong, and tinged with just the slightest amount of anger to it. She wasn't screaming, and she wasn't yelling. It was a loud, conversational tone that brooked no nonsense. Stacy knew her facts, stated them clearly and unequivocally, and would not admit nor agree with anything Jacob stated. To Laura, it seemed a little harsh, as Stacy was essentially blaming Jacob one hundred percent for the team's failure last year, but Laura had run the hair care division in a previous role, and she knew that sometimes, the market or consumer just didn't go your way, and there were unlucky bounces that could sink your year. Nevertheless, Stacy kept on the offensive, and Laura took a mental note of how she berated him. *"She never admits when he's right on a point, and she deflects to a new line of attack when there's truth to his counter argument,"* she thought. It was a powerful insight; one she wouldn't forget.

Jacob's face had gone ashen white, and his lips pursed into a tight, thin line. He was frowning and looked like he could chew nails right about now, but he finally caved to the assault. "Ok, so where do we go from here?"

"Look, forget the extra analysis. You're right, we've gone over it all and I've seen what I need to see. I'm going to support you on this one, and recommend you get the funds, ok? Is this the final PowerPoint deck, yes? Ok, great. We'll have it on our laptop for your presentation today to John at four. It's good, and I got your back."

Jacob stood up and gave a fake smile. Laura could see the venom behind those eyes. "Thank you, Stacy. I appreciate it. See you at four."

As soon as he left the conference room, Stacy turned to Laura. They were both still seated.

"You used to run a profit and loss statement. What did you think of the pitch? What would you do?" Stacy asked, pointedly. Inherently, Laura knew this was another test. A test of knowledge.

"Honestly, I don't think it's a good idea. It's true they need to tap into that demographic. They are the number one consumers of detergent in terms of frequency and dollar spend. But Jacob is missing the mark with their approach and ad campaign."

"Agreed. So, what would you do if you were the CEO?"

Laura paused. This was tough. On the one hand, Jacob was supposedly a rising star at the company. Well liked, well connected, and in the running to possibly be CEO one day in terms of succession planning, or so the rumors said. But on the other hand, he had missed budget for two consecutive years, and last year missed quite badly. That business unit had also underperformed for many years and was steadily losing market share.

"I would get a new business unit head to lead that team or cut bait and get out of that business altogether," she said thoughtfully. "They need some fresh blood to lead that team, and some new ideas that aren't so farfetched."

Stacy was quiet and was tapping the table with her pen. Her left arm was on the armrest and her hand was covering her mouth. Finally, she decided and looked at her. "I concur. And my decision is, we're going to cut bait and get out of detergents. We've been losing money and share on this business, and it's time to get the hell out. Jacob *was* the new blood. He was supposed to turn this thing around. He can't. Drop everything on your list and move this to the top. Get with Kristen, the chief HR person, and find out how much severance would be for Jacob."

Laura blinked twice to hide her surprise, but merely nodded and scribbled furiously. "But you'll still back him at the meeting with John?" she asked carefully.

Stacy shook her head. "Nope. That jerk is out. You have his final PowerPoint. I want to you go through the slides and change his numbers so that wherever he presents the same number on a different slide, make them not tie out. Make like three errors, understand?"

"What do you mean, not tie out?" she asked quizzically.

"Like, hmmm. See slide four? He shows operating income for next year at a projected eighty-two million dollars? And again, on slide five, the same eighty two million is referenced again? Change the number on slide five to like, ninety-six million. I'm going call him out for the mistakes and rake him over the coals. Make two more errors like that in the deck."

"Ah, ok. But won't he just point the finger back to you and say that you met with him this morning, and everything looked good?"

"I'll agree we met, but that we didn't go over the fine points, just the broad-brush strokes of his analysis. Then, I'm going to make him look like the idiot he is and recommend a 'no' to John. That will kill this go to market strategy. When his team leaves the room, I'm going to tell John that we need to shutter or sell that product line, and you'll give me the folder with the severance package. Make it effective one month from now. That will give us time to iron out the details on the rest of the team. Got it?"

"Yes, got it." It was then that Laura realized that Stacy was a much bigger fish than she had imagined. She was pulling strings and whispering the right, or wrong, things into the CEO's ear, and her power and influence were quite meaningful in this building. She had the power to advance or scuttle an executive's career, damn the consequences. Stacy got up and left the conference room, but Laura remained seated, contemplating everything she had just seen. This was the second thing she learned this day. In addition to how to compose oneself as you verbally attacked someone, she learned that a good ambush requires the opponent to think one way and trust you enough to give you key information. Jacob had walked out of the room thinking that he had secured Stacy's support. He didn't know that a storm was about to envelop him, and he had no means to combat it. Stacy and Laura had the final presentation, would soon have a severance package ready to go, and all they needed was to nudge John to sign off on the decision. It was almost a done deal, but the key was making Jacob think he was in the clear and allowing them access to his final PowerPoint. *"Trust, and information can lead to a good ambush,"* she mentally noted to herself.

After leaving the conference room, Laura made a beeline for Kristen's office. Though Kristen was surprised, she seemed to quickly recover her senses and came up with an appropriate recommended severance package for Jacob. Apparently, this wasn't the first time that Stacy had ousted an executive from the building. The rest of the day was filled with the other, less important tasks that Stacy had asked her to complete. By the time four p.m. rolled around, Laura felt a knot of nervousness in the pit of her stomach. It was her first time in the same meeting with John, and it was because of her sabotage, that a good executive would be fired.

She got to the board room fifteen minutes early and got her laptop setup. Five minutes to four, Jacob and his team showed up and filed in. There were four of them, including Jacob. She recognized Lindsay, the VP of marketing for detergents, and Lindsay gave her a smile. "I never got a chance to tell you, congrats on your new role!" she whispered to Laura. She smiled weakly back and gave a nod of appreciation. She hoped that Lindsay would make it out of this unscathed.

Just a few minutes past four, John and Stacy came into the room. They were wrapping up a conversation from their last meeting, apparently, and looked to be comfortable and at ease with each other. John took the seat at the head of the table, and Stacy sat to his right. She looked confident, and calm, just the opposite of what she herself felt inside. *"God, please don't let me throw up in front of everyone,"* she muttered.

"Alright folks. Sorry we're late. Let's get this going. Stacy says we're here to review your go to market strategy for detergents, yes? Please show me something good, Jacob. After last year, we need it." John was in his late fifties, tall, with thick grey and white hair that was combed neatly back with gel. He had on gold rimmed glasses, Gucci, and wore a Cartier watch on his left wrist. He wore a black suit today, with a crisp white shirt and a pale blue Hermes tie. He reeked of money, power, and slickness. He was born and bred in New York, and he liked to brag about how tough of a New Yorker he was, having been raised in the rough parts of Brooklyn, according to him.

"John, before we start, this is my new assistant Chief of Staff, Laura. She's a sharp one. I'll have her set up some time to speak with you, one on one." Stacy gave a smile, but there was no warmth there, just business, and John turned to look at her.

"Great. Welcome to the team, Laura. I've heard a lot of good things about you so far. Set up time with my assistant and we'll chat. Alright, Jacob. Show me something good."

Laura listened to Jacob present, and she was impressed with his smooth and articulate manner with how he comported himself. He talked briefly about the prior year, the problems that arose and how they dealt with them, and the general landscape of the detergent business for the upcoming year. John nodded, and asked one clarifying question about the lead competitor, but was pensive and thoughtful for the most part. Stacy took a few notes on her printout, and Laura saw that she had flipped ahead to see what the upcoming numbers were. As Jacob started into the new go to market strategy, he signaled to Laura to flip to the next few slides. Finally, the moment of truth.

"Jacob, just a sec. On the last slide, you noted an operating profit of eighty-two million, yes?"

"That's right."

"Yeah, but on this slide, your number is now ninety six million for the current year. Did you just magically create more operating income out of thin air?" Stacy said this dryly, without a hint of a smile.

Jacob blinked twice and looked at the slide being projected on the TV with confusion. "Hm, that must be a typo. It's eighty-two million. We'll get that corrected. At any rate, as I was saying-"

"Sorry, Jacob. I'm flipping through to slide seven and eight, and there's another error that isn't footing."

"Which one, Stacy?" asked John, as he looked down at his printout and turned several pages.

"The return on investments isn't tying out on slides seven and eight. I'm only calling it out because this is particularly important, the return on investment. We have to be completely sure that this will be ROI positive, and they just don't match. It's confusing as hell."

"No, no. You're absolutely right. We have to be sure that this will be an ROI of at least three to one, or I don't even want to see it." John was frowning, and he looked up at Jacob. "Which number is right here?"

"Um, let me see. This was all correct before…four to one, yes, four to one. Listen, let's get back on track. We'll get you a clean copy of the deck after the meeting, but the point I want to discuss, is our go to market strategy."

To his credit, Jacob didn't stammer or look as flustered as Laura thought he would, but he still struggled through the presentation, as Stacy jumped on him for the third mistake later in the presentation and made a big show of how the 'devil is in the details' and "If the presentation is this fraught with errors, how can we be sure of the strategy itself?" line of attack. Laura noticed that John shifted in his chair uneasily several times during the back-and-forth dialogue between Stacy and Jacob, and she also noticed that he rubbed his forehead in a perplexed manner when the numbers weren't footing. Again, it was Stacy whom she focused on, as she was much more polite than earlier in their meeting with Jacob. She sounded exasperated, but in a calm and toned-down manner. There was no anger in her voice, just a statement of facts, and again, she refused to acknowledge or give Jacob any credit on any aspect of the pitch. When the presentation was finally over, John murmured his thanks, and asked to chat with Stacy alone. Laura trudged out of the board room with the rest of Jacob's team, which were all eerily quiet. They didn't say anything in the elevator either, and merely said polite 'goodbye's when she got off on her floor. By the time she got to her office, her phone was ringing. It was Stacy.

"Hey, Laura. I just finished de-briefing with John. I got him to agree that we need to move on from Jacob, so go ahead and send the paperwork over to John, and he'll sign it tomorrow."

"Ok. And what about the business? Did John agree to sell it?"

"He's going to mull it over. But I need you to start conversations with the biz dev team, see if they can rustle up any interested buyers, quietly, that is. We'll catch up tomorrow. Oh, free up your lunch time. I'm going to take you out for lunch down the street. Italian sound good?"

"Yes, sounds good. Talk to you in the a.m."

She hung up the phone and sat down heavily in her chair. First, she had bribed the manager at Per Se. That had been an eye awakening moment in her life, as she had never broken the law before. It was almost a hazy dream, one that she almost forgot about. But now, she had helped orchestrate the exit of someone who, perhaps he wasn't a rockstar executive, but he was a smart guy, capable, had clearly done something right to get to be the lead of a product line, and now he would be unemployed in about forty-eight hours. It could have been her. All her life, she had worked hard, did her best, played by the rules, and it only got her so far. She had watched as other counterparts got promoted over her, mostly white, male peers, and she had ground her teeth and simply thrown herself even more into work. But it only got her so far. *"Was this the way people got ahead in the world?"* she wondered. *"Is this my way?"* She wasn't sure yet. But one thing she was sure of, while on the one hand she felt a pang of fear and doubt as she broke rules and laws she had always abided by, on the other hand, she loved the thrill of having the power to control other people's fates, and maybe someday, her own.

5

Power Plays

It took quite a bit of time to finally get onto John's busy calendar, but after six months as Assistant Chief of Staff, she stood outside his office. She was eager to make a good impression upon the CEO. Although she often was in any meeting that Stacy and John were part of, to this point, her role was mostly to watch, listen, take notes, and learn. She was sitting on a black leather sofa just outside John's office, which was on the twenty third floor of their building, and Janet, his admin, was quietly typing away on her computer.

"Laura, do you need any water? Can I get you anything?" Janet asked. She was a pretty brunette, about forty years old, with soft brown eyes and short hair that was just below her ears. She was dressed in a red and black dress that was just a touch too large for her petite frame. Her desk was cherry wood, and looked expensive, as did all of the furnishings on this floor.

"Oh, no. Thank you, Janet." She looked at her watch. *"Going to have to push my ten a.m. meeting. He's running behind,"* she thought irritably, as she pulled out her phone and opened up her calendar. She had just hit send when the door finally opened, and John beckoned her to come inside. Entering John's office, she couldn't help but feel envious of how enormous and luxurious it was. There was a black leather couch to her left, with a coffee table and two single leather seats across from the couch. On her right was a circular glass table with four chairs and a conference phone. Expensive paintings were on the left wall. She didn't know who the artists were, but she had no doubt they were at least six figures apiece. John took a seat behind his oak desk, and wall to wall glass windows stretched out behind him with a gorgeous view of Central Park. John's office was facing the same view as Stacy's, only much higher up. She hoped one day that she would be sitting in this office as CEO, and if not here, then elsewhere. She felt a momentary flash of hunger and ambition but dismissed it as she strode across the room and took the seat opposite John.

"Nice to see you, Laura. Your summary of the mid-year forecast update was nicely done. Stacy tells me that you've picked up things quickly. How are you feeling about the new role?" John was wearing a blue pinstriped suit today, and instead of his Cartier watch, was rocking a large IWC with an alligator strap. He took off his glasses and wiped the lenses with a microfiber cloth, then replaced them back on his face.

"Thank you. Yes, I'm pretty much up to speed. Stacy has been a great mentor and manager for me. She always has advice on how best to proceed with any task at hand. I've learned so much from her already." She gave a smile and hoped that she wasn't being too eager or friendly. She wanted to give off a confident but warm vibe, and not too obsequious.

"She is a tough cookie, and you should watch her every move. I wouldn't know where I'd be without her. So, tell me about yourself. What roles and positions have you had?" he asked with curiosity. He put his hands on his desk, with an air of "Impress me" written all over his face.

"Well, I've been with the company for six years now. I've had various roles here, including finance, strategy, marketing, and my last role was leading our hair care product line. That was especially enjoyable, as I got the chance to manage a profit and loss statement from top to bottom. Before here, I did a stint in investment banking for a couple years, consulting with McKinsey, and got my MBA from Cornell on a full ride. That's pretty much it."

John shook his head with what appeared to be a smirk. "That's it? Laura, I'll tell you, I'll never understand women sometimes. That's it. Hmph. That sounds like a pretty stellar resume and background, but you just downplayed it so humbly… so…second place like. Do you know what I mean? I mean, if it were a man sitting there, he'd be puffing his chest out, bragging about how he kicked butt in investment banking, finance, strategy, and come on, McKinsey? Don't be so meek and humble. Be proud of what you accomplished and brag about it a bit more."

Laura blinked several times, not quite sure if she should take offense at the "never understand women" comment, or if this was a back handed compliment instead of a sexist remark. Maybe it was a bit of both. "I…yes, I understand what you mean," was all she managed to croak out, and damn it to hell if it didn't sound weak and uncertain. Not at all the image she wanted to project about herself. "*Goddamn you, Laura,*" she thought. Inside her head, she was mentally gritting her teeth in annoyance at herself.

"What did you do in i-banking? And why did you leave?" John asked, with the smirk disappearing as he leaned slightly forward in his chair.

"Mergers and acquisitions. It was great work, and I learned a ton, but I didn't see myself getting to where I want, so I left."

"Oh? And where is it that you want to be?"

"I want to be you, John. CEO of a fortune 500 company. And someday, maybe more, perhaps."

"More? As in what?" he asked, one eyebrow raised as he titled his head to study her, this meek and too humble Asian woman who apparently had some big balls.

"I was thinking, well, perhaps a run in politics one day. After I've accomplished everything in the corporate world, of course," she hastened to add. It wouldn't be good to seem as if she were just using the corporate ladder as a steppingstone on her way to bigger things, which was the case.

"Ah, interesting! You know, it's tough being in politics. You can never please everyone, and eventually, they bring you down. Terrible people, the 'masses'. They never know what's good for them, and they never know what they truly need. Better to stick to what you can control, which is in the boardroom. At least, that's my advice to you."

"Thank you. You're probably right," she murmured.

"Alright. Listen, while I have you here, can we shift gears for a moment and talk about the proposed deal that was pitched on Monday? You have a banking background, what did you think of the deal parameters? In your own words and thoughts, and not what Stacy wants you to say. Speak honestly now," he said in an admonishing tone. Apparently, he knew Stacy all too well, as she had coached Laura on what to say if this topic came up, but instead of reciting what Stacy thought, she did as she was instructed, and gave her honest thoughts about the deal.

Though her meeting with John was only supposed to be thirty minutes, she ended up staying for close to an hour, and left the meeting feeling good about establishing rapport with the CEO and pleased with how she presented herself. This was just one small step in her master plan, and it was a good step.

Stacy was a great mentor and teacher, but Laura was an even better student. She only needed to see or hear something one time, and she could pick it up with the snap of her fingers. Laura realized that while John was the CEO and most powerful man at Abernathy Consumer Products, it was Stacy who was the quarterback of the company. Nothing of import happened at the company without Stacy's knowledge and say so. If a board meeting needed to be scheduled, Stacy checked all the calendars and booked the date, time, room, and attendees. If there were secret discussions with the mergers and acquisitions team about possible targets to purchase, she sat in and gave her thoughts on any potential deal. If John had a special off-site meeting with his direct reports, Stacy not only handled all of the details of the event such as which hotel and how many days, she set the agenda, ordered select members to create presentations, brought in guest speakers, and made sure everything went smoothly. In short, she was the engine that made it all go, and Laura was learning it all. In just a short amount of time in the role, Laura had taken over close to half of the duties and responsibilities that Stacy had. Although she was doing well, it wasn't enough, and she felt that she wanted more. More money, more responsibility, more power, and more upward mobility. It was a common theme for her, a flaw that she was self-aware of. No matter how great she did in anything in her life, she always felt like there was more to achieve, and her eyes always wandered upwards.

She had been about nine months in her role, when things started to get tense between Stacy, and John. John wanted to spin off the dog food division, and have the company take a majority stake in it, and Stacy didn't want to. She argued that the revenues and profits that it brought in were too valuable, and she was trying to get others in the executive leadership team to support her bid to keep the division. John was strongly against it and couldn't understand why everyone wasn't falling in line. The battle lines were clearly drawn. Things had gotten particularly nasty over the last several weeks, as John lashed out at Stacy during two different meetings and made a snide comment about how her britches were getting too big for her role. Laura felt that things were on thin ice and that at any moment, the two of them would break the ice and slip through to the depths of the dark, cold waters, never to rise again. It was after another tense meeting with John, Stacy, Laura, and Jeff who was the head of the dog food business, that Stacy revealed one of the aces up her sleeve.

Laura's desk phone rang. "Laura, can you swing by my office?"

"Sure thing, be there in a few," she replied into the phone. She grabbed her notebook and pen, sent out one last email, and then walked down the hall to Stacy's. She was now on the same floor as Stacy, but she had an office that was an inner one, and without windows. It was thoroughly depressing, and she burned up inside with envy whenever she walked into Stacy's broad, light filled office.

She saw Geoff, Stacy's admin, sitting in his cubicle with his headset on. He wore light pink shirt, grey blazer, and grey slacks that only he could pull off, and he gave her a warm smile as she approached.

"She's in a bad mood, Laura. Walk carefully," he warned with a grin.

"Thanks for the heads up. You got those printouts of the forecast for me?"

"Almost done printing. They'll be on your desk in twenty."

"You're amazing, as always."

"Don't I know it!" he chirped.

Laura walked into Stacy's office without knocking and closed the door behind her. She admired the spectacular view, and felt a twinge of jealousy, as usual. *"Someday, I'll have an office like this one,"* she thought bitterly as she sat down in the comfy leather chair across from Stacy's desk.

"What's up?" she asked as she flipped open her notebook.

Stacy was typing on her keyboard, and ignored her question for a moment, lips silently mouthing some words as she typed. Laura sighed and leaned back. It could be seconds, or it could be ten minutes, but she was at the mercy of Stacy's time now. Luckily, in this case, it was the former, as Stacy hit the enter button and turned to face her. She was wearing a beige suit jacket and matching beige skirt, with an ivory off white blouse. It looked expensive. Her hair was down to her shoulders and looked like there were even more streaks of grey than she remembered. *"Was it always like that?"* she wondered. Stacy wore a look of anger, and her eyes were narrowed and her lips in a tight, thin line.

"John has crossed the line. He is whispering behind my back about having me fired. Fired! I have friends up on John's floor, and they tell me that he's looking for the right reason to have me pink slipped."

"Why don't you just let this one go, Stacy, and fall into line with John? Let him win this one," she urged. Laura couldn't understand why this battle was so important to Stacy. But Stacy was shaking her head.

"No. Can't let this one go. We need the steady revenues that the dog food business provides. Besides, I want John to set his sights on something bigger. An acquisition that I think would be great for the company, and for me. If we can acquire Foster Brands, I think I can make a play to be named CEO of that division. But that acquisition only makes sense if we still own the dog foods business."

"Ah. That makes sense."

"It's time to bring out the big guns." Stacy opened her drawer and pulled out a business card, then slid it over on the desk.

"Go to this address. The man, Larry, is expecting you."

Laura picked up the card and read it. Larry Kudlow, licensed private investigator. There was an address in Brooklyn, along with a phone number, but no email.

"I don't follow. What do we need a private investigator for?" she asked curiously. *"Where is she going with this?"*

Stacy smiled. "Larry is an ex-cop. NYPD. He's got connections in the police department, and is a damn good P.I. He's on my payroll, and I use him to do my own background checks on anyone and everyone. From enemies to potential enemies, and even prospective business partners. If there's dirt, he'll find it. He's already pulled up everything on John, but I wanted to finally bring you in the loop on this resource that I have and wanted you to meet him in person. You can now use him at your discretion. He's expecting you."

Laura nodded her head thoughtfully. The computer pinged, as an incoming email alert sounded, and Stacy turned to look at the monitor, scanning the contents. Laura paused, and tilted her head as she processed what she had just heard, and then leveled a flat stare at her boss.

"Did you use Larry to do a background check on me?"

Rather than answer, Stacy pulled her keyboard closer and started typing a response to the email.

"Better hurry. He's waiting."

The L train to Brooklyn was roomy, and spacious. *"Why can't all the subway trains in Manhattan be this size?"* she wondered with disgust. She often took the seven train to Flushing to see her mother, and it often had delays, was packed to the gills, and almost always was behind schedule. At least if the train were this sized, she could live with it. She got off at Bedford station, and walked up to the street level. It was a brisk and cool winter night, and dark already at five p.m. She followed the map on her phone and soon came up to a door that was wedged between a cheese shop and a deli, with the letters LARRY KUDLOW, P.I. stenciled on the glass. Hitting the buzzer, she waited for the buzz and then opened the door, which lead up a long, narrow staircase. Trudging up the stairs with a sigh, she got to the second floor and was met with a short hall and another door. The door was solid metal, with a wire grate that was four inches square, right at her eye level. There was a camera installed up and to the left of the door, peering down at her as she rang the doorbell. Once again, there was another buzz, and she was through. *"What is this, Alcatraz?"* she muttered. However, the humble and rough exterior of the hallway and door belied the contents of the inside. The door opened up into a wide-open floor plan, with two desks on her left, two desks on her right, and straight ahead, one large wooden desk.

She walked down the aisle towards the desk at the opposite end of the room, where a middle-aged man in his fifties sat behind the desk. He was dressed in a drab brown suit, with a white shirt and an ugly brown and white tie. The desk had several monitors on it, and as she walked up to the desk, she could see that they were showing various camera angles of the street and hallway from where she had entered. Larry Kudlow was the classic definition of what Laura believed most middle aged, beer drinking, white males in America would look like. He had a slight paunch in the belly, that stretched his white shirt so that the buttons were protesting in pain, thin greying hair that was slicked all the way back with hair product of some sort, and steely grey eyes that looked at her with a sharp intensity. He wasn't what she would call 'handsome', but he was an average looking man who seemed about average in height, perhaps five foot eight.

"Laura, have a seat," he said causally, as he leaned back in his chair. He looked at ease and comfortable, and he put his hands on the arms of his swivel chair.

"Larry. May I call you Larry? Nice to meet you. Stacy asked that I come here to meet you," she said politely, as she sat down on the brown leather chair. Even the chair was nice, not at all what she had expected.

"Yes, I know. And how can I be of service today?"

She paused. *"What is the purpose of meeting Larry?"* she thought. *"She said to meet him and bring out the big guns. What am I supposed to do now? Just a meet and greet? There has to be more."*

"Stacy said you had pulled some info on John Lancet? Could I see what you gathered?" she ventured. *"Maybe this is what she wanted. That I see the info."*

He nodded his head and opened the drawer on his right side, pulling out a thick brown folder, about half an inch thick, and slid it over to her. Clearly, he had been expecting to give it to her.

"Straight and narrow guy, this John," he started to say, as she opened the folder. She saw a few photos of John entering their corporate headquarters, a few more of him inside a nice-looking apartment, and yet a few more of him seated at a table inside a restaurant. After staring at the photos for a second, she realized that all of these photos were taken from afar, secretively, without John knowing. She pursed her lips in thought, and scanned through the rest of the pages, which were to the point, concise, and incredibly detailed.

"He gets up early, around five a.m. or so. Heads to his gym in a nice luxury condo building that he lives in on the westside, near Hell's Kitchen. Works out for about an hour, then back up to shower and change. Usually in the office by eight, out by seven or eight at night, and if he doesn't have dinner plans, he's right back at home. No wife, no kids, never been married. No secret lovers, no hard drugs, no pets. Both parents, deceased. One younger sibling, a sister who lives in Connecticut with her husband and two kids. But he rarely sees them. He has a lot of acquaintances and friends, and he'll chat with them on the phone, make weekend plans, that sort of thing. He rides his bike on the weekends, goes for fancy meals with his friends, sometimes does some hiking upstate. Very normal stuff." Larry was speaking very casually, watching her with almost boredom, she had to say, as he rattled off all of John's habits and schedule. She was impressed, but also curious about how he knew all of this information. She now understood just how important Larry was in this game. With his knowledge and any dirt that he found, Stacy could influence and force people to do as she said. Quit the company, sabotage a presentation, call in a favor, anything at all.

"So, you couldn't find any dirt. But everyone has dirt. Have you dug deeper? How far back can you trace his contacts and connections?" she asked, confident now in what she needed to do. She needed to make John ease up on Stacy, somehow, and Larry seemed like the man who could find dirt to make that happen.

"My team and I have been tracking him for about a month now. We've started tracing back to his grad school friends and connections, but so far, squat, diddly, zippo," he said nonchalantly. He leaned back in his chair and tilted his head back to peer down his nose at her, not in a rude way, but just in a curious way, as if studying her.

"Can you go back farther, to his college days?" she asked. "There's got to be something there."

"I've been doing this sort of thing for a long time now. We can do that if you want. Going to cost quite a bit of time and money to hunt and find those college buddies and teachers. But my gut tells me that there's nothing there. This guy is pretty squeaky clean. Sometimes, you can get a feel for someone. That they're hiding something, or it's just a little too perfect, a little too clean. Those are the ones that are hiding a fucked up past or trying to get away from something. I can usually sniff those folks out, but this guy, you're not going to find what you need by going down that road." He stopped, and the last word in his sentence trailed off, begging for her to ask the follow up, which she did.

"So, what then, do you recommend?"

Larry sat upright, and opened up his left side drawer, pulling out an e cigarette. "Do you mind if I...?" She shook her head and waited as he put in a cartridge, and pressed the tab, inhaling deeply. He turned his head to the right and politely blew the smokey nicotine vapor off to the side and away from her. Still, she could smell the mint flavor as it hung, damp, in the air.

"Tried to quit, several times, but I missed the routine of lighting up, believe it or not. This is better. Different flavors too," he said conversationally. He studied her as he puffed one more time and then turned to discharge the vapor before addressing her.

"How badly do you need John to go away?" he asked calmly.

She stiffened slightly at the question. *"He couldn't mean...?"*

"Well, we need him ease up on my boss, Stacy. Or have him gone. But not gone, if you know what I mean. I just need enough dirt to make him stop hassling Stacy and stop him from firing her." She squirmed in her chair as she said those words, uncomfortable that the thought even crossed her mind, but she was put at ease when Larry gave a soft chuckle.

"Oh, no. We don't do that. There are limits, even for what Stacy asks of me. No, I mean, are you willing to get your hands dirty? Because that's the next step."

"Yes. I can speak for Stacy, and yes, I don't care if it gets dirty. What do you have in mind?" she asked.

"Ok. It will cost thirty grand for my services, but yeah, I think I can fabricate some minor dirt that will stick, and just strong enough to make this guy back off. Nothing that could get him fired or anything, but more embarrassing than anything else. A mistress perhaps, or we could get a fake record of public intoxication and indecency, something along those lines. Just very embarrassing info that wouldn't look good on the front page of the New York Post, know what I mean? If we present it to him, a man like this, he'll probably back off a little on Stacy if we agree to hand over all the evidence. But Stacy's future job prospects at the company will be dim unless she can leverage him to promote her or something along that line. Depends on how strong the dirt is." Laura nodded thoughtfully. Larry was right. If they tried something like this, Stacy would possibly lose any chance of moving up so long as John was the CEO. But, on the flip side, it sounded like she was on the cusp of getting fired. Might be worth the downside risk, she guessed.

"Tell me what you have in mind, specifically," she said, and leaned forward as he outlined his plan. It was a good one, and as she listened to him outline all the details and plans, she realized that Larry was an ace up the sleeve, a trump card that could turn the tables in any high stakes game. She liked him.

After they went over the plan again, this time with Laura asking many questions and probing on how it could fail, she stood up, satisfied that within the week, they would have enough fake dirt to make John ease off on Stacy. She turned leave, but before doing so, asked one last question.

"Larry. Did Stacy have you investigate me? Back when I was interviewing for the job?" She stared at him, and he stared right back, not a glimmer of anything showing behind those steely grey eyes.

"What do you think, Laura?" he asked quietly.

"What did you find?"

He stood up, put his vape pen on the desk, walked over to a coat rack that was off to the side of the room, pulled off a grey coat off the hanger, and put it on. He started walking towards the door at the far end of the room, the one that lead back to the stairs and out to the street, and she followed his lead and walked beside him. When they got to the door, he held his hand out, indicating that she should go first, and he followed her down the narrow staircase, until they were out in the cold winter night once more, standing on the street. There were people walking home from work, and a few snow flurries were lazily drifting down to the sidewalk, only to melt away once they touched down. Winter was her favorite time in the city, as it reminded her of snuggling up in her mother's bed, blankets pulled up to her chin as she lay on her back reading her favorite books.

"Larry, what did you find?" she repeated. But Larry only smiled and turned to walk away.

"It's getting late. Get home safely," he called out over his shoulder, and he receded away into the darkness.

6

A.F.U.

Laura never really celebrated Valentine's Day. It was for saps and morons. Those who were crazy in love, or maybe simply crazy, and she couldn't stand how restaurants seized on their madness to hike up prices. In New York City, many restaurants had prix-fixe Valentine's Day set menus, and they ranged from fifty dollars up to one hundred fifty dollars. To her, it was just another scam. "Don't go out to eat on Valentine's Day, ok?" her mother would scold her in Korean when she was in college. "So expensive!" But this year, Valentine's Day would take on a new meaning for her, and she would never forget the day ever again.

The day started off normal, with an eight-a.m. meeting with Stacy. Several days had passed since she had met with Larry, and she had been checking in with him daily. Partly because she was worried about how his scheme would unfold and go down, and partly because she wanted to gauge his skills and see how prepared he was when she questioned him. But she should have known and trusted Stacy. She only picked the absolute best, and Larry, well, he was the best, in her mind.

Stacy had asked her something.

"I'm sorry, what was that?" Laura asked as she blinked out of her reverie. She was in Stacy's office, sitting on her black leather sofa off to the side while Stacy was at her desk, notebook open as she read through the tasks for the day.

"I said, were you able to get the agenda for the eleven a.m. meeting with John? He's secretive as hell about it, and that's not like him. I usually pull the agenda together, but this one, he said there would be no need. I hate being blind like this." Stacy bit her lower lip and frowned. She was wearing a beige business suit and matching skirt, with a bright white blouse that was buttoned up to her chin. Her hair was hung loosely down to her shoulders, and it seemed to be greyer than usual, at least to Laura's eyes. These last few weeks had taken a toll on Stacy. The constant jockeying for position, the back biting, and attacks against her, all the while as she defended and tried to ease back into John's good graces had made her tense and on edge, seemingly twenty-four seven. She wondered why Stacy waited this long to get dirt on John, and with a guy like Larry in her corner, she didn't need Laura to run point for her on this. It was enough to pique her curiosity, and she asked it directly.

"Stacy, why did you wait this long to get some dirt on John? You and Larry could have hatched up the same plan a year ago. Why now?" she asked as she ignored Stacy's question about the eleven a.m. meeting. Stacy stopped typing and turned to look at Laura. Her eyebrows were furrowed, and her lips were in a tight, thin line of anger.

"To be honest, I never thought John would fire me. He made it seem like he would back me no matter what, and that someday, I would get promoted to head of the plastics business unit. I should have had a backup plan."

"Well, we have a good plan in place now. It's small enough to put him to shame, but big enough that he'll at least back off on firing you," she said with a small smile. She felt giddy and excited at the same time. Having this much control and power over people and situations was the best feeling in the world, better than even sex.

"Ha-ha. Your plan is a good one. It will kill any future job prospects here for me, but he probably won't fire me. But do me a favor, check in with John's admin, see what you can find out about this eleven a.m. meeting. I want to be prepared for whatever he's going to throw at me." Stacy frowned again, and then shook her head.

She took Stacy through the rest of her to do list, and then left to head to the executive's floor to see if she could sniff out anything about this mysterious eleven a.m. meeting that John was hosting. When the elevator door opened, she walked onto the floor and took a moment to appreciate the luxuriousness of it all. Whereas the rest of the corporate headquarters were a drab beige, and light oak color, the executive's floor on the twenty third floor was different. The waiting area right outside the elevators had two black leather couches, and the walls were made of a shiny cherry wood, polished to a high sheen. Even the wood trim around the admin's desk was made of the same cherry wood. Instead of the grey carpet that lined the rest of the building, the floor outside the elevators were white marble, and once you entered the hallway and waiting area, the carpet that lined the floors were a rich, and expensive looking silver. To the right and to the left of either side of the waiting area, hung oil paintings that were rumored to be in excess of one hundred thousand each, although she didn't recognize any of the artists. It was eerily quiet on this floor, but that just added to the mystique, and she took a deep breath. Even the air smelled of power and money, and it was intoxicating.

"Hey, Gabby," she said, as she walked into the waiting area and up to the admin's desk. Gabby was sort of a gate keeper. If you didn't have an appointment with one of the executives on this floor, she wouldn't let you by. But Laura had made in roads with her months ago and was now free to come and go as she pleased. She was in her mid-thirties, pretty, with straight long brown hair, brown eyes, and a curvy figure. Today, she was dressed in a dark blue business suit, with matching skirt.

"Laura, how are you?" Gabby asked with a smile.

"Oh, I'm good. Finally glad the snow stopped. Can't wait for spring, let me put it that way. You?"

"I'm good, thanks for asking. Yeah, I couldn't agree more. Spring in New York is my favorite time of year, and I can't wait for the weather to warm up. What brings you here? I don't think you're on anyone's calendar this morning."

"You're right, as usual. Actually, I wanted to know if you could tell me if there's an agenda for John's eleven a.m. with Stacy? Can you check to see if he has one?"

"Sure, let me see his inbox, one sec." Gabby turned her attention to her monitor and scanned it for several seconds. "Hmm. No, I don't see an agenda in the invite. All I see is, 'Meeting with Stacy'. That's it."

"Hm. That's odd. Did he say anything about it? Is it just the two of them?"

"Looks like it's just the two of them. Sorry. You could check with Janet though; she might have some details."

"Ok, I'll do that. Thanks, Gabby. Love the blue by the way!"

Gabby's desk was in the center of the waiting room and bisected the hallway. To the left, was the Chief Counsel, Chief Commercial Officer, and a few other senior Vice Presidents offices. To Gabby's right, was John's office, the Chief Financial Officer's office, and Chief Strategy Officer. She took the right hallway and admired the artwork on the walls as she glided down the hall. "*Someday, I'm going to own paintings like these,*" she muttered to herself. Her mother would drop dead in shock if she knew how much they cost. She reached another waiting area, just outside of John's office.

"Hey Janet, how are you? Quick question, do you know anything about John's eleven a.m. meeting with Stacy? Is there an agenda?"

"Hi, Laura. Let me see....hm, nope. Don't see an agenda."

"Ok. It's odd. Stacy normally prepares all the agendas for John's meetings, and this one, there's nothing there, and John hasn't said what it's about."

Janet looked up at her, and there seemed to be a flicker of recognition behind her eyes, something that she wasn't saying, but her response was smooth and natural. "Yeah, he hasn't mentioned anything to me. Sorry."

Laura nodded her head slowly, and was half inclined to probe further, but there was a look of determination on Janet's face, and she decided not to press it.

"Ok. Just wanted to see if we could prep anything for it. Alright, I'll catch you later then, thanks."

She sighed and turned to walk back towards the main

entryway. Another left, and she was back to the elevator bank, lost in thought. When the doors opened and the bell chimed, she walked straight for the opening, and almost knocked over Kevin Street, a senior VP in Human Resources. He was graying, in his late fifties, and had been with the company for close to thirty years. He had seen more dirt and buried more corporate gossip and bodies than almost anyone in the building, she guessed. He was dressed in a light grey Italian suit, and his black plastic Armani glasses framed brown eyes. His face was wrinkled and weathered, and his six-foot frame nearly bowled her over.

"Whoa, there! In a rush, Laura?" he asked as he gripped her elbow to steady her from falling.

"Oops! Sorry about that Kevin. Lost in thought. Where are you heading? Meeting with Kristen?" Kristen was the chief HR person, and her office was on the far end away from John's.

"Nope. Kristen's out on vacation. Have a meeting with John." Something about the way he said it, nonchalantly, piqued her curiosity.

"Oh? About the merit increases for March?" she asked quietly. She knew those raises had already been agreed upon, by the Executive Leadership Team, so that couldn't be the reason for his meeting.

"Er, no. Something else. Not too big a deal, but prep for a meeting later. Are you taking the elevator down?" Kevin stepped aside and held the doors open with one arm. He gave a fake smile and avoided looking at her. Something was up.

"Yes, thank you. Have a good one," she smiled back, with what she hoped was a less fake smile.

Back on Stacy's floor, she frowned when the elevator doors opened up to the drab beige walls and ugly grey carpet. "*Losers and nobody's get these floors. And I'm one of them, for now at least,*" she muttered. She took a right and then another right, heading past the cubicles filled with interns and newly hired MBA's, all eager and full of life. She caught the eyes of a couple of them as she passed, and she could sense the envy and ambition in at least one of them. Adam Thatcher, in particular, gave her a smile that didn't quite touch his eyes, and raised a hand as she passed.

"Excuse me, Laura? Hi, I know you're busy, but I was wondering if you had some time this week to have coffee, maybe chat about your career path and how you ended up in your current role?" He wore a crisp white shirt, probably Brooks Brothers if she had to guess, and neatly pressed grey slacks. He had brown hair, thinning, which was surprising given his youthful appearance, and brown eyes. He had a rather large nose, but it didn't look odd for his face, rather, it accentuated his mouth in a pleasant way.

"Hi, Adam. Sure. But this week isn't the best. Schedule something for the end of next week, ok? I have to run, but my calendar is up to date," she said rather hurriedly as she darted on by. She had no time for this bullshit. Adam was hungry and ambitious, and she recognized herself when she looked at him.

"Yes, will do. Thanks, Laura!" he called after her. She didn't bother to acknowledge the comment and kept on marching straight ahead. "*Ignorant babies. That's what they are,*" she thought sourly. Newly minted MBA's thought they knew everything about everything and were eager to please. She knew. She had been one of them, long ago.

She saw Geoff in his cubicle and gave him a wave. He was on the phone and smiled and waved back. Stacy wasn't in her office, so she kept on walking and made it to her own office several doors down. Laura's office was on the other side of the hallway and was an inner office without any windows. Whereas Stacy's office faced Central Park, Laura's office could have been a closet for Christ's sakes. There were two chairs for guests, her desk and chair, a filing cabinet, and another standing cabinet for other personal effects. She walked around the desk and sat down, then got busy, trying to manage John's meetings, agendas, reports, ad hoc requests, while taking care of Stacy's requests and trying to stay two steps ahead of them both. It was a tough and thankless job, but she knew the endgame and that this role would lead her to where she wanted to go. To the very top.

It was just around noon when she got the call. She was so focused on her monitor, that she almost didn't pick up the phone when it rang, but after several rings, she snapped out of it and picked up the handset.

"Hey, John. What can I do for you?" she asked as she saw the name flash on her desk phone.

"Hey, Laura. Listen, I want you to be the first to know. I just let Stacy go. It was time. I'm sure you have a lot of questions, and we'll setup time to talk, but for now, you'll report to me in the short term," John said confidently.

"Oh. Ok. Should I set something up today?" she asked, as her mind raced a thousand miles a minute. It was too late. John had acted first.

"No, I'll get it setup here. I have to run, but we'll talk soon," he promised, as he hung up.

She waited for a minute, waiting for her heart to stop beating so fast, then grabbed her cell phone and practically ran to Stacy's office. Geoff was sitting in his cubicle outside her office, and his face was pale.

"Geoff. Is Stacy back from her meeting with John?" she asked quickly. "Geoff! Snap out of it!" she barked. Now was not the time to hesitate.

Geoff blinked and turned his head to face her. His brown eyes were sad, and his brows were raised up in disbelief. "Mike from security just called. He said that Stacy is no longer with the company, and that he will be sending two guys up to pack her things to be shipped to her home. I can't believe this is happening. Why, I mean, what did Stacy do?" His voice was trembling, and he stared at her in shock.

She forced herself to take a deep breath and slowly exhaled. "She didn't do anything wrong, Geoff. She just…she ran into a formidable opponent here, and he took her out. Listen, call your husband…Ryan, is it?" Upon seeing his nod of affirmation, she continued with more confidence. "Take the rest of the afternoon off, call your husband, meet him for a late lunch or whatever, but just get out of here and I'll see you tomorrow, ok?"

"What about the packers coming to take Stacy's things? Shouldn't I at least be here to oversee that? I mean, what if there's something she doesn't want, or whatever?"

"That's not necessary, Geoff. They will pack up everything, and I mean down to the last pen that's on her desk and mail it to her. She'll figure it out from there. Take Ryan out, anywhere you want, and expense it to my account, ok?" She was an ambitious, and cutthroat person, she knew that, but in this moment, even she recognized that Geoff needed some reassurance that everything would be ok, so she leaned over and squeezed his shoulder. "Look, it's going to be ok. I'm going to find out what's going on, and we'll have some answers tomorrow. But right now, it's best if you take some time to gather your thoughts, yes?" He nodded and looked away. But her touch had the intended effect, and he nodded appreciatively.

"Alright, Laura. Thank you." He grabbed his cell phone, took his coat from the coat stand in the corner, and left quickly, his footsteps swishing noisily on the carpet.

Laura sighed and walked into Stacy's office. It felt cold, and lifeless. She wondered if the office would have felt the same to her, had she not known that Stacy was fired. Closing the door behind her, she walked toward Stacy's desk but past it, until she was face to face with the glass window and stared out the window overlooking Central Park. The trees were bare, and just brown bark and branches at this time of year. She could see miniature people walking along the cement pathways that carved and bisected through the park. Some were strolling alone, others were holding hands, and yet others were running or bicycling. She saw kids running and laughing, dogs being walked on leashes, and even a homeless man sifting through one of the trash cans. As she surveyed the scene playing out below her, her only thought was that it was all going to shit, her carefully crafted plan.

Her phone buzzed, and she looked at the number before she answered it.

"Stacy, what happened?"

She saw the homeless man score something to eat from the trash can, and he was now sitting down next to it, unwrapping something as he took a bite out of it. It brought back unpleasant memories.

She heard Stacy sigh. "He laid the groundwork a month ago, I think. You know the Kimura spinoff from a few months ago? He had the information technology team track and pull all of my emails over the last twelve months and dredged up a lot of shit that I ordered to sink the deal. Luckily for you, John half played by the rules, and agreed to abide by IT's rules of conduct. Meaning, IT only shared with John just the emails associated with the Kimura spinoff, and nothing else, and they only went back twelve months' time per their corporate policy on this sort of thing. Sort of like a statute of limitations kind of deal. Anyways, there were a lot of incriminating emails from me to you, and from me to others as well, as I tried to scuttle the deal. That's how he got me."

Laura was silent. *"What the hell? Am I am fucked too?"* she thought, and she briefly wondered if security would be waiting for her in her office. The homeless man on the street was done munching on whatever he had found and was now standing up to urinate next to the trash can while a horrified mother ushered her little boy quickly away. *"That could be me, soon."*

"What did John say? Did he offer you a chance to apologize?"

"Hmm. He was pretty cold. He said he has all the Kimura emails from the past, and it shows clearly that I went behind his back to try and kill the deal. 'Manipulation with the intent to harm the company, and falsify records,' he called it. Kevin from HR was there too. I tried to make amends, but I already knew their minds were made up. They gave me my severance package, and John left the room while Kevin took me through the details. Then security walked me from the building."

"Why didn't you try the fake bit of news that Larry fabricated? He might have backed off and let you stay," asked Laura, but she could almost hear Stacy shaking her head.

"No. I thought about it, but Kevin was there, and our plan was to have a one-on-one conversation with John about this embarrassing piece of news. Kevin would know it was a blackmail attempt. I think if John and I had been alone, I might have leveraged him with this lie that we made, but I didn't have time and I was a little stunned."

"What are you going to do now?" Laura had had high hopes that Stacy would leave someday, and that she could take over the Chief of Staff role, but this was not the way she envisioned it, with Stacy getting fired in disgrace and perhaps Laura soon to follow out the door.

There was a pause as Stacy thought. She could hear traffic in the background, and guessed that Stacy was walking home, as she often did after work. Her apartment was maybe a fifteen-minute walk from the office. "I don't know yet. Probably take a year off. I'm fifty-five years old, and I've been running so hard these last twenty years of my life, it's time to take a breather. Besides, the severance was fairly hefty." Laura was dying to know how much, but before she could hint at the question, Stacy volunteered the info herself. "A year's salary and bonus paid out at the end of the month, a million paid out in a year, and another million paid out in two years, if I agreed to sign a binding waiver to forgo any legal action at all against the company. No wrongful termination, no filing suit for unjust cause, etc. I thought about giving John and Kevin the finger and walking out without signing it, but the money was too good. I could have gone to court, but I measured my chances as less than fifty-fifty, so I signed." Laura was impressed. That was more than she thought Stacy would have gotten, but she *had* spent the better part of her career there and knew where all the dead bodies were buried. Metaphorically, that is.

"Congratulations…I guess?" She said with a smile, to take any sting off the comment. "You've certainly earned it. Stacy. Did John mention me at all?" She held her breath. The moment of truth. The next sentence would let her know whether her ambitions and plans were still intact, or whether they were garbage in the can, waiting to be sifted through by someone homeless.

Inside, she gave a mental bark of a laugh. *"Don't be so melodramatic, idiot. You can recover elsewhere if you're fired,"* she chastised herself.

"Yeah, Laura. Bad news. John said he's replacing you, in light of your willingness to carry out my orders behind his back. He didn't say who, but don't be surprised if you get a call from him, or his admin, asking to see you. I'm sorry." For all of her seemingly rough and cold exterior, Stacy was actually a pretty nice person, once you got to know her. She genuinely sounded sorry, and Laura appreciated her heartfelt response. But her mind starting spinning, and she wasn't done just yet.

"That's ok. It isn't over yet. Listen. Besides the small dirt we fabricated with Larry's help, is there anything more solid on John that I can use?"

Again, there was a pause, and then a murmur of assent. "You know…there might be something…a thread you might be able to dig into and pull. It's a little light on evidence, and you'll need to go back years and do some homework, but there might be something there. I never checked it out fully, as at the time, Larry hadn't hired his IT specialist, so I never ran it to ground. But, when Larry had initially investigated John some years ago, he found some very odd bank transfers to and from his bank account from many years ago. They were rather large deposits, that looked a little odd, especially since he was only a director at the time. You should have Larry drop everything and see if there is something real there."

"Yes, I'm on it, Stacy. I'm going to call Larry now. I'll stop by this weekend with your personal effects from your desk, yes? I'll call you later to check in on you." She hung up and stood looking out the glass window. The whole world, it seemed, was spread before her. The clear blue sky, the chilly February air that enveloped the people, the buildings, and the park itself. She stared out into the city, skyscrapers, and apartment buildings, and knew that she had a decision to make. She thought back to the little girl who had been raised in the streets of Flushing, poor, hungry, and ambitious. She had watched hustlers and pimps, drug dealers and junkies, and she knew that she could work hard, climb the ladder, and try to make it on her skills and good graces alone, but she also knew there were other ways to get ahead. But this juncture was dangerous for her, and she knew that she might take a long time to recover, if she tried what she was thinking, and it failed. She looked down towards the street as her mind went back and forth with how to proceed. There, she saw a little girl walking with her father, she supposed. The girl was holding a hot dog and was bundled up warmly in a brown winter coat, black scarf, and a red cotton cap that pulled over her ears. Suddenly, she half stumbled as she tripped on something, and the hot dog flew from her hands and landed on the sidewalk. Luckily, she caught herself and was able to stay upright. The girl's father bent over to say something, and although she couldn't hear the words, the body languages of the two told her everything, as she saw the man shake his finger at the girl repeatedly, and the girl's head dropped down and her shoulders slumped. Then, the man straightened up and walked forward, with his daughter slower to follow. She made her decision.

She went through her contact list on her phone and hit the dial.

"Larry? It's me. Yeah. Change of plans. We need some serious and real dirt against John Lancet. Stacy mentioned some strange bank deposits from many years ago. Can you find out what was going on there?" She paused as Larry described what he thought were odd and large bank deposits in and out of John's bank account, from an offshore account elsewhere. As she listened intently, she murmured her acknowledgment of what Larry was saying, but her eyes followed the little girl as she faded away in the distance.

7

The New Chief of Staff

It had come together very rapidly, but even still, Laura was amazed at how quickly she and Larry were able to pivot. Knowing that she was probably going to get fired, for her direct assistance in helping Stacy try to kill the Kimura deal, she had called in sick for the week. She knew HR's policies inside and out, having been on the other end of trying to fire people herself, so she knew that the company would never fire someone over the phone. They would wait until she was back in the office and fire her face to face. As soon as she sat down at her desk, an email invitation popped into her inbox, from John's admin, Janet.

Subject line: Chat with John

It was scheduled for thirty minutes, so she knew they were planning to fire her quickly and move on. Kevin was on the invite, she knew he would be there too, to give her severance. She was nervous, and butterflies were flitting in her stomach, but she was ready to take her shot. No more waiting around for another white male to pass her by on the corporate ladder, as executives smiled at her and told her how smart, how talented, and how great she was at her job. No more waiting patiently for her turn in line. It was time to take a chance, and if it didn't work out, then at least she tried and gave it her best shot. If it didn't work, she would restart at another company here in New York.

"I'll either be fired, perhaps sued for libel, or I'll be temporarily safe for a bit as the echoes of my power play reverberate throughout the walls," she muttered to herself. She was wearing a bright red business suit and skirt, with a black belt that rode above her hips. If she were going down today, she would go down in a bright red flame of fire, so the color suited her mood. She looked around her office, perhaps for the last time, and took note of the white painted walls, peeling in the far corner by the floor, the cheap Monet poster on her left wall, her coat stand in the other corner, the papers scattered on her desk, and her eyes finally settled on the desk photo of her and her mom. It had been too long since she had seen her, and she decided that regardless of the outcome today, she would go see her. She was in her black cap and gown, graduating from business school, and her mom was beaming proudly beside her, her short black hair and warm brown eyes bursting with pride. That was the day that she had fulfilled one part of her master plan, which was to get her master's in business, and she had been cocksure, confident, and hungry for power. Now, she was the same, just a little less sure of herself, and whether she would make it through the day unscathed. Time would tell.

She went about her business as best she could, firing away emails, setting up meetings, and trying to get ahead of what was left on Stacy's to do list. She didn't know if she would be here to supervise these meetings, but business wouldn't stand still for her, or anyone else for that matter, so she did her best to move things along. Finally, the time came for her to go meet with John. Standing up, she grabbed her notepad, a pen, and waffled a bit on whether she should bring her coat and purse but opted to leave them behind. Nevertheless, she neatly left her coat on top of her purse and set both on her chair. That way, she could succinctly tell security to gather her things from her chair rather than search all around for those two items.

Walking down the drab carpeted hallway, she passed by Geoff's desk and gave him a friendly wave.

"Hey, Geoff? I'm heading up to have a meeting with John. Just to let you know, so that you're prepared, I might not be coming back." Geoff's smile faded, and he blinked several times as he processed her words.

"You know, collateral damage from Stacy's departure… anyways, we'll see how it goes. But if I don't see you again, it was great working with you."

Geoff's eyes watered up, and he bit his lip before responding. "You too, Laura. I'm sure things will work out; you never know right?" She gave a wan smile in return but didn't answer and just turned to walk away.

In the elevator bank, she saw several coworkers, and made some polite chit chat that she couldn't recall by the time she made it to the twenty third floor. All of her thoughts were focused on how she would attack this meeting. But she had rehearsed her lines for the last forty-eight hours, and prepared for all sorts of outcomes, so she felt ready to face the news head on.

The marble floors on the twenty third floor never failed to

impress her, and today was no different. She gave a small smile at the luxuriousness of the waiting area in the elevator bank and walked quickly toward Gabby's desk.

"Hey, Gabby. I have a meeting with John. Everything good with you?" she asked.

"Yes, everything's great. Yes...I see you have an appointment, go on ahead. Janet's probably expecting you." Her long brown hair was tied back into a ponytail today, and she wore a light blue, long sleeved silk shirt with some elegant ruffles at the wrists, atop a black skirt.

Her heels made a familiar, sharp clicking sound as she walked quickly down the hall, towards the waiting area outside John's office. Janet was seated behind her desk and gave her a blank face as she approached. "*She knows,*" Laura thought.

"Hi Laura, go right on in. They're expecting you," said Janet loudly. She was dressed simply today, in a white sweater and black slacks, with pearl earrings.

"Thanks, Janet. Love your earrings, by the way," she said calmly, although inside, she felt like her stomach was about to turn inside out. She was about to try a twisted and fucked up power play, one she wasn't sure would work, but she was hungry to move up and move up quick, and this was the only way that she could see. "*Either this or wait and try to climb the corporate ladder like every other hard working, submissive and meek Asian,*" she thought bitterly.

"Thank you, good luck," was all that Janet said, as she pushed open the dark brown door that led to John's office. Stepping inside, she took the lay of the land with just a glance. As expected, Kevin Street from HR was there, at the round glass table to the right, and John was there as well, sitting at the table.

"Glad you could make it on short notice, Laura. Please, come have a seat," said John. She noticed that he didn't stand up for her. She walked over to the glass table, and John grabbed the TV remote and clicked the TV off. He was dressed immaculately, as always, in a light grey suit, pale blue shirt, and gold and blue tie. He wore black, plastic glasses, that stood out as a stark contrast to the grey hair he sported, combed over neatly to the right. Kevin was wearing a navy-blue sport jacket, white shirt, no tie. He gave her a tight-lipped smile, but to his credit, gave her strong eye contact. *"At least he has the courage to look me in the eye as he stabs me in the face,"* she thought. She pulled out the black leather chair and took a seat. She put her manilla folder on the table but didn't open it.

"Laura. First of all, I want to say that these things are never easy. You've done a tremendous job as the assistant Chief of Staff over the last year, and I'm really impressed with your work, attention to detail, and how you always seem to be several steps ahead of everyone in the room. However, as you know, it has come to my attention that Stacy's behavior was quite detrimental to the company. Although you were entangled in it, and I'm sure you thought you were doing what you thought was in the best interests of the company, your actions in executing Stacy's directives were misguided, and unfortunately, I have to go in a different direction in terms of filling the position that Stacy vacated. And, as part of the reorganization of the office of the Chief of Staff, I will also want to fill your role as well, and your term in that role has been reduced, effective today. Kevin?" John was calm, and quite matter of fact, the arrogant prick. He crossed his legs, with one ankle resting atop his thigh, and he drummed the glass table with the fingers of his left hand.

"Laura, I know this must be difficult for you to process right now. But do you have any questions about what was just said to you?" Kevin raised an eyebrow and leaned forward slightly. He had a blue folder under his left hand, and she knew that it was her severance package, along with other details about her health insurance coverage and most likely a waiver for her to sign, releasing the company of all legal liabilities or lawsuits, if she would accept her severance quietly and without fuss. Fuck that.

She took a deep breath. *"Now or never,"* she thought. *"Shoot, but don't you dare miss."*

"No, I understand everything that was just said."

"Great, then let me-" started Kevin as he moved to open the blue folder, but she cut him off abruptly.

"Wait. Before we get to that, can I have a few minutes to speak with John? Alone?" She turned to look at John, and now it was her turn to raise her eyebrow.

John blinked twice in surprise and stopped drumming his fingers as he considered the odd request.

"Ok, sure. But just a few minutes, Laura. We really need to proceed with this." Kevin turned to look at John with a frown, but John shook his head slightly and pre-empted whatever it was he was about to say. "It's ok, Kevin. I'll call you back in in just a minute."

Kevin hesitated for a second, then nodded his head and picked up the blue folder. "Alright. I'll be right outside. Take your time." He stood up and pushed his chair in, then walked out of the office, softly closing the door behind him.

John waited until it was shut, then cocked his head curiously and stared right at Laura.

"Ok? What's on your mind?" He had the look of someone who was taking what he saw and heard at face value, and nothing more. It was as if he was strolling through an exhibit, waiting to be intrigued by the next thing around the corner, but waiting, patiently, and without thought or prejudice of what was to come.

"John, I know that Stacy's tactics were…aggressive, to some. But trust me when I say that I was doing what was in the best interests of the company, and for you. I don't want to re-hash the past, but what I do want to say, is that you should promote me to be your Chief of Staff. You and I both know that I can do the role, and with me in your corner, we can accomplish more in the next two years, than what's been accomplished in the last two. Hire me to be your Chief of Staff." She knew what he was going to say, but she waited to let him say it anyway.

He shook his head and gave a firm frown. "Laura, I'm sorry. There's no chance of that. There's not going to be a promotion today for you. As I just explained, we are doing a re-org, and your time and your position here, is eliminated. I'm sorry, but as you'll see here shortly, the severance is quite generous, and I know you will land on your feet in no time. Ok?" He glanced at the door, raised his hand, and was about to call out to invite Kevin back in, but she cut him off.

"No. I don't think you understand, John." He lowered his hand and stared at her in shock at the audacity of her words and tone. The sight of his eyes widening were priceless and would be permanently ingrained in her head.

"You *will* promote me to be your Chief of Staff, effectively immediately. The reason I know this, is because you have been a very, very bad CEO. You see, I have some valuable friends. Friends, who have special skills in tracking down hidden information, and things that don't want to be seen in the light of day. Are you familiar with the Cayman National Bank?" She opened up her manilla folder and pulled out the first piece of paper. It was a bank statement, with the account holder's name at the top. John's name. It had taken Larry and his IT specialist a lot of hours trying to track down and trace all the connections, but she had all the evidence verified, checked again, and checked yet again. The dirt was good, and she knew it was too, when she saw the color drain out of John's face.

"You've made quite a few, large deposits, hm John? It's not unusual, I suppose. I mean, you're the CEO of a Fortune Fifty company. Your annual compensation, with stock and bonus is like, what, eight million? So, to see these discreet deposits of three million here, two million there, seem like no problem, right? Ah, but there is a problem. You see, these large deposits were made twenty years ago, when you were just a Director. Now how is that possible, John? Do you know how that could be? Directors make like one hundred fifty thou." She looked at John and she could see a small bead of sweat start to form on his upper lip. But he was smooth, and he didn't get to be CEO because he was dumb.

"I don't know what you are implying, Laura. But whatever you have on that bank statement doesn't mean much. As you said, I *am* the CEO of the company. A highly compensated one at that. The timing of those deposits doesn't mean much. I come from money, what's the difference?" But he was nervous, and she sensed his fear. She could smell it, like a cologne that you smelled when you stepped into an elevator, long after the person had left.

She pulled out several more papers and put them next to the bank statement. "That's a lie. You see, Stacy has more access to systems and paperwork than you know. And with that access, I went back twenty years and personally audited the Men's Haircare division where you were the brand lead of, and bingo! I found a trail of fake invoices, to a shell company that you setup. And to which you authorized payment to, under the premise of payment to an ad agency. Creative Cats agency, right? And that trail unwound, and my guys found you at the end of it. With some six million dollars of stolen money. Want to see the trail?" She pulled out several more invoices, bank statements, and statements of work with Creative Cats agency, all signed by John. There was no doubt now, as John was full on sweating, and he licked his lips nervously, as he leaned back in his chair. He started to say something, but the words wouldn't come out, and he remained silent instead.

Laura gathered up the papers, and neatly put them back into the folder. She paused, and then drove the knife home.

"I can take this to the press. The board will fire you, and trust me, they will come after all of that money, plus back taxes and interest. You can fight them in court, but you'll lose. They'll also come after all of your CEO pay, and you'll end up broke, and in jail. Embezzlement is up to twenty-five years in prison. I looked it up," she said matter of factly.

"You fucking bitch," he hissed. His face was now contorted in a sneer, and the hatred was visible for the whole world to see.

There was a knock on the door, and Kevin popped his head in. "Ready for me now?" he asked.

"Just a minute, Kevin, alright? I'll call you in when I'm fucking ready," retorted John loudly. The color had returned to his face, and it was a bright red now. Now it was Kevin's turn to blink, and he quickly removed his head and closed the door shut.

"Shut up, John, and listen to me carefully. The choice here is a no brainer. I'm going to sit on this, and it will *never* see the light of day. You'll remain as CEO. You'll make eight million a year for the next two years, and then you can walk away gracefully in retirement. Voila. All the money in the Cayman Islands? Yours to keep. All your board memberships, all your club and golf memberships, all your circle of powerful friends, nothing changes. But in return, you will do two things for me immediately."

"Oh? And what's that?" he spat out. She could practically hear his teeth grinding in anger and frustration. She had him over a barrel, and they both knew it.

"Number one. You promote me to Chief of Staff, today, effective immediately. Number two, you sign this letter of intent, right now. It says that you will step down as CEO in two years, and when you do step down, you will throw your full support behind me, to see that I succeed you as CEO." She pulled out the last piece of paper from her folder, and slid it over to John, with a pen.

He gave a short, mirthless bark of a laugh. "Fuck you. The board decides the next CEO, not me. I can't control that."

She gave a cold and ruthless smile in return. "Well, you better start buttering them up starting tomorrow then. Because if you don't throw your support my way and use all your power and influence to make it happen, I go public with this. If I don't succeed you as CEO, your shining face is all over CNBC and CNN, and all your money will be taken, and you'll serve jail time. Two years is a long time, John. You can make it happen."

John squinted his eyes at her but was silent. Laura waited patiently, staring hard back at John. The deal she was giving him was a good one. He could retire in two years and pocket the rest of his salary and bonus, and cash out his stock options. But he still needed assurances.

"When I retire, you hand over everything you've got on the false payments, right?"

"Everything. And the day I start as your successor, I'll go back, and scrub clear all traces in the systems that this ever happened. Wiped clean."

John pursed his lips and blinked several times as he considered his options. Then, he grabbed the pen, scanned the contract on the table, and signed it. He shoved the paper and pen back at her, and as he did so, she gave a sigh of relief. She hadn't realized that she had been holding her breath, and she felt lightheaded at that moment.

"Kevin! Come back in!" John shouted. Kevin opened the door and entered, closing the door behind him quickly as he made a beeline for the table with his folder. He took his seat again and waited for John to start the conversation.

"Kevin, there's been a change since you left. I've decided to keep Laura Park here, keep her on my staff. She is going to be the new Chief of Staff." They both looked at Kevin. "*John must be an ungodly good poker player, because his face is revealing nothing,*" marveled Laura. Truly, John had recovered from his shock, and the color was back in his face as he stared at Kevin's stunned expression.

"What...I'm sorry, what did you say?" exclaimed Kevin, as his eyes darted first to John's face, then to Laura's, and then back to John's.

"I changed my mind, Kevin. Laura's in. Scrap the termination, please." John frowned at Kevin, and Laura could tell that he was irritated. He didn't like having to repeat himself, she knew.

"Right...are you sure? Right, right. Ok. So...are we all done here...then?" Kevin's eyes were wide as saucers, and there was wonderment in his voice, as it was clear that he had no fucking clue as to what was going on right now.

82

"Well, not exactly, right John? With my promotion to Chief of Staff, we need to talk about my new compensation as a Senior Vice President, which is the level at which this role is graded for, is it not?" Laura's voice was soft, but direct and firm at the same time. She looked at John, who stared at her like he could chew nails, and she swore that she heard him grinding his teeth, but he just nodded his head.

"Of course. You'll have your new comp statement in the morning. I'll see to it that Kevin has that drafted up for you. Now, if you'll both excuse me, I have another meeting to prep for."

"Perfect. I'll take a look at your schedule for the week and set some time with you on what you want to prioritize for the month," she said calmly, as she gathered her folder and pushed the chair out, standing up. Kevin stood up as well and walked to the door first. No doubt that he wanted to get out of the cross hairs as soon as possible.

John glared at her, but merely grunted as she turned away.

She followed Kevin out of the office, past Janet's desk, and down the hall towards Gabby's desk. He paused as they made it to her desk, and he lightly touched her elbow and motioned her to the side, slightly out of earshot from Gabby's desk.

"Laura, um, congratulations. What exactly happened just now? I'm so confused," asked Kevin, as he shook his head. "What did you say to John?" He towered over her. She had forgotten just how tall he was, and a part of her resented him for that. He was another tall, white, male, promoted up the ranks quickly. She knew he was smart, and capable, but so were many others, who were short, nonwhite, and female. It was time to break the mold here, and she was going to do just that.

"Oh, you know. I just pointed out a lot of good reasons why

he should keep me on. And I made a very compelling case as to why I shouldn't be linked with Stacy, that's all. He liked what I had to say. Listen, let's catch up for lunch in a week or so." Without waiting for him to acknowledge the request, she smiled briefly and then walked past Gabby's desk, giving her a wink as she went past. This side of the executives' floor was equally tasteful, but with a slightly different feel to it. Whereas the hallway towards John's office was filled with Cubism art, such as Picasso, Paul Cezanne, and Henri Rousseau, this wing was filled with modern art. Claude Monet, Henri Matisse, and Frida Kahlo. She admired a copy of Frida's 'The Two Frida's', as she passed by it, the dark and ominous sky behind two women holding hands, and it suited her perfectly. "One day, I'll have this exact painting in my office," she thought. Today, was a good day.

8

Old Friends

Laura sighed as she sat on her seat on the seven train. It wasn't too crowded, since it was a Saturday morning, but the schedule was always more intermittent on the weekends, and it was now almost forty-five minutes since she had stepped onto the train. They were at the Mets-Willets point stop, the last stop before Flushing, and she stared out the windows at the platform as a few people boarded the train. This had always been a fun station stop for her. She remembered buying cases of bottled water, then dumping them into a large cooler with wheels and ice, then lugging it to this stop so that she could sell cold bottled water for a dollar during the hot summer days in August for the annual US Open tennis tournament. The best place was on the wooden boardwalk like walkway that led from the subway to the gates. Folks would often buy water on the way in or out, and it only took four hours or so to sell out her cooler, which she then used to buy ice cream pops back in Flushing. The train doors closed, and then the train slowly accelerated. Most of the seven train stops were above ground, unlike the majority of the New York City subway system, but the last stop in Flushing was underground, and as the train entered the dark tunnel, she felt a sense of comfort as she knew this area quite well.

Once the train stopped and the doors opened, she got up and started her brisk walk towards her mother's apartment. She took the long escalator up to the street level, oriented herself, and then started walking east, on Roosevelt Avenue. She couldn't believe that the same shops were still in business after all these years. There was the photo shop, the Coco tea shop, the natural beauty shop Faces, and even the street cart vendor selling roasted nuts of all kinds was still in its usual spot on the sidewalk. The sidewalk was dotted with dark grey and black splotches, where people had spit out their gum, and eventually they got stepped on, lost their color, and became a part of the cement sidewalk over time. It was almost like artwork, the way all the grey and black splotches randomly dotted the cement. She walked past three garbage cans, one with a blue lid for plastic bottles, another with a green lid for carboards, and then a solid green one for general trash. As usual, they were near filled to the brim, as it seemed that the city garbagemen always left Flushing as their last stop or cleaned the bins only when someone complained loud enough. There were a fair amount of people walking on Roosevelt at this time of the morning, as folks were heading to get dim sum or running errands, but she deftly dodged them as she walked quickly up Roosevelt. Most of the stores were run by Chinese, Korean, or Spanish owners, and she smelled the fragrant odors of fried rice, steamed pork dumplings, and chicken tacos as she walked past.

Once she crossed the intersection past the McDonald's, she entered the more residential part of Flushing. Here, there were many red brick apartment buildings, mostly three to six stories tall, and green bushes lined the sidewalks, periodically broken up by oak trees. She went past a familiar church on her left, which was holding a flea market in their parking lot that day, and she waved to the pastor who frowned uncertainly at her as she strode past. *"He probably doesn't recognize me,"* she thought, and she was right. When she had left Flushing for college, she had been a skinny Korean girl with glasses, wearing hand me down clothing from Goodwill or donated to her from her mother's friends, and now, she was wearing contacts, and had on some nice black slacks from Yves St Laurent, a white blouse from Gucci, and comfortable Prada platform slide sandals. Even she hardly recognized herself. As promised, John stepped down as CEO after two more years, and though it had required pulling some strings on her end, she had successfully become the new CEO of Abernathy Consumer Products. She was also on the board of directors for a mid-sized publicly traded company, and her rolodex had exploded as she used her ever expanding spheres of influence, power, and money to secure favors, cozy up to political allies, and start shaping her path for her future ambitions.

Finally, after about fifteen minutes of walking, she stopped in front of a small store, the Flushing Veterinary Hospital, on Murray Street. The vet clinic was on the first floor, and on the second floor of the red brick building, were residences. She used a key to unlock the door next to the clinic and revealed a flight of steps in a yellow wall papered hallway. She had urged her mother to move out and even offered to buy her another place here in Flushing, but her stubborn mother refused.

"All of my friends are in this neighborhood, and I'm too old to move!"

When she got to the second floor, she used another key to open the door, and was greeted by a clamoring of voices, as several women were talking and laughing in the kitchen.

"Umma! I'm here!" she shouted, as she slipped off her sandals. The kitchen was right next to the front hallway, and she stepped in to see her mom, and two of her mom's best friends at the table. They were eating pa-jeon, which were scallion pancakes, and her mom waved her over.

"Come. Eat some," she said in English.

"An-yong-ha-sey-yo!" Laura said as she bowed politely to her mom's friends. They smiled at her.

"Oh! Laura, you looks so pretty!" said Mrs. Kim. She was in her early sixties, with grey hair heavily streaked through black. She had glasses and her hair was permed and cut ear length.

"Wah! Your mom says you very important! How come you not married?" asked Mrs. Choi, also in her sixties. She was the tallest of the three at the table and had straight black hair that was cut at neck length.

Inside, Laura gritted her teeth. *How come a woman has to be married to fulfill herself? Why does marriage mean success?* But she smiled politely and deflected. "I'm still looking." She walked to the cabinet and found a plate, then walked back and helped herself to some of the scallion pancakes, using a set of chopsticks on the table.

"She's a CEO!" said her mother as she switched over to Korean. She was beaming at her.

"Oh, really? So smart! And you must make a lot of money

now, too. How much money do you make?" asked Mrs. Kim, who also switched to Korean.

"Oh, CEO's make a lot of money, of course. Probably more than one hundred thousand, isn't that right?" asked Mrs. Choi.

Laura felt her cheeks flush with embarrassment, but she quietly demurred in Korean. "Oh, the company pays very well."

Thankfully, the nosy friends didn't push the matter, and they moved on to other questions. But eventually, it always came back to marriage, and why she didn't have a boyfriend. After what seemed like five hours, but was actually only ninety minutes, she excused herself, and said goodbye to her mom and friends.

"Ya! Make sure you eat healthy, ok? Don't eat too much meat! Also, next time, can you bring the French cookies from that bakery you found?"

She promised yes to all those requests, and finally got out of the apartment. She loved her mother and was proud of the fact that she raised Laura as a single mom without much of an education here in the United States, but she could only take small doses of the constant nagging that her mom's friends bestowed upon her. But this visit wasn't the only reason she was here in Flushing.

She walked back down Roosevelt Avenue, and past the train station. She continued past familiar stores, weaving her way past the busy bystanders, as the street was quite crowded now. Cutting over to 39th avenue, she slowed as she walked past the alley right by the Hyatt. It had been a long time since she had been to this section of Flushing, and her old friend was no longer manning the sidewalk by the alley entrance. In truth, she didn't know what had happened to Charlie, and she had never bothered with trying to find out. She supposed he had passed away, homeless and on the streets, but sometimes, she tricked herself into thinking that he had made it out and had gotten himself off the streets somehow. It could have happened. But not likely.

Eventually, she was on 39th avenue and College Point Boulevard, and she was relieved to see a familiar sight. There were several black guys manning a card table, playing three card monte, and trying to hustle bystanders. One of them, she recognized.

"Hey, Randall!"

Randall paused, as did the two other black guys, and two white guys who were about to be hustled, then exclaimed, "Tiny?! Whoa! Tiny! What up, yo? Ay, yo. Keep on playing. I'mma talk to my friend." He gave a wad of twenty dollar bills over to the guy standing next to him and walked on over as the rest of the guys stared intently at the cards being whisked on the table.

"Yo, tiny! What up?" he shouted, as he held out his right fist for a fist bump.

"I'm good. Long time. Still hus- I mean, still working, huh?" she caught herself in time and gave a smile.

"Yeaaaaahhh man. We be working. All day, every day. Man, you been prospering! Look at them clothes. I smell money, lots of it," he said with a genuine smile. Although it was summertime, and already eighty degrees and starting to feel humid, Randall was wearing dark designer jeans, and a black v neck t shirt, probably Banana Republic from the looks of it. He was still as tall as she remembered, as he towered over her, well over six feet tall. But time had aged him, as he had more grey than black in his goatee, and wrinkles lined his forehead and around his eyes.

"I'm doing ok. Can't complain. Say, I need to talk to Mason. Is he around? He's still running this section of Queens, yeah?"

Randall stopped smiling. He was all business now.

"Yeah, he's around. He still runs this joint. What you need him for?" he asked succinctly with a raised eyebrow.

"Just to ask him some questions. I might need something. Do you know where he is? I thought he would be here."

Randall paused and looked around. She didn't know it, but he was looking to see if she was with anyone. Cops, friends, enemies, whatever.

"He's in the old Ashi plaza, right down the street. Can't miss him. He's too important to be on the street nowadays. Can't say more than that."

"Ok, thanks, Randall. I'll go check it out. Good seeing you!" She gave him another fist bump, awkwardly, in the way that only a corporate executive fist bumping a real street thug can, and then continued walking down College Point until she got to the old Ashi Plaza. At one time, years and years ago, it used to house a Korean grocery store, along with a Korean plaza full of imports from Seoul. You could find rugs, vases, spices, electric blankets, and all sorts of other things from Seoul, but the whole plaza had closed down as the owners went bankrupt. Now, the whole place was fenced off with a chain link fence, and the brick building that had been the plaza was mostly dark and boarded up. Boarded up...except there were people inside the fence. One was on his phone, talking to someone, two were sitting down next to a large tree stump, playing dominoes, and another was leaning against the door to the building. She saw another set of guys walk around the corner of the building and into a side door. She was a bit nervous, but she walked up to the fence, where there was a gate, and yelled to the guy on the phone.

"Hey, is Mason here?"

The man looked at her hard, and then nodded over to the

building, then continued with his phone conversation. He was young, maybe twenty years or so. She cautiously undid the gate, and walked in. The two guys playing dominoes stopped to stare at her, and one of them stood up and walked over.

"Gotta check you, spread your arms," he said. He looked to be Puerto Rican, or maybe Dominican, and he was tall, good looking, with brown hair that was slicked back, and slender. He was wearing a white t shirt and white jeans, with a fancy looking Hermes belt. She was a bit alarmed but did as she was told. This was their world, not hers, and she felt out of her element here. The man quickly patted her down, checking for weapons, and satisfied, turned, and went back to the tree stump to resume his game of dominoes. She looked uncertainly at the pair, but then continued to the brick building door, where another man was leaning against the wall. He was black, with black sunglasses, wearing a blue superman t shirt and blue jeans. His head was shaved bare, and he didn't straighten up when she walked up. He just kept his butt on the wall, with one leg raised and the foot leaning on the wall, the other supporting him as he stood, thumbs tucked into the pockets of his jeans.

"Can I help you?" he asked politely.

"Yeah, I'm here to see Mason."

"Does he know you're coming?"

"No, he doesn't. I'm a…sort of a friend. He knows me from a long time ago. Is he here?"

"Maybe. What's your name?"

"Laura. Tell him Laura from way back in the day is here. He used to call me 'Tiny', and I watched him, Zeebats, and Randall hustle three card monte after school."

The slender man chuckled and shook his head in disbelief.

"That right? Alright. Wait here." He opened the door, which she noticed was not in disrepair like the rest of the building. It was brand new, and was made of reinforced steel, with brand new hinges as well.

After a minute, the man came back out, and held the door open for her. "Come on in."

She walked inside, slowly letting her eyes adjust to the dimness of the room and saw a desk at the far end of the room, with a man seated behind it and two other men standing by the side.

"Go on, at the end of the room," said the door man, and he closed the door behind her as he stayed outside.

She walked confidently into the warehouse, her sandals making small echoes as she walked over. She noticed that on her left, were cages that were maybe ten feet high, and ten feet wide, one next to the other. The cages were empty, but all of them had doors with pad locks on them. She wondered what they normally held. The right side of the warehouse had cardboard boxes, some opened, some closed, and there were Styrofoam packing peanuts sprinkled on the floor, tape, scissors, and even a random bolt cutter. It all added to the mystique of the place, but she didn't dare venture over to see what was inside those boxes.

Finally, she stood in front of the desk. It wasn't fancy. Just a white acrylic desk, a little battered, and behind it, sat Mason. He was still as short as she remembered, but his hair was a mix of grey and black, and he had a goatee as well, also mostly grey. He had on a black leather jacket, white t shirt underneath, and black jeans. He looked up at her and gave her a smile.

"Laura! Tiny! Well, I'll be damned. Long time. Man, I remember when you went off to college. Didn't see you much after dat though. How's it going?" he asked warmly.

"Mason, good to see you. Yes, been a long time for sure. You're moving up in the world, I see," she said, as she glanced around and smiled back. He paused a good three seconds as he looked her up and down, before replying.

"As are you."

She squirmed a little under his intense stare but didn't show her unease. She was too polished and well trained. Afterall, she swam with the nastiest and biggest of sharks in her company.

"So, it's been a long time. And I know, that after all these years, you're not here to smile and chit chat about the past, am I right? What can I, Mason, do for you, today?" He leaned back in his chair and pursed his lips. The two black men standing to the side of the desk looked at Laura but didn't speak. One of them sat down on the desk, one leg swinging off the floor, and the other pulled out his phone to check a message, but otherwise looked bored.

"You're right. I'm not here to talk about the past. I'm here to talk business. Can we speak privately?" She looked at the two men, then back to look at Mason. She felt more comfortable now, as this was familiar ground for her. Negotiations, and deal making.

"Yo. Gimme some quiet time with my friend here. Give Zeebats a call and see where he at."

"You want me to see about lunch?" asked the man who had sat on the desk. He now stood up and stretched.

"Yeah. Get dem Cuban sandwiches from the deli down the street. But no Swiss cheese on mine, aight?"

The two men sauntered off back towards the door that Laura had entered, then disappeared outside. She waited for the door to close, then turned back to face Mason.

"Zeebats doing well?" she asked.

"Yeah, he doin' aight. Running an errand for me right now.

So, what's dis bidness you talkin' bout?"

She took a breath and dove right in. Negotiations, and deal making.

"You know, there's a crackdown on cocaine these last few months. Feds and DEA have been all over it. Busted up the drop in Miami last week. Fifty tons. Another shipment caught in Texas last month, twenty tons. Very, very little has made it into the port of New York. Can't find it anywhere on the street these days. At least, not in Manhattan…" she said quietly, and then waited to see Mason's reaction.

He chuckled, then it grew, louder, and then it was a full-on laugh. But he eyed her up and down, then stopped laughing and asked a question. "Ok…And? What's this got to do with me?"

She walked over and pulled out the chair that was across from his desk and sat down.

"You run point here in Flushing, right? I need a kilo. Straight up. My contact says that there is hardly any coke at all in the city, and he was skeptical that you would have any, but I said that I would give it a shot."

Mason was calm, and if he was shocked, he sure as hell didn't show it on his face, but his words showed it. "You? Tiny Asian Laura. Need. A. Kilo. Are you for real right now?"

"Look, I know it seems like an odd request. I'm not with the police, I'm not undercover or anything like that. But an immensely powerful person is literally dying to get his hands on this. And if I can get it, then this person will owe me a very, very, big favor. Multiple favors. I will own this man."

"And you think I got it?"

"Yes. And if not, then I know you can get it."

Mason paused and looked at her. He leaned forward and

stared into her eyes. Laura didn't flinch or lean back. She held strong eye contact and also leaned forward, unafraid, and confident as fuck. Twenty seconds passed, then thirty, and finally, after a minute, Mason made up his mind.

"Yeah, I got access. You right, there's not much on the streets. I got prolly half a key, and I can get my hands on another half via…partnerships. But I'm 'posed to be dealin' it on the streets. What make you think I'mma sell it all to you?" He leaned back and tilted his head.

"How much does one key cost?"

"Street value? Normally like thirty large. But there's a drought you see. And I gotta go secure the other half key from someone else, which will cost me more. So I'mma make prolly ninety off this one key."

"I'll buy it for one hundred."

"You got cash? One hundred large? Cuz I don't take that American Express bullshit."

"I'll get it in cash. One hundred large."

He shook his head. "I said ninety large for one key. But *I* still gotta go get the other half key, which will cost *me* forty-five, street value. Add in a markup for getting that half key, plus my half at street…call it one thirty-five."

She did some quick math in her head, and then shook her head in reply. "You're charging me a hundred percent markup on the other half key. That's too much. Let's call it one ten."

"You got someone else you can call to get a half key from? In this drought? Like one eight hundred cocaine? Huh? You think if I don't hurry up and pick up the phone, like right now, and put a stop to the other connection, you don't think they will sell out their half key by dinner time?"

She knew that he had a point. She didn't have any other connections, and she really, really wanted to pull the rabbit out of the hat on this one. If she could score a kilo now, she would forever own this person. He had a habit, a bad one, and she would have Larry make sure to get it all on video tape, the handoff of the coke, and he would be in her pocket for as long as he lasted in his role. Still, she had played enough big-time poker games, to sense a bluff when one was being played. She could afford the one thirty-five, now that she was making millions as a CEO, but she didn't want to give so easily this time. It would mean Mason would feel like he could do it again, in the future.

"Hm. You're right, Mason. You're right. But I got one twenty-five, cash, and I can have it to you as soon as you get the full key. You'll make more on your half key, and a markup on the other half key, and there's no risk of your dealers getting busted on the street. This is low risk, all reward. Everybody wins. One twenty-five, or I walk." She added a lie at the end. "This is a nice to have deal for me, not a must have."

Mason pursed his lips and frowned. Laura stood up and pushed back the chair, but she didn't move yet. She sensed a fold coming, and she was right.

"Aight. One twenty-five. Cash. Gimme yo number and I'll have Zeebats call you when I got the full boat. He'll call you, then direct you to a pay phone, and then setup the exchange once you get to the payphone. Gotta be careful, you know."

Instead of giving her number, however, Laura pulled out a card from her pocket and slid it over the desk, whereupon Mason picked it up and squinted at it. Her mind raced ahead to how she would have to get such a large amount of cash out of her bank, but she would figure it out.

"Just call this number when you're ready, and my guy will be ready for the exchange. He's exceptionally reliable. He wanted to come to do the negotiations, but I knew you wouldn't trust a stranger, so I came in person. From now on, you'll only deal with him, not me." She turned around and started to walk away, relieved that she had done it. She was going to own the Mayor of New York City.

"Yo. Who da fuck Larry Kudlow?"

9

The Exchange

It was about ten p.m. when Larry finally got the call.

"Is this Larry?" said the deep voice on the other end of the line.

"Yeah," he said cautiously. "It's Larry."

"Write this address down. Meet outside there in one hour. Bring what you owe." Larry grabbed a pen and post it, then scribbled the address that was given, and hung up. He had tried to convince Laura not to go this route, working with some street drug dealer and hustler that he didn't know, as it introduced risk to the equation. Risk of the unknown. But Laura was convinced that her early friendship with these guys would pay dividends in scoring the drugs. He had one of his guys do a quick check to find what he could about Mason, and even in just a few short hours, he learned much. He found out that Mason was one of the key lieutenants running point in Flushing, and that he worked for a drug kingpin named Luis. Long rap sheet, did some jail time, but from all accounts, smart, cutthroat, and not to be messed with. He opened his drawer, grabbed his .38 special revolver, and put it in his holster under his left armpit. He also grabbed the black duffel back on the floor, full of cash, and quickly made his way out of his office and onto the street level.

He checked his phone and put in the address to see how long it would take. About forty minutes, due to traffic. He unlocked his sedan and put the duffel bag in the passenger seat, then started his lonely drive. He took the 278 to Grand Central Parkway, and then slowly circled the address a few times, checking out the building. It was a rundown coffee shop, it looked like. There were a few customers inside, drinking tea or coffee, and one rather large black guy, standing out front, smoking a cigarette. He figured that might be his guy, but only one way to find out. After he parked down the block, he grabbed the bag and walked towards the coffee shop, and stood outside, making eye contact with the large black man, who came up to him promptly.

"Larry?" he asked in a deep voice.

"Yeah," he said simply.

"Alright. Follow me." The man looked up and down the street, then crossed it, and over into a dark alley between two small residential buildings. Larry hesitated, but quickly followed the disappearing man's back, into the darkness. The man went to the end of the alley, where there was a steel door on the left, then rapped on it several times. The door opened, and the man went inside, jerking his head to indicate that Larry should follow him, which he reluctantly did. As soon as he entered, two sets of hands grabbed his arms, and roughly escorted him forward to the middle of the room, which was lit by a single bulb. There was a rickety wooden table there, and a rather short black man was standing behind it, hands on the table, leaning slightly forward. He had a few streaks of grey in his short hair, and a goatee as well. Black leather jacket, white t-shirt, and jeans.

"Check him," the man said, and Larry felt the two guys release his arms and give him a quick frisk. One of them pulled out his gun and laid it on the table, along with the duffel bag.

"No wire, boss."

"Aight. Zeebats, go outside and walk around the block. Check for any funny looking dudes, vans, anything suspicious. Call me if you see anything even remotely funny."

The tall black man who had met Larry, and who was off to his left, grunted and walked back out the way he came, slamming the door shut behind him.

"So. You are Larry Kudlow, eh? How you know Laura?" asked the short man. There was no smile or mirth at all. Just a cold and matter of fact tone.

"I work for her. She uses me to do…jobs that she otherwise couldn't."

"Is that right? Like…what kind of jobs?"

"You mean, other than picking up drugs? This and that," he said sarcastically.

"Oh, you're funny, huh? Funny white guy, eh? Give me an example. What else she got you do? I need to know more about you. I can't just hand over product to someone I ain't met before," said Mason coldly.

"Just stuff. Mostly investigative work, research, digging into people's pasts. That sort of thing."

"That right? And you're good at that sort of thing, huh?"

Larry didn't answer. Rather, he just tilted his head and stared flatly back at Mason.

"So. You got the cash?"

"Yeah. I got it. In the bag," he said as he nodded at the duffel bag which had been put on the table. "You gonna count it?"

"Oh, we gonna count it alright. Not that I don't trust you, Larry," now it was Mason's turn to sound sarcastic. "But I don't trust you. Until we do some mo' bidness, that is. Trust got to be earned, ya feel me?"

"I feel you," he said dryly, as he watched Mason unzip the bag and pull out the stacks of bills. It took a while, but Mason was satisfied. He nodded to the man on Larry's right, who tossed Mason a brown paper bag. Mason pulled out a saran wrapped block of white powder, and a knife, which he plunged into the block and slid it over the table towards Larry.

"Check it," he ordered. Larry shuffled forward, dipped a pinkie into the opening, and tasted it on his tongue.

"It's good," he said, and he sealed the hole over and stuffed it into the bag but stopped when Mason's hand clamped down on top of his.

"I know. Just one mo' thing. Who's it for?" Mason leaned closer, staring into Larry's eyes.

Larry considered his answers and options carefully, before replying. "Someone powerful. Someone that Laura needs in her pocket. Someone, that she wouldn't appreciate me telling you."

Mason gave a small smile, then let free his grip on his hand. "I heard the mayor has a habit. I hear, that perhaps, this might be for him."

Larry finished putting the coke back into the bag and then stuffed it under his coat. He pursed his lips and cocked his head to one side as he answered. "Careful about rumors. The rumors you hear about someone are as true as the rumors you hear about yourself. I'll see myself out now. Can I have my gun back?"

Mason narrowed his eyes at the rumors comment, unsure of whether it was just a glib comment, or an insult. He decided on the former and slid the gun back over to Larry.

"Be seeing you soon, Larry."

"Maybe. Maybe not," he answered over his shoulder, as he thankfully got out of the building in one piece.

10

Rumors in the Air

Three Years Later...

Ever since she had become CEO, Laura had tightened up her
ship. She learned from Stacy's firing, and didn't send any
dangerous emails which could be later traced by IT. Whenever
she wanted to undercut someone or steer the board a different
direction, she relied on face-to-face conversations, or phone calls.
No more paper trails. She hired a new Chief of Staff, Jennifer
Jones, a friend from her MBA class, and she trusted her implicitly.
She no longer generated fake invoices herself whenever she
needed to tap into her slush fund. Instead, she had Jennifer
generate them with Geoff's help, and she had Jennifer sign off
on approving them. She didn't want any links of her approving
fake invoices. She also deleted all records of her past approvals
of invoices linked to the slush fund. Internally, she had
consolidated her power and sphere of influence, by firing or

navigating her enemies out of the company and hiring and promoting her friends and those that she trusted. One more year as CEO, then a Senate run. She wanted to run for Senator, and after that, President.

"*I'm going to be the first Asian American President of the United States, and a female one at that!*" she grinned. From rummaging around the trash bins of Flushing, to President. She knew she had a long road ahead of her, but she had excellent advisors surrounding her, and, she already had political allies in her corner. Like, the Mayor of New York City, for example. When she had first thought about making the announcement that she wanted to someday run for the Senate, she thought of no better person to call than her old boss.

"Stacy, hey, it's me, Laura," she said.

"Laura! Good to hear from you. I saw the earnings last week. Nice call on Brazil, by the way. Fastest growing country for the company, and far outstripping Proctor and Unilever by double."

"Thank you. Yes, we did well down there, and we're going to push even harder this year in that market. How's retirement treating you? What have you been up to these days?"

"Oh, you know. This and that. I'm on several boards. The most interesting one is being on the board of Carnegie Hall. Those people are so arrogant and pompous, but it's funny at the same time. Just last week, one of the more senior board members, this guy name Joseph Calderon, got into an argument with another member, Caleb Weinstein, you know, the CEO of Time Warner? Anyway, they are arguing about who gets to sit at the head of the table for the board meeting quarterly dinner. Ridiculous. They are literally arguing for fifteen minutes straight, and I'm sitting there thinking, 'Really? This is what we are talking about?' And finally, this woman, Jessica Kennedy, I think she's one of the nieces of the Kennedy clan, she jumps in. I'm thinking, great, finally, someone is going to put a stop to this nonsense. Then she goes off on how *she* should be sitting at the head of the table. My god."

"Ha-ha. Well, at least you're making some good connections. I may need to tap into them one day," she said with a smile.

"You're doing well, Laura. You had a good teacher. What's up? You didn't call me to talk about my boring board meetings."

"That's true. I didn't. Listen, you know that I want to make a run in politics, sooner rather than later. I'm thinking of announcing it publicly, in the press, that when the Senate election for New York comes up next year, that I plan to run. This way, I figure I'll start to get a lot of airtime, media requests, questions as to where I stand on certain matters, etc. What do you think?"

There was a long pause on the other end. She knew that Stacy was considering her question carefully, and thoughtfully, as she always does. "I don't think that's the best angle," she offered simply.

"What do you mean?"

Another pause. "You can do that; I'm not going to be mad at that approach. But I think it's better to hint at it. Make people wonder, 'Who the hell is this Laura Park?' Instead of blatantly announcing your intentions, a better way is to leak it to the press."

"Hm, ok. So, leak the news that I'm running next year, and then confirm the rumors?"

"No, exactly the opposite. Leak it to the press, and then *deny* the rumors."

Normally, Laura was able to piece things together very quickly, but on this one, she wasn't following. It didn't make sense.

"Wait. Leak it to the press, and then deny the rumors? I'm

not tracking. Why would I do that, and what does that even accomplish?"

"Hmm. Ok, check this out. You know when you go on a first date with someone? That nervousness, the anticipation? Right? You go on the date, and then…you wait. You wait for the next call, the next text, the next email, whatever. But there's this heightened sense in that waiting, as your body and mind tingle, anticipating, going back, and dissecting everything, and you become almost obsessed. The waiting kills you. You just want to know, is the second date coming or not? So, by leaking it, and then denying it, firstly, you cause people to google and read up, 'Just who the hell is this Laura Park anyway?' You build up your profile, you do the charitable events, you make good noise and press in Abernathy, you start fleshing out your policies and what you believe in. Soon, people start reading up on you, who you are, how you grew up, and they believe in you, they want you to run. But still, you coyly demur, you deflect, you make them wait. You keep up the media presence and you keep the noise going that folk close to you are saying you'll run, but when you finally do announce it, it will be a huge roar of approval, a large groundswell that you can ride as you hit the primaries hard. It's about momentum."

Laura thought about it. It kind of made sense, but she wasn't one hundred percent sure. But what she was sure of, was that Stacy's opinion was usually on point, and that tipped her decision. She made up her mind, quickly and decisively, as Stacy had taught her, long ago.

"Alright. I'm doing it. Should I use my contacts at CNBC to get an interview?" she asked.

"No, no. I have a contact at CNN. I'll put them in touch with your office to setup an interview with you. We'll have the pretense be, 'The most powerful Asian woman in business you've never heard of', but then you have Geoff or Jennifer casually mention that this is strictly about business, and not to bring up a possible Senate run. That will get the reporter's ears perked up, and immediately, he will home in on that, either in the middle, or end of the interview."

Laura pictured how it would go down, and it all fit neatly. "Set it up."

It took a few weeks, but the day finally came when the reporter from CNN was coming to do the interview. She was wrapping up her staff meeting and looked at her watch. Eight forty-five in the morning.

She was in John's old office, and she had redecorated it, but not by much. She had replaced John's wooden desk and replaced it with an acrylic white desk and a modern bungie cord chair from Room and Board. Her desk was immaculate, empty save for the keyboard, mouse, and monitor. She had kept the same black leather couch and leather armchair, along with the glass coffee table over to the right side of the office, and the TV was playing CNBC on mute above the couch. There was a white orchid on the coffee table, and just one magazine for show, National Geographic. The other side of the office had the same round, glass table with four white chairs, also from Room and Board, but she had had all carpeting removed from the office and it was now just grey ceramic tile, not small squares, but large squares about twelve inches square. Geoff was still her administrative assistant, and he had also moved up to the twenty third floor as well, replacing Janet, who Laura had moved to another part of the company after John's retirement.

She was seated at the glass table, and Jennifer, her Chief of Staff, and Adam, the director in the team, were taking notes. She recalled five years ago, when Adam had persistently tried to get onto her team. He was young, smart, ambitious, and eager to learn. Although he was sometimes a little too aggressive, he was capable. Jennifer was her classmate from business school. She was tall, black, and spoke with a level voice that just oozed confidence and commanded respect. She trusted Jennifer implicitly, and she knew that she would have her back no matter what.

"Alright. Make sure the board materials are printed out, laid out neatly on the board room table, one in front of each seating," she said as she looked at her notebook.

"Yes, all printed out, and will be taken care of," said Jennifer as she looked at her. She knew the drill by now. Even though both she and Adam knew how to handle a board meeting by now, she still went over every detail. It soothed her, they knew.

"Refreshments outside the room on the table by ten a.m. Coffee, tea, snacks. Oh, and make sure you have the Chobani yogurt this time, ok?"

"Yes, we have the Chobani. And lunch will be ready to go in the adjoining conference room, catered from Del Frisco's, precisely at eleven forty-five," said Adam as he took a note in his notepad. He was only thirty-five years old, but he was extremely ambitious. He was an NYU Stern business school alum, and so far, had proved very capable.

"Great. Afternoon refreshments?" she asked as she looked at Jennifer.

"All set with that as well. We have pastries, cookies, and madeleines from Le Pain Quotidien, as well as cupcakes and banana pudding from Magnolia bakery."

"Ok. And black Lincoln town cars for each board member in the back side of the building, right? Those need to be ready to go at three p.m., but the meeting ends at four. The meeting will be focused on the quarter results, so I may text you to track down some details if I don't have them handy." She checked her notebook. *"Damn, almost forgot."*

"Yes, cars will be ready. I called the limo company yesterday and they confirmed the reservations." Jennifer was sharp, and on it, as usual.

"Ok. Sounds like we're all set. Oh, Jennifer, one last thing. Can you ask Geoff to call Anna Wintour's office, and request two more tickets to the Met gala? She's expecting my request, as I hinted at it last week when I had lunch with her, and she said she could make two more tickets available if I absolutely needed it." She snapped her notebook closed and stood up.

"Wow! You're going to the Met gala!" exclaimed Adam enviously. He had an incredulous look on his face. "How in the world did you get tickets?"

"They're not for me. It's for one of the board members. I got introduced to Anna several years ago, and we made a large donation to her foundation. I made sure she knew it was me who orchestrated it. Alright, Jennifer, you clear on the last bit for when the reporter comes by?"

Jennifer stood up and flashed a bright smile. "Oh yes. I got it covered. I'll just wait outside by Geoff's desk for when she arrives."

"Alright then. Let's get to it. Text me if you need anything today. I'll be in with the board pretty much all day, but I can step out if you need me to put out any fires."

"I doubt it. All the fires start because of requests from the people in that room!" laughed Jennifer, a deep and powerful laugh that started from the gut. She smiled wryly and shook her head, but she was right. She walked back to her desk but didn't sit down right away. She wanted to enjoy the view out the window. Behind her, she could hear the muffled voices of Jennifer and Geoff, chatting as they waited for the reporter to check in and come by for the interview.

The sun was straight ahead of her, and it would start its ascent as it climbed up, up, and then over Central Park, making its way westward and over her head. The sky was a bright azure blue, with long grey colored clouds that filled up the horizon and heavens. Spring was in full swing now, and the trees were budding green with leaves and the grass was getting thicker and greener. It would need to be cut soon. There were joggers below, running on the cement sidewalk along Central Park West, and also along the pathways that snaked into the park itself. Most of the buildings on Central Park West were old co-op residential buildings, but Abernathy Consumer Products was one of the last holdouts along this coveted street. She inhaled deeply and smiled, for perhaps the thousandth time. She sometimes had to pinch herself, as she couldn't believe that she had made it this far, unscathed.

The phone on her desk rang and interrupted her reverie, and she turned and pressed the speaker button.

"Yes?"

"Hi, Gale Marsden is here to see you? From CNN," said Geoff pleasantly. She could hear Jennifer's voice softly in the background. She knew that she was warning the reporter not to mention a Senate run, and please, please, don't even bring it up.

"Ok, send her in." She clicked off the button just as Geoff started to reply, but she didn't catch what he had been about to say. She sat down on her chair, opened her desk drawer, and put her notebook inside it to leave her desk clean and barren except for her keyboard, monitor, and desk phone. The door to her office opened, and in walked a short, blonde haired woman, with blue eyes. She wore her shoulder length hair pulled back in a ponytail, and was wearing a grey blouse, and black slacks that hugged the curves of her hips suggestively. Her nose was small and very slightly upturned at the end, and she smiled as she crossed the room in comfortable Eloise black leather flats. In a word, she was beautiful, and Laura was taken aback.

"Hi, I'm Gale Marsden," the short woman said as she extended her hand. Her handshake was firm and strong but contrasted with how soft and smooth her actual hand felt like.

"Nice to meet you. Laura Park. You're not exactly what I was expecting," she said and as soon as the words left her mouth, she was kicking herself for showing her surprise. "*Stacy would not approve right now*," she thought with a wry smile.

Gale settled into the chair across from her desk, and pulled out her phone, setting it on top of a notepad. "Why is that?"

"Oh, nothing. Anyways, glad you could make it. I'm looking forward to this interview."

"Me too. Listen, I don't know who you know in my office, but my editor gave me this assignment and made me drop all of the other projects I was working on. Priority numero uno, she said, and I'm not going to let her down. This is going to be front page on the CNN homepage, according to her. Do you mind if I record our interview, by the way?" Gale tapped her phone, unlocked it, and quickly found the voice memo recording, and without waiting for Laura's assent, hit the record button.

"Not at all," she said, and she found herself staring at the top of Gale's blouse, where the top two buttons were unbuttoned, and she could see some of Gale's cleavage. Though she was petite, maybe only five foot two if she had to guess, she had pleasant curves to her toned and athletic body.

"Ok, great. So, the article we're working on is with the theme of, 'The most powerful Asian American woman in business that you've never heard of.' Can you start by telling me your background, where you grew up, what your childhood was like, where you went to school? Let's start there." Laura blinked and looked up from Gale's cleavage and she noticed that she had been caught looking, as Gale was staring right at her with a raised eyebrow as if to say, "*Up here, lady. Look up here.*"

"Absolutely. Well, I'm a native New Yorker, born and raised in Flushing, Queens. I was raised by a single mom, and we struggled for a good part of my childhood."

"What happened to your dad?" asked Gale, as she opened up her notepad and started scribbling some notes.

"He left us when I was young. I think I was in the fourth grade."

"Why? Was it another woman?" asked Gale sympathetically as she looked up to gauge Laura's expression.

"Oh, no. Nothing like that. My parents were immigrants from Korea, and they had a really hard time when they moved here. My dad…he had a hard time finding work and supporting us. And my mom, she didn't really speak much English at the time, so she did odds and ends for money, but it was difficult. My dad, he just blew up one day at my mom, and he left. We never saw him again."

"That must have been really stressful. Do you think about him at all?" Gale was looking down at her notepad and taking notes.

"Yeah. Sure, I guess. Listen, this isn't a psychology session, ok? Can we just move on from talking about my dad?" Gale blinked and raised her head, but if there was any surprise, she didn't show it.

"No problem. So, Flushing born and raised, and you went to school there I assume, what about college and work?"

Laura subconsciously breathed a sigh of relief. "Yes. I went to the University of Maryland on a full ride and studied business and economics. After graduating, I did several years in investment banking at Deutche bank here in New York, in their mergers and acquisitions team. Went to Cornell for my MBA, then McKinsey, then here."

"Very nice. Tell me about banking. I hear it is very cutthroat to be in i-banking, and I've heard from several friends that it can be quite hard for a woman."

"It was very intense; I will say that. All the stories you hear about investment banking are true, mostly. You work crazy hundred-hour weeks, work on Thanksgiving day, Christmas, New Year's, all of that is true. But you learn a ton, especially right out of undergrad. They had us doing all the modeling, all of the deal prep and analysis, PowerPoints, etc. I learned so much from my time there, and it has served me quite well in this role." She thought back to those long ass hours and imbalanced work life balance and was thankful that she got out of the rat race when she did.

"Ok. What about the second part to my question? Was it tough for a woman?" Gale looked up again, to see what kind of reaction Laura would show her.

"You know, the expression of 'you have to work twice as hard to get half as far'? There is a little bit of truth in that. And for a minority, doubly so, but I kept my head down and worked as hard as I could to get noticed. But then I realized something. Working hard and keeping your head down only gets you so far. It's the relationships you make and cultivate that are more important. Who you know, and the information you know, is just as important as the what you know. So, I started branching out and making friends, gathering information, and doing my best to accelerate my career there."

Gale made some notes and a noncommittal 'hm'. "You still didn't really answer my question though. Was it tough for a woman? What was the culture like? Did you ever face any sexism or racism while you were there?"

Laura frowned and drummed the top of her desk with her fingers. "Mmm. Nothing that I want to go on record at this point. Let's just say it was tough being a woman in that team, but I'm a tough woman. I can dish it as well as anyone, and you have to, if you want to fit in and thrive. Honestly, I enjoyed being as good or better than any of my male peers."

Gale nodded her head and scribbled some more in her notebook. There was a pause as she stuck the tip of her tongue out, touching her top lip in concentration, and Laura found it incredibly sexy. She squirmed a little in her chair, as it dawned on her just how attracted she was to this reporter. *"God knows I haven't been in a relationship in forever,"* she thought to herself.

"Tell me what you did after investment banking, and how you ended up here as CEO," said Gale as she looked up once more. Her blue eyes were inquisitive, piercing, and contrary to most people with blue eyes, looked warm and inviting as opposed to cold and distant.

"Sure. I went back to business school and studied at Cornell, graduated, then did a stint at McKinsey consulting for about six years. Met some incredibly bright people there and found a mentor who I still keep in touch with. While I was there, I was working on a project for Abernathy Consumer Products, and I impressed the head of the hair care division so much that they made me an offer to come join them and I accepted. I did a lot of various functions in that team, from finance, to marketing, to market research, and eventually, I became the head of that division when Ely retired. Did a stint in strategy here, then finally made my way over to being the Assistant Chief of Staff, to Stacy Atkins, who later retired. When she left, I became the Chief of Staff, and later, accelerated to CEO after John retired."

Gale was furiously taking notes, but was looking up now and then to read and follow Laura's facial expressions, and stopped to ask some follow up questions.

"Very impressive. I think I have read or heard a lot of what you just said. Homework," she added. "But I want to know why you are the most powerful woman in business that we've never heard of. Which circles do you run in, what do you mean when you say you are powerful, and why is that we don't know about you at all?"

Laura tilted her head and considered the myriad of questions that were thrown her way. She knew that she wanted to be private, but at the same time, she had to divulge some of her background and what made her influential, otherwise there would be no point to the article. *"How do I share just enough without giving away too much?"* she thought. It had been a struggle, as she prepped for this interview, but she thought she had found just the right balance of what to share.

"I think the words 'powerful' or 'influential' can mean a lot of things. My sphere of influence expands outside the company.

I have staunch support and a close friendship with the mayor of New York, Joe Gaundino. I can pick up the phone and call any number of CEOs who will take my call. I can't really divulge who my connections are in the media and entertainment business, as they are very private, but let's just say that I can secure a meeting with most actors or actresses if I need it, or any sports figure as well." She stopped, to see if Gale had any questions. If she was in awe or surprised, she didn't show it. *"God, she is so beautiful,"* she thought. She wondered if Gale had ever dated a woman before.

"I see. I do want to come back to that, about just how you were able to get these connections and how you became so influential. But let me ask you this. Are you also considering a career in politics? I heard you may be making a run for Senator next year, is that right?" Gale was staring at her, waiting to get a reaction of some sort with this shift in the conversation. She acted as if she was caught off guard.

"Hm. Who told you that? That wasn't supposed- Let me just say, I'm not running for Senator at this point. I don't know who told you that, but I am not running." She looked at her watch. *"Time to cut this short,"* she thought. *"Make it seem like it was an important discovery but that I wasn't prepared to answer."*

"You said 'at this point', what did you mean by that? Does that mean you will at some point, run for Senator?" Gale asked curiously. She was leaning forward slightly, and damn it all, her cleavage was distracting Laura to no ends.

"I can't answer that right now. Listen, I'm sorry, I have to cut this meeting short, as I have a board meeting to get ready for. Can we finish up your other questions later?"

"I understand. We can do that." Gale tapped the stop button on her phone and gathered her notebook and started to stand up.

"Ok. How about we finish up over dinner? I should be finished by eight. Grammercy Tavern at eight thirty?"

Gale looked at her, and Laura felt naked and vulnerable under that one second glance, as if Gale could see right through her and into her darkest and deepest recesses of her being.

"Sounds good! See you then," and Gale leaned over to shake her hand once more, her skin soft and smooth, her grip strong and confident.

When she had left, Laura felt the tension in her shoulders release, and she sighed, but whether it was from longing or relief, she couldn't tell.

11

The Demon Within

Larry listened intently on the phone and was writing notes with his right hand.

"Yup, got it." He leaned his head to the left and cradled his cell phone between his shoulder and cheek as he pulled open the drawer on his left and rummaged for his wallet.

"Yes, yes. We're on it. I'll have something over to you in a couple weeks. What? I see. Well, listen, Laura, if you want things done right, then you have to trust me when I say we'll need a couple weeks." Laura could be really pushy sometimes, and this was one of them. "No. Yes. Give me two weeks, and you'll have a full report. Ok. Talk then." He grabbed his phone off his shoulder and ended the call. At this point, five years in, he and his team were on an annual retainer, and his firm only worked exclusively for Laura. For a million dollar per year retainer fee, his team of four did whatever Laura needed, plus expenses and travel. Any work or projects that exceeded the retainer, eventually got billed to Laura, or these days, to Jennifer, and she ensured prompt payment for anything beyond the initial fee. It was a good life, he had to admit, far better than being in the police force. He did background checks, found dirt, made up and planted dirt, bribed folks that Laura needed to either go away or vote or push a project of hers forward, blackmailed certain folks if push came to shove, and did generally everything that she couldn't legally do herself. Because he was an ex-cop, he knew all the angles, all of the pitfalls, and because he had been a stellar cop, he had friends in high places. Yes, life was good.

"Hey! I need your guys' attention for a minute," he yelled out into the room. His office was the same as it was when Laura had first walked in, five years ago. There were two desks to his right, which faced the center walkway towards the exit door at the far end, and another two desks to his left, also facing the walkway, such that the two desks on either side of the aisle faced each other. Farther down on the right-hand side, there was the familiar brown leather sofa that faced the red brick wall, with four flat screen TV's hung on the wall and playing various channels. Across the aisle on his left-hand side, was a foosball table, a refrigerator against the wall, and six tall metal filing cabinets. One of the men who had been lounging on the sofa looked over, yawned, then stood up and walked over toward Larry's desk. Two other men were sitting at their desks. One had been playing solitaire on his computer, and the other was on his phone, but he said, "I gotta run" and hung up and came over. The solitaire player grabbed a piece of gum off his desk, popped it in his mouth, and stood up, casually making his way over to stand by his left.

"Where's Jocco?" Larry asked.

"Bathroom," said the tallest of the three, the one who had been watching tv. Gary was perhaps six foot four inches tall, with light brown hair that was combed neatly to the right. He had steel grey eyes, and was built like a linebacker, which was true, because he had played collegiate football back in the day. He was dressed in a white Brooks Brothers business shirt, with his sleeves rolled up, and khaki slacks with black leather shoes. He was handsome, and perhaps in his late thirties. Gary was an ex-cop like himself, and was great at tracking down people, sniffing out lies, piecing together leads, and coercing people with brute force, if need be.

"He's always in the bathroom. Mother fucker be eatin', like, plain yogurt, and still that shit makes him get the runs," said Jerome. He was black, six feet tall, and had his head shaved to the skin. He had a wide nose and equally large nostrils, that always flared even wider when he was laughing, which was often. He was the prankster in the team. Jerome was wearing a grey hoodie and blue jeans, with some brand new, white Jordan sneakers. Jerome was his street man. He could talk to anyone, befriend even the meanest of people, and he had all the hookups and contacts. He knew where dope was being slung on the street, he knew where all the secret brothels and gambling parlors were, and he could get meetings with anyone in the street world. These were people not in the news. In short, you didn't want to be friends with the people Jerome knew. They would kill for you something as simple as stepping in front of them in line.

He looked at Samuel, the one who had been playing solitaire. He was of average height, maybe five foot eight, Jewish, and he was the smartest of anyone on his team. He was always quiet, understated, and very calculating when he spoke. In a word, he was like himself. Samuel was his technical forensics guy. If there was anything electronically they needed to track down, erase, or manipulate, Samuel was the guy. Text messages, emails, GPS tracing using cell phones, anything that plugged in, Samuel was like God. No, scratch that. He *was* God. Samuel didn't say anything, but just shrugged when he looked at him as if to say, *"That's Jocco, whattya want from me?"* Samuel was dressed in a blue shirt, no tie, and grey slacks. He had brown hair that was receding, and a kind expression.

The bathroom door to Larry's far left opened, and Jocco came out, wiping his hands on his shirt. He was Puerto Rican, or New Yor'rican as he liked to call himself, and he was short, a little chubby, and had tan skin. He had black hair that was a little unkempt and bushy, along with thick black eyebrows. Wearing a plain black t-shirt and khaki cargo shorts, Jocco looked like he had rolled out of bed, and had miraculously found a job. He was Larry's logistics guy. Anything they needed, supplies, travel, fake or real documents, Jocco could get it, no matter how impossible it seemed. He was useful to have around, but sometimes, very annoying.

"Larry, there's no more toilet paper in there," said Jocco as he walked up to the group to stand next to Samuel.

"Sheeeet man. You da logistics guy. Fuckin' go get some more. And make sure you put extra under the cabinet sink, fuckin' tan ass 'Rican motha fucka," said Jerome. He said it in jest, without any real malice, but his face was scowling.

"Hey, fuck you, man! I'm the logistics guy, but I ain't no bitch neither! You 'spect me to run down to fuckin' Duane Reade and get that shit? I got it last time," Jocco whined. He whined. A lot.

"Just order it online. They deliver," said Gary, shaking his head.

"Yeah, man. Order dat shit. And hey, yo, you be the one

fuckin' usin' it all up! Sew your asshole shut or summin', cuz I'm tired o' yo ass blasting away on that toilet, ya feel me? Go see a doctor or sumpin', cuz you got some prollems." Jerome was snickering as he said this, shoulders shaking slightly as he laughed at his jokes.

"Fuck you, man. I got that, whattya call it? That irate bowel symposium, you know, that's what I'm talkin' about. So, fuck you, Jerome."

"Alright, alright. Enough. Listen up. We got an assignment," he said with a sigh. *"These kids will be the death of me,"* he thought with resignation. But they were *his* kids, and they were good at what they did. "We need to run a full background check on one Gale Marsden. Her full name is Gale Tabatha Marsden, and she is a reporter at CNN. Samuel, see what you can find electronically. Facebook, IG, LinkedIn, the whole nine. See if you can tap into her texts, emails, all of it. Gary, see what you can find about her past. Connections, contacts. Talk to the landlord, talk to her friends, see if you can talk to folks in her office, discreetly of course. Jerome, same thing, but help out Gary if he needs it. See what you can find out in her neighborhood, both where she lives now, and her hometown too. Chicago, Illinois. Jocco will get you setup with the flights and car rental. If you need any of the fake licenses, Jocco's got you covered. Give all the receipts to Jocco at the end. I need a full report in two weeks. Any questions?"

"How far back do you want us to go?" asked Samuel.

"Five years should be good. Don't go chasing deep down the rabbit hole, unless you see a thread that merits chasing."

"Anything in particular we should be looking for? Drug use? Some scandal, cover up, what?" asked Gary. He looked at his watch, and then back at Larry.

"Not sure yet. Just a general inquiry at the moment. But let me know if anything funky comes up. Oh, and check her finances and bank statements," he said as he looked at Samuel. Sam nodded.

"Alright. Text or call me if you need anything. I'm heading out." They all nodded their heads, but Samuel stayed a few seconds more, rooted in his spot, and was that a look of…what was it? Concern? He couldn't tell. But before he could say anything, Samuel had turned and walked to his desk, closing out the solitaire game and opening up his spyware programs. He rummaged in his desk drawer for his keys as he heard the guys teasing Jocco.

"Yo, don't gimme no connecting flight to Chicago," warned Jerome as he stood over Jocco, who was seated at his desk on the right. "Man, you smell like diarrhea! Shit! What's wrong with you man!" yelled Jerome as he pulled the front collar of his hoodie up to cover his mouth and nose.

"Hijo de puta! I just farted, that's all, man! There's still some gotta come out, geez," whined Jocco.

"Fuck! Ay yo. I'mma be over here. Email me my flight shit." Jerome scrunched his face up in a scowl and went over to his desk across the aisle, next to Samuel's.

"Sammy! Gimme the girl's hometown address where her parents live. Let me see if O'Hare is the closest airport or not," yelled Jocco.

"Working on it," said Samuel with a small smile. Nothing ruffled that man.

Larry found his keys, stood up, and went over to the coat stand to the right. He grabbed his light grey wind breaker, pulled it on, and walked down the center aisle towards the exit on the far end.

"See ya, boss!" yelled Jocco. He grunted a goodbye and walked down the steps, closing the door behind him. He knew that they would do a good job, and have a draft report in two days, with the full report in ten. He used to do all of this himself, but as Laura's needs became more and more frequent, he had hired out his team years ago, and now he only got involved if they needed an extra pair of hands to chase something down. This was how Laura grew so powerful, so quickly. First, it had been the mayor of New York. He had done the deal with Laura's contact in Flushing and secured the goods, then videotaped the exchange between Jerome and the mayor, had video surveillance of him using the drugs, and now they owned him, lock, stock and barrel. The mayor, in turn, had introduced Laura to his key political allies and hot shots. She had met Darren Johnson, the governor of New York, and cultivated a true friendship with him without having to twist his arm. Sylvia Trejo, the state attorney general, she had met at a fundraiser with the mayor, and it had taken some dirt, but they owned her as well. James O'Malley, the Commissioner of the New York City Police Department had been a tough nut to crack, as they had to tip toe carefully around him, but Laura had found a weakness in his defense, as he had a son with a rare blood disease. She had made an exceptionally large donation to the Dana Farber Boston Children's Cancer and Blood Disorder Center, and met their CEO, eventually joining as a board member. From there, she was able to promise James unlimited support and care for his son, if in return, he would do certain...favors for her when she needed them. He jumped all over it. Soon, she had been able to get meetings with the most powerful CEOs, agents of sports figures and actors, and even horse traded her favors for other I.O.U's and favors down the road. For example, she used her connection with Emma Stangrove, the President of the board of directors for the Dalton school, a very prestigious private school on the upper east side, to get John Steinbach's son enrolled there, and now, John owed her a very big favor. As New York City Comptroller, that was a nice I.O.U. to have in her hip pocket. Much of this was made possible by Laura's hustle and careful machinations, but some of it couldn't have been done without Larry's team who worked in the shadows.

Larry looked down the street and hailed a yellow cab as it passed by. He got in and gave the driver a cross street in nearby Brooklyn. He felt the same knot in his stomach. It was a mixture of excitement, fear, depression, and anger. He knew that he shouldn't be going to this game, but he couldn't help it. It was out of his control, much as he tried to control it. Years ago, he had been on the police force, and was one of the brightest, most promising detectives in his precinct. But the story he had told Stacy Atkins, when she hired him, was that he had been caught up in an illegal gambling sting and was trying to protect his partner. In the end, he got fired along with everyone involved. That wasn't really the truth. Only partially true. His partner had left New York, gone back home to Seattle to try and pick up the pieces, but Larry had stayed in New York, and Stacy had resurrected his career. Laura, however, had put a turbo charger on his back, and he was now making more money than he ever dreamed of. But that was both a good thing, and a bad thing.

"Right here?" asked the cab driver, an Indian man with a grey beard.

"Yeah, this is good. Here, keep the change," he said as he put a twenty-dollar bill in through the hole of the thick plexiglass divider.

Larry got out and looked around. He was in a tree lined street in Brownsville, Brooklyn. There were townhouses lined up next to each other in this part, and it was quiet, and mostly empty save for a mother walking hand in hand with her son. This section was run by the Russian Jews. They had a brothel in the area, did some loan sharking business, smuggled some contraband like Cuban cigars, and dealt in weed and ecstasy. Minor stuff, not big enough to get a crackdown yet by the police department. Oh, and they ran a very large gambling parlor in the brown townhouse in the middle of Amboy Street. Larry walked up the set of brown concrete steps up to the townhouse and rang the buzzer. The door was solid metal, painted all white so that it looked mostly normal, but there was a camera at the upper left by the frame that was discreet and hardly noticeable. He looked up at the camera. The door buzzed open, and he pushed on it.

Walking into the foyer, he was met by a rather large white man in a black suit, sans tie. He had a buzz cut, and some stubble on his face. "Arms out," he instructed, and Larry obliged. The man patted his arms, under his armpits, around his back, down over his hefty belly, down the sides of his legs and a quick once over between his legs. "Ok." The man could have at least given him a 'hello' or 'nice to see you', as Larry was here almost every fucking night, but the man acted as if they had never met, and so Larry simply did the same and walked down the hallway. The first room on the left was the living room, and there were several men seated on the sofa, drinking beers, and watching baseball on TV. The Yankees were playing the Mets, and someone was winning, he didn't know who, and he didn't care. He passed a bathroom, the door closed with someone inside, and saw the kitchen at the end of the hallway. It had white cabinets, but the walls were decorated with an off-white wallpaper filled with the same pattern of flowers every few feet, and the weird offset of colors was jarring to his eye, as usual. There was an old, obese, Russian woman with her grey hair in a bun, stirring a large pot on the stovetop, and whatever it was, it smelled good. She wore a simple grey dress, also with white flowers printed on it, and she looked to be someone's grandmother. Another woman, much younger, was seated at a small two-person kitchen table that was shoved along the wall and in direct line of sight down the hallway, and the woman smiled a friendly smile at Larry as she recognized him but said nothing as she peeled garlic with her bare hands. She was speaking in Russian to the older woman, and they were engrossed in their conversation.

He smiled back, and before the kitchen entrance, there was a stairway leading downstairs. He took the stairs and walked down towards the basement. The room was dimly lit, with several professional poker tables set up around the room. There were also two blackjack tables, and one craps table in the far corner. On his right, there was a full bar, maybe twenty feet in length, and a beautiful black haired Russian girl in her early twenties was manning the bar in a black shirt and black knee length skirt. He walked over to the bar, and the girl, Svetlana, smiled and grabbed a clean glass from behind her.

"Hello, Larry. Same as usual?" she asked, and without waiting, she reached for a bottle of Jack Daniels and gave a generous pour into the squat whiskey glass.

"Hi, Svetlana. No blackjack or craps today?" he asked as he took a sip and scanned the room behind him using the mirror on the bar.

"Not yet, Larry." Svetlana's thick accent was adorable, and he gave a half smile. "Only game is one hundred, two hundred no limit." He recognized Slim, Jenkins, a guy who he only knew as Dominoe, and Ralph. The others playing poker, he didn't recognize. It was still early, only one p.m., so maybe they would open up the blackjack and craps table later. In fact, he knew they would.

"Ok, thanks. Keep my glass full, ok?" he said, as he peeled off a twenty-dollar bill and left it on the bar. He brought his glass with him, over to the left side of the room, where there was a metal cage that was eight feet by six feet. Inside the cage, was a middle-aged man with wire rim glasses. He was seated at a wooden table and had a leather notebook in front of him. Behind him, were racks and racks of chips in all various colors, as well as one large safe. The bars of the cage were thick, maybe half an inch, but there was an opening about the size of a large envelope, in front of the man where transactions took place.

"Larry, good to see you," said Alex. He was one of the bookkeepers here.

"Alex. Just poker for now, huh?"

"Yes, for now. What can I do for you?"

"I need twenty."

Alex frowned, and opened up the notebook, peering at the contents. He sighed and looked up.

"Larry. You owe two hundred thousand dollars. You know this, right? I thought you were here to make payment, and instead, you ask for money. Where is the money you owe?" Alex was speaking softly, and was unhurried, with a Russian accent. He was just the bookkeeper. The real powers that be wouldn't have been so polite. The Russian Jews who ran this place, sooner or later, would get their money, or get their pound of flesh.

"I know. I'll get the money. You know I have always paid my

debts. Ten years you've known me, and I always pay," said Larry confidently. He just had a bad streak, that's all. All it takes is one good run, and he'd be back in the black, like usual.

"Yes, yes. But this time, been much longer since you cover and make whole. The juice is running, you know this, yes? Ten points a week. You know this, and still, you let it ride? I suggest you make payment, yes?"

"Alex, I will cover and make whole. I promise. But today, I need twenty. I'll sign for it, and next week, I'll make a payment. Fifty thou next week. I have a job that just came in, and I'll have more money next week." He stared at Alex, who stared flatly back at him. One word, and the two muscle heads standing quietly and discreetly in the back corner would grab him, take him upstairs to the third floor, and beat the shit out of him.

Finally, Alex looked down at the ledger, made a note, initialed it, and flipped the notebook around to Larry. He took the pen, initialed next to Alex's, and set the pen down while Alex turned around and counted out twenty thousand dollars' worth of chips. He sighed with relief, and the nervousness in his stomach turned to excitement. Grabbing the rack of chips and his glass, he walked over to the only poker table that had people at it, set his things down on the felt table, and got comfortable in his seat.

"Slim. Jenkins. Dominoe. Ralphy. How's it going?" he asked politely. Now that he had chips, they greeted him like a long-lost friend.

"Heeeeeyyy! Big Larry is here."

"Larry! Alright, now we got some new blood."

The men at the table had been quiet when he entered, and he knew it was because they weren't sure if he was going to be allowed to play. Everyone knew that he had been borrowing heavily and was deep in debt, and there was a particularly good chance that Alex would have turned him away and signaled for a beating. What Larry didn't know, was that folks were secretly betting when he would go bust and the Russians would call in their debt. The pot was up to almost thirty grand on that side bet.

"How's the table going?" he asked, as he took another sip of his drink and then put it down as the dealer dealt out the cards.

"Eh, you know. Slim's been catching cards like a mother fucker. Jenkins too. So, watch out!" said Dominoe.

"Oh, I will," he said, as he peeked down at his hole cards. Ace, ace. Maybe today was the day his luck would turn. The demon inside him grinned.

12

Lovely Ladies

Laura was running a little bit behind, but she finally hopped out of the black town car at eight thirty-five, in front of Grammercy Tavern. It was one of her favorite restaurants in the city, and she was a regular here. The restaurant was not right on the main street, but on an east west street near Grammercy. Grammercy Park was a tony neighborhood, with old school co-op buildings that surrounded a small garden. The garden itself was fenced in, and only residents of the immediate surrounding buildings had keys to enter the garden. It made it seem very exclusive and private, but in reality, Laura rarely saw anyone actually use the garden. She saw Gale standing outside the doors to the restaurant, on her phone and texting. She was wearing the same outfit from the morning and had a black laptop bag slung over one shoulder.

"Hi Gale, sorry I'm a few minutes late," she said as she walked up to Gale. She looked at cute as she remembered.

"Oh, hi! Not a problem. I wasn't waiting very long. Um, it looks really busy here, and I didn't make a reservation. Do you want to go somewhere else?"

"Let's check with the host. We might be ok here."

Gale arched an eyebrow. "What's that supposed to mean? It's packed." She looked over to her left, where there were four or five couples waiting on the street, like themselves. There were maybe six or seven people already in the foyer right inside the restaurant doors as well. But instead of answering, Laura just gave her a wink and a smile, and opened the tall door to the foyer.

"Excuse me, pardon me, just need to speak to the hostess," she said as she politely nudged her way through the crowd to the front podium. She felt rather than saw, Gale closely following behind her.

At the podium, there were two staff members. A tall man in a black suit, pink shirt, and blue and pink paisley tie, and a short brown-haired woman in an elegant black cocktail dress. The man wasn't familiar to Laura, but the woman was.

"Hi, Stephanie. I don't have a reservation, but can I get a table for two? The back dining room please."

Stephanie gave her a warm smile, but before she could reply, the man jumped in brusquely.

"I'm so sorry. The restaurant is completely booked up tonight. You *must* have a reservation in order to dine in the back dining room as well. Would you like to put your name on the list for the front bar room? It is more casual and is first come, first served, but the wait is only about an hour," he said with an arrogance that she could only surmise came from going to the absolute best private schools, an expensive private college, and perhaps training at only the best, and most exclusive restaurants.

She felt Gale tug the sleeve of her blouse. "Come on. An hour is crazy. Let's go around the corner on Park Ave, I know a great diner there." But now it was the hostess' turn to cut in as she shot the man standing next to her a dirty look.

"Miss Park! Of course. We always have a table ready just for you." She looked at her computer screen, and pointed to something on it, and with her other hand, she raised it in the air and made a 'come here' motion with four of her fingers. Another woman in a modest silver looking cocktail dress appeared from nowhere.

"Jen, please take Miss Park and her guest to table twenty-eight in the back dining room. Accept my sincere apologies on behalf of my colleague here, and I hope you enjoy your meal." Stephanie flashed her another smile, and Laura smiled back and nodded her thanks. As they walked into the front bar room, she overheard Stephanie scolding her colleague.

"You dumb ass! Miss Park is friends with Danny Meyer, the owner. We *always* give her a table whenever she stops by, which is like twice a week. Now call the Geumwalts and tell them that we had a VIP come in and we have to bump them an hour. Dumb, stupid…" the rest of her diatribe was lost as they walked through the loud and boisterous bar room. The room was moderately lit, and was primarily a dark wood, that lined the floors, matched the bar on the far side of the room, and matched the walls. The tables here were also wood, and metal chairs accompanied them. The room fit maybe about a hundred diners, and it was packed to the gills, with every table full, and even people sitting on bar stools eating their meals on the bar. The chandeliers were modern, Edison bulb lights that hung down across the room at varying heights, and the room was loud and filled with laughter, people talking, the clinks of glass, and silverware on plates. The menu was different than in the back dining room, but the food was cooked by the same chefs, so the quality was still excellent. Everything was a la carte, and entrees ranged from thirty dollars for the farm raised chicken breast with leeks and cauliflower puree, up to forty-five dollars for the day boat diver scallops with two-ounce wagyu beef and truffle mashed potatoes. They walked past the tables, which were on their left, and on their right-hand side, was an open kitchen where they could see a long counter where the head chef was plating dishes, and behind him, a long cooking station filled with plates, chefs, pans sizzling on the stovetop burners, and four or five wall ovens to the far left. It was quite impressive, and she guessed there must be at least seven chefs back there that she could see. They followed Jen, who walked them past the bar room, past the kitchen, and into a formal dining room. Here, it was noticeably quieter, and the whole vibe was quite different. The room was bathed in a soft yellow light, and even the wallpaper was an off white and yellow vertical stripe that gave a natural, soft, and welcoming atmosphere to the room. All of the tables were covered with white tablecloth, and all of the men in the room were wearing jackets or suits. The women, elegant evening dresses or modest cocktail dresses. There were perhaps thirty tables here, and all of them were filled as well, except for a handful. Business was brisk, it seemed. They were led to the back of the room, and Jen swept her hand to gesture to their table.

"Here we are. And here are your menus. Your server, Jack, will be here momentarily. Enjoy your meal," said Jen with a smile.

"Thank you very much," Laura said as she went around the

table to sit on the booth side. Gale took the chair opposite her and hung her laptop bag on the chair back.

"My, my. It seems you might, maybe, have a little bit of power. Ok, I'm very curious to know. Just how is it that you are treated like a VIP?" Gale had a smirk on her lips and was trying to show that she wasn't impressed.

"Well, I met Danny at a fund-raising event for the United Nations, and I said I wanted to invest some money into his next restaurant. I met with him in his offices, and even though the investment banker in me knew that the deal he was proposing was exorbitantly expensive, and that I should pass on it, I agreed to his deal terms after he refused to budge. After that, I asked what he wanted to accomplish, and then-"

"Wait, wait. Back up. You agreed to his deal terms, even though you knew it was unfavorable? Why did you do that? Did it ever occur to you that he was being sexist, and that had you been a man, he would have negotiated?" Gale pulled out a pen from her laptop bag, and also brought out her notepad as she started writing some notes.

Laura pursed her lips and thought about it. "Hmmm. No. I never got that feeling. I don't think it had anything to do with me being a woman. But I wanted to do a deal with him."

"Why? Why him, and why at his price?"

"Because sometimes, you only get asked to the dance once. If you pass, you might not get asked again. Sometimes you will, but in this case, my gut told me that if I passed, he would forget I ever existed and tap into other folks he knew. As for why him? I needed a contact in the restaurant industry, and he's connected to everyone, and now, I'm connected to everyone." Laura noticed Gale writing furiously in her notepad.

"Oh, wait. Please don't write down. That makes me sound like some ego maniac. Please, scratch that."

Gale looked up and paused mid scribble. "Listen, we never said this was off the record. Unless we agree it's off the record, I can write it "

Laura narrowed her eyes and considered her next move. "Okay…. But here's the thing, I didn't know that. So, can you give me a mulligan and let that one go? From now on, I'll know when to ask to keep something off the record." Speaking to a writer and having your life exposed was something new for her, and normally, she wouldn't share anything. But the whole article was about how powerful she was, so she had to give something.

Gale sighed. "Ok. Mulligan. I'll scratch that one, but you have to give me warning if something is off the record, deal?"

"Deal."

"Ok, so you said something about Danny…?"

"Yes. Getting a deal with him was just part of the equation. Now, I needed to give him something he needed, and only I could provide. This makes the ties that bind, incredibly strong. Like, a million times stronger."

"So, what did you provide?"

"This is off the record."

"What?! No! You can't just pull it out anytime you want like that," exclaimed Gale as she looked at her with eyes wide open. Her blue eyes were annoyed, and Laura found herself lost in the depths of those blue pools of openness. She wanted to lean forward and caress Gale's cheek and laugh at her, in jest, but she smiled and winked instead.

"I'm a quick study, huh?"

"You are Ok, listen. Now *I'm* going to negotiate. You tell me what it was you offered him, and then we decide if it goes on or off record, deal? If you say 'no', then we keep it off, but let me see how bad it is before we decide."

"Ok, deal. The thing I offered...." She decided to have some fun. "Oh, no, no, no. I just can't." She coyly smiled and picked up her water glass, hiding her smirk in the lip of the glass.

Gale blinked slowly, several times, and she narrowed her eyes at her.

"Ok, ok. I got his son into Harvard. I pulled a lot of strings, called in some favors, and got his son into Harvard. There, you happy? But like I said, that's off the record. For real. Just say that I forged a strong and deep relationship with various members of New York society, in all sorts of industries."

"Hm. Ok. For now. We'll come back to this one." Gale leaned over her notebook, tongue once again sticking out so that the tip was touching her top lip. It was freaking adorable.

"Hello! My name is Jack, and I'll be your server tonight. Have you had a chance to look at the menu? Any questions that I can answer for you?" Jack was a short man with a stocky build. He had dark brown hair that was cut short, a wide face with slightly plump looking cheeks, and he was wearing a starched and crisp white shirt, and black slacks.

"Oh, just a second, I haven't looked yet," said Gale. She put her pen down and quickly opened the menu.

"Ok, I'll be back in just a second then." He smiled and left to attend the table next to theirs.

"Uh, there's no prices next to these. What the hell?" Gale was looking in confusion at the menu.

"It's all prix fixe here. There's a five course or seven course tasting menu. Are you vegetarian?"

"Nope."

"Ok, great. Let me order then." Laura waited for Jack to finish with the other table, and she caught his eye and signaled that they were ready.

"Hi. We'll both do the five-course tasting menu. And we'll also do a bottle of the '97 cabernet? The Portsmith, yes, that one."

"Great. You'll love the lamb saddle dish, it is amazing. I'll have the sommelier come right over with the wine." Jack took their menus and disappeared.

"Ok, ready for the next question?" asked Gale as she picked up her pen.

"Later! Time to relax and get ready for a fantastic meal. You're going to enjoy it."

"Ok, your highness. Your royal VIP master ness," teased Gale with a grin.

"Yeah, yeah. VIP, whatever."

"You know, you're never going to live that down, you know that right?"

"On the record, or off the record?" she said with a smile.

Gale picked up her napkin off her lap and threw it at her, hitting her in the face. Time seemed to fly by for Laura. The dishes came out, and each was more delicious than the previous. They had lobster bisque, angel hair pasta with fennel and rock shrimp, dover sole with a lemon beurre and minced daikon radish and leeks, day boat diver scallops with mushroom risotto, and vanilla cheesecake with fresh berries and cream. The conversation was light, funny, and tit for tat. Gale had a quirky sense of humor, and an innocence to her that seemed at odds with her inquisitive reporter nature, which one would think would make a person hardened and jaded. Rather, she was curious and surprised by some of the stories Laura told her about behind the scenes in the boardroom.

"Wait a minute, wait a minute. You mean to tell me, that you found out that one of the board members was having an affair, in their kid's school?! Like in a classroom? How the hell did you find that out?"

They were walking south along Park Ave, and even though it was close to eleven p.m., the street was still busy with pedestrians, and cars and taxis whizzed by on the busy four lane street. They had been walking for just a few blocks, and they were nearing Union Square, one of her favorite places in Manhattan.

"Well, and seriously, you can't write this anywhere. I just… had someone investigate him, that's all. A good resource of mine checked him out. And the parent was taking night classes from a French teacher at his kid's school, yes. But apparently, there was a lot more than just French language lessons happening in class. So, we got it photographed, discreetly, this romantic encounter. It was supposed to be private one on one lessons with a teacher, but they would meet up twice a week for "class", and he was having sex with her on the teacher's desk. Dirtbag," she said with a smile.

"There you go again!"

"What do you mean?"

"Like, when you found a secret or got over on someone, you have this sneaky smile. Like you won a game or something. Tell me that you are not going to actually use that photo. That would be blackmail," Gale said with a frown.

"No, no. I'm not going to use the photo," she lied. "*At least, I don't think I'll have to use it publicly,*" she thought. "I just keep it, just in case. Just in case something happens where I need to push a little, that's all. No one gets hurt, and no photos will get released, trust me."

"So, you…threaten them with it?" Gale's tone was subdued, and a little soft. Laura sensed that this bothered her, the thought of using it for her own purposes, so she tried to deflect it.

"Not at all. I think you are misinterpreting. I don't…use it for ill will, or to harm anyone. It's only protection for me. It's a cutthroat and nasty world, particularly the closer you get to the C suite. I've had folks try to cut my legs out from underneath me, simply because I'm a woman, or I'm Asian, or I'm just in their way. Whatever. In that case, I need a little something to protect myself. In case I'm unfairly attacked. Make sense?" They were walking into the park at Union Square. Instead of heading south along the left-hand side of the park, where there were benches under the oak trees, she turned to the right, towards the western side of the park, where it opened up to a wider cement plaza. The left-hand side pathway was dark and tended to have a few homeless people and junkies either high on drugs or looking to score drugs. The plaza to the right was safer, as it had a lot of foot traffic down to the subway station, and was well lit.

"Hm. Ok. Not really, to be honest. But we'll chat more. I still need to wrap up my interview with you." Gale brushed a lock of her blonde hair that had fallen across her eyebrow, back and behind her right ear. It was the last straw for Laura, and she stepped forward, hoping that this wouldn't end in embarrassment for both of them.

"We can finish the interview. Later," and she reached up and cupped Gale's face and leaned in to kiss her. She was shorter than Laura by a few inches, and her lips were warm, soft, and tender. She wasn't sure if Gale would recoil or push her away, but to her surprise, she felt her body press closer to hers, and her lips pressed firmly back, slightly parted, with the split-second slip of her tongue into her own eager and waiting mouth, and then it was over.

"Do you want to come over for a night cap?" she asked breathlessly.

Gale laughed, and nodded, but teased her one last time. "Yes. But seriously? Who uses the word night cap these days?" She didn't know, and she honestly couldn't have cared less.

13

The Bear and the Bull

Things were going exceedingly well for Laura. In fact, they were going so well that she lost sight a little bit, of keeping extra close tabs on things at work, and it almost derailed her whole career, and her ambitions. But she would never forget the day it all snapped back into focus for her. It was the day she first met the man that people called "The Bear." Gale had to recuse herself from the article on Laura, as it wouldn't have been right to do the article with someone she was in a relationship with. Nonetheless, when it had been published, it garnered well over three hundred thousand views in the first day.

In the month after the article's release, she had her phone ringing off the hook, nonstop, asking for interviews, meeting requests from people high and low that she had never heard of, and requests for her stances and opinions on various topics around the country. She denied all of the interview requests and continued to deny an upcoming Senate run. In the meantime, she was photographed having dinner with the mayor of New York. Of course, her team had tipped off the photographer at the Daily News. She was seen at the John F Kennedy Center for the Performing Arts in Washington, DC, watching the National Symphony Orchestra and then chatting amicably afterwards with Senator Ormsby from California, and Senator Stein from Maryland. And then last week, she was seen at a fund-raising event for the Democratic Party, hosted by billionaire New York financier, Jay P. Moss. All of the signs were there, and it sure looked like Laura Park was contemplating a run at the Senate. True to Stacy's advice, it generated a buzz and raised her profile overnight. It was a meteoric rise, and she was thrilled with how it was going.

"Hey, you, are we still on for dinner tonight?" Gale was on her speaker phone, and Laura was multi-tasking, getting ready for a meeting with a group of investment bankers from JP Morgan Chase, who had a deal pitch that they claimed, "would unlock a tremendous amount of value for Abernathy."

"We sure are. Eight p.m. at Le Bernardin. Be there or be square," she said as she re-read through the email threads from the investment banking team. *"What the hell could this be about? And why didn't Jennifer do her homework and get the exact details of this meeting?"* She sighed and made a mental note to sternly remind Jennifer that all meetings have to be clearly vetted with an agenda. This meeting was vague, and she had no clue who would be in the room. None of the names were familiar to her, and it irked her greatly. But she had been delegating more and more to Jennifer and Adam, focusing her time outside the company, and coyly dodging the press.

"Ugh. French again? You know I'm only blah on French. But for you, ok. But next time, we're doing Italian!"

"You get it, Gale. Italian next time. Maybe Carbone? You haven't been there yet right?"

"Nope, not yet, but I've heard good things about it."

"Not just good. Fantastic! Alright, gotta run. Have to head to my next meeting, which I have no freaking clue what it's about, and I'm irritated to no end. Besos," she said, and Gale gave a verbal smooch in reply and hung up.

She shook her head in annoyance one final time, as she squinted at the last email thread from these bankers, and then stood up, grabbing her notebook and pen. It was fall, one of her favorite times of the year in Manhattan, and the leaves in Central Park were turning yellow and orange. She turned to look down at the park, and smiled, as she always did, when she looked at the vast sky sitting atop the park, and all of the buildings lining the edge. She turned back and headed for the door of her office, stepping out to see Geoff sitting at his desk dressed smartly in a dark blue blazer with silver buttons, crisp white button-down shirt, and khaki slacks. He had a glossy black belt to match his black leather oxfords. His brown hair was neatly combed to the side, and he gave her his usual cheerful grin.

"On your way to the nine a.m.? Jennifer and Adam are already there. It's in the boardroom and you're free until your eleven a.m. with Lindsay Backus."

"Thanks, Geoff. Hey, can you do me a favor and make a dinner reservation for Carbone, for two? Preferably tomorrow night, eight p.m.? They'll say they're booked but ask to speak to the manager and tell them that I'm friends with the chef, Rich Torrisi. Say that I have a standing invitation to dine in the kitchen chef's table any time of the week. It might be booked but get the next best available if it is. Thank you!"

"Ok, you got it."

She made a second mental note to herself, to get Geoff a really, really nice watch at the end of the quarter as 'thank you' for all of his hard work over the last six months.

She walked briskly down the gleaming white marble floor, her heels clicking on the stone as she turned left towards the executive boardroom. The walls were dark stained wood, and the paintings were all modern and contemporary, a change she had implemented last year. The first conference room on her right was the one, and she opened the door and entered. Jennifer and Adam were sitting with their backs to the window, facing the doorway. She could see they had an agenda placed at the head of the table, for her use. The conference room was large and had a long oak table that could seat twenty people on either side, and one at the head and foot of the table. Two conference call speaker phones were on either end of the table, and small white microphones were discreetly hanging several inches from precise three-foot intervals all throughout the room, to pick up anyone's voice clearly from anywhere in the room. This room was where they held their quarterly earnings calls.

"You're looking quite sharp today, Jennifer. Like the suit." She was wearing a navy-blue windowpane plaid Italian suit jacket, with a pale light blue shirt.

"Adam, you too. Like the cufflinks," she noted approvingly. Adam was wearing a light silver suit, with white pin stripes, no tie, and a white French cuff shirt with silver knot cufflinks. His brown hair was lightly tousled, as if he had just rolled out of bed, but he somehow pulled it off. This was it. Her team of two that she trusted the most within the company. Only Jennifer handled the dirtiest of work, while she kept Adam in the dark. He was just a little too junior, a little too ambitious, and besides, she had known Jennifer for over a decade.

There was a polite knock on the door, and one of the building security staff opened the door and poked his head in.

"Laura? Your guests have arrived," said Oliver. He was a wide set man, thick through the shoulders, chest, and gut, and tall. She thought he was Puerto Rican, if she recalled, and he always had the most spot on info about the weather, and traffic delays on the seven train subway.

She motioned him to come in, but Oliver stepped back, and the door opened fully to let the guests spill through the door and into the conference room. There were four men, one of whom looked really familiar to her, but she couldn't quite place. All four men were dressed in fine Italian suits and wore expensive looking watches. You could tell a lot about a man just by looking at their shoes, and their watches, and Laura took note of the International Watch Company, Patek Phillipe, Breitling's, and Prada and Gucci leather shoes. The group of men smiled, except for the man in the rear, who was the oldest of the group, and walked forward to shake their hands. Laura, Jennifer, and Adam stood up and walked around to greet them, returning their firm handshakes and fake smiles that didn't quite reach their eyes. She could always spot an investment banker when she met one. Unless they were freshly minted MBA's who just started out, many of the Vice President's and Managing Director's that she met were cold, and battle hardened by years of grueling hours and nonstop deal pitches that often times went nowhere. They were polished, smooth, eloquent speakers, but their smiles never reached their eyes. They reminded her of the Borg from Star Trek. Calculating, methodical, and robotic.

"Hi, Jesse Rothenberg." Jesse was rather short, Jewish, with light brown hair that was fairly curly. He wore a modern looking set of glasses, that were plastic on top of the lens and on the frame, but rimless on the bottom half of the lens.

"Hi, Eric O'Shea, nice to meet you." Eric was tall, over six feet, and had light blonde hair that was combed to the side. He was good looking, with high cheekbones and a strong jaw that jutted out prominently. His blue eyes were sharp, and clear, and full of intelligence.

"Matthew Kim, a pleasure." A fellow Korean! What a pleasant surprise. He had long black hair that was down to the nape of his neck and covered his ears as well, and wore it parted in the middle, oddly enough. But he looked handsome, if she had to say, and had a narrow face that fit well with his slender frame.

"Darbear Markovic." Now she knew that familiar face. He was sixty years old if she recalled, and was a wealthy corporate raider who worked with investment banks to do hostile takeovers of smaller companies, and loudly agitated for changes in corporate management in order to drive up share prices of companies he was invested in. He was worth close to a billion dollars, and the press and everyone called him 'The Bear', both for his first name, and for the fact that he was ornery and unpredictable as a bear. Time had not treated him well, as he looked far older than his age. His hair was completely grey, but slicked and combed straight back over his head. He had mottled brown sunspots on his face, especially near his eyes, and harsh crow's feet and deep wrinkles lined his forehead and cheeks. He had a wide and round face, as he was ever so slightly overweight, but he was tall, maybe six foot four, and he wore his extra weight gracefully. Unsmiling, he barely acknowledged her as he briefly gripped her hand and let it go.

"Welcome, please have a seat," said Jennifer, and the men sat opposite Laura, Adam, and Jennifer.

"What a remarkable view! Do all of your offices have this view of the Park?" asked Eric with another fake smile.

"I was thinking just the same thing, in fact-" started Jesse, but he was cut off by Darbear.

"Ok. Let's get to business, shall we?" He was seated in the fourth chair, furthest from Laura.

Laura raised her eyebrows in silent annoyance at his brusque demand but pulled out the chair at the head of the table and took a seat. Everyone else followed suit and quickly sat down. Eric at least had the decency to smile apologetically at Laura. After a moment, the bankers turned to look at their leader, Darbear, who took the opening to start the meeting.

"I have some good news for you," the old man said nonchalantly. Laura doubted that it was good news for them, the way he said it.

"I have bought up five percent of the shares of the company, and registered with the SEC. I'm going to accumulate even more, if need be, so that I can get what I think is right for this company." He was staring blankly at Laura now, lifeless, but she knew he was coming in for the kill.

"You see, there is a severe lack of shareholder value being generated here, and I want a new CEO. And I want a new board, and a new CEO of my choosing."

Laura felt as if Mike Tyson had gut punched her, but she blinked once, and thought through the corporate governance of the company structure. There was a long pause, and Eric, Matthew,

Jesse, and Darbear were all staring at her. Finally, she spoke.

"The board won't go for it. They won't want an outsider they don't know, installed as a puppet CEO. The shareholders won't approve such a vote."

"With all due respect, Laura, we believe we can get such a vote approved," said Jesse. He leaned forward, arms comfortably resting on the table in front of him. "We've run multiple scenarios, and we think the operating expenses of the company are inflated. We see room for operating margin improvements of five to seven percent. We also believe that the strategic decision to focus on the Brazil market instead of China is a huge mistake. Those two changes alone will easily cover any executive payouts or parachutes." Laura couldn't believe what she was hearing. These guys were smart, but they had no clue about what they were talking about. Their operating expenses were best in class in their industry.

She shook her head in disbelief. "I don't know what comps you are using, but your analysis is way off. You'll have a fight on your hands if you initiate a hostile bid."

"Laura, you should really think about our proposal. We can get the shares up significantly with the right leadership." cooed Matthew softly. Clearly, he was the good cop.

"We have some financials and some strategic decisions that we'd like to share with you, here in this presentation," said Eric, as he handed out several copies of a thick printed PowerPoint deck. She glanced at it but didn't open it.

"No, I don't need to see it. I'm sorry. Agitating for changes in how we run our business, and also a change to management, just won't fly. We know our business, and our operating profits are growing steadily," she said calmly, although her heart was beating much faster than she believed it could.

"Listen to my team. They have some good ideas, and your company will benefit. And if you don't do as I say, we'll go for a hostile takeover. Trust me, no one wants that," said Darbear with a cold smile.

The meeting went on for another half hour, with the bankers pitching their ideas from their presentation. Mostly, Laura was silent, allowing Jennifer and Adam to ask questions and take notes. Instead, she watched Darbear, who was intently watching her. Sizing her up. Taking stock of his opponent, just as she was taking stock of him. She didn't like what she saw. Here was a man who could not be swayed by money or favors. He wanted to win at all costs, and he wanted her gone. Finally, when there was a break in the conversation, she cut the meeting short.

"Is this it then? If you don't get your way, you intend to make a hostile bid for the company? I've heard everything I need to hear, and I will relay your intentions to the board. Now, if you'll excuse me," she said as she stood up. Everyone stood up with her.

"We'll just leave our business cards here with you," said Jesse as he pulled out a small stack of cards and placed them on the table. "Please feel free to reach out to us, if you want us to talk you through any of the details of Mr. Markovic's plan for changes within the company."

She nodded curtly, and walked over to shake each of their hands, as was customary, even among business enemies. Darbear was the last to shake her hand, and this time, he gripped her hand in an iron, vice like grip, crushing her palm which made her wince.

"Laura. Don't wait too long on this one, eh? I always get what I want." The man sneered and gave a soft chuckle, and then he was gone. She waited for a good thirty seconds to ensure they were down the hall in the elevator bank, and then turned to Jennifer and Adam who were standing beside her.

"What the hell just happened? And why didn't you know about the context of this meeting?" she demanded angrily, staring first at Jennifer, then at Adam, and back to Jennifer.

Jennifer shook her head and licked her lips. "I'm sorry, Laura. I couldn't get ahold of you last week, and then all they would say is that they had a tremendous deal, an 'opportunity of a lifetime' they called it, that would unlock enormous shareholder value and lead to a thirty percent rise in our stock. They said it was urgent, and they needed to speak with you. I'm sorry," she repeated.

"They never told us about Markovic," added Adam. "He came out of left field. But I can go verify if he's truly bought up five percent of the company, because that has to be made public. He has to file a schedule 13D within ten days."

She nodded. "Ok. Get on it. Find out everything you can about his team, and everything you can about the bankers too. I'm sure this is not the first high profile hostile bid they've worked on together." She looked at her watch. "Move this to the top of the list, and we'll regroup at four in my office. I've gotta break the news to the board." Jennifer and Adam nodded grimly, and they left the boardroom towards the elevator bank where the two took the elevators down. Pulling out her phone, she fired a text over to Larry.

Urgent. Need your team to find and dig up as much info as possible on Darbear Markovic. Get me whatever you can by eleven p.m. tonight and give me a call then.

After thinking about it, she sent another text, this time to her former boss.

Stacy, need two things from you. Can I call you around six? Urgent.

14

The Gathering Storm

Laura called Larry again, but as with the other times, it went straight to voicemail. She hadn't heard back from him all afternoon, so finally, she called Samuel to see what was going on.

"Samuel, where the hell is Larry? He hasn't been answering my texts or phone calls. Is he there?" she demanded.

"No, no. He's not here. We haven't seen him since yesterday. He never came in this morning," said Samuel calmly. He was always levelheaded and calm, much like his boss, Larry. "But I'm sure he's fine. He does this sometimes."

"What do you mean, he does this sometimes? He just doesn't come in?" she asked with surprise. There were sometimes days or even a week or two where she didn't need Larry or his team's services, but it never dawned on her that he might simply not come into his office in Brooklyn. But it kind of made sense to her. When it was quiet, it was really quiet, and when the shit hit the fan and she needed some dirty work done, it all of sudden heated up to a maelstrom.

"Yes. He sometimes just takes off for a day or two, and no one sees or hears from him like this. It's normal. What's up? Is there something perhaps I can help you with?"

"Damn. Ok. Yes, I need you to find out as much as you can about Darbear Markovic. He's a wealthy financier, and he's about to make a hostile bid for Abernathy. Give me everything you can find out in the next, oh, six hours and then call me back after ten p.m. You want me to spell his name?"

"No, no. I got it. Everyone knows this man. He's Czechoslovakian. There are lots of Czechs in my neighborhood, and they talk about him a lot. But it's good you called me because Larry would have assigned this one to me anyways. I can find more through the dark web and my technical searches in this short amount of time. Hey! Jocco! Put it down. Put. It. Down. Is that it?" he asked, clearly distracted now. She heard laughter in the background as Gary, Jerome, and Jocco were hooting and hollering about something in the distance.

"Yeah, that's it. Thanks." She hung up, just as she heard Samuel yell profanities at Jocco.

She looked at her watch. *"Four p.m. Too much to do, and I really need to talk to Stacy,"* she thought. She made a snap decision and walked briskly towards her door and out.

"Geoff! I'll be back by six. Clear the rest of my day and clear my morning tomorrow as well. Did Jennifer draft up the email for the convening of the special board meeting?" she shouted over her shoulder as she walked away, not waiting for the answer.

"Ok! And yes, she said it will be in your inbox in two minutes!"

yelled Geoff to her retreating back. She gave a thumbs up over her shoulder and kept on her brisk walk until she made it to the elevators. Once she was down in the lobby, she exited the turnstiles and went to the curb, looking for a taxi. Although it was perhaps a fifteen-minute walk, and she could have used the fresh air, she didn't want to waste any time.

"Riverside and seventieth street, please," she said to the cab driver as she hopped in and closed the door. She was fairly sure that Stacy would be home, and it would be best to speak in person. The cab ride was short, and she gritted her teeth at the slow traffic on west 66th street as pedestrian's lolly gagged across the crosswalk. *"Walk faster, goddamit,"* she muttered. The upper west side was home to beautiful tree lined streets, high rise apartment buildings, cute shops, well off married couples with kids, and also home to Lincoln center. It was one of her favorite neighborhoods in Manhattan, and she absent mindedly noted with a quiet joy, the familiar red awning of the Gourmet Garage on 66th just past Broadway, the brown, black and beige mosaic tile of the High School of Arts and Technology on her left, and finally, the sweeping skyline that sat atop the Hudson River and looked westward towards New Jersey as they made the right turn onto Riverside boulevard. When they pulled up to Stacy's building, she paid the driver and stepped out to see the white stone and glass condo building that she had been to before. A doorman opened the door to the building for her and she entered a modern lobby that was almost entirely white. White marble floors, white quartz counters where the concierge desk was, white plush sofas off to the right, and two white pillars that made up part of the foundation that went from the floor to the thirty-foot ceiling. The only nonwhite item was a six by eight-foot grey carpet in front of the door, just inside the entryway, presumably to soak up dirt or rain from tenants walking in.

She walked up to the concierge manning the front desk and introduced herself.

"Hi, here to see Stacy Atkins, apartment 16F."

"Ok, just a moment. May I ask for your name?" asked the man politely.

"Laura Park, thanks."

He picked up the handset and punched a keypad. "Hello? Yes, I have a Laura Park here to see you. Ok, thanks. You can go on up."

She nodded and walked to the left where the elevators were situated and grabbed the first one. When she got to the sixteenth floor, she turned right and knocked on the door to 16F.

Stacy opened the door and gave her a sincere smile.

"Laura, I wasn't expecting you to swing by. I thought we were going to chat on the phone! Come in, come in!" she exclaimed as she gave her a brief hug. Although she had been fired years ago, she looked much the same, except her hair was slightly greyer now than she remembered, but still was half dark brown. Her brown eyes measured her up and down in one critical glance, as she ushered her into her apartment. Stacy was wearing comfortable grey slacks and a dark blue blouse, with pearl earrings completing the ensemble. Laura hadn't been to her apartment in perhaps a year or so, and it had been changed since the last time she had visited.

"You made the living room look more modern, huh? I like it," she said with a smile. It was her taste exactly, and she felt at ease and comfortable at once. The kitchen was off to the left immediately as one entered, and it was large and spacious, enclosed on three sides. There were stainless steel appliances, Paykel and Fisher for the stovetop and Sub Zero for the refrigerator, and the countertops were a beautiful Calcutta marble. The cabinets were sleek, white lacquered, with no handles to speak of. You just pulled from the bottom edge of the cabinet and the doors or drawers swung open effortlessly. Straight ahead was the living room, with tall nine-foot-high ceilings, and the view opened up to the Hudson river and the New Jersey skyline. The floor to ceiling glass windows brought in a ton of natural sunlight, and the view was spectacular when the sun set in the evenings. The taupe leather couch and love seat were from Bo Concept, she thought, and fit the room perfectly.

"I did a refresh maybe six months ago. Changed out all of the furniture. Want any coffee, tea?" Stacy asked as she went into the kitchen.

"Hm? No, I'm fine, thanks. How have you been? What's new?" She walked over to inspect a tall black wooden bookcase, filled with books. Most were fiction, with a handful of nonfiction titles, but nothing that she recognized.

"Traveling a bit here and there. Went to Germany in the spring, which was surprisingly fun." Stacy poured herself a cup of coffee from the Keurig machine that was tucked in one corner of the counter and walked over to the sofa where she took a seat. "Sit, take a load off."

Laura smiled and turned around to take the love seat opposite her former boss.

"So. What brings you here? It couldn't wait until the evening to chat?" As usual, Stacy got right to the point. She had always been direct, blunt, and forceful, and all of those qualities were things that Laura admired, as one always knew where you stood with her. But it also had hindered her career, as others with Abernathy had labeled her a bitch, or cold and rude.

"Listen, we had an unexpected turn of events today. Do you

know Darbear Markovic?"

"Hm. The corporate raider? What about him?"

"That's the one. Well, he brought his team over today for a meeting with me, and he announced that he's taken a large position in the company and that he wants changes in the management. He wants me out, and someone of his own choosing to be the next CEO. Otherwise, he's going to make a hostile bid to take the company private."

Stacy whistled. "Wow. The balls on that guy. From what I can recall, he doesn't have enough capital to take it over himself. He'll need a lot of other investors and will need to leverage up quite a bit to do that."

"You know, that's what I think too. I think he's bluffing, possibly, but he might have enough connections to raise that kind of capital. He brought a team of investment bankers with him, so I'm sure he can tap into the bank for a large loan as well."

"It almost doesn't matter. As long as the threat is there, he can play a pretty solid high stakes poker game. What's your next move?" Stacy asked thoughtfully as she narrowed her eyes.

Laura pursed her lips tight and looked to her left, where the sun was starting to set over the Hudson, casting a soft orange glow over the river and cars whizzing by on the streets below.

"I'm going to fight it. Have to brief the board, but I'm not going to roll over on this one. I've worked too hard to get to where I am now, just to have someone take it away from me."

"Why not just give in and run for the Senate, like you've been mentioning to me?" asked Stacy.

Laura gritted her teeth and turned to glare at Stacy. "Because I'm not going to have this...this... *man* tell me what to do. I'm not going to let him stand in the way of *my* plans. He thinks he can walk in and dictate terms, just like that? I'm going to fight him on this, and I'm going to win."

Stacy nodded, as if she had expected to hear nothing less. "Ok. I get it. What do you need from me?"

Laura gave a small smile. "I need you to be my Chief of Staff. Not at Abernathy. But for my campaign that I'll be running next year. The earlier I can get sorted out and up and running, the better. There's no one better that I can think of to run my campaign." But to her surprise, Stacy shook her head.

"I'm honored. Truly, I am. You have a tact, polish, and public speaking ability that I just don't have, and hell, I even think you might win when you run. But while I can run a tight ship and keep things moving, I don't have any idea of how to navigate a campaign trail. We'd be running blind in the dark on what to do."

"You can figure it out. You always do, and I have faith in you," Laura pleaded. She hadn't expected Stacy to say no. Again, Stacy surprised her.

"I'm not saying 'no', per se. I'll be your Chief of Staff, and I can keep your schedule, make sure you're where you need to be, put out fires, handle all the dirty items, but we need a political campaign advisor. Someone who knows how this shit works, and has done it before, and handles all the politics. Who to talk to, what fundraiser to throw, who to invite, what policies to run on, how and who to attack, and how to defend. That's the only way you can win, is if you have someone like that to pair up with."

"I don't know anyone like that, but I can tap into my resources to find someone," Laura said thoughtfully. She would need to setup a lunch with the mayor, asap.

"I've already got someone in mind," Stacy said with a grin. "Ever since you told me where you wanted to go, I've been thinking on this puzzle, of how to navigate the political jungle. There's a person I want you to meet. She was big in the Democratic party, and helped run the campaign for Forrest Newton, Senator of Delaware. She even had a role in the last presidential campaign, but she quit. I'm not sure why, but I think you'll like her. She knows everyone in D.C. and knows what it takes to win."

"Sounds great! What's her name? Do you have her contact info?"

"Mary Chatsworth. I'll text you her info later. Have your office setup time with her."

"I'll do that." She stood up, and Stacy did the same, still holding her coffee in her right hand. "I'm so excited you said 'yes'! I know that everything will be taken care of with you in my corner."

Stacy smiled, and then her smile faded. "Listen though. There's one more thing."

Laura, who had started walking towards the door, turned and raised an eyebrow as she searched Stacy's face. "Yes?"

"I don't know how to say this, so I'll just say it. You know that I had Larry investigate you before I hired you, yes?" she asked softly.

"Yes. What did you find?" Laura asked quietly, unsure that she wanted to hear the answer.

"Not much. But…I do know that you happen to like the company of women… Not a problem, especially if you just had eyes on a Senate seat. But if you want to go all the way…well, I would ask Mary what the polls and odds say of a lesbian president, that's all." Stacy stared hard at her, and her face revealed nothing. Laura blinked twice and turned away.

"Thank you, again, Stacy. I'll be in touch soon. Oh, if you have anything on Darbear, can you text or email me? I need all the ammo I can get." Stacy murmured her assent, and she left without saying another word.

15

The Action's to You

Larry winced and gingerly touched his left eyebrow. The black eye was slow to heal, but it was getting better, he supposed. He had a cut on his lip, the black eye, but worse were the black and blue bruises all over his stomach and back. He had been back to the townhouse in Brownsville, played on credit for forty thousand, and lost it all. The bookkeeper that day had been a man they called Mouse, and Mouse had demanded that Larry front some cash for the juice, or interest, running on his debt when he had tried to leave. Of course, he didn't have it, and so Mouse had signaled the two strong men to take him away. To the third floor. Where he promptly had his body beaten over the course of two, long, painful hours. When they were done with him, Alexander had come in. He was a Russian gangster, and it was his gambling parlor that Larry partook of.

"Larry, Larry. You know the rules. When payment is demanded of you, on the last day of the week, it must be paid. Today, is Sunday. The last day of the week. And, you don't have my money. Why you do this to me, eh? Why you make me do this? You think I like having my men beat you to a pulp, eh?"

"Fuck you," he had mumbled, as he lay on the floor on his side, blood dribbling from the cut in his lower lip. His wrinkled and drab tan suit had been ripped and rent in a few places during the beating, and there were pink stains on his once white shirt where blood, saliva, and sweat had commingled.

"Ah, yes. Fuck me. *Mudak*." Alexander slapped him hard on his face and stood up. "Listen, *perdoon stary*, you make payment for the juice, tomorrow, ten a.m. sharp. Otherwise, the interest gets added to the principal, yes? Your bill, up to three hundred large now. Better make payment, get the balance down, or I cut your penis off."

"Fuck you," he croaked out again.

"*Yob tvoyu mat*," said Alexander with a smile, and he kicked Larry hard in the ribs, eliciting a groan of pain.

That had been two days ago, and now, things were back to normal, for the most part. He had missed Laura's calls and texts, and when he had finally gotten to them, he forced himself to quit gambling for one goddamn minute and focused on what he was good at. Detective shit.

He dabbed his left eye with a paper towel one more time, and then exited the bathroom and walked over to his desk. Jocco, Jerome, and Sam were at their desks, typing away and occasionally chatting with one another. They had learned not to ask questions of him when he sometimes showed up with new bruises or cuts, so they tactfully ignored his badges of dishonor and pretended they didn't exist, for which he was grateful for. He looked at his watch. Almost noon, time for a quick huddle up. He walked down the center aisle between the four desks and made his way to the water cooler, which was tucked onto the wall underneath the TVs, poured a cup of water and then made his way back to his desk, where he sat on the front part, one leg on the floor and his other leg dangling in the air.

"Alright, guys. Let's huddle up real quick, have a debrief."

Jocco, Jerome, and Sam stood up and made their way over, standing about four feet away as they pondered their boss.

"Alright. I'm about to go have a chat with our boss. She wants a personal update on the Darbear investigation. Sam? What have you got?"

Sam was dressed as he usually was, in khaki slacks, and a pressed white shirt from Brooks Brothers. His glasses had a slight smudge on one of the lenses, and he pulled them off and wiped it down with a microfiber cloth that he produced from his pocket.

"Not much, I'm afraid. Darbear is fairly squeaky clean. Had one DUI back in the nineties. No jail time, no outstanding warrants or anything. Divorced, no kids. Doesn't even speak to or see the ex. No corporate fraud or malfeasance that we could dig up. Nothing sinister online that I can track or find. I'm still checking everything out, going back even farther, but I can't find hardly anything."

"Ok. Thanks, Sam. Jerome?"

Jerome was dressed in a jean jacket, but the sleeves had been cut off, with a black t shirt underneath, and green camouflage pants tucked into black combat boots. His head was shaved bald, freshly done this morning by the looks of it, and his white teeth gleamed in the rays of sunlight that streamed into the office from the windows.

"Man, this mutha fucka be clean as a virgin's ass, know whut I'm sayin'? I can't find no nothing on him. Checked out round his building and hood. Spoke to the doorman, concierge, all dat shit. They wouldn't say shit, and far as I could tell, they didn't seem to be hidin' nothin' neither. Checked out all my contacts, dis and dat, on the street, nothing. No drugs, no prostitutes, can't trace him to any o' dat shit. Squeaky clean, seem like." Jerome sniffed loudly to signify he was done speaking and make a loud sucking sound with his tongue and teeth, as if he were trying to suck out a piece of food stuck between his teeth.

"Figures. Man like this, he would use someone else if he were into that stuff. Where's Gary?" he asked.

"He's out checking all the white collar connects. Country clubs, business connections, neighbors out in the Hamptons, that sort of stuff," said Sam.

"Ok. Have him call me as soon as he's back. Jocco? What you got, anything?"

"Nah, boss. Ain't got shit. I checked all my airline and limo connections, but this guy, he flies private everywhere on his own jet. So, I checked where he flies in and out of. The only thing I could find was that he goes up to Martha's Vineyard, a lot, flying out of a small airfield up in Westchester. So, I called my contact up there, see if he knew anything about who he flies with, that sort of thing. But this guy wouldn't say shit. Clammed up real tight. Other than that, I couldn't find out anything."

Something about what Jocco said stirred something in his memory, but he couldn't quite pick it out, like a fuzzy thread that he just couldn't quite grasp. Anyway, he let it go and took a deep drink of his water.

"Keep checking all the leads you can. This one is high priority, but I'll have a better sense of what needs to get done after I meet with Laura. Call or text me if you find anything important." Larry stood up, essentially ending the meeting, and Jocco and Jerome turned and went back to their desks, with the latter teasing Jocco about his unkempt hair. Samuel, however, lingered and followed Larry to the coat stand in the corner.

"Hey, Larry?"

"Yes, Samuel?"

"Hey. I know this might be awkward. But some of the guys on the team, they're worried about you."

Larry didn't respond at first. He turned away and took his coat off the stand, and swung it around and slipped into it, the comfortable and cool blue liner fitting snugly on his arms and back. He nodded his head towards the door at the end of the room, indicating that Samuel should follow him. They walked down the center aisle between the four desks and heard Jocco laughing at something Jerome said as they made their way down the long rectangular room to the exit. When they got to the door, Larry turned and spoke softly, so that no one but Samuel could hear him.

"Worried about what?"

Samuel shrugged. His brown eyes unreadable behind his wire rim glasses. "You know. This and that. Your bruises. Your late night...habits. They all know, Larry. It's not a secret, I mean, you hired an ex-cop and a street thug. They know all the dirt."

Larry narrowed his eyes and winced again due to the black eye. *"Fucking Russian animals,"* he thought to himself.

"Listen, there's nothing to be worried about. Everything's under control. Just find some dirt on this Darbear sonofabitch, and life will be good. Call me later." He heard Samuel grunt an acknowledgement, and he left, walking slowly and gingerly down the long stairs until he was out on the street. It was busy as usual, with a few hipster cool young thirty somethings walking towards the cheese shop, an elderly couple walking their dog, some kids running down the street off to God knows where, and a few other locals out and about running errands. He flagged down a yellow cab, hopped in, and gave the cabbie a location that Laura had given him.

"Fifty third street between fifth and sixth," he said.

"You got it. Midtown tunnel or Queensboro bridge?"

"Queensboro bridge, please." He was still a cheapskate in some things, despite being a degenerate gambler, and he hated paying for the tolls through the midtown tunnel, even if it was sometimes faster. In this case, the Museum of Modern art was pretty close to the fifty ninth street bridge anyways, so it wouldn't really take him much longer to go the long way, and it would save him on the tunnel toll.

The ride was pretty quick, and he absent mindedly admired the views of Manhattan as they crossed the Queensboro bridge. He could see the East River up and down from his back seat, and the skyline was impressive with all of the tall buildings cutting up and pressing up against the sky. The traffic wasn't too bad on this day, being a Friday afternoon before rush hour, and he was able to make it to the Museum in just about twenty-five minutes, not too bad. He paid the cabbie and got out and stared up at the façade of the building. The doors were all glass, with long stainless-steel handlebars that went from the top to the bottom of the door. There were square panels about four feet square that were made of a not quite translucent glass, and these went all the way up to the top of the building, which was only six stories tall.

He supposed they were windows. Going through the revolving door rather than the regular door, he paused as he squinted and looked at the crowd of people who were milling about in the lobby or standing in line waiting to pay for entrance.

"Larry! Over here," he heard, and he looked to his right to see Laura, dressed smartly in a cream-colored blouse and black slacks with black heels. She waved him over and then strode confidently towards the entrance, past the reception desk where folks were waiting to buy tickets.

"I have your ticket," she said, and handed over two tickets to the attendant.

"Thanks," he murmured as he followed her. She took another right and they went down a hallway, lined with oil paintings, and then got to another glass door that led back outside to a courtyard. It was a beautiful courtyard, he had to admit. White marble with swirls of black, cut into rectangles that were connected together, formed the walkway through the courtyard. There were four rectangular reflecting pools, and the pools were created with black marble, adding a nice contrast to the white marble sidewalk tiles. The walkway even crossed over and bisected two of the pools, so that patrons could walk over the pool itself. Throughout the courtyard, were small pockets of grass, and trees that sprouted up from the ground. Cryptomeria and birch trees if he wasn't mistaken. Laura led him all the way to the far end of the sculpture garden, where there were a set of chairs that were unoccupied. She took one chair, and he followed suit and took the other.

"How's it going, Larry? What the hell happened to your face?" she asked calmly. That was the thing about her. She never seemed rattled, and never showed her surprise. Stacy had trained her well, he mused.

"It's going well. This? Bah, it's nothing. Just a little accident at home. Wife left her knitting materials on the floor and I tripped over them in the night is all." He watched her carefully to see her reaction. She paused, and then answered him carefully.

"I know you're divorced, Larry. So, what really happened?"

"Don't worry about me, ok? Everything is fine," he muttered, his voice tinged with a bit of anger. "Why am I here? We could have handled this over the phone." He hoped the subject change would get her off his back, and it worked. She gave him a sour grimace but let the subject drop.

"We're here because I needed to get out and stretch my legs, and I wanted to see you in person. You've been hard to get ahold of these last couple weeks, and Samuel is telling me that he's worried about you. That's rare for him to speak up like that, and that's got me concerned too. But at any rate, there's two things we need to discuss. First, tell me what you've got on Darbear. Your team has had a lot of time on this, and I can't wait any longer."

He frowned and grumbled. "We've had a lot of time because we needed it. There's nothing on this guy. You keep telling us to dig deeper, go back farther, but I'm telling you, we've found nothing. Either he's clean, or he has been really, really good at hiding it. Perhaps he even has a Samuel of his own, neh? Clean up all his bad histories and stuff. Do you want to manufacture some dirt?" He paused to look around and made sure no one was too close to eavesdrop on them.

She shook her head. "I don't know that it will work. This kind of guy, he's got lawyers crawling everywhere, and it would have to be legitimately tight dirt to make it work. We would need something really solid. So, that's it? You really couldn't find anything? I thought for sure this asshole would have some buried skeletons." She was disappointed, he could see, and her shoulders slumped slightly.

"Nothing that we can find. But it's a little too clean."

"What do you mean?"

"There's something about this guy. Everything I've read, all the reports my team has compiled. I don't know. Just a gut feeling, there's something there, but we can't see it yet. Everyone in the business world hates this man's guts, and he's an asshole by all accounts, but then when we dig, it's just a little too...buttoned up, clear, church like, I don't know. I feel like something will come up, but we just have to keep searching."

"Ok, then. Keep searching. Do you need to hire more investigators?"

He shook his head. "No. Just give me free rein on the budget, carte blanche, and let me see where my team leads us to."

Laura hesitated. Not because of the free rein on the money, but rather because she wasn't sure she could trust Larry to use the money properly. By now, she knew he had a gambling problem, as Samuel had told her last week, and things weren't going well for him, from what Gary had been able to track down. But she was desperate, and she had no choice.

"Ok. Carte blanche on the budget. Just get me something to work with, either real dirt, or a solidly fabricated piece of dirt that will stick in the media and get him to back off."

"Right. What's the other thing you wanted to chat about?" he asked.

She looked around the sculpture garden and then turned to lock gazes with him.

"You kind of hinted at it before, about Darbear having his own Samuel to wipe his slate clean. I need Samuel to do that for me."

He raised an eyebrow and leaned forward so that his elbows were on his knees, hunched over slightly as he peered up at her from an angle. "How do you mean?"

She was quiet for a moment but was still intently staring at him. "I know Stacy had you investigate me years ago, back when she was about to hire me for the assistant Chief of Staff role. I know you found out about my past. I want Samuel to go through my complete file, all the way back as far as internet records on me go, and wipe out any references or anything at all, linking me to liking the company of women. Everything. Dating sites, blogs, anything at all. There shouldn't be much, but I want it all erased, permanently."

Larry pursed his lips, and then nodded his head. "Yeah, ok. Consider it done."

"This is important, Larry. Have Samuel do it tonight, and for as long as it takes. I just hope Darbear hasn't dug into my past yet, and I don't think he has. He considers me an insignificant fly, just a buzzing gnat that he has to shoo away before he makes his move. He's still slowly accumulating more shares of Abernathy, building up his stake as quietly as possible before he makes his move. I think he'll do that very soon, likely this week. He's gathered close to fifteen percent of the company, with the help of his investment bank and some wealthy backers. Now is the time that he'll agitate for management changes and make his threats."

"Understood. I'll have Samuel prioritize this. But tell me why? You never bothered to hide who you are before? Why now?" he asked curiously as he straightened up and zipped up his coat. It was getting chilly.

She stood up and blew some warm air on her cupped hands.

"Just precautions, Larry. I don't know yet how I'm going to campaign, whether I'll be myself…or be who the public wants to see. I just want some options and I don't want the media to find out on their own. If I go public, then I want the world to hear it from me first, that's all. But first things first. Call me when it's done." She walked briskly away, leaving Larry to sit alone on the chair in the suddenly forlorn sculpture garden, wondering to himself how he had ended up here.

16

Balls in the Air

Laura unlocked the key to her apartment and opened the door to a wonderful mix of aromas. Chicken, simmering in a pan with some type of broth and herbs, truffle with mushrooms mixed into a risotto, and dill with carrots sizzling in the pan.

"You're early!" shouted Gale, who was wearing a white apron atop her dark blue merino sweater. She came to greet her at the door and gave her a full kiss, leaving her aroused and panting for breath. "I thought I'd surprise you with dinner. You've been so busy these last few weeks, I knew you'd be exhausted and would just want to order that Chinese takeout place you always get. Phoenix? Phoenix Garden? Whatever. Anyways, I'm almost done. Surprise." Gale smiled at her and looked her up and down.

"Gotta tell you, babe, you look like shit. Seriously, you have dark circles underneath your eyes."

"Gale?"

"Yes? You want me to tone it down? I know you're stressed like hell, so you want me to take it easy on you? Serves you right, for telling me that I walk like a duck. Karma, baby, karma."

"Someth_ng's burning."

"Oh shit. The carrots!" yelped Gale, as she scampered over into the galley kitchen that was off the hallway by the front door.

Even as tired as she was, Laura still managed a smile. Gale always could cheer her up, no matter her mood, and she was a breath of fresh air in an otherwise intense, male dominated, power hungry underworld, where only the strongest and most brutal survived. She was her fountain of youth. She took off her coat and hung it in the closet opposite the entrance to the kitchen, then walked down the hallway and through the living room to her bedroom. She lived in a large, eight hundred square foot one bedroom apartment, large at least by New York City standards, and although she could afford more, she decided that less was more in this instance. She knew that if she upgraded to a two bedroom, that she would just stuff and fill the second bedroom with clothes, luggage, and other crap that she really didn't use or need. Besides, she liked being alone, and this way, she didn't have to host out of town guests as much. She freshened up in the bathroom and came out into the living room, where Gale was setting the table for dinner. Her living room and dining room were all just one large space, where she had a small round glass table that could seat four, right in between the kitchen and the living room. The kitchen had a pass-through window that peeked from the kitchen and into the living room. Laura's tastes were minimalist and modern. Kind of like IKEA, kind of like Bo Concept, but with very few pieces of furniture. There was just the couch, a coffee table, two armchairs, a bookcase, an end table with a lamp, the round dining table with four chairs, and a sideboard for dishes and other glassware. There wasn't even a TV or a computer desk in the living room to speak off. Very simple, clean, and high-end modern furnishings, just the way she liked it. Gale called it 'boring' and 'super Nordic', but she enjoyed the couch, as they spent many nights just snuggled up together on the couch, streaming Netflix, or Hulu.

She decided to change out of her work clothes and went back to her bedroom and into her walk-in closet, switched into her PJ's, then walked out to find the dining table set, and food already plated, as well as a bottle of chardonnay opened and ready to pour. Gale was scrolling through her phone, seated at one of the chairs, the one that was back to the wall. She pushed her phone away, though, when Laura came out and took the chair opposite her.

"Thanks, babe! Wow! This looks and smells so good. I am famished," she said, as she leaned closer over her plate and took a deep breath of the wonderful aromas.

"You are most welcome! You know, when I started dating you, I was expecting to eat all this amazing, homemade Korean food, but all you can make is like, mac and cheese. Such a disappointment. Tsk, tsk," her girlfriend said with a smile. Her blonde hair was tied back with a scrunchy, and her blue eyes twinkled with mischief. Gale was still in her work clothes, as she wore her comfortable dark blue jeans, and her favorite fall sweater. She didn't have much makeup on today, but that made her look all the more appealing to Laura.

"Hey, listen. I was too busy studying, and working my tail off, to learn how to cook. Besides, don't put me in a box. Just because I'm a woman, doesn't mean I have to be able to cook, you know that. Now, let's see how good of a cook you really are," she said as she used her fork to taste the mushroom risotto. "Mmmmm. Delicious. I gotta say. You are like, probably, the fourth best cook that I've ever dated. No lower than fourth, for sure."

Gale's eyes widened in mock shock. "You are so rude, you know that?"

"And that's why you like me so much, right?" she said around a mouthful of carrots.

"Meh. So. Anyway, what's new at work? Any head way on Danbear?"

"Darbear, not Danbear. Ugh. Terrible today. He went public today and announced that he had acquired close to nineteen percent of the company. The stock took off, on hopes that he will be able to agitate for change, or possibly do a hostile takeover. He also announced that while he doesn't want to do a hostile takeover, he's not shying away from it. My office and also the investor relations team got flooded with phone calls today, and it was all about damage control. Want some wine?" She poured herself a generous pour and did the same for Gale when she nodded her head.

"So, what does that mean for you then? Are you going to get fired?" Gale raised an eyebrow and had a look of concern on her face. She loved how genuine and sincere Gale was. She really was worried and hopeful for her, not for herself. It made her feel good, knowing that someone cared this deeply for her.

"Well, it depends. If he just postures, and makes demands for changes in the company, the board might acquiesce and give in to the strategic demands. I might be ok there. But if he asks for heads to roll and wants a new management team in place, yeah, I'll lose my job. Lastly, if he manages to do the hostile takeover, I'll also lose my job in that scenario too. So yeah. I'm in a bit of trouble here."

"What a jerk! And he can do all this legally? I don't follow corporate raiders." Gale frowned and bit into a carrot with gusto.

"Yeah, unfortunately. He's got power, money, and influence. He's a queen on the chessboard, very powerful. But I'm a queen too, and I'm still formulating my plans." She took a sip of the wine. "Mmmm, very good."

"So now that Darbear is openly attacking Abernathy, what are your next steps?"

"That's the tough part. I don't have a lot of options at the moment. I have a research team, looking into all sorts of angles that we could pursue, but they haven't found anything yet. The board already met, and after a couple hours of back and forth, they basically came back to square one, which is, they don't have a clue of what to do next. They want to reach out and meet with Darbear and his team, and they want to set that up soon, but that's about all that they could agree on. So, for the moment, it's a bit of a holding pattern for me and my team."

"Hm. That sucks," said Gale as she wrinkled her nose and shook her head. "Well, if you get axed, you could just start up your campaign early for the Senate run, right?"

"Yeah. I could do that. If I get fired, that's what I'll have to do, but it's not my first choice. We'll see. I have a meeting with Mary Chatsworth, tomorrow."

"Whoa. Really? Mary Chatsworth?" exclaimed Gale. She had both eyebrows raised, and her blue eyes sparkled.

"Yeah, you know her?" Laura had been so busy with Darbear, and having Larry and his team solely investigate him, that she had done little research at all on this political campaign manager that Stacy had connected her to.

"Yes, everyone knows her. At least, in my circle they do. All the reporters on the political campaign beat talk about which campaign managers are solid sources, or which ones have all the scoop, or which ones are the best to work with. Mary's name comes up all the time, or at least, it did. She sort of disappeared over the last couple of years."

"Why, what happened?"

"She helped that Senator from Delaware get elected years ago. Then, she was a huge player on the presidential campaign, but she left before it finished. No one knows why. I think she's been running a consultancy down in D.C. the last few years. But you should look her up tonight before you meet with her. I hear she's brilliant, and supposedly one of the best at what she does. But the reason I'm excited for you, is that she's connected to all the power players. The last two Democratic presidents, all of their billionaire donors, movie stars even. She's a good person to run your campaign if you can get her onboard."

Laura mulled over what she had just heard and chewed thoughtfully on a bite of chicken. It was juicy, and well cooked, and she decided that she would indeed, have to do some reading up on Mary tonight.

The next morning started off rough. It was raining and fall in New York. She hated these cold, rainy, fall days. There were some orange and brown leaves on the sidewalk, and even though she could have taken a cab, she had decided to get some fresh air and walked from Columbus circle up to her office building, walking along Central Park West. Luckily, she wore her Hunter rain galoshes, dark green, and had her umbrella and tan raincoat to keep her dry. The doorman opened the tall glass door in the lobby, and she quickly folded her umbrella, stuffing it into one of the plastic rain sleeves that were in a stand by the door, so that rain water wouldn't leak onto the marble floor and cause colleagues to slip and fall. The lobby was full of people. Colleagues coming into work, visitors waiting for guest badges off to the side in the reception area, security guards standing by the turn stiles and checking badges, and even a few kids, waiting to get checked in with their parents into the office daycare center which was adjacent to the lobby. It was one of the company perks, one which she had never had the need for. The ceiling of the lobby was tiled in a mosaic blue tile and went well with the grey marble floors and black walls.

By the time she made it up to her office, she was already five minutes late for her eight a.m. meeting with Jennifer and Adam. She found them waiting for her, seated at her round glass table off to the side and she had them jump into the days to do list while she shed her raincoat, and switched her rain galoshes for her comfortable, red Romy 60 pumps from Jimmy Choo.

"Alright. Give me the highlights of where you guys are at. Start with the Darbear situation," she ordered briskly.

"Nothing new to report on that front. The board has setup a meeting with him, his team, and you for next Wednesday, nine a.m., but you already knew that. Media and news outlets are reporting about his acquisition of the company's shares, nineteen percent, and speculating on whether he'll go hostile or not. Not much else new to report at this point," started Jennifer. Her voice was full of disappointment.

"The only other thing is that one of his investment bankers unexpectedly quit on him. Remember the short guy with glasses? He resigned and left for another investment bank, I think Deutche," said Adam as he stared down at his notes. He was dressed casually today, which for Abernathy, meant a button-down dress shirt and slacks. But something clicked in her head, and she threw it out there to see if it made sense.

"Wait. Adam, didn't you say you were in investment banking before business school?"

"Yeah, for about seven years, why?"

"What did you do?"

"Mergers and acquisitions, deal structuring, some leveraged buy outs. But it was up or out in banking, and I was getting burned out by the hours. Why?" he asked again, his curiosity piqued.

"Listen, just throwing it out there. But what if you applied to Chase investment banking. Basically, your angle would be that you know all of the ins and outs of Abernathy, and everything that we strategically want to do, so you would be an invaluable resource to assisting Darbear with this deal. He'll hire you, but secretly, you'll still report to Jennifer, and we'll have an insider's view of every tactic they're about to try. What do you think?" she asked. It was a long shot but could be worth it if Adam could get into their graces, and then give them a heads up on everything Darbear was attempting.

"Hmmm. What about my benefits, 401k, all that stuff here? My stock options? I mean, what if they find out too?" he asked as he leaned back in his chair. She realized it was a big ask. He was essentially leaving the safety and comfort of an extremely high profile and highly compensated role here at Abernathy, where he was building his profile and becoming an important player in the company, to be a mole at an investment bank where there was no guarantee he would get staffed onto Darbear's team, and where he could be fired at any moment without anyone there to vouch for him. It was a risk, a big one.

"Look. Don't answer now, just think about it. I'll take good care of you. If you get fired, or they don't staff you on his team, either way, you can come back here and resume your current role, with a promotion here and a salary bump. Just think on it, ok? I could really use an ace up the sleeve, that having you on the inside would allow us to outmaneuver the fox," she implored. The more and more she thought about it, the better she felt. *"This would give me a huge advantage,"* she thought.

Adam hesitated, then nodded. "I'll think on it," he promised.

"Ok, great. What's next on the list?"

The next forty minutes was filled with to do's and yet more to do's. She had to check in with the Investor Relations team about a follow up from the last earnings call, then she had to meet with the Chief Operating Officer about a round of layoffs in their London office, and finally, she had to get ready for a global townhall that she was going to deliver in the following week. Of course, Jennifer and Adam had to make sure she had all her notes and Q&A ready for these meetings, so that she was prepared and ready to lead these meetings. There were a lot of balls to juggle, especially now, with the Darbear situation throwing a monkey wrench in her carefully laid plans.

Finally, though, she dismissed Jennifer and Adam, and got ready for her meeting with Mary Chatsworth. Mary worked from her offices in D.C., but she happened to be in New York for several meetings and had agreed to stop by for a meeting with her. She sat down at her desk by the window, and quickly scanned her notes from last night. It was everything she could find online herself, as she didn't bother with pulling her investigative team off their Darbear investigation to check out Mary. No, Darbear was too big a target to siphon off even one or two hours' time for this political campaign manager.

Mary had led a charmed life, it seemed, at least if all the articles online could be believed. Her family came from wealth, and she had never wanted for money. She had gone to a private boarding school in Massachusetts when she was just a freshman in high school, at Bard Academy. There, she had been class president, graduated valedictorian of her class, and went to Wellesley women's college, also in Massachusetts. Graduated near the top of her class, having studied political science, and then went to work in D.C. She had joined as a junior staffer for Congressman James Mahoney, a Democrat of Virginia, then worked her way up in his staff, eventually becoming the Chief of Staff to the Congressman himself. She left his employment after he retired and went to work on the re-election campaign for Senator Julie Shenk, Democrat of Connecticut. After her successful re-election, she joined her staff in various roles and capacities, until she became Chief of Staff there as well. Never satisfied, Mary then went to serve on the campaign of Forrest Newton, a first-time challenger for the Senate seat in Delaware, and to the amazement of everyone, her candidate won. This was the peak of her political rise, however, as she went to serve as a senior campaign advisor for Senator Brandon Charnock, the Democrat from Massachusetts as he made a run for the Presidency. It was here, that the articles were conflicted about Mary's time in this role. Some articles stated that she did her job well, while others hinted that there was turmoil within the campaign, and whispers of in fighting and a power struggle. Ultimately, she left, or perhaps was fired, it was unclear, and the Senator failed to make it past the third round of the Democratic primaries. After this failure, Mary had opened up her own political consulting practice in D.C. and was doing quite well. The

Washington Post named her one of the top ten most powerful women in D.C., in 2018, and her net worth was estimated at around five million plus. Life was good.

So, when Geoff buzzed her desk phone and announced that Mary Chatsworth was here to see her, she felt prepared, and felt as if she knew her target well. How wrong she was.

"Laura? Miss Chatsworth is here to see you."

"Thanks, Geoff. Send her in, please." She smoothed her beige business suit jacket and matching skirt with her hands and folded them on her desk as she waited for the door to open. In walked a short middle-aged woman, in her forties, with short brown hair that had a few streaks of grey in it, steely grey eyes, and a determined look on her face. She wore a simple grey raincoat, London Fog, and a Calvin Klein one button blazer in black, white pleated blouse, and black trousers with short heels. Laura stood up and extended her hand, but Mary didn't accept it at first. She came over, set her briefcase onto the adjacent chair, took off her raincoat and set it atop her briefcase, then eyed Laura up and down for several seconds, looking at the watch on her wrist, sizing up her skirt and suit jacket, then looking at her face, actually, at her earrings and lipstick. There was an awkward ten second silence while this all took place, and Laura just stood there, her welcome smile frozen on her face, as she debated whether to drop her hand or to say something politely about the rain. Before she could do either, Mary finally gripped her hand and gave it a firm handshake.

"So? You're running for Senator?" Mary asked casually as she sat down in the chair opposite her and watched her face for a reaction.

Laura gave a thin smile and sat down, already disliking this woman who had no manners whatsoever. *"I thought boarding school and Bard meant cultured, and refined, but clearly not,*" she grimaced to herself. To her credit, she didn't stammer or appear surprised, and instead, she decided to directly answer the question.

"Soon, I'll be making a run next year. The-" but she was interrupted before she could finish.

"I know. The Senate seat here in New York. It's the only viable play that makes sense. Maryland's seat just got re-elected, so that won't open for six years. You have no other ties, and your residency is here."

"Pardon my asking, but who told you I was running anyway? Did Stacy mention this?" She would be surprised if Stacy had, because Stacy never shared anything with outsiders.

"No. Stacy just called in a favor, and I agreed to meet with you. But it doesn't take much to put two and two together. There was the article by CNN, and I read it. It mentioned rumors of a foray into politics. I checked in with my political contacts, and I've seen all the groundwork you've been laying. The lunches with the mayor. The hob knobbing with congressmen and senators down in D.C. The carefully planned photos of you at Democratic fund raisers. It's a good plan, but you can only play it out so far, the coyness of 'will she or won't she run'? Sooner or later, you have to announce, and then, you'll need a platform to run on. And that's why I'm here. So, what's your pitch?"

Laura was surprised at how blunt and direct this woman was. She was used to Stacy's no bullshit, no nonsense approach, and Stacy was at times, crass and foul mouthed, but this woman was direct in a different way. Her eyes pierced into you and even though she was asking a question, it seemed to Laura that she already had an answer formulated in her head. Mary had reviewed all the angles, and now, she was waiting to see if you had figured it out too. It was like being quizzed, only, you didn't know what the subject was ahead of the quiz.

"Well, I'm still ironing out the details, but the broad-brush strokes? Senator Thorpe here in New York has had a few stumbles lately, particularly around job creation and the economy. My platform is going to be two pronged, centered on creating jobs for the middle class here in New York, and then increasing wages for women and minorities. There's no one better equipped to talk those two areas than me."

Mary nodded her head approvingly. "That can work. The devil is in the details, but you can win on that platform. I know Justin. He's getting soft, and left his belly exposed recently. If not you, someone else will unseat him next year. Why do you need me?" Again, the unrelenting stare into the deep parts of her brown eyes.

"Can I ask for confidentiality here? That nothing said will pass these four walls?" she asked firmly. Mary paused, then nodded her head.

"Listen, Stacy said that I needed someone on the inside of the political jungle. Someone who knows all the ins and outs of D.C., and how to navigate a campaign. She suggested you, and I trust her instincts. To be frank, I have my sights set on something higher."

"The Presidency," said Mary calmly. "You want to run for President." It was a statement, not a question. Laura was not sure if Mary had read her mind, or if she was simply good at guessing.

"No need to sit there blankly, trying to hide your ambition. I can sense it. You're a power broker, and you make things happen. I've been around enough people like you to know one when I see one. But let me ask you this. How long after you win a Senate seat, do you think you'll make the plunge and go for it all?"

"I'll play it by ear, but I want to try right in my first term, after I get some experience of how things work."

Mary chuckled and gave a smile. "You've got some big balls, lady. No one knows who you are yet, and you're thinking you'll run for President during your first term? You think you're another Obama?"

Laura smiled sweetly in return and pulled herself closer to her desk, putting her hands on the table. "That remains to be seen. Do you want to be my campaign manager?"

Mary turned to the adjacent chair and opened up her briefcase, pulling out a folder.

"Normally, I would say 'no'. I've already had my fill of this sort of thing. I've helped people get elected to Senate seats, Congressional seats, and almost got a President elected. I know how to pick winners, and I know how to run a great campaign. But you've got me intrigued, I have to admit. We don't have enough women and we don't have enough Asian Americans in Congress. Here's the thing though. I don't know you. And we need to know each other, to see if we believe in each other. I need to know everything about you, and your past, and your present. Are you willing to open up and share everything, what you believe in, and show me who you really are?" Mary opened up her folder but didn't reveal the contents yet.

"Yes," she said simply. She would need Larry and his team to do a quick and dirty investigation into Mary, but her gut told her that she knew what she was doing, and she would be best served if Mary was in her corner.

"Ok then. Here is a schedule of fees. If I agree to be your campaign manager, this will need to be my salary. Also, I'll want you to hire my political consultancy as a full-time staff. They're a great team, and they will bring all sorts of great analysis and polls and strategies to our fingertips. That being said, I won't charge you or the campaign until you announce. Until that point, we'll hold all the billing until that date. Take some time to review it, and when we meet again, you can ask me any questions you have about it. Since you'll be running in New York, I'll get a rental here, and hire some local staff so that we can run point out of New York. Let's meet this weekend. I'll plan a hike for us upstate, and we can talk and get to know one another. I want to hear about your ideas and plans for the future. I want to know what kind of person you are, and vice versa. Let's see if we are a fit." Mary slid the paper and the folder over and stood up.

"That's it? You don't want to go over some of these things now?" Laura asked with mild annoyance. She was trying to stay afloat among everything going on, and a hike upstate sounded like a waste of her precious time.

"Nope. We need a good six, eight hours together. Let's save it for the hike," Mary replied cheerfully as she pulled on her raincoat and grabbed her briefcase. She was already walking towards the door when Laura asked her one more question.

"Mary. I couldn't quite figure it out from the articles I read, but why did you leave the Presidential campaign? What happened there?" Laura stood up and walked around the desk, leaning against it as she waited for Mary's reaction. Mary turned around and studied her for a moment before replying.

"I had a nasty run in with the Chief of Staff, Marc Trumbo. I'm a lesbian, and he said some extremely negative and homophobic things when he didn't know I was in earshot. We had…some harsh words. Anyways, I quit. We'll chat more on Saturday. I'll get your info from Geoff and pick you up. Nine a.m. sharp." With that, Mary left, and Laura had much to consider.

17

Calling in a Favor

Larry and his team had been sprinting for the last several weeks. Everything they checked on Darbear had led to a dead end. His ex-wife had nothing to say. All the leads going back to his college and high school days, zippo. Ex colleagues, rivals, peers, hell, he even had sent Gary over to Czechoslovakia to run down some leads, and nothing there either. Jerome had even tried talking to the gardener and lawn service guys who did Darbear's yard work, and same result. It seemed this guy was squeaky clean. Checking accounts and transactions were all legal. He had a couple Swiss bank accounts, but Samuel couldn't crack those, so that was a dead end too. But even though everything seemed on the up and up, something smelled a little funny to him. He had been a cop, and later a detective, for far too long. His senses were tingling, and he just knew that there was something not right about this guy.

It was all *too* tidy. This guy, however, made him uneasy, and he knew to trust his gut. Larry had found out where Darbear was eating dinner one night and scored a table right next to him and eavesdropped carefully. He had watched the man eat, drink wine, laugh, and talk with a colleague. And through it all, he came away feeling that this man was not as he seemed. There was a look around the man's eyes. A hard look, filled with cruelty. He had seen it before in murderers he had locked up, thieves, and the wicked. Hell, he saw the same look in the thugs and bodyguards in the gambling parlor that he frequented all the time. It was easy to spot. So, he knew that Darbear was no angel. It just meant that he was hiding something. The only thing was, he didn't have all the tools to find out this time.

"Samuel," he had asked last night.

"Yeah, boss?"

"Can you hack into the police department system, get me access to all their files and reports?"

"Hmmm. Not a good idea, Larry. I mean. Theoretically, I could hack in. But there's a good chance, more than fifty percent, that I could get spotted. And if I do, they'd be able to trace me all the way back here. They have a pretty decent team over there, and they've been beefing up the security over the last several years." Samuel looked worried.

"What if I got you another resource? Couldn't two hackers find a way to get in unnoticed?"

Samuel shook his head. "Maybe...I don't think it's a good idea. They've set some nasty traps in that system. I wouldn't risk it. If you did, you would want to pack a bag, get ready to run, because there's a good chance they'll come crashing on top of you. What are you looking for?"

But Larry clammed up. He didn't know exactly what he was looking for. So instead, he decided to call in an old favor.

"Joe, hey, it's me, Larry."

"Larry K? What the hell, how've you been you old sack o' shit?" exclaimed the voice on the other end of the line.

"Oh, you know me. A little bit o'this, a little bit o'that. Same, same. How's Nancy and the boys?"

"They're great. Nancy's packed on twenty more pounds, but don't tell her I told you. Every fuckin' week, it's 'does this dress make me look fat?' No! Your fat makes you look fat, Jesus. Boys are good. Harry's a senior in high school. He's going to electrician school after he graduates. Paul's a freshman, playing JV lacrosse. What about you? What you been up to man?"

"I've got a private shop now. Doing P.I. work. Got a great client though. She's smart, pay's really good when there's work to be done. Keeps my team on retainer."

"Sounds good. Who is it?" Joe asked curiously.

"Bah, just some rich businesswoman. You don't know her," he had said. He was careful not to reveal Laura's name. He knew she would be pissed if she ever found out.

"Say. I need to call in a favor. A big one," he said.

"Uh, oh. Five fuckin' years you don't call, and this is how you do me? What favor?"

"C'mon, Joe. It ain't like you don't owe me. This will clear all debts."

"Fuck you. You did it to yourself. You and your gambling ring. You said you wouldn't get caught," Joe said uneasily.

"Yeah, well. Karma's a bitch. Anyways, I kept you out of it. You stayed clean, kept your job, your pension, all your benefits. I never snitched, and we both know you owe me," Larry said calmly.

"Fuck's sake. What's the favor?" Joe demanded.

"I need you to get me in to the precinct, at like midnight on Friday night, when there's no one there. And I need you to get me a master login and access. I need to see all the files in the system, even the private or hidden files or reports in the Comish's computer. Do this, and we're all square."

There was a long silence, followed by a long low whistle. "Wow. You really want to get me fucked. You know the shit I could get in if anyone finds this out? I'll be fired instantaneously."

"Joe, you can do it and stay clean. No one will ever know it was you, and how can they? I'll be in the system under a real id, not yours, and no one will be the wiser."

"Yeah. Where have I heard this before?" snarled Joe with anger.

"Trust me. Just get me in."

"Let me think." Another long pause. "Ok. I can get you into the precinct. That's not the issue. But I can't get you a master login with admin access. I can only get you a guest login and access, best I can do. You'll be able to browse through some of the files and reports, but not the Comish's computer."

"That'll do. Set it up. Call me back with the details."

"And then we're all square?"

"Promise."

After he had hung up, he had called over Samuel.

"Hey, Samuel? If I can physically be at the precinct, with a guest login and access to the system and files, can you hack me in and get me admin access to everything? Even the Comish's private files and folders on his computer?"

"Well, yeah. I mean, if you can really be logged into the system without me having to hack in? I can then work my program from the inside of the firewall without triggering any of the traps. How are you going to get in?" Sam had asked with one eyebrow raised doubtfully.

"Forget that part. Assume I can get in. You can hack all the files? The ones I need the most might be on the Comish's private computer."

"I'll write some code now and put it on a USB flash drive. Just pop it in once you've logged in, and it will do the rest."

"Ok. Great. I'll be inside on Friday at midnight, so I'm going to need you here, just in case I need to call you for help."

Samuel grinned. "Sure. I'll be your IT help desk for a day."

Larry took a drag on his e-cigarette and blew it out in a white puffy billow of smoke. He looked around the street and saw only one person walking down Madison Street, heading away from him. It was dark, and almost eleven forty-five p.m. He was sitting on a bench, up on the raised steps just outside the small security stand that was in front of the police headquarters in downtown Manhattan, just to the right of Tribeca. There were young oak trees lining the concrete walkway here, with small square plots of dirt and grass poking through the cement to allow the trees to take root. He had always thought it odd, that Manhattan, a city of steel and concrete, could still have these small pockets of dirt to allow trees to sprout and grow. Just didn't seem natural to him, but whatever. There were trash cans on either side of his long bench, and he waited patiently, sitting comfortably in his thick grey coat. Finally, a man walked out of the police building, past the security gate, and over towards him. Joe was a little heavier in the paunch than he last remembered, with a bald head, thick set jowls, bushy grey eyebrows, and a wide bulbous nose. He had on his blue police uniform, hat, and looked grumpy as hell.

"Hey, Larry. Good to see you."

Larry stood up, pocketed his e-cig, and stuck out his hand, gripping Joe's thick, meaty fist with a strong shake.

"Joe, good to see you, old friend. You got my things?"

"Yeah. Here's a badge, and the login. The badge will get you in through security and swipes through all the doors inside too. I told the guard in the shack there to keep his head down, and read the newspaper, and don't look up at the guy walking through. Left him a thou, so you owe me."

Larry nodded, and pulled out a manilla envelope, handing it over to Joe.

Joe weighed it up and down a few times, then raised an eyebrow.

"Feels heavy."

"Yeah. There's ten g's there. The extra is yours. I know how much trouble and risk this is for you. I promise you though, you won't get linked at all, and I'm not doing anything harmful to the department. I'm just looking for information is all."

Joe nodded gratefully, and the envelope disappeared. He looked Larry up and down approvingly. "There shouldn't be anyone in the building. I made a quick check of all the floors, and it's empty. But on the off chance someone should swing by, just tell them you are internal affairs, doing a check on a file for the Shapiro case. You look the part. It was a big case several years back, but the whole precinct has been whispering that internal affairs is looking into the case again for some unknown reason. We've had a couple folks come by last week, so one more guy poking around shouldn't raise any alarms. The IT room is open, you remember where it is? Good. There's a computer that I left on there. Just use the guest login from there, and you should be all set. Make sure you're gone by five though. Always a few assholes who clock in early, trying to impress the man. Capiche?"

"Sounds good. What about the cameras inside?"

"No one reviews the footage unless something goes wrong. So just make sure…nothing goes wrong, got it?"

Larry nodded again. "Got it. Thanks, Joe. We're good."

"Yeah," he muttered. "Don't get caught, or you're on your own."

Larry was about to reply that he never gets caught but shut his mouth. He had been caught. Once. And the gambling sting had taken him, and his best friend down.

"I'm going to take a walk, stretch my legs, before I head back to the security desk inside. I'm on duty til six, so just make some noise when you're about to leave the building, by the elevators, ok?" said Joe. He didn't wait for Larry's nod, and started to walk away.

He waited for Joe to walk down the street towards Madison, then took the three steps down to the main walkway towards the security shack. He pulled his collar up to shield his face a little more and walked past the guard shack. There was a security guard inside, but true to Joe's word, the man had his back turned to the window, and was intently reading a newspaper which was opened up in front of him on his desk. The man turned his head ever so slightly as he walked past, so Larry knew that he at least acknowledged him, but he never turned around to see who it was. *"Thousand dollars goes a long way these days,"* he muttered.

He kept walking steadily towards the entrance, and looked up at the square, brown brick building. It was twelve stories tall, with windows evenly spaced every two feet apart in neat rows. Larry had been in the nineteenth precinct on the upper east side and had rarely come down to One Police Plaza downtown. This was the official New York City Police Headquarters, and this was where the commissioner's office was located. Luckily for him, he had friends in all the precincts, and Joe was one of the old guards here. The man knew everything about this building, the people inside, and how the access and systems worked. He walked towards the glass door, and used his badge to swipe in, waiting for the audible 'click' to signify the door unlocked. Pulling it open, he walked into the lobby. The lobby was a huge, open space, with ceilings that went up thirty feet. There was a wooden concierge desk at the front, that was currently empty and unmanned. Joe had taken the watch this night, just for this purpose. He would be back in fifteen minutes to re-man the desk. White marble with black flecks lined the floor, and soft light brown wood made up the walls, giving it a somewhat soothing presence, oddly enough. He walked past the concierge desk and towards the elevator bank. There was an elevator that was open and waiting, so he went in and hit the tenth floor, where all the IT servers and offices were. When the doors opened again, he walked out and saw glass doors to his left, and to his right. He had to stop and pause to get his bearings but decided to take the right set of doors. He swiped in and found himself in a drab looking hallway with grey carpet and bland, white painted walls with no artwork. He had been up here only once, but Joe had been clear in his instructions. "Tenth floor, room one oh two. That's the IT shop." So, he shrugged, and turned down the left hallway, figuring that the floor must loop around since each floor was a square, and eventually, he would wrap around and find the right room. He was right. He walked past an open area with cubicles, down another hallway, past a coffee break room, past a row of offices, and finally, he found room one oh two. He swiped in and found himself in a square room, where rectangular tables had been pushed up against the walls, and desktops and monitors were spaced apart through the tables. If one stood in the center of the room and turned in a circle, you would see chairs, monitors, and keyboards, all evenly spaced apart. There were about twenty computer rigs setup, and each station had personal effects there. Some had framed photos of families, or kids, others had binders with reports, another area had a used coffee mug with stale coffee, and so on. Clearly, these were workstations of department IT employees. All of the monitors were dark and off, except for one. In the far-right hand corner, one monitor was on, and bright. He walked toward it and found a post it note on top of the keyboard. All it said was, "This one."

He took off his grey coat and set it on the back of the chair, then pulled it out and sat down. Looking at his note from Joe, he quickly typed in the login id and password, and found himself staring at a windows home screen. He was in. Pulling out his phone, he called Samuel and put it on speaker, setting the phone on the desk.

"Yeah?"

"Hey, Samuel. I'm in the precinct and logged in to the mainframe."

"Great. Alright. You got the flash drive I gave you?"

"Yes."

"Put it in, and then open the folder for it."

"One sec…Alright, it's open."

"Ok, there's a file there called zorb.exe. You see it?"

"I see it."

"Double click it and let it run. I'll hold. Should take a few minutes."

Larry double clicked the file, and saw it a folder open, then another folder, then another folder, and then the screen turned all blue for twenty or so seconds, then flashed back to the windows home screen.

"Ok, I think it's done," he said.

"Ok. Let me check something here…Hm. Yes, it worked. I can access the mainframe from here too. How long you going to be searching their files?"

"Not sure. Probably a couple hours at least, why?"

"Well, I figure, since we're in, I might as well start to download and make a copy of their files. I won't get everything, but we can start."

"And you won't get caught?" he asked.

"No. I'm in as a real user and I can now cover my trail. There's no way to find us," Samuel said confidently.

"Ok, in that case, download their most recent cases. No, wait. See if you can download all their confidential informants first. I want a list of every snitch that's working with them. Secondly, get a brief of all their most recent cases that are open, starting with the most high-profile ones. Third, if you can get to it, get me a list of all their open internal affairs investigations, and find out all the dirty cops, or potentially dirty cops. That will come in useful for us down the road. Actually, make that number two, and the case work number three."

"You got it, boss."

"Be ready by your phone, in case I need you," he told Samuel, and then hung up.

He blew out a big breath. He didn't know where to start, and this was going to be looking for a needle in a haystack. Firstly though, he wanted to check the white crimes unit. If there was any dirt on Darbear, that would be the most likely area to find something, even it wasn't yet on the record. He found the white crimes unit folder and started searching for anything related to Darbear. Nothing showed up. He looked in recent cases, he looked in old cases, and still nothing. He popped out of the white crimes folder and decided to peek in vice. *"Maybe there's something with drugs or prostitution,"* he mulled. *"Solicitation of a prostitute, come on, give me something,"* he muttered. But try as he might, he couldn't find anything related to Darbear. An hour had gone by, and he had nothing to show for it. Leaning back in his chair, he stared up at the ceiling and thought about his target. "Wealthy guy. Tons of lawyers. Nothing in plain sight. Private jet..." Something tickled his mind, something that he had heard when Jocco had been giving his debrief a couple weeks ago. *"Guy flies in and out of Martha's Vineyard quite a bit. Private jet."* He stared at a cobweb on the popcorn ceiling. It was old, and dusty, and likely had been there for years and years. Wait a minute. Years and years. He blinked, and then his eyes got wide.

"No fucking way..." he whispered. He sat up and stared at the computer screen. He didn't know if the computer files would go back that far, but he could check. He went back to the vice folder and searched for cases from the year 1989. For the specific type of case he was looking for, he searched them all, but didn't find what he was looking for. He checked again, going slower, and searching for it. "God damn it. I know it has to be here. I was there," he said through gritted teeth. The realization hit him suddenly. *"It's been erased,"* he thought. *"Either that, or..."*

He elevated out of the vice folders and went over to the Comish's personal folders. Sam's coding hack allowed him access to the entire system, even the Comish's. If it weren't erased, this would be the only place it could be. He looked through the mountains of folders, old cases, some interesting info on a few confidential informants, and finally, he found it. He opened the folder, and found three video recordings tucked away in a folder labeled D.M. He held his breath as he opened and played them, one by one. "Fucking jackpot," he breathed. He copied the three videos over to the flash drive and then also copied over the police reports associated with the recordings as well.

"*Three a.m. Time to get out of dodge,*" he thought. He called Samuel.

"Hey, I'm all done. What about you?"

"Good progress here. Got all the confidential informants. Names, addresses, phone numbers, and what they've been snitching on. About halfway through all the internal affairs lists of suspected dirty cops, and what they are suspected of. Give me like twenty more minutes."

"No go. I've got what I need, and I'm bouncing. Time to get a move on."

"Alright. Just unplug the flash drive, and power down the desktop, and you should be set," said Samuel.

"Go home, and I'll see you tomorrow."

"You got it."

He hung up, powered down the desktop, pulled on his coat, and made a beeline for the elevators. While he waited for the doors to open, he fired a quick text to Laura, knowing she wouldn't get to it until the morning.

"*Jackpot. Got real dirt on Markovich. Call you tomorrow with the details. Going to watch the videos in full tonight and read through the police reports. He'll back off with this evidence.*"

When he got down to the lobby, he saw Joe manning the concierge desk, but rather than acknowledging him, knowing that there were cameras watching them both, he just coughed loudly, and Joe turned his back to him, bending down to tie his shoes, and Larry quickly sprinted past and out the doors, not bothering to look back. He just walked past the security shack, and didn't turn to look in the window, so he didn't know if the man inside saw him or not. It wouldn't matter. Everything had gone smoothly, and he knew no one would review the footage from last night because of that.

At Madison Ave, he hailed a yellow cab, and gave the cabbie his directions to his townhome in Brooklyn. While the taxi navigated the mostly empty streets of downtown New York, he exhaled loudly. He couldn't believe that fate brought him to this juncture, this moment in time. Of all the police officers who could have interviewed Markovic twenty years ago, it was him. He had been the one to interview him, and he had written up the police report. Back then, the suspect hadn't been listed as Darbear Markovich. He had been David Milanovich. When the commissioner had told him to let him go, he had been incredulous, and infuriated, but there was nothing he could do at the time. Fate, it would seem, had decided to balance the scales.

"Here we are."

He snapped out of his reverie and mumbled his thanks as he peeled off a twenty.

"Keep the change," he said, and he got out and slammed the door shut. The taxi drove off and he climbed the few steps up to his front door, put in his key, and entered his home. He had time to close the door and was about to switch the light on when he felt his head explode in a burst of stars and pain, and he collapsed to the floor.

"Larry, Larry. Out late, huh? Alexander wants to speak with

you. You know, you owe a lot of money, my friend." The big Russian thug who had hit him with a billy club leaned down and smiled at him. His name was Oleg. And he was a mean motherfucker.

"Alexander hasn't been paid in over a week, you know. And I've got some good news, and bad news for you. The good news is, you're going to live. For now. The bad news. Alexander wants to speak with you. And let's hope you make it out alive, yes?"

18

Friends and Enemies

Laura had time to talk to both Jennifer and Adam before she left for the weekend. Tomorrow was her hike with Mary, and she wanted to pack and get a good night's rest. For Jennifer, she asked her to focus her energy and efforts on running the day-to-day operations. Set up meetings, take notes, lead certain meetings that she couldn't attend, run down follow ups that she had asked for. Adam was doing her ad hoc requests. Most involved helping Jennifer, but she also had him do some financial modeling on various take over scenarios in the event Darbear did go hostile. They were seated in her office at her circular table, and she was tired and ready to go home. The sky was already dark outside. She hated late fall and early winter in New York. It was usually dark when she woke up at six, and dark by five p.m. as well, so she rarely got to see any natural sunlight, unless it was through her window. She looked at her watch, and stood up, but Adam remained seated.

"Hey, Laura?" he asked. He was dressed in a navy-blue blazer, gold buttons, and grey slacks. His brown hair was combed over neatly to the right, and his brown eyes looked serious but calm. Jennifer continued walking to the door, and waved goodbye as she slipped out and shut the door behind her.

"Yes? I think that's it. Go home. Have a good weekend. Try to forget about work for once, ok?" she said with a tired smile.

"Yeah, I will. Listen. I thought about your offer. I'll do it. I'll see if I can get hired onto Darbear's banking team at Chase." He paused and put his hands on the table. She sensed that he was about to insert a 'But…' qualifier, and she was right.

"But I need some guarantees."

"Like what?" she asked. She went around to sit in the chair at her desk and started powering down her laptop and getting ready to go home. Gale was waiting for her, and she had promised not to be late today, so that they could go see a movie.

"Well, first of all, I need a promise that if I don't get hired, or if I get hired but don't get staffed onto his banking team, that you'll hire me back into this role."

"Of course. That's easy. I can hire whom I please, and I'll make sure HR keeps this role open. What else?" she asked. She turned around and looked out the window to see if it was raining. It wasn't, thank goodness.

"Next, I want your guarantee that when I come back, I'll be promoted to Vice President, with all the salary and benefits befitting the position."

She turned back around to face Adam, paused, and tilted her head. *"That will be much tougher,"* she thought. *"Even Jennifer just got promoted to V.P. just several months ago, and it would look odd to have yet another V.P. promotion in the team, since it's so small.*" She thought about her answer carefully and wanted to see how strong Adam's resolve was on this point.

"Is that a deal breaker?"

"It is. I need to be assured that I'll come back to a promotion." His chin tilted up slightly, and his lips were in a tight line.

She nodded. "Ok. That's it, right?"

He craned his neck forward and shook his head slowly. "I also want your promise that after a year, you'll get me placed as the head of a business unit. I want to run a P&L full stop, and something big, not a small unit."

She wanted to whistle and say what she was thinking, which was to the effect of, "*Wow, you got some nerve,*" but she just stared at him in silence. He was asking for too much, with this last request. There weren't many of the BU head roles available at Abernathy, and when one opened up, usually ten or more highly qualified candidates stomped their feet and navigated with their political capital to secure it. Almost all of the candidates had prior P&L experience too, running a brand. Adam on the other hand, had zero experience in that regard. If she pulled such a stunt and got Adam placed in such a role, she was almost sure to cause deep discontent and possibly a riot internally. She would have to mend a lot of fences. "*But is it worth it? I could have Adam buried on Darbear's personal investment banking team. He would give me the scoop on what they're planning…*" Laura mulled it over, and then decided that it *was* worth it. She was flying blind right now, and she needed a light. That light was Adam.

"Ok. I'll make that promise. But you only get the BU head position if you make it onto Darbear's personal team. Otherwise, you only get the first two items that you asked for. That's the best I'm willing to offer, take it or leave it." She was gambling here a little, because Adam could have refused to go, and then she would be stuck back at square one, sailing without a light, but her gut told her that Adam's ambition would win the day, and her guess was right.

"Ok, deal. And I want everything in writing, please. I just want to cover my bases," he said, somewhat apologetically. She noticed for the first time, that there were small beads of sweat on his upper lip. *"He didn't know if this would work, and how I would react to this strong-arm tactic. He knows I hate being forced like this, especially coming from a man."*

"I'll draft it up over the weekend, sign it and have it notarized. This assumes, of course, that I'm still gainfully employed when you come back. Otherwise, if I'm fired or let go, you'll be stuck there. So, let's plan to beat this jerk at his own game, yes?" she said with a wry smile.

He gave a relieved smile and laughed. "Yes. Trust me, I don't want to be stuck over there if I don't have to be."

"Alright. Great. Have a good weekend with Emily, and we'll chat on Monday. Text me or call me if you need anything."

By the time she got to Gale's building, it was nearly six p.m., plenty of time to catch the seven p.m. showing of the latest Tom Cruise movie playing at Kips Bay theatres in Murray Hill. Gale lived in a high-rise condo building in Murray Hill, on East 34th street. It was a convenient location, between Second and Third Avenue, so Gale could easily catch a bus heading downtown on Second, or uptown on Third, and close enough to the 4, 5, and 6 lines on 32nd Street if she needed a subway. Her building was tucked in between two other apartment buildings, both around twenty stories high, and was across the street from a liquor store, and a nail salon. Young oak trees were planted in small, square earth plots, spaced about twenty feet apart, and the beige brick building looked as new and fresh as the day it was built, just a few years ago. Personally, Laura wasn't the biggest fan of Murray Hill, as it was full of late twenty, early thirty-year old's who still were into the party scene, at least as far as she could tell. Although Gale was always quick to point out the mom and dad's pushing around babies in their strollers, telling her that it was a good mix of singles and families.

She went in through the revolving doors and into the brightly lit lobby, which was bathed in a gentle yellow glow. The wallpaper was a stylish yellow and gold, with a linen like texture, and the ceiling was tall, more than thirty feet if she had to guess. The dark wood paneled concierge desk was to the right, and two sofas were on the left. Mark was standing behind the concierge desk in a black suit and tie, and he looked up at her as she entered.

"Hey, Laura. How we doin'?" he asked with a friendly smile. He was about six foot tall and had black hair that was yearning to be curly, but couldn't be, because Mark had trimmed his hair short and gelled it back in such a manner that the hair was wavy and undulating. He was good looking, and according to Gale, had at least three girlfriends, all of whom didn't know about the other.

"I'm good, Mark, and you? Busy today?" she asked as she walked up to the waist high desk. The building concierge were asked to stand all day, and not sit down while in the lobby.

"Oh, yeah. Real busy. New tenant moved in, so we had movers back and forth. Package deliveries as usual, you know. Plus, there was a car accident like right outside the building. Yeah! Police and ambulance were here for like an hour, cleaning up the mess."

"Oh, no! Anyone hurt in the accident?"

"Nah, not really. Minor injuries. No one was killed, thank God. You here to see Gale? Alright, go on up, I'll let her know you're here." He picked up the phone and she waved goodbye and walked down the lobby and to the left where the elevator bank was. The wood panels here were stained the same dark brown, and the elevator doors were stainless steel. There were beige colored leather love seats behind her as she waited for the elevator, and when it opened, she took it to the twelfth floor. Exiting the elevator, she found herself in the familiar hallway with white wallpaper, and light sconces spaced throughout on the walls. She turned right, and then another right down a narrow hallway, and used her spare key to open the door.

"Gale! I'm here!" she announced loudly as she closed the door and stepped out of her heels. She took off her coat and hung it up in the front closet and put her laptop bag on the floor. Gale appeared from the bedroom, dressed casually in dark blue jeans, and a tight white sweater, looking gorgeous as usual. Her blonde hair was tied back into a ponytail and her blue eyes twinkled with laughter as she came over and gave her a welcome home kiss.

"Hey, babe. Listen, are you hungry? Or can you wait until after the movie? You didn't answer my last text messages. I figure we can eat after the movie, does that work?"

"Yeah, that's fine. I'm just going to check some emails and texts, and we'll go in like twenty?" Laura walked into the kitchen, and grabbed a clean glass, then filled it up with tap water.

"Ok, but no more work after the movie. C'mon, I haven't seen you in a few days, and its work, work, work. I'm getting grumpy," said Gale with a sigh.

"I promise. But I do have go back to my place tonight. I have to pack for the hike with Mary tomorrow, remember? Anyways, tell me about your day. Did you get the green light on your article?" Gale had been investigating the business practices of the DuBois Group, and had uncovered some highly questionable business decisions that had been made by the executive team. Extortion, fraud, shell corporations. Nothing too shocking for Laura, but for Gale, it was appalling and shocking, all at once. As Gale talked on and on about her findings, Laura tuned out and sipped her water with one hand, absent mindedly nodding, checking her emails, and typing away on her phone with her other hand.

Larry, I need the latest on Darbear. Call me with an update.

She was worried about Larry. She thought back to the conversation she had had with Samuel some time ago.

"It's getting bad, Laura. Larry's usually always on time. We were supposed to have a team meeting today, and he didn't show up. So, the four of us, we went out for lunch, and when we came back, Larry was in the office at his desk, but he had bruises all over his face and cuts on his hands. We didn't mention it, of course, but we know it's from his gambling problems. I asked Gary to investigate, and he said that Larry is in for over two hundred G's to a Russian gangster in Brooklyn."

"Are you serious? How the hell...how often is he gambling, do you know?"

"We don't know for sure. He used to be very discreet, and he must have been up and down, up and down, but never in the hole like this. Jerome says the word on the street is that this gangster, Alexander, is going to cut him up and spread him out in the East

River, to make an example, if he doesn't get his money soon. But then, things get better, the bruises go away, we work on the case, and then...he comes back with new bruises. What do you want us to do? We're concerned," Samuel had said quietly.

"Ok." She sighed deeply. "Thanks for telling me, Samuel. Keep me posted. I'll have a word with him. We'll get him out of this mess, together, ok?" That had been two weeks ago, and with all the things she had been juggling, she hadn't been able to get back to this one. She had wanted to see him in person, which was why she had setup the meeting at the museum, but now, he'd disappeared again. He had been her most trusted, most reliable person, but now, she didn't know if she could trust him with anything, anymore. It was frustrating her to no end.

"Laura? Babe?"

"What? Oh, yes. What?" she asked as she looked up to see Gale staring at her with one eyebrow raised.

"I've been talking nonstop for like ten minutes, and all you keep saying is 'mm hm' and 'oh yeah?' Are you trying to piss me off, or just accidently doing it? Because it's very annoying."

She put her phone down and set her glass of water off to the side of it.

"I'm so sorry," she said, and she walked over to her girlfriend, wrapping her up in her arms. She brushed away a few stray strands of hair from Gale's face, and leaned in for a soft, tender kiss on the lips. She felt Gale lean into the kiss, her lips opening, tongue probing her own lips, and for a moment, she wondered whether they would make it to the movie at all, but Gale pulled back, breathless, and laughed.

"Ok. Apology accepted. Now, let's get to the theatre, or else we'll never make it out the door."

"Is that such a bad thing? We could just..."

"No, no. You promised! Tom Cruise, baby. He's my man crush, you know that. Now, get your coat, let's go."

"Gale," she groaned, as Gale grabbed her elbow and steered her to the front door by the closet. "Who cares about your man crush? What about your girlfriend crush?"

"I got you, babe! You're already mine. But Tom on the other hand..."

The next morning was cold and pale. She yawned as she sat on the leather couch in the lobby of her building and checked her watch. Mary had said she would pick her up by eight, and they would head to Bear Mountain to hike the trails. The movie last night had been fun, and Tom had lived to save the day yet again. Though she had wanted to spend the night over at Gale's, she had come home late last night to finish packing for the hike and had promised Gale that she would come over later Saturday night. She was dressed in a red and white North Face jacket, with comfortable blue jeans, tan hiking boots, and she had a backpack filled with snacks, water, a portable power bank for her phone, lunch, and an extra sweater in case it was colder than she expected.

Right at eight a.m., a black SUV pulled up in front of her building, and Mary hopped out from the back seat and waved to her through the glass door of her building. Laura gave a small smile and hauled herself out of the comfortable couch and shouldered her backpack over one shoulder.

"Hi, Mary, how are you?" she asked as she stepped outside in the chilly fall weather. It must have been about forty-five degrees outside, if she had to guess. There were only two people on the street at this early hour, walking their dogs. The sky was murky and grey, with not much in the way of clouds. It just appeared to be a grey haze more than anything, and the sun was blotted out from the sky.

"I'm doing well, and you? Here, hop in the backseat with me. I'll take your backpack and stow it in the trunk." Laura handed over her pack and shimmied her way over to the far side of the back seat. She heard Mary open the trunk and file away her pack, then slam the door shut before she hurried into the car next to her.

"Ah, great. Andre? We're ready," Mary said cheerfully.

"Yes, ma'am."

The car sped off and headed west down seventy second street, and then turned right onto the West Side highway, heading north towards the GW bridge. Laura turned to subtly take in Mary's appearance. She was still as short as she remembered, and was wearing a dark blue Patagonia jacket, and a loose fitting but comfortable looking black trail pants by Columbia. She wore sturdy white Nike sneakers, and they looked almost new. Her brown hair hung straight down to her just past her ears, and she wore no makeup or jewelry today.

"How has life been, with this whole Darbear situation?" asked Mary casually as she turned to stare back at Laura.

Laura raised an eyebrow and gave a wan smile. "It's certainly made life interesting, that's for sure. But you know, it's also been a tremendous learning experience as well. I had gotten a little too cozy the last year or so, and this has sharpened my senses so to speak. I've really had to re-prioritize my life, and this brought a lot of clarity to what I needed to do. We'll see what the next few weeks bring, but I'm feeling more and more confident that we'll be able to get past this and come out stronger on the other side."

Mary nodded and tilted her head. "That's nice, the way you speak, and the way you deflect the question without really answering it. There's a polish to your words and demeanor, from the way you sit, to the way you carry yourself. It speaks volumes of confidence, assurance, and calmness. Public speaking, and how you carry yourself, can be taught, but it's nice to know that you are a naturally good speaker. One less thing I would need to worry about."

Laura gave a wry grin. She hadn't known that she was being tested already.

"So, what do you want to know about me? Should we start with the platform that I intend to run on?" Laura asked.

"Nope. Let's save the serious stuff for when we hit the trails. Exercise clears the mind, and I want an unfiltered peek into that head of yours. Tell me about you. What was it like, growing up in Queens?" Mary asked intently.

Laura turned to look out the window, pretending to admire the view of the Hudson River as they traversed the GW bridge. The water was a dark, dark blue, almost blue grey, and quite calm. There were a few boats on the river, even at this early hour, and she could see the trees on the far side, which were colorful with orange, yellow, and red leaves. There was some traffic on the bridge, but everything was flowing smoothly, and she guessed that it would only take about an hour to get to the mountain.

"Queens was a great place to grow up. I'm Korean American, as you noted, and there's a pretty good-sized contingent of Koreans, and Korean Americans living in Queens. It's mostly Chinese, but there are Koreans, Thai, Russians…you name it, you can find people from all over the world there. So, it was nice to be able to eat food from your country, and find Asian groceries, pretty much anywhere you went. Nowadays, while it is still filled with immigrants who in many instances, speak little English, you do find a that a lot of folks from the other boroughs come to eat there. The food is delicious, and much more affordable than in Chinatown in downtown Manhattan." Laura paused and waited to see if Mary had any questions. But instead of asking a question, Mary made a statement.

"C'mon, Laura. That's the political, made for TV answer. If I were a reporter, or you were being interviewed, that's the answer you would give. But tell me the truth. What was it really like back then? It used to be a real dump, right? Dirty, full of shady business, illegal immigrants and happenings, right? Tell me what it was like to live in those conditions." Mary's eyes narrowed and she pursed her lips into a tight line. She was sharp, this one.

Laura thought for a moment, then opened up. "Yeah. It was kind of a dump. But you know what? It was home," she said simply. "We grew up extremely poor. My father left us when I was young, and we always struggled for money. I remember a lot of times going hungry, and you may not believe this, but I had to scrounge for food in the dumpsters in the alleys. It was hard times."

Mary nodded. "I'm sorry to hear that. That must have been tough on a young girl. But, that kind of story is a good one to have. You can tell that story and earn a lot of sympathy. What else? Was it rough and tumble? Did you get into any trouble?"

"Rough, yes. I mean, there were street hustlers, drug dealers sometimes. But I stayed on a pretty tight and narrow path. I couldn't afford to screw up, you know? My mom needed me to stay out of trouble, so that she could focus on putting food on the table."

They talked back and forth about Laura's upbringing, her friends growing up, what things she did in her free time, but ultimately, there was one topic that Mary focused on at the end.

"Tell me something. I get it. You're ambitious, you're a hard charging go getter. You want to be a Senator, to effect positive change for the lower income and middle-class folks, just like you were once upon a time. But, why the ambition for President? I don't get that. You can do everything you want to do, social wise, as a Senator."

Laura pursed her lips and nodded her head. It was a fair question. "I *am* ambitious. But one thing haunts me from my childhood, and that is the lack of a father figure, and the physical and mental abuse we endured at his hands. It's shaped my thinking, my emotions, and made me who I am today. But it also scarred me. I still yearn for that fatherly figure and love that I never had. I think as President, I can enact stronger laws and measures to put that sort of domestic violence to bed."

Mary looked unconvinced. "You can push through those laws as a Senator. You don't have to be President to do that."

Laura shrugged. "You're probably right. But that same yearning I have, for the strong, powerful, loving father figure that I missed out on, I think deep down, I feel like making it to President would kind of put those feelings of unworthiness and powerlessness to the side. At least, that's what I think."

They sat in silence for the next thirty minutes. She hadn't really thought about her father in close to twenty years or so and thinking about him now dredged up a lot of buried feelings. Resentment, anger, sadness, hurt, and confusion. She honestly couldn't remember what his face looked like, and to this day, she probably never would. Her mom had burned any photos with him in it, and she had never heard from or seen him again. She wondered if she should see a psychologist and try to bury the hatchet with her father figure, because deep down inside, she knew that she was fucked up in the head because of him. *"It probably explains why I'm such an asshole to powerful males with authority,"* she thought with a frown.

When they finally made it to Bear Mountain, the sun was shining, and the temperature had risen to a more palatable fifty degrees. Bear Mountain state park is situated in some shallow but rugged mountains rising from the west bank of the Hudson River. The park has a field, picnic areas, a lake, swimming pool, hiking and biking trails, and even an outdoor ice-skating rink that is open in the fall. Atop Bear Mountain, is the Perkins Memorial Tower, which affords spectacular views of the park, and that is where Laura assumed they were heading, but she was wrong.

Andre drove them past the historical museum, which was nothing more than a one-story stone building. Small boulders about the size of a man's head lined the road towards the museum, and a flagpole was off to one side of the building. The grass was starting to turn yellow, but still had most of their green color. A wooden, brown sign read, "Historical Museum", and there were several folks walking up to the building as they drove by it.

"Andre, I'll call you when we're heading back down. Should be around two p.m. or so."

"Yes ma'am," he said again. Laura was beginning to wonder if that was all the words in the English language that he knew.

They hopped out of the SUV and walked to the back. Mary popped the gate and grabbed their backpacks, and they were off. Instead of taking the trail to the right, leading up a concrete pathway towards Perkins's tower, Mary went to the left, down a well-worn dirt trail that was quickly engulfed by trees and vegetation. Although it started heading downwards, very soon, it sloped upwards, and they were huffing and puffing their way up to the top of a ridge. The trail was damp, and muddy in some parts, with rocks and boulders sticking out on either side of the narrow footpath. The trees were numerous and on either side of them, forming a large canopy that shielded them from most of the sunlight. There were birch trees, oak, maple, and chestnut oak, and they were tall, fifty feet or more. Leaves were sprinkled and covering the floor of the forest, yellow, red, and brown, and everywhere one looked, was an amazing color palette of these yellows and reds. As they hiked, Mary asked her more questions about her youth, what it was like growing up without a father, how school was in Maryland as an Asian, why she decided on her career path, and so forth. They walked up the trail slowly, methodically, taking time to pause and catch their breath. Laura, in turn, asked about Mary's past, why she chose to be in politics, and what she enjoyed about it the most. Her answers, unlike Laura's, weren't really surprising in any way. Mary simply found her passion to be in politics, and she had a born skill in navigating that particular jungle.

By the time they made it up to the ridge, it was nearly noon. They made their way over to a humongous beige boulder, built into the side of the mountain, but bare to the sky like a bald man's head, and sat down, admiring the views of the lake below. The lake was perhaps a mile or two away, but they could see people walking along the shoreline, and nothing but trees as far as the eye could see on either side of them. They sat down on the boulder and took off their back packs. Laura fished out a bottle of water and sipped from it, and was tempted to check her phone, but resisted the urge and instead sat quietly, taking in the scenery.

Mary offered her a granola bar, and she accepted. They sat in silence for a bit, munching on their snack.

"I'll do it. I'll be your campaign manager," said Mary thoughtfully.

Laura turned to look at her, and Mary did the same.

"You've got the right skills to be a good political leader. And you can win this race. I only pick winners. I can help shape your platform, and I believe in you as a person. That's enough for me to get behind this campaign." Mary stuck out her hand, and Laura looked at it for a moment, then grasped it and shook it firmly.

"Alright. I'm glad to know that I passed muster. What are the next steps?" she asked, relieved that she could cross one more thing off her never ending to do list. Mary seemed competent, and sharp. She knew that Mary would run a tight ship, and with Mary steering the political landscape, and Stacy putting out all the other fires, she felt unbeatable.

"I'll hire a team here in New York, and also get my staff down in D.C. shifting gears. We'll run some polls on the issues here in New York, find out what the people want fixed, and get some basic numbers in front of you. We have some time before the actual election, but we'll do some research on what the best platform to run on would be and find the recipe for your success. My recommendation is that you'll want to announce that you're running, in six months. So, you'll need to tidy up any loose ends with your company by then. Tell me about your love life. Any boyfriends I should know about?" Mary put away the wrapper into her backpack and pulled out a bottle of water.

Laura paused. She had been expecting this question and was ready with a response. "No boyfriends to speak of. But… hypothetically, what if I had a girlfriend?"

Mary locked at her with a side glance, and then turned to stare down at the lake below them.

"Hypothetically speaking? You could win a Senate seat if you had a girlfriend. New York is very progressive and there are more and more Senators and congressmen and women who are LGBQT. That's not an issue at all. But if you want to run and actually win the Presidency? There's still a lot of racism and bigotry out there in America. More power to you if you want to run and try to win from that angle. Let me run some polls for you and get back to you. If you really, genuinely want to be President, it'll be an uphill battle if you run as an LGBQT member. Not impossible, just really, really hard."

Laura was about to say the exact same words, but she instead simply nodded. She had time to think about whether she would run as an openly gay woman. Right now, she had to solve this issue of Darbear, and time was running out.

19

Spinning

A week had gone by, and still no word from Larry. It was if he had disappeared from the face of the earth. He didn't answer her calls or texts, he hadn't shown up for work, and neither Samuel nor anyone else from his team had seen or heard from him. She had only received one text from Larry early Saturday morning on the day of her hike with Mary, stating that he had found genuine dirt, but that was it. Radio silence ever since that one text.

"Samuel. I want you to lead the team in Larry's absence. Do you know where he was, the last time you spoke to him?"

"Yes, I know where he was." Sam's voice was hushed and quiet on the phone. "He snuck into the police headquarters late at night. He called me from inside, said he found what he was looking for, and told me to go home for the night. But he never came into the office the next day."

"Did he say what it was he found? Anything at all about it?" she asked. She hoped that Larry was ok, but at the same time, she didn't want to call the police. Who knew what kind of dirt could come up if they searched for Larry. No, better for her team to try and find out what happened.

"No, he didn't say. I've checked all the police reports over the last week. There's nothing about Larry in there and no missing person that fits his description or anything."

"That's not a good sign," she sighed.

"I mean, Laura. There is the possibility…" his voice trailed off.

"What? What possibility?"

"It's possible that the Russians…collected their debt via other means."

She didn't answer right away. It was possible. This Alexander was a gangster and had ties to the Russian mafia. Still, it made her shudder to think that Larry could have been murdered.

"Have Gary and Jerome check out Alexander's hangouts. See if they can carefully sniff out if Larry was…you know. If that is what your gut is telling you, then I trust your gut. Keep me posted, ok?"

"I will. You can count on me."

She hung up the phone and stared blankly at her computer screen. *"If Samuel is right, then Larry is possibly dead. And with him, this supposedly great piece of evidence to use against Darbear. I need to find out what it was."* The problem was that she had no clue as to where to start looking. The police headquarters was a big place, and he could have been homing in on any number of leads there. *"One thing at a time,"* she muttered. Today was the meeting with Darbear and his team.

"Hey, babe? You ok? You look like you're coming down with

something," Gale said to her as she came out of Laura's bedroom. She was dressed in a white sweater, Banana Republic, and her main stay blue jeans. Her blonde hair was down and hung freely to just below her ears, blue eyes twinkling with mischief as always.

"Hm? I'm fine. Just the meeting today with Darbear and his team. Second time we're meeting with them, and the board is anxious to try and get to some amicable resolution." She powered down her laptop and started to pack it away in her bag. Gale came over and rubbed her shoulders as she stood behind her.

"Good luck. I know you'll find a way."

"Mm, that feels good. Alright, I gotta run or I'll be late. Don't wait up for me tonight. Might be working late."

Gale sighed. "Make some time for me this weekend. Your girlfriend is getting tired of hanging out by herself all the time."

"I will. Love you," she said as she gave Gale a quick kiss.

"Yeah, yeah. Love you too. Break a leg," Gale said with a grimace.

Laura hurried out of the apartment and slipped on her black Burberry winter coat as she shifted her laptop bag from one shoulder to the other. She nodded politely to her neighbor, Franz, and they rode the elevator down in silence. Once at the street level, she luckily found an empty cab driving by and hailed it down.

"Seventy second and Central Park West, please," she said as she slammed the door shut. She stared out the window at the grey sky, and the various people on the sidewalk as they walked to work, ran errands, or went off to school. The city was always busy and vibrant on a weekday morning, especially on Mondays, and today was no different. It never ceased to amaze her, how this huge city always had life and energy, no matter the weather, season, or time of day. She saw an Asian mom, dressed in a beige winter coat, plaid scarf, and black earmuffs, walk hand in hand with her daughter, who must have been five or six years old. The child was over dressed, it seemed, with mittens, scarf, hat, thick winter jacket, and multiple layers on her legs, as she walked stiffly and uncomfortably next her mom. Seeing the two brought a small smile to her lips, as she recalled those days when *her* mother took her out in the winter, to play at the playground near their apartment in Flushing. She remembered seeing her friends and their parents there, and the only pang of regret she felt was remembering that her friends' fathers were there too, pushing her friends on the swing, or talking to the other dads. Her mom, on the other hand, stuck mostly to herself, or chatted with one of the other Korean moms. She had been the only one of her group without a dad, and it made her feel uncomfortable to think back on it now.

"*Fuck him,*" she thought angrily.

"Here you go," said the cab driver. She swiped her card through the machine, and then hopped out, ready to do battle. Today was going to be an important one. She would know whether Darbear meant to negotiate in good faith, or whether he wanted to go hostile. She guessed it was the latter, but they would soon find out.

She nodded hello to Jonathan at the turnstile and made polite small talk with several of her colleagues as she passed them in the lobby and in the elevator, but her mind was elsewhere. She needed to focus, and time was short today.

By the time she got to her office and powered up her laptop, Jennifer was knocking on her door.

"Hey, boss. I made twenty copies of the proposal and put one in front of each chair in the boardroom. Bottled waters there too.

We have croissants, bagels, coffee and juices on the table outside the room, and I have drivers on standby for when the board members are done for the day."

"Great, thanks. Might be a long day, so those drivers could be needed in an hour, or at the end of day, not sure yet. Just be ready."

"Board members are all here too, but some are working in their offices, while others are taking calls in various empty conference rooms." She looked at her watch. "We should get going in a few."

"Right." Laura checked her phone to see if Larry had called or texted. Nothing. "Ok. Let's go." She grabbed her laptop, a pen, and her notebook, then they left her office and walked down the hallway to the boardroom. Just outside of the boardroom, she saw several of the board members in the waiting area. Two were sitting on the sofa, chatting in low tones, and several more were on their phones, either checking emails or news, coffee in hand and waiting in a relaxed manner it seemed.

"Max, Gerta. Hello, good to see you. Bobby. Vanessa. Shall we go in?" she said confidently and loudly. They looked up at her and gave her warm smiles.

Once inside, she gave the room a quick once over, and nodded, satisfied with Jennifer's work. The room was meticulous, everything just so, and just how she wanted it. She sat at the head of the long rectangular table as the board members shuffled in after her, talking to each other as they caught up on each other's children, significant others, weather, stocks, and other boring, non-essential news.

Finally, there was a knock on the door, and one of the assigned runners opened the door and in walked Darbear's team.

Darbear himself was first, and he strode in and started greeting folks by name, shaking their hands, and coldly nodding his head to their pleasantries. Three other folks followed behind him, and she recognized all three of them. There was Eric O'Shea, the tall Irishman, Matthew Kim, the fellow Korean, and then there was Adam Thatcher, formerly her assistant Chief of Staff. She held back her grin, but it was difficult.

"Hi, good to see you again, Eric. Matthew. Adam, what a surprise. I didn't know you had gone back into investment banking," she said calmly and with what she hoped was a surprised tone.

"Hi. Yes, went back to i-banking, and joined up with Darbear's team. Good to see you again, Laura," he said with a small smile.

After all of the introductions and pleasantries were dispensed, Darbear and his team took their seats, with Darbear sitting directly across from Laura, with the rest of his team sitting next to Darbear. Laura jumped right into the heart of the issue.

"Darbear. Thank you, to you and your team, for meeting with us last week, and again today. We've had several productive discussions on the phone, and last week, and it's time now, for our proposal to you. We understand your position, and while we don't necessarily agree with everything that you contend, we have what we believe, are very fair and equitable terms to discuss changes within the strategy and company org structure, that should alleviate your concerns for shareholder return. In exchange for implementing these change initiatives, it is our recommendation that we set an end date, whereby you agree to exit your position in Abernathy Consumer Products," she started. She spoke confidently, and with gusto.

Darbear, who had been flipping through the presentation

print out laid before him, frowned, and looked at her. "Hmph. Yes, these changes are a good start. They should drive the stock price up when they are announced. But there's no guarantee that I'll make any money if I exit my shares by an agreed upon end date. Why would I do that?"

"That certainly is true, that the share price might not move enough for you to generate a sufficient return on your investment. Our proposal then, is that should the share price not meet a minimum threshold, the company will buy your shares at a twelve percent premium to what you paid for them. This way, it will ensure that you generate a profit, and also ensure Abernathy of an end date to external factors." The words 'external factors' had been hotly debated amongst the board, but ultimately, it came out better than 'hostile threat' or 'unwanted financial advances', which essentially was what Darbear was creating with his share purchases and threats in the media.

"Twelve percent is too low. I'm looking for a twenty percent return on my investment. Eric?" Darbear looked to his left at his team.

"A twenty percent premium from today's stock price would put the valuation at eighteen times forward earnings, something that we think is fair, and where the stock traded just two years ago." Eric's voice was soothing, and silky smooth, like all investment bankers. At the heart of it, Laura's estimation was that investment bankers were just cars salesman at the end of the day. Extremely sharp and smart salesmen, but still, salesmen at their core. He was selling now.

"You've already seen a three percent bump in the stock price since the news that you came out that you were acquiring shares. Along with the twelve percent minimum guarantee we're offering, that puts you at a healthy fifteen percent gain here. That would put the valuation at fifteen times earnings, right around the S&P 500 average," she argued back, firmly and without any heat in her voice. *"Fifteen versus twenty percent, we're in the ballpark. I think we can settle somewhere in the middle,"* she thought hopefully. But it was Adam, her former subordinate who surprised her.

"Actually, a fifteen percent gain from the time of the announcement wouldn't be a sufficient return on our money. We happen to know that you have solid plans for an expansion of your business in the EU region, which should lead to a double-digit percent increase in earnings in your international business unit. Twenty percent would be a more accurate and fair reflection where Darbear could exit with a reasonable profit." Adam locked eyes with her, and there was nothing there. No sympathy, no regret, no "Sorry I just took a dump all over your negotiation." He was using insider information, divulging internal plans for expansion that were known only to a select few in the room, as part of how they calculated their deal terms. It was a shocking turn of events, at least for Laura, and she could tell by the faces in the room, for almost everyone there.

"Adam, that information is privy only to a few select folks within the company. Nevertheless, those expansion plans and revenues that come with it, are far from guaranteed. There is a lot of risk in what we are trying to do, and there's as much a chance of failure as there is success. So, basing your valuation on that, would be misguided." Laura frowned at Adam and narrowed her eyes ever so slightly.

Darbear laughed, the dimple in his chin winking devilishly at them all. "All is fair in love and war, as they say. Adam joined Chase investment banking, and the managing director immediately suggested that he be staffed to my team. So what if he has some great information? I would be foolish not to use it. But I want some other things implemented too." He smirked now.

"What else would you want implemented? We've already conceded on a handful of some of your strategic suggestions. Certainly, you are not going to come back on the point of selling off the cosmetics division, are you?" asked Catherine, one of the more senior board members. She looked calm, but was leaning forward on her forearms, staring intently at Darbear.

"Matthew? Can you share the one pager?" Darbear asked casually, as Matthew passed around a one-page memo for each member at the table. When she got hers, she skimmed it and shook her head in denial. It was absurd.

"You want two board seats, and the removal of the CEO and COO?" she asked. "This is ridiculous."

"Not at all. I need to ensure that the future state of the company is proceeding along my vision," said Darbear loudly. He looked smug.

"But if you exit and sell all your shares, what difference does it make whether the company follows your vision or not? You'll have profited at the minimum guarantee," she argued.

"I never said I would sell *all* my shares. I'll keep some. See if I can generate an even higher return. I mean look, the other option is that we throw this deal in the trash, and I do a hostile takeover. I can pull the resources and capital together to make it happen, you know this. I have the right connections. But I want to clean house, and make sure this company has the right leadership in place."

Laura looked around the room and decided that she needed to discuss with the board. She didn't want to get fired, and she wanted to fight, but first, she needed to make sure the board was behind her.

"Can we discuss amongst the board? There's a room down the hall you can be in while we chat. Just need a few minutes," she said politely.

Darbear stood up, and had the audacity to leer at her, staring at her breasts momentarily before moving his eyes up and smirking one last time. "Come on, boys. Let's talk business in the room they suggested, while they gather their panties, eh?" He laughed at his own joke, while his team smiled politely and also stood up. Adam stood up, but Laura was quick to corral him.

"Hey Adam? A word?"

He turned to look at her and was not surprised in the least, it seemed, as he nodded. They followed Darbear, Matthew, and Eric out into the hallway, but while the three turned right, she went left, towards another empty conference room, and went inside, flipping on the lights. Adam entered and closed the door, but he didn't come in any further, opting to stand by the door in case of a quick exit.

"What the hell, Adam? I mean, seriously. What. The. Hell?" She did her best to maintain her composure, but her eyebrows were furrowed, she knew, and she immediately calmed herself and made her face go blank.

"I did what you said, Laura. I got onto his team. I tried to find out what they were doing. But Darbear is much, much smarter than you give him credit for. He sniffed it out right away. And you know what?" He paused and pursed his lips thoughtfully. "He made me a better offer. I'm sorry, Laura."

She was stunned, for the second time that day. She blinked several times, but quickly recovered, and said coolly, "What did he offer you?"

He turned slightly, and turned the handle of the door, cracking it open an inch, getting ready to leave. "He offered me a million dollars if I told him everything that I knew here. And then he had his lawyers draft up another document, where he'll give me another two million when he completes the takeover. I'm sorry, Laura. It's game over. You played it well, but he's two steps ahead of you, and he won't stop at anything to win." He at least had the grace to smile sadly, and it seemed genuine, before he opened the door and left.

Her mind was spinning, and she sat on the edge of the conference table, looking out at the drab grey sky. *"Game over, huh?"* she mused. *"Is it? Maybe it is, but Adam did let slip one piece of information. Darbear wants the hostile takeover. Why else would he put it in the contract for Adam? He expects the negotiations to fail. No, he wants them to fail, so that he can push me out. The rest of this morning will be a waste of time then."* It wasn't much to work with but knowing that Darbear wanted to end his game a certain way, at least gave her something to think about.

20

Room Seven

"Detective Kudlow!"

"Yeah, Lieutenant?"

"I need you to interview a suspect in interview room seven. It's that case you just opened up last week. The one with the mom who brought her daughter in, claims her daughter was sexually abused by some rich guy. Guy came in voluntarily for questioning, and I want you to process him."

"C'mon, L.T. Yesterday was my last day in the special victims unit. I just started with homicide, literally today. Give it to Frank." Larry smoothed his white shirt over his flat stomach, and adjusted his brown shoulder holster, which held his Glock 22 handgun.

"You don't think I fuckin' know you started in homicide today? I signed your fuckin' paperwork. I know exactly where you work, dipshit. Frank's out sick, and I want you to process the interview." Lieutenant Antoinetta was of medium height and build and had a thick head of black hair that was poufy and unkempt. He was wearing a threadbare tan suit, well-worn and in need of repair, a white shirt like Larry, and a thin black tie to match his black belt and black leather shoes.

"C'mon, Lieutenant," he pleaded again. "I'm outta S.V.U."

"You know the rules. Lieutenant decides whether you finish off a case or hand it off. In this case, I need you to wrap this one up. Quit yer bitchin'. You know Joey just made detective, so he's liable to miss something. And Frank's out sick, like I said. So, do me a favor, will ya, and just process the interview? I got enough shit to worry about without you whining like a little baby. Room seven."

"Freakin' unbelievable," he muttered under his breath.

"What's that? Did you say somethin'?" Lieutenant Antoinetta said as he cupped a hand to his ear. "You want to go back to special victims?"

Larry glared at his boss, opened the left-hand drawer to his desk, pulled out a stick of gum, and popped it into his mouth angrily, but he wisely kept his mouth shut. He wasn't a detective because he was stupid, after all. He looked at his suit jacket, which was hanging on the coat rack in the corner but decided against wearing it. It was hot as shit today, being the middle of July, and the air conditioners were just barely keeping up as it was. Already, he started to feel some perspiration underneath his armpits, not a good sign. He shook his head and sighed, then grabbed his notebook and pen as he stood up. Before he spoke to the suspect, he needed to refresh his memory on the case, which meant he had to go track down the case file, another annoyance of his L.T.'s request.

The NYPD 19th precinct was on the upper east side of Manhattan, on 67th street between Lex and Third Ave. It was a relatively small five story building, with the outside first level nicely done in white granite, and the rest of the exterior of the building done in a tan and red granite. The first floor was where the lobby and reception area were, as well as a few administrative offices. The second floor, where Larry sat, was known as the bullpen, and it was nothing more than a square open floor plan with desks interspersed throughout the floor, and offices lining the outer ring of the square, where superior officers sat and gave directives to the sergeants and detectives like himself. The third floor housed more administrative offices, as well as the Captain's office. He almost never went to the third floor as it usually meant someone was in trouble, and he sure as hell didn't want it to be him. The fourth floor held multiple interrogation rooms, the armory, conference rooms, and a situation room for larger audiences. The fifth floor was mostly storage, as well as evidence, while the basement held several jail cells which were usually empty, save for the occasional drunkard or low-level offender. Anytime there was a serious arrest, those suspects almost always got sent downtown to headquarters.

Larry picked his way down the aisle of black desks, nodding his head to a friend here or there, and eventually made it to the far side of the room, where a young thirty something black man was sitting on the side of a desk, leaning over, and chatting with a grumpy looking, middle aged white guy who was leaning back in a chair behind a different desk. Both were dressed in plain clothes, which for the black guy was jeans, sneakers, a grey t shirt, and his badge was flashing on a lanyard around his neck. The white guy was balding, but looked fit, wearing jeans, sneakers, a white polo t shirt, and he too, had his badge on a chain around his neck. He knew both men, though not well. Lieutenant

Antoinetta's team was commingled. Larry had worked in S.V.U., Frank was in homicide, and Joey was in narcotics. Even while in special victims, Larry had known most of the other detectives in the unit, but he hadn't gotten to know them all. Jay and Robert were two that he didn't know that well.

"Hey, Jay, Robert. What's up?" he said politely. If his memory served him, Jay had just transferred over from Queens, and was new to this precinct, maybe like six months. Robert, the white guy, had been here for maybe fifteen years, and was sort of a prickly asshole, from what he could recall. He honestly never chatted with the guy much, because Larry's circle of friends was on the other side of the bullpen, and almost all of his close friends played poker with him or gambled. Robert did neither, and so that precluded him from even being on Larry's radar in terms of friendship.

"Oh, shit. He needs something. You see that look?" sneered Robert. His hands had been resting on the arm rests of the chair, but he now folded his arms across his chest and leaned even further back in his chair, looking up at Larry with contempt.

"What up, Larry." Jay flashed him a quick look and then turned back to Robert. "I'm telling you, man. They're running a brothel up in that joint. You heard the doorman. He said it's a never-ending stream of dudes just coming and going at all hours of the day, apartment 12B."

"Look. I'm not saying you're *wrong*, Jay. Hell, I even think you might be right. All I'm sayin' is, you ain't got no proof! And with what we got, we don't have shit for a warrant. So, unless you can get some evidence to go to the judge to get a search warrant, it's gonna have to drop to the bottom of the pile. We got other fish to fry, capiche?"

"Call it in as a 9-1-1," said Larry casually. Jay and Robert swiveled their heads to stare at him, eyebrows raised.

"What do you mean," ventured Jay.

"You, Jay, go out to the pay phone across the street. Call 9-1-1. Tell them you've heard furniture break, and a woman screaming in apartment 12B at wherever the fuck. Give them the address, then hang up. Dispatch has to send a unit to go check it out, and as soon as they put out the call, Robert, you jump on it, saying you're two blocks away. Doorman will have to let you up, and when you knock on the door, you make sure you get in the apartment. That's when you see...whatever it is you think is up there, and now you have probable cause to search. Though if it's a brothel, you probably won't find all that much. You need the madame, or whoever is booking the appointments. Just my two cents." Jay was nodding slowly as he listened, a thoughtful look on his face, but Robert rained on his parade.

"That's dirty. That's not how we do it."

"Hey, man. Look. That could work. We could get in there," said Jay.

"That's not right. That's not how we do it. We're police officers. We don't just make shit up," he said haughtily, but his words were directed squarely at Larry, as Robert was glaring daggers at him.

Larry shrugged. "Do whatever you want, guys. But sometimes, rules are meant to be bent."

"Yeah? I hear you like to do that, a lot. Bending rules that is." Robert's eyes narrowed as he stared up at Larry, and Larry froze. "*He couldn't know about my gambling thing...? Can he?*" He chose to ignore the comment.

"Anyway. That case I dumped on you last week. The last one

I transferred, with the mom who said her daughter was raped? You still got that case file?" he asked coldly.

"Yeah, I got it. What of it?" asked Robert stiffly.

"Suspect voluntarily showed up today, and Lieutenant Antoinetta wants me to interview him. He's waiting upstairs, but I want to review the case file first."

"You're no longer in special victims. It's my case now." Larry wanted to grind his teeth, but instead, he simply nodded.

"You're right. Go tell that to my L.T. He says he wants me to wrap it up, since the suspect is here. Had he not shown up, this thing would have been all yours. But I'm just following orders here. So. You want to give me the case file or what?" Larry put his hands in his pockets. It was his way of keeping himself from balling up his hands in frustration.

Robert hesitated, looked at Jay, who gave him a shrug, as if to say, "Your call," and then he sighed. "Fine. Whatever. One less case to worry about. But it's yours again. Finish it up and don't expect you can drop it off to us again, deal?"

Larry nodded, and stepped closer to the desk while Robert pulled open his lower right drawer and searched through the file folders. He pulled out a green folder, thumbed through it quickly, and then handed it over.

"Thanks, Robert. See ya, guys."

Jay nodded, but Robert merely grunted and then ignored him as he turned his attention back to his partner.

Larry looked at his watch as he walked back towards his desk on the other side of the room. Twelve fifteen. He needed to get up to speed quickly, as he didn't want to keep the suspect waiting too long. He sat down at his desk and opened up the folder, skimming his notes and making mental notes of some key questions that he would need to ask.

"Maria Olazabal. Mom. Age 39. Brought her daughter in last week. Claims her daughter was sexually assaulted by a wealthy man. David Milanovich. Daughter, Alexa Olazabal, age 14. Claims this man flew her daughter to a private residence on Martha's Vineyard where the assault happened. Claims the man bragged that she was just one of many girls he'd done this to, and that no one would believe her." He read through his notes, and now the details came swarming back to him. The mom had been believable. Frantic, upset, genuine tears. The daughter had been silent, head and eyes cast down to the floor, depressed, shamed, and her voice had been barely audible. Just a few whispers here and there. Now he remembered. He made a few scribbles in his notebook, snapped it shut, along with the folder, and stood up. He was ready to do the interview now, and he sure as hell hoped that the guy was the one. He was a damn good detective, one of the best in the city, certainly the best in his precinct, and he always could smell a rat when he saw or got near one. *"Let's see if you're the one, David,"* he muttered to himself as he walked over to the elevator.

He politely waited as the doors opened and two of his colleagues stepped out, then walked in and pressed the four button. The elevator was newly installed, as the old one had been a prewar, dingy elevator that seemed like it would collapse at any minute. This one was silver on the inside, with stainless steel walls and matching railing, and bright LED lights in the ceiling. When the doors opened again, he found himself on the fourth floor, with a reception desk in front of him. He nodded to Mary, who was manning the desk, her blonde hair done up in a beehive circa 1950. He walked up and noted her attire, which was GAP if he had to guess. Denim jeans, blue merino sweater, and a gold necklace with a heart pendant.

"What's with the hair do?" he asked nicely.

"Oh this? You like it? I'm going to a party later tonight, and I won't have time to go home and make it to the party in time, so I figured I would just come in to work like this. It's a 1950's theme party," she said with a smile. She was in her late twenties, good looking, and almost all the cops in the precinct had hit on her, at least once. So far, she had declined every overture. She was a civilian, not part of the police force, and that made her even more attractive to most.

"It's nice. If you cut it short, like to your ears, and get rid of the tall beehive, you'd look a lot like June Cleaver."

She stared at him blankly. "Who?"

"You know. June Cleaver. From the show, Leave it to Beaver?" He raised an eyebrow. Still, nothing, as she blinked twice at him. "Oh, never mind. It's way before your time. Anyways, where's David Milanovich? I'm here to interview him."

She gave him a fake smile and looked down at her computer. "He's in interrogation room seven. Camera's on, just so you know."

"Yup, thanks," he said as he waved goodbye. The cameras were always on, he knew. He walked down the grey hallway, which was lined with a grey and white tile, past a break room which had a few vending machines, a refrigerator, and a couple tables, past a conference room that held an oval table and enough chairs for ten, past a couple empty interrogation rooms, until he stood outside the room he was looking for. The door was a dark green, made of metal, and had a small square window about eye level, with wires embedded in the glass to resist shattering. He peeked inside, and saw a rather tall man, sitting down on a chair at the table. He knocked twice, then opened the door and entered.

David Milanovich was relatively good looking, he had to

admit. He was perhaps forty years old, with dark brown hair that was combed and slicked back, dark brown eyes, and a dimple in his chin that made him look roguishly handsome. There was a stern and confident look to him, as the man stared up at him coldly from his seat. He was dressed in a fine blue and white pinstriped suit, with a white shirt, no tie, and light brown crown Windsor leather oxfords.

"Mr. Milanovich? Hi, I'm Detective Larry Kudlow. How are we doing today?" he asked cheerfully, as he walked over to the table and held out his hand. The man didn't stand up to shake hands with him, he noted. David's grip was strong, and firm, and the man made solid eye contact with him as they shook hands.

"I'm fine. But I've been waiting for thirty minutes, and now I'm annoyed. What took you so long?" the man asked imperiously. Larry could tell that this was a man used to giving orders, and not used to waiting around on someone else's time.

"Well, I was out grabbing a coffee, and my Lieutenant only grabbed me like fifteen minutes ago. So, apologies for making you wait." Larry pulled out the opposite chair and sat down at the small, rectangular metal table. The room was only eight feet by seven feet, with nothing but the table and the two chairs. He surreptitiously looked in the upper right corner, where he could see the video camera watching their every move. There was a small red light housed under the lens, which meant that everything was being recorded. He opened up his folder, and also his notebook, and looked down at his notes one more time, before he looked up and fixed his gaze on David.

"Just to remind you, our conversation is being recorded, and you came here of your own volition, without an attorney, but should you feel the need to get legal counsel, you are free to stop the interview at any time. So, Mr. Milanovich. Why did you come down to the station this fine summer day?"

David cleared his throat, and crossed his legs, lightly drumming the table with his right hand.

"I came down here, because I understand that I have been accused of something that I am not guilty of. I came down here, to see where the case was, and to clear my name."

"I see. And the case that you speak of is related to what, may I ask?" Larry asked coolly. He wanted to see David's reaction, and wanted to see how he would talk about 'rape'. Many people got squeamish or uncomfortable whenever they uttered the word 'rape', and he wanted to see how David reacted.

"You know damn well. I see your folder in front of you. I'm being accused of rape! It's fucking preposterous!" He had an accent, Slavic, maybe eastern European, but he couldn't place it. David's face contorted into anger, and his tone was loud and sharp. But the man's eyes were cool and under control. There was no loss of control that he could discern, and no discomfort with the word 'rape'.

"Yes, you are right. This is the accusation. And where have you been the last week? My partner and I tried to contact you, but your office said that you were traveling internationally and was unreachable."

"I had business overseas, in London, to be exact. That's why you couldn't reach me."

"And when were you in London, from when to when?"

"From the fifteenth to the...twenty second. I just got back last night."

"Ok. So, you've been out of the country for about a week, and unreachable. Let me ask you then, how do you know the case is about rape? The case was filed on the fifteenth, and you were out of the country supposedly. How in the world do you know what you are being accused of?"

David blinked rapidly a few times but recovered quickly. "My office said the police were looking for me, and I had my team investigate as to why. They were able to find out that I was wanted for questioning in a rape, that's all I know."

Larry made some notes in his notebook. "And your office can verify the flight info, provide proof of your travel?" He didn't really need this bit of info, but he wanted to probe and see what kind of reaction it would draw.

David made a 'hmpf' sound before he answered. "Of course! But I fly private, on my private jet, so you'll have to check the logs from where I flew out of."

"Which is...?"

"Westchester county airport."

"Ok, noted. So, tell me, Mr. Milanovich, can you tell me how you know the accuser?" He wrote down in his notebook 'Westchester airport' and 'flies private'.

"I have never seen the girl before, in my life," David said with contempt dripping from his voice.

Larry paused and looked up at David, narrowing his eyes. "Are you sure you want to go down this angle? Because the accuser described in great detail, things about your body. Like a tattoo on your chest, over your heart. And she attested to your genitals, whether you were circumcised or not. That would be rather remarkable, don't you think, for someone who has never met you, yes?" Larry spoke slowly, and softly, but with precision and confidence. David hesitated, and right then, Larry's gut told him at the very least, the man knew the girl.

"No, I have never met her. Many things about me are public,

and anyone can find those things out, if they truly put their mind to it. I've dated many women." David snapped his mouth shut and pressed his lips together into a thin, tight line.

"What about the mother, how do you know her?"

David paused, and took a moment to carefully consider his answer. "I know her. She is a house cleaner, at my apartment on the upper east side."

"I see. And how often did she clean your apartment?" Larry already knew the answer.

"Once a week, on Tuesdays."

"And did she ever bring the accuser to your apartment, as part of house cleaning?" Larry tapped his pen on his notebook.

"No. I'm not sure. Like I said, I've never seen the woman before." David shifted on his chair and rubbed the back of his neck, massaging it.

Larry made another note, and absent mindedly adjusted his gun holster under his left armpit. "Tell me about Martha's Vineyard. What's up there?"

The man gave him a glare before answering. "I have property up there. It's my summer retreat, and I fly there often on the weekends."

"I see. And the accuser, she says she can describe this property in detail. She claims that you said you would help her, give her some money, fly her to your beach property, and then you whisked her away. Only, she claims that you plied her with alcohol, and you raped her. In your master bedroom. Can you tell me where you were last week, on the night of the fourteenth?"

The man frowned and leaned forward. "Listen. I did not rape anyone! This accuser is just trying to shake me down for money. I have never been accused of anything, go check my records.

Everyone knows I have money. And my property has been featured in Architectural Digest. It's easy for anyone to read that article and describe it. Even a monkey could do that. So, this accuser is lying. Write that down." David used his index finger and was stabbing the desktop vehemently as he spoke.

Larry looked at his notebook and did write something down. He wrote, *"Strongly denies the rape, but body language is showing that he is hiding something. Need to question the pilot."*

"Let's go back to the question. Where were you on the fourteenth?" Larry paused and looked up at David, who was now leaning back and straightening the lapels of his suit.

"I was…" he paused, carefully considering his next sentence. "Yes, I was up at Martha's Vineyard. I did fly up there that night."

"He knows I can get the flight logs out of Westchester airport and I'll see that his plane departed that night," he guessed. "Ok. So, you flew up there for one night? Because you said you flew to London on the next day, the fifteenth."

"Yes, of course. I'm a busy man. I wanted to get one last night in my beach house, and then I had business in London." He sounded confident, and he looked relaxed now. He gave Larry a Cheshire cat's grin.

"I see. We'll have to interview your pilot, of course. I'm sure he will remember if you had any guests onboard your plane that night. It's a good thing you came here today and told us where you flew out of. We had a hard time finding that out, because the accuser said she couldn't recall which airport it was, and our searches at La Guardia, JFK, and Newark didn't turn anything up." Larry twirled his pen around his thumb, casually.

"Go ahead. His story will check out with mine, I'm sure," said the man, again, with confidence.

"If he is guilty, then the pilot has been paid off already. That's the only way he can look so confident," he thought sourly.

He asked a few more questions, got the address of the house in Martha's Vineyard, the name of the pilot, his address on the upper east side, and a few other things, but he was starting to lose hope. The man's story was fairly tight. Now, he didn't think the mom and her daughter were lying, per se. She had seemed traumatized by an assault, and the rape tests confirmed that the woman had been through a rough sexual encounter, but that didn't mean the man across from him had been the one to do it. His gut only told him that the man was hiding something.

He snapped his notebook shut and put his pen into his shirt pocket. "Alright, Mr. Milanovich. I think I've got all my questions answered so far. I'll be sure to call or stop by if I have any other questions. Thank you for stopping by today." He stood up, and David did as well, and they shook hands again. David was buttoning up his suit jacket while Larry politely waited for him to finish.

"You know, how is the girl anyway? Fucking liar, I tell you. Hopefully, she's ok, but what balls it takes, to accuse a wealthy man for money, huh?" He snickered. "She'll get what she deserves, I'm sure. People like this, I tell you, they always get what they deserve."

Larry gave the man a stone-faced stare but replied noncommittedly. "She's recovering. Getting better. We'll get the bottom of this, rest assured."

David pushed his chair in and stretched his arms, yawning. "Fucking high school teenagers. They're all liars."

Larry stiffened up, and cocked his head, thinking back on the last twenty minutes of questioning. He had been about to walk towards the door, but he turned and faced David, notepad in his left hand, dangling by his thigh. He knew now that David had done it. He was the rapist. His tone, his words, and now, his last sentence.

"I never said she was underage," he said softly, staring at David intently.

"What?" David frowned at him, as he tried to walk past him to the door, but he was stopped as Larry stepped in his path, blocking him.

"I never said she was a teenager," he said. Now David realized his mistake, and his face flushed pink, though from anger or fear, he couldn't tell.

"You said it earlier. You said the accuser was a girl," he said haughtily.

"No. I never said she was underage. You did. You know her. You raped her, didn't you?" His voice was calm and measured, and he studied David carefully.

"Impossible. You...No... I heard from my team, they said I was wanted for questioning, so I had them check out with the police what it was for. That's how I know." He had started out stammering, but as each word came out, he sounded more and more sure of himself. But Larry knew it was all lies now.

"No. Even if your team came here, which I now doubt, our police officers would never tell you the age of the accuser. Only that a Jane Doe had filed a case for rape. The only ones who would know the age, are me, my Lieutenant, and the rapist. You."

The door to the room opened suddenly, and in walked the Captain of his precinct, Captain James O'Malley. He was tall, with dark blonde hair that was starting to thin and turn grey, with a sharp angular face that looked worn, and creased with age. He was dressed in a suit today, tan, white shirt, black tie, remarkably similar to his L.T. Although Larry didn't interact that much with him, he knew that Captain O'Malley was a rising star, and had ambitions to be Chief of Police one day.

"Alright, that's enough, Detective. I'll take it from here." He had a walkie talkie in his hand, and he spoke into it now. "Dan? Make sure the cameras in room seven stay off. I need a word in private. Detective...Kudlow, right? Good work, son. But I'll take it from here." He stepped to the side, to allow Larry to walk out, but he refused.

"Captain. This man here, he is guilty-"

"I said, that's enough! I watched you conduct your interview. Fine work, son, as I said. But now, I'll wrap this up. Out!" O'Malley gave him a stern warning look, and Larry was stunned. He had never had anyone barge in like this, especially not his Captain. He felt uneasy, and he wasn't sure why.

"Of course, sir. I'll be right outside." He walked towards the door, but as he walked past Captain O'Malley, the case file was snatched from his right hand.

"That won't be necessary. I'll take the case file, and you can go back to the bullpen. Tell your L.T. that the case has been re-assigned, and that you are to start in homicide today. Effective immediately. Understand?" Immediately, his stomach felt like it had done a somersault, and he knew something dirty was about to go down, but he just nodded silently, and pulled the door shut behind him.

As soon as the door closed, he sprinted to his right, down the hallway towards the control room. It was about eight doors down, and he busted through the door, into the small ten by ten room filled with monitors on the wall, two chairs, and the control technician, Dan Slombowsky, with a walkie talkie in his hand. The room smelled stale, like nacho chips and microwaved burritos, and it fit the personality of the heavy-set man sitting in the right chair. He was bald, with thick glasses held in a square, wire frame, and his blue police uniform stretched tightly over his belly, straining to not burst open.

"Dan! Which one turns the video recorders back on for room seven!" he shouted.

"Jesus Christ! You scared the shit out of me. Cap'n was just in here and was watching you do your interview. Like ten seconds ago, he said to turn 'em off, watched me do it, and ran out. What the fuck?"

"Where is the button to turn it back on!" he yelled as he scrambled into the small room.

"I don't know, man, I'll get in so much trouble-"

"Tell me right now, or I swear to God, Dan. Fucking show me," he growled as he stared a death stare at the man, who was now starting to sweat.

"Alright, alright. Jesus. It's there," he said nervously as he pointed to a black switch that was in the 'Off' position.

"Good, now get the fuck out. Here's twenty, go get a coffee and don't come back for twenty minutes, get out, get out. Now! Move it!" he yelled. Dan scurried hastily up from his chair, grabbed the twenty from his hand and hauled ass out of the room, slamming the door shut behind him as he flipped the black switch up. One of the monitors, which had been a blank grey screen, turned on, and he could see Captain O'Malley leaning over the table, hands on the top, and David was now seated again. Picking up the headphones on the station, he pressed 'Audio' next to the black switch, and listened in.

"God damn it. I told you not to come in. The case was being

re-assigned, and I was going to kill the investigation," said O'Malley.

"Yes, yes. I thought I could clear my name faster. But that little prick caught me in a word slip up. It doesn't matter. Just burn the video and this never happened," said David casually.

"It does matter! Fucking bring your lawyer next time, if you decide to act like an idiot and present yourself for questioning," hissed his Captain.

"Watch it. Watch your tone, Jim," warned David quietly. He stared daggers at the Captain of the precinct.

The Captain threw up his hands and turned around, showing his back to the seated man. "Fuck's sake. Get a prostitute. Get a girlfriend. Something. But stop luring these underaged girls and raping them! This is the last God damn time I'm going to cover for you. You hear me? The last fucking time."

David chuckled. "But what's the fun in that, eh, Jim? The younger, the better. They like it, trust me. Besides, these girls, they're sexually active, most of them. The last one? The fourteen-year-old? Her cherry had been popped already, so don't look at me like some monster. They're already doing it, and I'm sure she loved every minute when I was fucking her."

Captain O'Malley turned to face David and glared at him. "You *are* a monster. But this is the last time I am covering your ass. Cover your tracks better, because next time, I won't be there to wipe them away. God's truth."

Now it was David's turn to show anger, as he stood up and slammed his fist on the table. "Well, that works both ways, fucker. I'm not going to help you make it to Chief of Police!"

"I'll make Chief of Police on my own. We're through. No more help from me, and I don't ever want your help anymore

246

either." Jim started for the door and pulled it open, just as David called out to his retreating back.

"Be careful, Jim. If I find you are now my enemy, I will crush you. Be incredibly careful what you say about me," warned David.

"I won't say anything, Darbear. I want nothing to do with you. But if you get caught, it's on you." The Captain left the room, and Larry pulled off the headphones and flipped off the switch to room seven. He didn't know how to get a copy of this tape, but he would have to ask Dan to make him one. He waited a few minutes, then snuck out and went down to the bullpen.

"Who the hell was he talking about at the end? Darrear? Dar-nair?" he wondered. He figured he would wait a bit, then butter up Dan and get a copy of the tape. You never know when it could come in handy.

Larry woke up and blinked his eyes groggily. He was lying on his side, on a concrete floor, and his hands were bound behind his back. He coughed loudly and felt the coppery taste of blood on his lips as he struggled to sit up. He had been in this room for close to a week now. The room was dimly lit with a low wattage light bulb, as if the owner of the building had decided to save electricity by putting in a low illuminating bulb instead of a bright one. He looked down at himself and shook his head in disgust. His white shirt was untucked and smudged with dirt and grime. His tie was nowhere to be found, and he had a rip in his pants just above the left knee. His wrists ached something fierce, and he tested the bonds to see if they would slip or give at all. Nada. He leaned back against the wall and waited. Luckily, he didn't have to wait too long. He heard footsteps coming down the hall, and a bolt being drawn back as the thick steel door swung open. Two men entered the room.

"Larry, Larry. You look filthy. Trust me, you don't look good at all. Am I right?" Alexander said to the big Russian man who entered the room with him and moved off to the side.

Oleg sneered but didn't say anything. He simply folded his arms across his massive chest and kept quiet. He was dressed in a black t shirt that was one size too small and stretched tight across his chest and around his biceps, and dark blue jeans, with black combat boots. He was probably six foot five inches tall, with a crew cut, and a stern look. Larry knew he was former military, and rumor had it he had been special forces. He sure looked the part. Oleg had been here every day, asking him questions about how much money he had available, and when Larry's answers failed to please him, he got a beating. Mostly punches and kicks to his stomach and back, but a few vicious right hooks to the face as well. Until today, however, he hadn't seen Alexander at all, despite his repeated requests to see the gangster.

"Larry. You know why you are here. You know this. You owe me a fuckload of money, yes? And before I had Oleg drag you in, it had been well over a week, and still, you don't come to pay me the juice. I have to come chase you down, like a rabbit. You make me call Oleg here, to bring you to me, like a filthy cur from out in the street. Do you have anything you want to say?" Alexander squatted down, resting his butt on his ankles and his forearms on his knees as he peered into Larry's face. Alexander was dressed in a white shirt, black trousers, and black oxfords, but no jacket. He had slicked his hair back with gel of some sort and was smiling at him without warmth.

"I'll get you your money," he said softly. He knew this was no time to fuck around. He owed half a million dollars to this man across from him, and he knew that this time, he was in serious trouble.

Alexander pursed his lips and itched the scalp of his head with his right hand, itching just above his right ear. He then grimaced and rubbed his chin with the same hand as he turned his head to peer at Larry from a slightly different angle.

"I don't know, Larry. I just don't know," he sighed. "My gut says you won't pay me back. That if I let you go, you'll just run away into hiding, and I might never see you again. Normally, I would listen to my gut, and just have Oleg here take care of business, you know what I mean? But you're an ex-cop. That makes me think twice." Alexander sighed again and shook his head.

"I said I'll get it for you. I swear. Give me three days, and I'll have fifty thousand for you to cover the juice and part of the principal. I can get it from my boss, I have a big job I'm working on." He spoke calmly, but inside, he was panicking. He had never ended up in this position before, bound in a basement somewhere, with his executioner standing off to the side, just waiting on the word to... 'take care of business' as Alexander called it. He knew that Alexander was not messing around this time. This was for keeps.

Alexander narrowed his eyes and glared at him. "You know how many fucking times I hear this? Please, please. Just a little more time, I'll pay you, I swear it! I know when people are tapped out. You, my friend, are tapped out. You are banned from my gambling parlors, so if your...boss...doesn't come through, you are out of luck. So now I have to weigh your word, and whether this boss of yours will give you fifty large, or whether it's worth the risk to take care of business on an ex-cop." Alexander turned to look to the side, thinking about his options. The room was quiet, and then he made up his mind and turned to look at Larry. "It's going to bring a lot of heat on me, and my operation, but I can't let you skip town without paying. Sets a bad example. So..." He stood up.

"Wait! Wait!" Larry yelled.

Alexander turned to Oleg, and nodded his head, then turned around, heading for the door. Oleg pulled out a wicked looking knife, and his face was now blank, and stone cold, emotionless.

"Five hundred thousand in three days! You'll have it in three days, I swear it! You just have to let me go, so that I can convince my boss. She has access to that kind of money," he shouted. He was sweating now, and he dared not look up at Oleg. Instead, he focused intently on Alexander's back as the man paused in the entrance of the door. Five seconds went by. Ten. Thirty. A full minute before Alexander turned his head slightly to look back over his shoulder at Larry.

"All of it?" he asked softly. "She will give you half a million... because you ask?"

"All of it, every nickel. Not because I ask. But because I have valuable information for her. Valuable *only* to her, that she will pay dearly for." He made it clear that only she would find it useful, otherwise, Alexander might want this information for himself.

Alexander thought for a moment. With his head still looking back over his shoulder in his general direction, he made his final decree. "I won't let you go. Too much of a flight risk. You get one phone call. Oleg will be by your side. If you scream for help, you die on the phone. I suggest you make it a very persuasive pitch. If she agrees to pay on your behalf, give her this phone number and have her call me. One of my associates will pick up and give her instructions on how to make payment. In cash." Larry saw a piece of paper fall to the floor, and then Alexander was gone. He leaned his head back against the concrete wall and stared up at the ceiling, breathing a sigh of relief. He wasn't out of the woods yet, but at least he had a chance. One very slim chance.

21

A Slim Chance

Laura awoke to hear her cell phone buzzing on the nightstand. Groggily, she reached for it and peered at it with squinted eyes. "Two a.m. Who the hell is calling me at two a.m.?" She didn't recognize the number, but on a whim, she decided to answer it.

"Who is it?" asked Gale sleepily. She was naked beneath the covers, and Laura pulled them up to cover her girlfriend's chest.

"Not sure. Go back to sleep. I'll be right back," she whispered as she stood up, also naked, and picked up the call.

"Hello?" she said with a dry and parched voice. She walked out of the bedroom and over towards her kitchen to get a glass of water. Winters were always dry in New York. She decided that this weekend, she would finally head over to Bed Bath and Beyond and get a humidifier.

"Hey, boss. It's me, Larry."

Laura stopped in her tracks and blinked. She pulled the phone away to look at the number one more time and put it back to her ear in disbelief.

"What the hell, Larry? Where have you been? Why haven't you been answering my calls or texts? I thought you were dead!" she exclaimed in shock, but as each word tumbled out of her mouth, faster and faster, her tone switched over to anger. This man had been the lead for her team, her most trusted ace up her sleeve, and he had disappeared for close to a week. She was pissed.

"Well. About that. I may still be dead." She heard a muffled voice in the distance on the phone, and heard Larry coaxing the other person gently. "Whoa, whoa. Relax. It was just a joke. Alright, alright. I'll keep it straight."

She heard him shift his tone back to her.

"Sorry. Hey, listen. I don't have a lot of time to talk. Can't go into details. But I need a big favor from you."

She walked over to the kitchen and turned on the light, wincing as the light blasted on. "Really? You disappear for nearly a week, without a word, and now I'm supposed to do you a favor? You forget that you work for me, not the other way around?"

There was a silence on the end of the phone, and then Larry's voice came through again, tight, but with a hint of desperation in it. "Yes, I know that. But I really, really need this. More than you know. I need you to bring half a million dollars, in cash, to settle up my debts to someone. And I need it in three days."

Laura paused, unsure if he was somehow joking, or if he was serious. But the way he was speaking, and the absurdity of the whole situation made it clear that this was not a joke. She leaned back against the refrigerator, the cold stainless steel almost bringing a yelp from her, but it sharpened her senses and cleared the fog from her sleepy mind.

"Hold up. Did you say you need half a million dollars? In cash? In three days? What the hell, Larry? Explain yourself," she demanded. She knew that he was deep in debt, but now it was clear that he was in over his head. And from what Samuel had said, he was in debt to a Russian gangster with ties to the Russian mafia. Not good. The earlier joke about being dead made sense now, and she guessed that he was being held hostage somewhere.

"You heard correctly. I can't really go into details, Laura. Just ask Samuel, he probably can fill you in a little here. But... everything depends on this. I need this favor."

"Larry. I want to help you. But I don't know that I would just fork it over like that. That's a lot of money."

"You can get it. From your slush fund, just expense it and get it."

"You and I both know that would be extremely hard to do. I mean, to draw out five hundred thousand in cash? That is nearly impossible. I won't risk my job like that."

"Maybe not for me. But there is something else. Remember when I said I found it? I had the evidence against Darbear?" Larry waited a second, then continued. "Well, I found it. It's legit too. You get this recording, and you'll have him by the balls. He will back off and do whatever you want, no questions."

Laura blinked. It was too good to be true. There couldn't be anything that solid and that dangerous for Darbear. Samuel had checked all his leads, and there wasn't anything even remotely that juicy.

"Prove it. Tell me what it is," she whispered.

There was a sigh on the other end. "About twenty years ago. I was still a detective with the N.Y.P.D. One of the last cases I ever worked, was a rape case. A mom came into the precinct with her daughter. Her *underaged* daughter, mind you, and claimed that her daughter had been a victim of rape by her employer. The accused was a man by the name of David Milanovich. He came into the precinct about a week after the accusation, with the intent to try and clear his name on his own. He thought he was a clever son of a bitch, and he was. He almost fooled me. Long story short, I caught him in a lie, but the Captain of my precinct stepped into the interrogation room and shoved me out. He had the video recorders shut off, but I got them turned back on in time. Just in time to hear this man admit to the rape and suggest there were others. You with me so far?"

"Yes, keep going," she said.

"David Milanovich. He's Darbear. Darbear's middle name is David, and he changed his last name from Milanovich to Markovich, right around this time. It didn't click in my head, because I didn't even realize the two were the same guy. I never knew the man as Darbear, and I only found out about the name change when I logged into the police precinct about a week ago. But he's a rapist, and he raped an underaged girl, and it's all recorded." Larry was speaking calmly and quietly, but Laura's heart was racing. *"Could it be? Is this real?"* she wondered.

"How sure are you on this? You seriously have this on tape?" she asked forcefully. She had to be one hundred percent sure this was real.

"It's him, Laura. The same man. And yeah, it's all on tape. My Captain at the time was in on it, and covered the guy's tracks, but not for much longer it seems. They had a falling out, and the Captain went on his merry way. But the thing is, I got caught up in a police sting about a week later, and I was forced out, so I never got a copy of the tape…until about six days ago, when I hacked into the police main frame with Samuel's help. My Captain found out that I had flipped the video back on, and right or wrong, he kept the video recording in his private files. Maybe for leverage in case Darbear ever went after him, but it implicates him as much as it does Darbear." There was more muffled talking in the background.

"Where's the tape or recording? Do you have it?" she asked breathlessly. If this were true, it would change everything.

"I had it. But it got destroyed…when I was detained. I know where you can still get a copy though."

"Where?"

"Five hundred thousand, Laura. In cash. To clear my debt, and then I'll tell you where and who has it."

She shook her head in disgust. Even if she could get the cash, five hundred thousand was a large sum of money. It was easier for her to have fake invoices made and then have accounts payable pay electronically, but cash was a much harder thing to cover her tracks with. Not impossible, but it would leave her exposed, which she didn't like.

"Laura, you there?" asked Larry with concern in his voice. He was worried, and that was not like him. He was always unflappable and collected. Not today, however.

"I'm here, just give me a minute to think." She could have Jennifer setup a shell company, have them invoice Abernathy, and then process the payment through accounts payable. Jennifer would then need to get to the bank to withdraw the cash, but that would draw a lot of attention. Instead, if Jennifer then used those funds to buy, say, gold bars, she could then wire the money over to the jeweler and then walk out with gold instead. It could work.

It would have to work, as she just didn't see a scenario of Jennifer walking out of a bank with half a million dollars.

"Ok, I can get half a million dollars, but in gold bars. You know the one-ounce gold bars that jewelers in the diamond district sell? I can use that as payment, but I can't get cash. Will that work?" There was silence on the other line. *"I'm going to have to make sure this account never gets audited, and afterwards, destroy any trail of this happening,"* she thought.

"Ok. That will do. Write this number down. You'll speak to a person who will setup the drop, and then I go free."

She walked over to the counter and grabbed a pen and post it, carefully writing down the number that Larry relayed.

"Two more things, Larry. First, after this is done, we are done. You no longer work for me, and I never want to see or hear from you again. Agreed on point one?"

"Agreed," came the somber reply. She just couldn't trust Larry anymore.

"Point two, tell me at least who has the video or recording. I need to know who I'm up against."

There was a soft chuckle on the other end. "It's someone you know, but I'll tell you after I'm free. Call the number when you have the gold." She heard the call drop and tried to puzzle out who the person could be, but quickly gave up. The possibilities were too many. She picked up her phone and made another call. It was late, but she knew this person would still be up.

"Hey, Mason. Long time. Listen, I need your help with something. There's money in it for you, and it's easy work. Just a drop of goods to another person in about three days' time…"

22

Fractures

Laura hopped off the subway and stepped onto the platform. The station at Bryant Park was much like the rest of New York City's subway stations, which was to say, old and worn out. Only the newer station stops at the end of the seven line and the new second avenue subway stop were clean and new. The metal pillars were a drab beige, and had been painted over countless times, to the point where any chips or dents that managed to pierce through to the aged steel underneath revealed layer upon layer of paint, much like the rings of a tree trunk when a tree is cut down. The subway system in New York was over a hundred years old, but she enjoyed riding it, nevertheless. For all of its faults, delays, or occasional homeless man occupying a whole subway car to him or herself, she still appreciated the relative quickness with which you could navigate to any part of the city. The tiles were a tan color, and only the yellow caution rubber panels that lined the edge of the platform broke up the monotony of the cold and impersonal platform. She hiked up a short set of stairs, then walked towards the turnstiles, up another set of stairs, and out into the dark New York night. Bryant Park was one of her favorite places in New York. It was centrally located in midtown, on forty second street, and abutted the public library on one side. There were often events or things happening in the park. It could be yoga in the park, or summer movie nights, or during December, winter holiday stalls and a temporary outdoor ice rink. She loved it all.

There were a fair number of people walking the streets, as usual, from tourists, to people just getting off work, even a mom pushing a baby in a stroller, as she walked west towards sixth avenue. She was a bit late in meeting Gale for dinner, so she hurried along, stopping to jaywalk across the street to the north side of forty second street. Gabriel Kruether, the upscale French Michelin starred restaurant was on forty second, between fifth and sixth avenues, and her mouth was already watering by the time she pushed through the doors.

"Good evening. How can I help you?" asked the host, a short man in a grey suit. He had a slight French accent, and smiled politely at her.

"Yes, I have a reservation. Laura Park, party of two for eight o'clock."

"Ah, yes! Your guest has already been seated. Follow me, please," he said as he stepped out from behind the lectern and briskly walked her into the dining room. The dining room was elegant, modern, warm, and inviting. The carpet was a light brown, with large gold circles about the size of a stop sign, that barely touched each other but never overlapped. The ceiling was also light brown but appeared to be a shiny lacquer of some sort, and had recessed, soft lighting. The chairs were made of leather, soft and luxurious to sit in and touch, and also in the brown spectrum, albeit a medium dark beige with dark brown, wooden legs. Even the long wooden table in the center of the room, which held several vases of flowers, was brown as well. To offset the earthy feel of the room, white tablecloths adorned each table, and a small foot tall lamp sat in the center of each, giving off a soft and gentle yellow light. The chandelier above the long wooden table sprinkled down from the ceiling, which must have been close to twenty feet high, and was silver strands and silver rectangles that quietly twinkled in the light. The room was about three quarters full, and the diners were dressed impeccably, with men wearing blazers or suits, and the women in dresses or modest cocktail attire. The host lead her across the room towards the tables where one diner sat in booth style seating, although there were no partitions to separate one section from another, and the other person sat across from them in one of the leather chairs. She saw Gale already seated on the booth side, and she smiled at Laura when she saw the host leading her.

"Here we go, madame. Your server will be with you shortly to tell you about the specials," said the host, as he pulled out the chair and helped her get seated.

"Thank you," she said. "Hey, babe!" she said as she leaned over and gave her girlfriend a quick kiss.

"Thank, god! I'm starving! I was about to gnaw off my arm, I'm so hungry," said Gale with a grin. "I ordered for us both, already."

Laura gave a grateful smile in return and laid her napkin in her lap. "Great. How was your day? Did you get your idea for your next article approved by your editor?"

"Hm, no. Well, not exactly a 'no' per se, but an almost 'yes'."
Laura raised a confused eyebrow and took a sip of her water.

"Confused. What do you mean?"

Gale sighed. "Matt said I need to have something more solid
than a rumor. You remember how I said that Lynn James was
illegally using company funds to donate to one of her charities?"
Lynn James was the Chief Counsel at an exceptionally large
investment fund in the city. Laura nodded her head.

"He said that the story is good, if I can prove to him that I
have a solid lead. Something more than just scuttlebutt from
somebody in the office. He said that any disgruntled employee
could make stuff up just to spread dirt, and he's right, but I really
thought he would give me a pass on this one, because he knows
I went to school with my source. She's trustworthy, and I know
she's not telling a lie here."

"What kind of proof does he need? I mean, she's the freaking
Chief Counsel. She's smart, and probably hid her tracks really
well." Laura looked up at their waiter as he stopped by with a
breadbasket and tongs.

"Hello! Today, we have a homemade sourdough bread, and a
mini baguette with black olives," he said cheerfully as he proffered
the basket.

"I'll have the sourdough," she said.

"Me too. And can I have the baguette too?" asked Gale.

"Where was I? Oh yes. Yeah, Matt said I need something more
than a whisper from a college buddy. So, yeah. Now I have to get a
little more evidence before he'll green light the article and research."

Laura chewed thoughtfully on her bread, then gave her
girlfriend a nugget from her playbook. "Why don't you make it up?"

Gale wrinkled her eyebrows in confusion. "What do you mean?"

"Well, you pretty much know that Lynn is doing something shady. You just need to dig and find it out. So, make up something stronger. If you want, I can make up an email, something from Lynn, asking a subordinate to transfer the monies posthaste, to that certain you know what account. I can make it sound very… underhanded and as if she's trying to conceal something, without explicitly saying what it is. That way, you can show it to Matt, and he'll sign off on your article."

Gale's face was shocked, and Laura knew that she had crossed the line.

"Laura, that's- I don't know even where to begin, but that's so not right, and I could get fired! You can't just lie about something like that!" Gale blurted, and truth be told, hearing those words and that tone from her stung Laura a bit.

"Hold on now. You won't get fired. Don't be so melodramatic. You're just speeding up the process. Lynn is the one who is doing something wrong here, not you, not me. So…we're just getting the process started so that Matt will sign off, and then you go find out the dirt. That's all I'm saying," she said, a bit defensively, she realized.

"Even still. You can't make up an email! That's…that's… lying essentially. You'd be lying, and as a writer, I won't go down that path, no matter the gain." Gale was frowning, and behind her blue eyes, Laura felt as if she was judging her. It made her feel slightly ashamed, but more so, angry. Laura had done far worse in her career, and who was Gale to judge her?

"Alright, alright. Forget I mentioned it. It will just take longer for you to get your article greenlit," she said with annoyance, and Gale answered right back in the same annoyed tone.

"So be it, then. I can live with that," she snapped.

Laura shook her head ever so slightly, but Gale noticed it and pursed her lips in silence. Laura decided to change topics and hopefully shift the mood back to a positive light.

"Hey, so I finally made a breakthrough in the Darbear situation."

"Oh, yeah?" asked Gale a bit coldly. She was spreading butter on her sourdough bread and wasn't looking at her.

"Yeah. So, get this. Larry finally called me, out of the blue. He was…being detained somewhere, is my guess, and needed me to get bail for him to get out, essentially." She decided not to go into the details of the money he owed, and the amount of money she was embezzling from the company to set him free. Gale didn't know about her slush fund account.

"He finally called? Where was he being detained, like in a jail?" Gale asked with an arched eyebrow. Her reporter senses were tingling, Laura knew, and she moved quickly through those lesser details.

"I think so. It's not important. He needed some bail money, and I'm going to get it to him so he can get free. But get this part. He has solid evidence on Darbear," she said excitedly.

Gale took a bite of her bread and mumbled out some words around her full mouth. "I thought your team had looked into Darbear with no luck. And now something comes up? Sounds odd."

Laura grinned. "Yeah, all true. My team had checked, but this one was secret. Only one or two people knew about this. You remember Larry had been on the police force, right? Well, he had interviewed Darbear years ago, way back like twenty years ago, only he had forgotten. Darbear hadn't used his real name, and he had secretly changed his last name. It wasn't on any public records that my team could find."

"Ok. I find that a bit hard to believe, what with legal documentation required to change names, but I'm with you so far," Gale said a bit skeptically. She had polished off the sourdough and was now nibbling on the baguette.

"That's fine. Believe what you will. But when he was being interviewed at the police station, he was caught on tape admitting to raping an underage girl! It's all on tape!" Laura smiled triumphantly and eagerly awaited her girlfriend's response, which was slow in coming.

Gale blinked several times and digested this information, eyes opening wider than normal. She took a sip of her water and then blankly stared at Laura's smiling expression. "Who has the tape, and what will you do with it?" Gale finally offered. There was no smile or hint of congratulatory emotion. Just a curiosity if you will.

Laura smiled quizzically, eyebrows slightly furrowed in confusion. "Well, that's what I need to do next. I have to get the video tape. Aren't you excited for me?" she asked breathlessly. Laura had been running in circles over the last six weeks, trying to get something, anything, on this opponent, and she had been this close to admitting defeat, when this miraculous piece of evidence was nearly in her grasp, and tilted the table suddenly in her favor. Why couldn't Gale see that this was a boon?

Now it was Gale's turn to look puzzled. "I mean, I guess I'm excited for you. I don't see how it's going to help that much. I mean, say you get the tape. You have to turn it over to the police, right? And they'll investigate, and I'm not sure how rock solid the tape is anyway, but let's assume it's got a full confession on it. There will be a trial, and lawyers, and debates on whether the tape is real, or if that man is really him, et cetera. I mean, all this will play out in court, and it could be a year plus. Meanwhile, he still does all those things you told me about. The hostile takeover, you getting fired. So, I don't know how this tape helps you.

Maybe it's him, and he does go to jail, but you still lose, right? What am I missing?"

Laura was dumbfounded. *"How can Gale not see?"* she wondered. She decided to voice out loud her initial plans, but she wasn't sure how Gale would receive the news.

"Babe. If I get the tape, I have humongous leverage. Don't you see? I'm going to parlay that tape into Darbear backing down. He won't want that tape shown to anyone. He'll lose business and would do jail time. It's a huge bargaining chip."

The blood from Gale's face drained, and her lips formed a small "o", but before she could say anything, their server came by with their soups.

"Hi, for our first course, we have a butternut squash soup, with wild elder flower petals, and a dollop of crème fraiche. Enjoy," he said as he placed a wide rimmed bowl in front of each of them. Gale murmured a 'thank you', and then picked up her spoon, but she was staring at Laura pensively.

"So, you won't hand it over to the police? You'll use it, against him?" Gale finally asked.

"Yes! He'll have to back down, and I can still do everything that I planned. Better yet, I can make it so that he owes me a future favor. It's genius," she said with small smile. But Gale's face said otherwise. She was horrified.

"Laura. If that tape truly has a confession of rape, on an underaged girl mind you, you have to turn it in! You can't- I mean are you serious right now? You would negotiate with a rapist, and let him walk? For what? So that you can still have a job? Big fucking deal! I'm so shocked at you right now. What the fuck?" The color had returned to Gale's face, but it was flush now, with anger.

"Gale-" she started but was quickly interrupted.

"No! I'm serious, Laura. You can't just blackmail someone into backing down, and then handing over evidence of a crime to that suspect. He'll get away with it and think about that poor girl he raped! What about her, huh? Have you thought about what she must feel like? Having been raped, but her rapist never got caught? Never got punished? Never faced the consequences? I mean, we live in a society of laws. And not only did the rapist break the law, but you are about to as well. You want to blackmail someone, and then hide evidence of a crime. Is that what you're really saying right now?" Gale had put her spoon down, soup untouched, and was staring at Laura with big eyes and a stern, cold look. She wanted to yell back, scream, say something, but for once, she was without words. It was one thing to operate like a cutthroat person without morals, it was far different to hear it spoken in the light of day to your face, and then having to think on what it actually meant you were doing, all for the sake of power.

Laura stared back at Gale, thought carefully about her next sentence, and spoke calmly. "I'm still thinking about what to do," she lied.

Gale shook her head and gathered her purse and slid out of the booth, standing up. "It shouldn't even be a question. There's only one right way to handle this, and the fact that you are 'still thinking about it', isn't a good sign. Babe, I have a lot to think about, and I have lost my appetite. I'll see you back at home, ok?" Shocked, Laura started to stand up, but Gale was already walking away, and Laura sat back down, heavily, wondering what had just happened.

As she had predicted, the rest of the negotiations on getting Darbear to exit his position by a certain end date, failed. He wanted a guaranteed twenty percent return on his money and wouldn't budge. When the board relented and caved to the twenty percent floor, he then pushed to have Laura removed from the company, immediately. But Laura was able to wrestle the board into fighting back, albeit it was a split vote. Darbear and his team agreed to talk again in the coming weeks, but Laura already knew that he would eventually make a hostile bid. The rest was just a charade.

Mason had agreed to do the drop of the gold over to Alexander's associates, for a fee of course, and Larry had made good on his promise by calling her with all the details and specifics of the video recording and how Commissioner Jim O'Malley played his part in covering for Darbear. After that phone call, she hadn't heard from Larry. Samuel said that he got one call from Larry, but that was it. He didn't show up to take anything from the office, and no one saw or heard from him again. She suspected he left the tri state area, but when Samuel asked if she wanted him to try and track him down, she declined. Although Larry knew a lot about the dirt she ran with her team, she also knew that he would keep quiet about it. Just a hunch. Besides, she had bigger fish to fry.

"Laura?" Geoff popped his head into her office. "Mary is here to see you; do you want to meet her? She doesn't have an appointment."

"Yes, send her in, thanks." Mary had done a remarkable job in the few short weeks since she had come onboard as her campaign manager. Although she hadn't announced yet, Mary had already hired two staff members in New York City, and sent along a few articles to read, poll results that her team had already compiled from earlier in the year and started setting up lunches and meet and greets with various folks that were influential in the donor sphere. She didn't have time yet, to fulfill or meet anyone just yet, but Mary had already scheduled the meetings far enough in advance so that she could focus on settling the Darbear situation.

Mary walked in, dressed demurely in a black skirt that was just below her knees, modest black Bottega Veneta suede heels, a white silk shirt, and she carried her black London Fog coat over her forearm. Her hair was as short as she remembered it and hung down to just below her ears.

Mary put her coat on the back of the chair across from Laura's desk, and Laura stood up to greet her with a hug and a warm pat on the back.

"How are you doing? We couldn't just chat on the phone?" she asked with a tired smile.

"Phaw! Some things we can do on the phone, some things are best said in person. This is one of those times," said Mary with a snort. She walked back to the chair and sat down with a thud. For someone who had a reputation for being well heeled and in all the right circles, she lacked a certain decorum and etiquette that continually surprised Laura.

"Hm, that doesn't sound so good. How's everything going? How's your apartment in Tribeca so far? Are you enjoying it?" she asked as she too, sat down in her chair. She flicked a quick glance at her monitor to see if there were any fire drills that she needed to handle, but it looked clear, and she turned her full attention to her campaign manager.

"It's nice, everything's nice. Just a bit hard to get to and from Tribeca, but you warned me on that front. Anyways, enough with the niceties. Let's get to brass tacks." Mary sat up and turned serious. "Do you remember when we were up on Bear mountain, and we talked about your plans, that you wanted to go all the way on this one, see if you can make it to President?"

Laura nodded slowly. "Yes, I remember that conversation. We talked a lot about the platform I could run on, and you made it sound like I had a good shot, if a lot of things go my way that is."

Mary nodded impatiently. "Yes. You do. And I admire the balls on you, lady. You're ambitious, hungry, super intelligent, and cutthroat. You can play this game and you have sharp elbows to muscle your way to the table and stay there. I've gathered this much from my homework, speaking to employees here, and also to those you've managed to oust."

Laura's eyes narrowed a bit at that last comment, and she tilted her chin up, a little defiantly. "Oh, really? And what is your point, Mary?"

Mary paused to study her for a moment, and Laura stared back with a quiet confidence. "Well, there was one thing I wasn't certain on. If you want to stop at Senator, you can win as a gay woman. But if you want to go all the way to the Presidency, that's where I'm not sure you can pull enough votes and grab enough states to get to the finish line. Remember, I said I would run some polls for you on this and get back to you. Well, now I have the data."

"Hm, by the way you're framing this up, the data isn't good, is that it?" she asked as she leaned back slightly in her chair.

Mary shook her head and pulled out a folder from underneath her coat. She opened it up, pulled out several sheets of paper, and slid them across the desk to Laura.

"No, 'fraid not. I had my team run several polls, framing up the question differently each time, but essentially asking if they would ever vote for a gay woman as President. We targeted red states and also toss up states, because those will be the ones you'll need to win if you want to make it to the top. Unfortunately, the results were putrid. Worse than putrid. Only twenty two percent said they would vote for a lesbian woman to be President of the United States. Now, it's only three thousand households that we managed to get solid data on, but if you extrapolate it out…" Mary shook her head again. "You won't carry enough states and get enough electoral votes to close this out. So, my question to you is, how do you want to proceed?"

Laura looked down at the poll results in front of her. She quickly skimmed through the three sheets, which she appreciated were concise, clear, and to the point. If what she was reading was true, she wouldn't have much of a chance to win the Presidency. She brushed her black hair back behind her right ear, and then looked up at Mary. There was a look of sympathy there, but in flash, it was gone, replaced by a stone-faced look that was expressionless.

"You're my campaign manager, what do you recommend?" she asked loudly.

Mary nodded her head with satisfaction. "Good question. Look, I'll tell it to you straight. I think you've got a good platform to run on, and I think you can win the Senate seat here in New York. Lesbian or not. But to be honest, if I were a betting woman, you're not going to make it to President if you run as a lesbian. Just being honest. So, you have two options here, the way I see it. Either you set your sights a bit lower, and just go for the Senate seat. Or…you ditch your girlfriend, find a husband to marry, and play it straight, like what Americans expect and want to see in the office of the President." She paused and waited for Laura's reaction.

Laura stood up and turned away, walking towards the wide expanse of glass windows that showed her Central Park. The sky was grey, again, a worn-out winter day that held no warmth or solace for Laura Park, not this day. She clasped her hands behind her back and stared down, twenty-three floors to the Park where she could see brown and empty branches, some green pine trees sprinkled throughout, patches of white where some snow had yet to melt, and green grass interspersed with yellow. She saw people walking through the park, on their way to various errands in the city, or out for a stroll during the workday, or just grabbing coffee. This was a big decision, she knew. Mary was asking her to toss aside someone she loved and fake it. She was giving her a choice, but one was to pick love and aim her sights lower, or pretend to be someone she was not, and aim higher. How could she decide something like this? It wasn't fair.

"What you're asking me…" she started.

"I know. It's a tough choice, but only you can decide. I'll stick by your side, either way," said Mary softly. *"Of course, Mary knows how hard this is. She's a lesbian too,"* she thought.

She turned around and faced Mary. "I can't decide right now. I need some time to think. But…if I were to play it…straight, as you say, can you help me find a good…" she trailed off. If she decided to pretend to be a straight woman in a loving, heterosexual relationship, she would need help to find that person. She just didn't know where to begin.

Mary pulled out another folder from under her coat and slid it over the desk. "If you decide that is the way you want to go, I have a list and profiles of some high profile, excellent matches. They are all single, eligible bachelors, Democrats, and all of them have some pizzazz and bring something to the table."

Laura walked over, and opened the folder, staring at the first match. "Greg Washington. Male, black, aged forty-two. Harvard law school, practices law at a big law firm in Georgia. Father was the governor of Georgia, and uncle was a cabinet member in the early nineties."

"Greg would be a great match. He would help secure the African American vote, and I happen to know that he is partial to dating Asian women," said Mary matter of factly.

Laura turned the page to look at the next picture and profile. "Franklin Kennedy. Male aged forty five. Yale and Princeton. Nothing else here?"

"He's a distant family relation to the Kennedy family. The name alone will give you cachet. He's also ambitious, and I'm sure we could set you up on a date."

Laura sighed. "I see you are very prepared. The fact that you have these profiles already scouted out, tells me where your head is at."

"Not at all. I don't envy the decision you have to make, Laura. I'm only here to give you options," said Mary quietly.

"Alright. Let me think on this. I'll take a look at these profiles tonight, and let's talk again in a week or so, ok?"

"No problem. In the meantime, I'll have the team craft up your political stances on every issue in the world today. You can review and edit them later but let me know if anything is way off the mark or not." Mary stood up and grabbed her coat. They hugged one more time, and then Mary was gone.

Laura sat back down at her desk and opened up the folder of eligible bachelors again. She sighed. *"Is she really asking me to pick a bachelor, forge a love interest, and get married, just like that? Just like picking a menu item at a restaurant, she thinks it's that easy?"* she wondered. She had tried dating men when she was younger and through her college years. It just hadn't been for her. She knew her interests were elsewhere, and she had dated a few women to know that she preferred women to men. But if the poll results were correct…she wouldn't have much of a shot to make it to the office of the President if she ran as who she truly was.

"Who am I, exactly?" she murmured softly aloud, to no one in particular. She was the daughter of immigrant parents. She had been poor, smart, hungry to succeed, and willing to do whatever it took to survive and win in the process. She thought back to when she had to forage for food in the dumpsters after school. *"Anything it takes to win,"* she thought. But what about now? She genuinely loved Gale. Gale was her bright light in her male dominated world, and she made her laugh and brought true joy to her life. How could she just throw her away?

"I can't. She brings out the best in me, and I feel happy when I'm around her." She decided, and the decision brought her relief, as she pushed the folder away. If she only made it to Senator, then so be it. There were other, worse things in life. Decision made, she picked up her desk phone, and punched in the number from her contacts list from her cell phone. It was time to go to war.

23

The Chief of Police

Laura was standing outside the entrance to the newly built library in Long Island City. Officially, it was called the Hunters Point Library, and it was aesthetically beautiful. From the front, it looked like a big rectangle, made of white concrete that was painted with aluminum to give it a silvery finish. Steven Holl Architects designed the library, and it was years in the making. In fact, it finally finished construction in 2019, about five years behind schedule. Large, irregular cut outs in the concrete gave way to glass windows that had broad, expansive views of the Manhattan skyline. Inside, it was six stories, made of light-colored bamboo wood, glass, and steel, with huge ceilings that gave it a cavernous feel. There was a café on the fourth floor, and even a rooftop patio. She checked her watch. Just about noon. She watched the various passerby's, many of whom were moms pushing strollers, or kids walking hand in hand with their mom or dad. Long

Island City had been an industrial city, many years ago, but had been gentrified and changed in the last decade. There were still old warehouses and car repair shops that were sprinkled throughout the nabe, but it was largely tall, residential condo and co-op buildings now, at least along the waterfront. Nowadays, it was a family friendly neighborhood, as many parents opted to move out to Queens for more space. LIC was still a short hop on the subway, or one stop on the East River Ferry, allowing easy access to Manhattan without all of the energy and excitement.

Finally, she saw the tall, lanky figure she was expecting to meet. James O'Malley was in his late fifties, perhaps six foot four inches tall, of Irish descent, and had thinning grey hair. He had a few strands and wisps of blonde that still managed to come through, and she could tell that he had been a handsome man when he was younger. Now, his face was weathered and lined with creases from fatigue, stress, and work. His face was lean and angular, with narrow cheekbones and a tapered chin. He wore a tan raincoat, even though it wasn't raining. As a matter of fact, the sun was shining brightly in the cloudless blue sky, although it was brisk and chilly at fifty degrees Fahrenheit. He had charcoal slacks under his raincoat, which was buttoned up tight. When she had called him and asked to talk about a certain tape from twenty years ago, he had insisted on meeting in person, rather than discussing anything on the phone. He had suggested here, out of the city, and away from prying eyes and ears. He wasn't famous, but at the same time, a lot more people would recognize the Chief of Police in Manhattan as opposed to Queens.

"Laura, how are we doing today?" he asked amicably as he strode up to her. He stuck out his hand and gave her a strong, firm handshake.

"Just fine. No troubles on the seven train?" she asked politely.

"None whatsoever. A little bit of train traffic at Grand Central, but nothing too bad. Come on, let's go for a walk, shall we?"

"You don't want to go inside the new library?" she asked curiously. She thought that was one of the reasons he had asked to meet here.

"Nah. I've already been inside, just a few weeks ago. It's nice if you haven't seen it. But I like the fresh air. I'm stuck at my desk all too much," he said casually.

"Alright. Let's walk down to the water and loop around," she suggested. He held his hand and arm out as if to say, "*Lead the way.*"

She walked to the right, towards the water. The path was a white brick pathway, and it opened up into a broad expanse or courtyard almost, where the East River kissed several wooden piers, and two huge black gantries lined up where the water met the concrete walkway.

"You see those gantries over there?" James pointed to the two black structures. "Those gantries supported cranes, and there were boat slips that jutted under the gantry, and goods were loaded and unloaded using those gantries, a long time ago. Back during Prohibition, a lot of alcohol was smuggled into boats right there, and at various other gantries along the East river all the way down to Brooklyn as well. They'd go up to Connecticut, or down to Atlantic City. But now, the gantries are either just rusting away, or revitalized, like these over here. Just artwork, in a sense, for blossoming neighborhoods like this one. But trust me, twenty years ago, Long Island City was nothing like what you see here today. It was full of warehouses, lots of petty crime, and they didn't really have a lot of these high rises that you see now." James looked pensive, and he had his hands clasped behind his back as they strolled up to the water, and then took a right turn down another brick pathway.

"Were you here in Long Island City? I mean, did you ever work a beat out here?" she asked. She glanced at him, and then looked to her left, out across the East River. The Manhattan skyline was magnificent at this time of day, with the sun sparkling on the water, and sending beams of light prancing and skipping along the glass high rise buildings across the way. It was a magical sight.

"Me? Nah. I worked a bit in the Bronx, some in Brooklyn, but never did a stint here in Queens. Mostly, I worked the Upper East side. Then I made Commissioner, and ever since then, I've been downtown at headquarters." He sighed. "But I miss the simpler days sometimes when you knew who and what you were fighting. Once you get to the top, the game changes, and you never quite know who it is you're up against."

"I know what you mean by that," she said with a wry smile. "When I was just a poor college kid, I'd come back home to Flushing during my breaks, and there was always a sense of calmness, a sort of peace, knowing all the ins and outs of my neighborhood, which parts were safe, which weren't, who ran which section of Flushing. I could always count on the safety of knowing; do you know what I mean?"

James gave a small smile and nodded. "You're a Queens girl, eh?"

"Yes. Born and raised."

There was a fork in the pathway ahead, with the straight portion leading past a small green area with grass and some willow trees, or the left turned towards the river, where a railing guarded people from falling into the river. They took the left path and walked towards the water and the skyline.

"That makes a lot of sense then. You know, there's a lot of rumblings and rumors that you are going to run for the Senate seat here in New York. It ties together." James peered at her from the corner of his eye, to gauge her reaction, but she looked up at the sky, and ignored the comment. James chuckled quietly. They kept walking until they got to the corner, where the pathway made a ninety degree turn to the right once more and continued, following the East river north. But here, they had a vast, unimpeded view of Manhattan. She guessed they were about where forty second street would be in the city, and she could see the United Nations building to the right, somewhere around forty seventh street or thereabouts, way across the water. There was an East River ferry, heading towards the city, having just left its stop here in Long Island City, and the blue and white hull cut a clear path through the calm river current.

"So, you called me the other day, asking about a certain tape from twenty years ago. Can you elaborate?" The Chief of Police looked around before he asked the question, and there were a few folks, such as a jogger, a mom pushing a stroller, and two teenagers laughing as they strolled the wooden boardwalk, but no one that seemed suspicious.

"Yes, I did. Let me be frank with you. I have it on particularly good sources, that you happen to have a video tape of Darbear Markovich, at the time, he went by David Milanovich, where he confesses to raping an underaged girl. I need that video tape, and I'm told that you're just the man who can give it to me." Laura watched his reaction intently, but if she thought that she would see some sort of giveaway, she was wrong. His face was blank, unmoving, and revealed nothing.

He shrugged and blinked once. "I'm not sure what you're

talking about. If such a tape existed, that would mean several things. One, that he is a rapist, and two, that I'm the one hiding the evidence. Why would I do that?" Laura applauded him in her head. He was a cool customer and knew how to bluff with calmness.

"I don't know, James. Maybe, perhaps, there's something on that tape that you don't want the world to see, other than the fact that Darbear raped a girl."

James narrowed his eyes, ever so slightly, and paused to consider her words before answering. "Who is your source?"

"Why does that matter? I know I'm hitting on all the right spots here, Jim."

"It matters, because I can see how credible your source is."

"So you admit there's such a tape then?" she asked.

"I admit to nothing. There's no tape that I'm aware of, but let's hear who your source is. Maybe I can connect the dots on why something like this would even come up."

She shook her head. "No, I'm not going to go back and forth on this. The source doesn't matter. What does matter, is if you have this evidence or not. I think you have it, and you know that I need it. What's it going to take to get it?"

James turned away and stared out towards the city. He looked left, south down the East River towards Brooklyn, and then stared straight ahead, leaning on the metal railing with his elbows as he bent over it. "Let's just make an assumption and assume that such a tape existed. If it did exist, what would you do with it?"

Laura mimicked her guest, and leaned on the railing with her elbows, staring out at the dark brown, blue water. "I'm going to use it to twist Darbear's arm and make him back off this hostile takeover. I'll get it in writing, have the lawyers make it bullet proof, and then hand over this tape. I just need him to back off so that my other plans can fall into place."

James turned his head slightly to peer at her from the corner of his eye. "You see, that's no good for me. I can't have that happen, if such a tape existed," he said softly.

She turned her head to look at him. He was calm, but tense, hands clasped as he leaned over the railing and peered down at her. She knew that this tape implicated him as much as it did Darbear, because it showed that the Chief of Police knew about the rape, helped to cover it up, and had done so over the course of twenty plus years. He would be fired, perhaps even face jail time, but he couldn't let such a tape get out of his control.

"You're on the tape. That's why you can't let it go," she said. "But if this tape could harm you as much as Darbear, why keep it?"

James shook his head slightly. Partly in disgust, partly in defeat. "To protect myself. You don't know what type of enemy Darbear is, Laura. He will go to any lengths to crush his foes. As much damage as this tape would do to me, it was my only safeguard to keep him off my back. He goes down, but I would go down with him. He's not stupid though. He tried to get me to protect him again, for another rape he did, but I wouldn't do it. When he got outraged, I showed him the tape. He managed to somehow bury the noise from that last rape accusation, the files and reports were deleted, and we never spoke to each other ever again. It was an uneasy, unwritten alliance. He knew to steer clear of me, and I knew to do the same. It's been sitting in my files for years, collecting dust, and I never thought it would ever see the light of day. But now, you come asking for it. And my answer is 'no'. I'm sorry, Laura."

Laura frowned. She suspected it would come to this. Afterall, she put herself in his shoes. Would she give away a tape that implicated her as well as her enemy? No. But she had one last card to play. Her trump card, but she wasn't sure how strong it would play. *"Only one way to find out,"* she thought.

"How is Damian doing?" she asked, abruptly changing the topic.

James blinked, but smiled at the thought of his son. "He's doing fine. Just turned nine last week. He doesn't have much energy, as you know, from the thalassemia he's got…but he's doing well. Thanks for asking."

Laura took a breath to steady herself, then plunged the knife. "I'm glad to hear that. You know, it took a lot of effort and using up my political capital to get Damian into the Dana Farber Boston Children's hospital. It would be a shame if I had to unwind that… you know, just a few phone calls here or there."

For the first time since she had known Jim, his face lost its color. "You don't have that kind of power," he whispered.

She nodded. "In fact, I do. I'm on the board at that hospital, Jim. The head of the hospital has ambitions, just like me, and I promised him a big role when I go further in my career. Dana Farber is one of only six hospitals in the U.S. designated for clinical excellence in thalassemia. I can make sure that Damian gets removed from the hospital system, and just a few strings to pull, to make sure that he gets rejected from the other five as well. He'll be back in the system here, in New York. Good hospitals, to be sure, but not among the elite when it comes to rare blood disorders for children. How long do you think he'll live? A year? Two more at most?" She winced inside. This was cruel, even for her she knew. Her ambition knew no bounds.

Jim's lips curled into a snarl as he stood up straight and balled his hands into fists. "You fucking cunt!" he yelled. A jogger turned her head to stare at them as she ran past, and Laura waited for her to disappear before she addressed her friend.

"I want the evidence, Jim. All of it. The video, and whatever else my source said you had on Darbear. Look, he'll back off the takeover, I'll give him the evidence, and it won't see the light of day. He'll be safe, and you'll be safe. Everyone wins. And Damian gets to stay at the hospital where he can get the best care. Don't you want that?"

"You're disgusting. You would jeopardize my son's life so that you can get what you want?" he said with heat in his voice.

"Look in the mirror, Jim. You hid a rapist for twenty plus years, all so that you could climb the ladder yourself and make it to Chief. Isn't that also getting what you wanted? You ruined lives just like I do." She looked at him and waited.

James shook his head and turned to walk away. "Let me think about it. I'll let you know in a day or so," he said.

"Don't wait too long, Jim." She said loudly at his back as he walked back the way they came. She didn't trust him. To her, it sounded like he was just buying some time, to think of another way to outsmart her, so she plowed ahead. Better to push him hard now, right to the edge so that he had to make a quick decision, she decided.

She pulled out her phone, found the contact she was looking for, and dialed the number.

"Doctor Raj Singh, speaking," came the mellow voice on the other end.

"Hey, Raj. It's me, Laura Park. How are you?"

"Laura! Good to hear from you. I'm doing well. The next board meeting isn't for another month or so. Is something up?"

"Yes, something's up. Can you speak privately?" She heard some voices in the background, likely at the hospital.

"One second, let me close the door. Ok, I'm alone. What's up?" he asked seriously.

"Listen. I need a big favor. I'm pulling some strings here, and I need you to contact James O'Malley. He's the father of the boy I had you help to get into the hospital. Damian O'Malley is his son, you remember, the one with-"

"Thalassemia, yes, I remember." Raj was whip smart.

"Yes, he's the one. I need you to call James, and tell him that unfortunately, due to patient and staff circumstances, the hospital can no longer treat his son."

"Wait, what?! I pulled some big strings on my end to get that boy in here, and now you want him out?" he exclaimed.

"No, no. It's just a threat. Keep up with the treatments, but just call the father, keep it short, and say that he'll need to be moved to a hospital in New York. He'll ask why, and what can he do to keep him there. Just tell him that he needs to chat with Laura. He'll know what that means."

"Just that? That he needs to chat with you?" Raj was incredulous but speaking calmly now.

"Yes. I'm painting him in a corner for a favor that I need. Also, I need you to make sure that Damian won't get accepted at any of the other five hospitals that specialize in thalassemia. Put in some preliminary calls, make something up, call in whatever favors you need, but he can't get into those hospitals. Do you understand?" She knew this was a much harder ask.

There was a long pause on the other end. "Laura, that's a big ask. I don't know if I can pull that off…even if I tried, it would require some major favors being called in. What are you offering?"

She smiled. Raj was brilliant, and as ambitious as she was. But she knew how to deal with people like him. Offer him a big reward. "Listen, Raj. I'm going to run for Senator of New York. And after that, I'm going to run for President. When I win, I'm going to nominate you to be Secretary of Health and Human Services. You'll be a Cabinet member."

Another long pause, as Raj calculated the odds and whether this was a good bet to take. "That's a long road, Laura. There's no guarantee you'll win. Why should I burn up my goodwill now, for such a slim chance?"

"Secretary of Health and Human Services, Raj. I know you want that job. Do you have any other horses you can ride in this race? I'm going to win, and you'll get that Cabinet position. Trust me, I don't lose," she said confidently, although inside, she was much less sure. It *was* a long road, and she hadn't yet started.

"Hm, ok. I'll call James, and get your message across, then make some calls to the other five hospitals. I'll see to it that Damian can't get admitted there. But you owe me, Laura. I want a guarantee."

"You'll have it in writing from my team, and I'll send you a copy of the guarantee."

"Done. Talk to you soon." He hung up.

Laura exhaled with a sigh of relief. James would try to see what he could do, but once he found out that Laura had been true to her word, he would be forced to make a hard choice. Go down with the ship and move Damian back to New York, or hand over the evidence and keep his son at Dana Farber. She didn't know which way he would jump, but time would tell. She decided to keep walking, and she strolled down the wooden boardwalk towards the north end, with Manhattan to her left, and Long

Island City to her right. There were kids, moms with strollers, joggers, and other people just casually walking like she was. The boardwalk was nice, with smooth wooden planks that had yet to be worn down by time and nature. Eventually, she made her way to where the iconic Pepsi sign was located. It was huge, maybe ten feet tall by fifty or sixty feet wide. The sign read Pepsi Cola, in red cursive letters, and a huge Pepsi cola bottle cut out hung askance to the right of the letters. At night, the letters shone in bright red, illuminating the night sky, such that when you were driving on the FDR in Manhattan and looking east, one could easily see the sign. It was a landmark now, one of many in New York City. Behind the sign, were tall residential condo buildings, where folks who wanted more space for their dollar made their way from Manhattan living to Queens living. There were wooden benches that lined the boardwalk here, with the benches facing Manhattan and the Pepsi sign behind them, so she sat down at an empty bench and admired the view.

She was thinking about how to use the video tape, assuming she would get it, when her phone rang. It was her girlfriend. Things had been tense around the apartment ever since dinner at Gabriel Kruether's. Gale had been touchy, and short with her answers whenever they spoke in the apartment, and they hardly even spent much time together, as Gale cited the need to work late at the office. Laura almost let the call go to voicemail but decided at the last second to answer it.

"Hey, babe," she said softly. Gale was the only girlfriend she had ever fallen in love with, and she knew that relationships like these didn't come around that often. Whatever their disagreements were, surely, they could overcome them.

"Hey. I've been thinking a lot. About our last conversation

about the video tape. And about us too," Gale started. Laura tensed up subconsciously. This had all the beginnings of a breakup phone call.

"Yes?"

"And…I want to get back to how things used to be. I don't like how we are now, all tense and short with each other. This isn't who we are." Laura breathed a sigh of relief. It wasn't a breakup. Yet.

"Me too. I'm really glad you called to say that. I've been thinking about us a lot lately, and you're the only person, aside from my mom, that I've ever really loved," Laura said quietly.

"I love you too. And I know what kind of person you are. You're strong, ambitious, kind, funny, and you do the right thing. Which is why it's important for me to say, that when you get the tape of Darbear… I mean if you get it…you have to turn in the evidence. I know you'll do that. For you. For me. Because *it's the right thing to do*." Gale stressed the last sentence and stopped, waiting for Laura's reply. What could she say to that? She wasn't a good person. She didn't always do the right thing. Playing by the rules and obeying the rules and standards that these men set, that got her nowhere. She was making up her own rules now, and she was thriving. Who said that she couldn't bend the rules anyway?

"I love you. And I'm so grateful for you in my life," was the only thing she could think to say. "I'll see you at home for dinner tonight, ok?" When Gale hung up, Laura's stomach twisted inside. She didn't want to disappoint her partner, and let her see the ugly, ambitious, do anything to win side of her, but she didn't know how to appease both Gale, and the hungry demon inside of her. The one that wanted to win at all costs, who would do anything to get to the pinnacle. She thought about how much Gale meant to her, and how much she loved her. There was no one else who came close to fulfilling her like Gale did.

"I can get this tape, turn it over to someone in the police department who will take action on it, and Darbear will move ahead with his takeover and oust me. Then I can run for Senator and still have Gale. Even Mary said I could do all the social changes that I wanted to do, as a Senator. I don't need to be President," she thought wistfully. *"That's the right play."* Her mind made up, she got up from the bench and made her way back to the office.

24

Leverage

When Laura walked into the office the next day, she felt nervous. Raj had called her last night and confirmed that he had been able to pull some strings, and now Damian O'Malley would have no chance of getting into any of the other five hospitals that specialized in thalassemia. Raj had also called James, and he relayed that James had been angry, and menacing on the phone, but Raj simply directed him to call Laura. Now, it was just a waiting game to see if James would follow through or not. He had to decide if his career, or his son, was more important to him. She found out around noon.

"Laura, there's a package here for you. Came by courier delivery," said Geoff, as he walked into her office and placed a large manilla envelop on her desk.

"Thank you, Geoff," she said as she turned the envelope over in her hand. It was rather plain, and there was no return address. She used a pair of scissors from her desk drawer to cut it open and poured the contents out onto her desk. There was a handwritten note, and a USB flash drive, nothing else. She read the note first.

Call me when you get this.

That was it. No signature, no greeting, nothing else. She put the flash drive in her computer and clicked it open. There was one video file in there, and when she saw that it was a video extension, her heart started to race. She double clicked it, and waited for it to load, mouth slightly open in anticipation.

There. The footage was a little grainy, as it was from technology from twenty years ago, but there was no mistaking Darbear's face, and voice, as she heard him talk with a much younger looking James. She sat in rapt attentiveness, as Darbear laughed, and then mocked James, acknowledging the rape, and then threatening James to do his bidding. To James' credit, he was infuriated, and vowed never to help this man again. She rewound it and watched it again. Then one more time, for good measure. It was clear, and unmistakable. This was Darbear Markovich, even though he was younger, a jury would be able to see the match. Bingo. She had thought her mind was made up, but seeing the video made it real, and she changed her mind.

She picked up her cell phone and made the call.

"Yeah?" came the curt greeting.

"I got it. Thank you. Trust me, Darbear won't let this see the light of day, so you're safe," she said, as she oozed gracefulness. It was like the tone of a mother cooing to her toddler, that everything would be ok, and the bad guys would stay out at night.

"Damian stays at Dana Farber hospital. For as long as I need it," said James coldly. He had probably reached out to the other five hospitals to test her and see if she had as much pull as she intimated and found that she did.

"Of course. Damian will continue to get the absolute best care in the world, and I'll personally see to it that all of the best doctors see him round the clock." She pulled out her notebook and scribbled a note. *Call Raj, Damian to stay.*

"There's one other thing. After this Darbear business gets snuffed, we're through. I no longer help you, and you forget we ever knew each other," he said in a gruff and angry tone. But Laura was not one to forgive and forget so easily, and she let him know who was running the show here in New York.

"Tsk, tsk, James. You refused my hand the first time around, and only came around today. I won't forget that. Damian stays at Dana Farber at my beck and call. I crook a finger, and he's out of there. So, don't act like you have any leverage here, James. You should have helped me from the get-go. I'll be in touch if I need anything. Until then, be well." She hung up and made another note in her book. *Have Geoff send a huge gift basket to James O'Malley, with my thanks.* With one hand she cracked the whip, with the other she soothed the scars.

"*Time to swim the sharks. Let's see who's the biggest shark in New York City,*" she breathed quietly to herself. She opened up her email, searched for the contact info, and then dialed it into her desk phone.

"Solenium Private Equity, Mr. Markovich's office, how may I direct your call?" came the sweet voice on the other end of the line.

"I need to speak with Darbear, is he available?" she asked.

Although her voice was calm and strong, inside, she was a touch nervous. Today would bring clarity to her future, and although she felt that she held all the right cards, she was unsure if Darbear would cave, or tell her to go F herself. He might feel like the videotape wouldn't hold up in a court of law, or that he could drag the case on for years and leave the U.S. if things got dire. Who knows?

"May I ask who is calling?" asked the young admin. She sounded like she was in her early twenties.

"Tell him that Laura Park is calling, and I have an offer for him that I think he'll want to hear."

"One moment." She clicked the 'play' button on her computer one more time, and while the video ran, she used her cell phone to take a video recording of the video playing on her computer.

"Hello, Laura! Is good you called me, yes? Been enough time for you to come to your senses. You finally agree to my terms, eh?" Darbear chuckled loudly and snickered. "You didn't put up as much of a fight as I thought. Your reputation is embellished, I think."

"I have a video of you, given to me by James O'Malley. You know him, right? Chief of Police?" she asked nonchalantly. There was silence on the other end of the line. A pause, and she could almost hear the gears turning in his head, all the way across the phone connection as he struggled to gather if she was talking about *the* video. The one that James had hidden years ago, which Darbear knew existed, but had almost forgotten about. Until today.

"Meet me in Central Park in thirty minutes. Right at the entrance to Heckscher playground. I'll let you see the video tape, and we'll talk business." She hung up the phone without waiting for his reply and looked at her watch. She knew his offices were in midtown east, and it would take about twenty minutes or so for him to get to the Park, plenty of time for him and for her. She stood up, grabbed her cell phone, her coat, and then headed for the door As she exited, she saw Geoff glance up at her with one eyebrow raised.

"Um, you have Jennifer in a few minutes -" but she cut him off.

"Tell Jennifer I need to move our meeting. Move it to the afternoon. In fact, clear my whole morning. If you need me, text is the best way. I'm going to an offsite meeting, back in about two hours or so. Oh, and can you lock up this flash drive in your file cabinet? Tuck it under the folders and put it way in the back, top drawer, ok?" She waited for Geoff's quizzical acknowledgement, then gave him a smile and briskly walked towards the elevator bank. She knew that Geoff would do as she instructed.

When she got to street level, she took a right turn and then quickly crossed the street so that she was right on the sidewalk lining Central Park. It would be faster to walk on this side of the street, instead of having to navigate the crosswalks on the other side. She had walked hundreds of times through Central Park, and she knew that walking to Hecksher playground from her office would take about fifteen minutes. She walked with determination, and at a moderate pace, but her mind was racing a thousand miles a minute as she envisioned how her meeting with Darbear would go. *"Will he bite and take my deal? He has to, right? He can't let this tape get out to the police. Or will he chance it and simply leave the country? If he goes to Eastern Europe, can the United States even extradite him back here?"* She didn't know how strongly Darbear feared the evidence on the tape, but the fact that he hadn't called her back to refuse the meeting meant something.

"Or will he simply not show up and then laugh at me over the phone?"
Darbear was a multimillionaire, worth several hundreds of
millions of dollars. If he wanted to live a life on the run, he could
do that, and comfortably. But his reputation would be tarnished,
and he would never be able to step foot inside the United States
again without facing the consequences of an arrest warrant.
*"James and Larry seemed to indicate that this was a pattern of his, and that
there were others after this tape. Yet, Darbear has managed to keep it squeaky
clean, and nothing has come to the light of day, so that must mean that he
does care about being accused. He does want to be free from accusation and
jail time, is my guess."* She was unsure, but inside, she decided to
assume that this tape would be especially important for Darbear,
and she made up her mind to play it as if it were a winning trump
card. There was no other way. If he laughed at her and said it was
useless, she would have no leverage, and it would be game over.

She passed by a hot dog cart, and although she disliked street
food in general, her mouth nevertheless watered at the smell of
hot dogs and pretzels. The sun was shining brightly in the
morning, and the oak trees planted in the sidewalk were green
with leaves. The familiar green wooden benches on her left were
mostly empty, although she did see a few people parked on them,
either reading a newspaper or sipping a cup of coffee. The
buildings on her right, across the street, were mostly brown or
red brick residential coops, prewar, she knew. Almost all of them
were manned by doormen and concierge, and despite the age of
the buildings, she knew they would fetch a lofty price, simply for
the fact that they were right across the street from the park. When
she reached 64th street, and the Ethical Culture School, with its
red brick façade lined by white stone, she saw the opening that
she wanted to take into the park itself. There were green benches

on the left side to the entrance, where an elderly couple were sitting down, munching on bagels. She walked into the park, onto the black asphalt pathway, and followed the meandering path generally heading south, and east. There were gray squirrels aplenty, foraging for food and hardly moving at all when she walked within a few feet past them. New York City squirrels were the boldest and bravest of all, she noted for the hundredth time.

Heckscher playground was Central Park's first, and also largest playground. It spanned almost two acres, and was built in 1927, named after a real estate tycoon and philanthropist who had a fondness for children's causes. Laura remembered her mom bringing here on special occasions, like when she got all As on her report card, or if she had a day off from school. They would hop on the seven train in Flushing, take the forty-five minute ride into Manhattan, then transfer at Times Square onto the A or C line, riding it up to Columbus circle. She remembered being in awe every time she came up the steps at Columbus circle, seeing the flurry of yellow cabs flying around the circle, hearing the murmurs and laughter of people talking as they walked past, and seeing the bright colors of people's clothes. When she was little, she wore hand me downs and whatever her mom could afford out of the goodwill or thrift stores, and her mom typically picked drab blue, grey, or black clothes that fit her size. Rarely did she ever get anything vibrantly colored, and so it amazed and delighted her to no end, seeing women dressed sharply in red, yellow, and greens as they either headed to work, school, or just out and about. She remembered pleading for sweets or a treat inside one of the shops inside the Time Warner center, but she also remembered her mom always sadly shaking her head 'no' when she asked. They couldn't afford extras like treats. They could go inside and look and browse, but inevitably, they never bought anything. After window shopping, or 'eye shopping' as her mom called it, they would cross 59th street and enter the park, eventually making their way to this very playground. At first, she always happily entered and played for as long as her mom would let her, often begging her mom to stay 'just a little longer'. But as she got older, and just as she was entering the phase of not really enjoying these childlike playgrounds anyway, she became self-aware and self-conscious when she came here with her mom. She must have been around eleven years old, and even then, her mom was still not very well off. She knew, even at that young age, that there was a gap between her and the other kids. Whereas her clothes had threadbare spots or patches where her mom stitched up holes, the other kids were neatly outfitted in GAP, Carters, or other nice-looking clothes.

"Ok! Ga-ja! Ka-suh nol-luh wah," her mom said, during the last time they came here. *Go play.* Only, she didn't budge. She just stared at the entrance and looked away.

"Wheh-gu-reh?" *What's the matter.*

"Umma. I don't want to play. I'm too old for this place," she said quietly. Her eyes darted furtively at the put together mom in yoga pants and blue t-shirt, wearing a gold bangle bracelet and pushing a Bugaboo stroller into the entrance.

"Uh!? You love this place. This is for getting good grades, that's why we came here!" her mom had said in Korean. She was dressed in a sturdy but tired looking blue pea coat, found in the goodwill store. Her hair was cut short, straight, and just above her ears, and she looked old. Wrinkles had set in around the corners of her eyes, and small brown sunspots had just started to appear on her face. They would only get bigger and more pronounced as she aged. Her mom had been carrying a worn-out brown purse, with the buckle broken so that it no longer latched closed, and she remembered feeling ashamed right then. Ashamed that they were poor. Ashamed that she had no father. Ashamed for feeling ashamed.

"Can we just walk around the park and then go home?" she had whined pathetically. Maybe her mom sensed something in her daughter. Or maybe she just didn't want to push and prod that day. Either way, her mom had sighed, and they had walked around for half an hour, then made the long trek back. That was the last time she had been here. Until today.

The entrance to the playground was a small red brick building, with beige or cream-colored stone pillars that guarded the opening into the playground. The same cream-colored paint wrapped around the eaves of the building, wrapping around the top section of the structure. Bathrooms for men and women were on either side of the building, and there was the same green park bench off to the left-hand side. A Hispanic man had a bucket full of balloons tied to a plastic stick. He was selling them for eight dollars each, and extended one to her, hopefully, but she shook her head and instead sat down on the bench. On the right-hand side, another Hispanic man was manning a cart, which was selling popsicles, ice cream, and juice boxes. Being a weekday, she didn't expect to see many kids, but to her surprise, there were a handful of kids already inside, playing, and she watched several more kids being pushed in strollers by what she guessed were nannies. Most of the kids were young, maybe up to three years old, so she assumed that they were too young to be in school. The bench she sat on was shaded by trees, and she was grateful for the shade as she glanced anxiously at her phone and waited. Finally, after about fifteen minutes, he showed up. Darbear Markovich.

He was dressed in a suit, but no tie. It was a black suit and tapered to fit snugly around his lean frame. He had a presence about him. An aura, like when a commanding officer walks into a room full of subordinates and everyone takes notice and straightens up. His hair was graying, as she remembered, and even for his age, he still looked roguishly handsome. His eyes narrowed as he spotted her, and he tilted his head to follow her, as he walked through the pillars and into the playground itself. Emerging through the building and onto the other side, she smiled as a wave of nostalgia swept over her. It had been thirty plus years since she had stepped foot inside. Looking to her left and up at the sky, she could see tall buildings over the treetops, and the Essex House sign in red letters. That would be 59th street she knew. Straight ahead, was a wide, circular patch of fake grass, where a couple toddlers were running around, oblivious to the gravity of her situation. There were swings and a slide on the left, a raised concrete maze like structure ahead of her with more slides, and a sand pit and water splash pad area to the right. Darbear looked around, and then veered to the right, towards the sand pit area, where he found an empty green bench and sat down. He didn't look at her as she calmly took a seat on his left.

"It's amazing, eh? This playground, right inside Central Park. You know how much this land would be worth, if one could buy it and develop it into buildings? But no. Just used for simple kids to play in. Unbelievable." He shook his head with disgust.

"There's more to life than just money, Darbear. Everything is not just a transaction or opportunity for you to make money. This playground, and the park, brings joy and recreation for millions. I used to play here myself when I was a child," she said softly. She watched a young boy, about two years old, fly off the slide and land on his butt in the sand, and stunned by the result, took a couple seconds before he decided that it was worth crying over.

"Joy?" he scoffed. "What good is joy? It's *always* about money. Money, and power. You know this. That is why we are sitting here. And so, tell me, what is it that we are sitting here for?" he demanded as he finally turned to stare at her. His eyes were piercing and cold, and she knew many a man or woman had withered under that haughty, calculating, and ruthless gaze. But not her. Not this woman.

"I have it, Darbear. The video. The one where you confess to raping the young underaged girl."

"Show me," he said sternly.

She pulled out her phone, and quickly brought up the short video recording of her monitor and played it for him. Darbear's eyes were steady, but there was just a second where he blinked his eyes quickly, and then recovered. It was him. It was the video.

"How did you get this?" he asked, his voice tight with anger and eyebrows furrowed in concentration.

"It doesn't matter how I got it. We both know who was in charge of it, but let's just say that I forcefully got it into my possession. I own the only copy now," she said, without a hint of smugness. She knew men like Darbear. Push them too far, taunt them too much, and they would burn everyone and everything around them, just to see it burn, even if it meant burning himself. Better to ease him into the decision she wanted, rather than strong arming him, even though that was what she was doing.

"Fucking O'Malley," he muttered under his breath. "So now what? How much do you want for it?" He glared outright now, a half snarl on the left side of his mouth.

"I think you know, Darbear. It's not going to come cheap," she said.

"You want me to sell my shares, back off the takeover," he huffed.

"That's right. And there's more for you to do, in order to get the tape."

He scowled and cursed at her. "What the fuck? Fuck you, there is more. What more?"

She gave him a sweet smile. "A political donation. Three million dollars for when I run for the Senate. Another ten-million-dollar donation for when I run for President."

For the first time that she could recall, his eyes widened in surprise. "You're fucking nuts. You? Run for President?"

"Think about it, Darbear. We don't have to be enemies. I'm going to win the Senate seat. You'll have an ally in the Senate, and I'll add another rich and powerful ally in the business world. One hand washes the other. You said it yourself. Money, and power. Just think what happens if I actually win the Presidency. Think of the favors you could ask of me, and which I will help you with."

He leaned back and stared at her from the corner of his eye, re-measuring his opponent. It was not the first time she had seen this look. The one that said, *Goddamn. I underestimated you, you fucking bitch.* She had seen it in business school. In investment banking, in consulting, at Abernathy, and now, here, in Hecksher playground.

"I do this, and I get the tape. How do I know you won't make a copy of it?" he asked, but with no heat this time. He was considering new opportunities. One that now included Laura as a future ally.

"You won't know for sure. But let's draft up a contract. Let's get this in writing, have it signed, and I'll give you the tape. What's it gonna be, Darbear? Are we friends, or enemies? How badly do you want me out? If we're enemies, I'll still run for the Senate, and I'll still have the tape…" she trailed off. No need to explicitly say what she would do with the tape, which would be bad for him.

He pursed his lips once again, and looked at her, deep in thought. Finally, he stood up, and she stood up with him.

"Draft up the contract and have it sent to my office for my attorneys to review. Just say that in exchange for one videotape, contents of which are not detailed here, Mr. Markovich will donate three million and ten million to whatever cause Ms. Park deems appropriate, with an expiration date of six years." He straightened his jacket and looked at her one final time.

"I was right. It's always about money, and power," he said, and he walked away, heading for the exit of the playground. But he stopped suddenly and turned to say one last thing.

"By the way. You should re-think exactly who your allies are."

"What do you mean?" she asked cautiously.

"You know. Adam, sending him to me. He spilled his guts voluntarily from the first meeting I had with him. Offered to switch sides if I made him a sweeter deal." He grinned, and this time, he walked out for good, leaving her much to think about.

She waited for him to leave, and then, exhaled a sigh of relief. She had done it. She had won. It cost her soul, but she had won. *"But maybe I had lost my soul long ago. Maybe it can't be chalked down to this day, could it?"* She honestly didn't know. And it didn't matter at this moment. Slowly, she walked around the playground, happy, but at the same time, a little bit sad. She found herself in front of the swings, which were atop a mulch ground so as to cushion any falls. She saw a woman pushing a little girl on one of the swings, and for a moment, she thought it was her mom and did a double take. But it was just a Korean woman pushing a girl. The woman was wearing a nice sweater, blue, and her daughter was giggling with glee as she soared up to the sky and back down again. Smiling sadly, Laura went inside and sat down on the far end on one of the empty swings. She stepped back several steps, and then let fly, swinging on a set meant for little kids. And in that moment, she was just Laura Park again, not the power hungry, conniving, and brash businesswoman that people knew her as.

25

Loose Ends

It took about a week to get everything in order, but finally, she was ready. Her attorneys had drafted up the contract for Darbear, and he had countersigned it. She had made a copy of the tape, but sent him the original, although she lied and told him that there were no other copies. You never knew when it could come in handy again. When she had received the final contract, she gave Darbear a call, and they had chatted for about thirty minutes. She then put Samuel and his team to work around the clock erasing any traces of her illicit activities within Abernathy. Laura's personal attorneys had also been hard at work. Today, all loose ends would be tied.

In her personal life, things had gotten back to normal, for the most part. She hadn't told Gale yet about getting the tape and aligning herself with Darbear, but that would come later. They had apologized, patched things up, and this week had been blissful. Lots of snuggles and kisses, laughter, and joy, and she had soaked up every minute of it, for she knew that all good things must come to an end.

She heard voices talking outside her door, some laughter, and she looked at her watch. Nine a.m., right on the dot. He always had been punctual.

There was a knock and the door opened. Geoff, Jennifer, and Adam walked in, all of them smiling, as thick as thieves.

"Look what the cat dragged in!" said Jennifer loudly with a genuine smile. "He returns! The stealthy assassin, from his secret mission." Jennifer was dressed sharply, as usual.

"Laura, as you can see, your nine o'clock is here," said Geoff. He had on a dark blue blazer with gold buttons, light blue shirt with silver cufflinks, and charcoal slacks to go with his black Ferragamo's. "Oh, and just a reminder-" he started, but she cut him off.

"Yes, yes. I remember. You're heading out early today to head to the Hamptons. Just text me when you're leaving so that I know to answer my own phone line," she said with mock exasperation. It was all he had been talking about for the whole week.

He smiled sheepishly and ducked out, partially closing the door.

"Hey, Laura, I'm not early, am I?" asked Adam. He was dressed in a black suit with white pinstripes, an off-white shirt, and a red Hermes tie, a power color. *"He wants to project power, huh?"* she mused to herself. His brown hair was longer than usual and swept back neatly with a slight undulating waviness to it. He looked like a young Christian Bale, with the same sharp and angular facial features.

"No, you're right on time."

"Hey Adam, good to see you. See you at lunch, alright?" said Jennifer. She gave Adam another pat on the shoulder and left the room, closing the door behind him.

"Come on over. Good to see you, Adam," she said as she stood up and waited for him to walk to her, extending her hand to give a firm handshake. Adam smiled, shook her hand, and took the seat opposite her at her desk.

"I forgot how amazing the views from your office are," Adam said with admiration. "Much better than what we had at Chase."

She smiled. "Yes, thank you. You know, I always admired these views myself, back when John was still here. I always dreamed of having this office, you know."

"Yes, I remember."

"Right. So. You asked to see me this week. It's your show. How can I help you?" she said warmly.

Adam cleared his throat. "Well, first of all, I want to apologize for how I behaved when I left and went over to join Darbear's banking team. I shouldn't have taken his offer, and I shouldn't have divulged key strategies to his team that helped them in their negotiations. That was the wrong thing to do, and after a lot of thought and deliberation, I just firstly wanted to apologize." He waited expectantly for her reaction.

She pursed her lips into a thin line. "That was a shock. I was extremely disappointed in you, Adam. You know how much I trusted you, and you betrayed me."

"I know. It was a horrible thing to do, but I know now, that I shouldn't have done that. In fact, that brings me to the second thing, and the reason why I'm here. I quit Darbear's team. I gave up everything, and I wanted to see if you could find it in your heart to forgive me, and bring me back on here, under you." He sat up even straighter and looked at her hopefully.

She decided to let him squirm a little bit. "What do you mean, you quit?"

He shifted slightly in his seat. "I quit. I decided that I was on the wrong side of history, and I told Darbear that I can't in good conscious, continue on his team. So, I wanted to make amends, and see if you would re-hire me again."

She nodded slowly, one eyebrow raised. "I see. And what role do you see yourself coming back to? Surely, not as a promotion to Vice President? And surely, the agreement we had about you getting to be a BU head someday, that is off the table too, right?"

There was a faint, but barely noticeable sheen on his forehead now, as he started to sweat slightly.

"Well, I think you're right, that the BU head is probably off the table. But even the Vice President role...?" his voice tapered off.

"Adam. You screwed me over, remember?" she said softly.

Clearly, he was expecting her to say more, but when she didn't, he cleared his throat again and back pedaled. "Of course. I would be happy to resume my role here as before, senior director. That would be fine."

She smiled slightly, to give him hope, and it worked, as he the outlines of a smile started to blossom on his face as well.

"Adam, I'm afraid not." The color that vanished from his face and the drop of the corners of his mouth as his smile faded were priceless.

"You see, I talked to Darbear. Yes. Several times this week, in fact. I know that it was you who volunteered to switch sides. I know everything. That you were fired this week, and that Darbear put a hold on his payments to you, so that you haven't gotten any of the millions that he promised you. That he terminated you with no severance, and that you are crawling on your belly, back to me, to ask for a job. And you know what? I made Darbear do all those things to you. Now, why would I ever welcome you back, Adam?"

Adam's eyes were getting bigger and bigger with each word, and his mouth was agape now. "What? How....?" His voice was steady, but she could see that he was visibly shaken. "I have a contract, that you signed, saying that you'll re-hire me," he finally managed to say.

"I know. And I had my attorney's pore over that contract, every word. And it says in an iron clad guarantee, that should I still be employed here at Abernathy Consumer Products, that I will in fact re-hire you. But, very soon, I'm going to be resigning. I have other things to do, Adam."

His face was pale now, and he blinked several times.

"By the time your lawyers and my lawyers argue and finally get a court date months from now, I'll have resigned. That contract doesn't hold, Adam. I don't owe you anything." She gave him a smile. A pearly, white, sharp, toothy grin.

He sat up, and now the color had somewhat returned to his face. His expression was blank, and he was now trying to play poker. "I know things, Laura," he started with a low guttural voice. "I know about your slush fund here, and all the payoffs and things you use that account for. I can blow the whistle on you."

She laughed, and the laughter caught him by surprise as he leaned slightly back in his seat.

"Adam. I'm way ahead of you. You see, I have experts on my team, really, really good technical experts, who wiped away any traces of that, and any connection to me. It's gone, my friend.

There is no account here that you're referring to. You could have a team of auditors here, tomorrow, going through every account here in the company, and they won't find a thing. Nothing out of the ordinary. So, go ahead. They'll find nothing, and you'll be in the media as a whistle blower who got it all wrong. See who will hire you then."

His stunned expression almost made her give pause. Almost, but she was Laura Park. Nothing could stop her now.

"I lost it all. I gave up my stock options here, my position, everything. And Darbear didn't give me any of the money he promised. I did this for you," he lamented softly.

"You did this to yourself," she said harshly. "You messed with the wrong woman, and you picked the wrong side." She stood up, grabbed her notebook, and walked to the door, opening it, where security was standing outside.

"Geoff, please have security escort Adam downstairs." She didn't wait for Geoff's embarrassed nod, as she left for the elevator bank. Geoff and Jennifer had both known what she was going to do, and she had made them pretend to be nice to Adam. It made digging the knife in that much sweeter.

Eight p.m., and she was right on time for a change. She told the hostess that she had a reservation, and the hostess smiled and said, "Your other party member is already here. Follow me, please." Daniel, a high-end French restaurant on 65th between Park and Madison, was one of her all-time favorite restaurants. The service was impeccable, the presentation stunning, and the food was to die for. She and Gale had celebrated their one-year anniversary here, some years ago, and they regularly came back when they wanted to celebrate something special. The dining room was bathed in a warm ambiance, with an off-white paint over the elaborately sculpted and carved ceiling and walls, a soft yellow light from the wall sconces, and a reddish brown rug with oval patterns that interlocked. The tables had white tablecloth, and the chairs were oak, stained brown, with a muted red leather backing. The room was nearly full, even for a Monday night. She saw Gale wave to her from one of the tables off to the left.

"Here we are. Someone will be with you shortly. Enjoy your meal!" said the hostess with a smile.

Laura sat down and gave Gale a smile. She soaked in every last detail. Her blond hair was pulled back into a ponytail, but a stray wisp of hair had escaped and was dangling over her left eyebrow. Her blue eyes were twinkling in the candlelight, and as always, there was a hint of a smile on the corners of her lips, as she was always quick to laugh or smile. She wore a white merino sweater, and black pants, but no jewelry. She had a little blush on her cheeks, but that was about it. Gale, in general, didn't really wear much makeup. In short, she was beautiful, and she wanted to always remember her this way, today.

"Hey, babe. Wow, you're actually on time. Can't believe it. No traffic?" Gale teased playfully, as she opened up her menu.

"I know. I was thinking the same thing as I walked in, that I was actually on time for a change. You look beautiful..." Laura said softly.

"Oh! Thanks! You know, you're the second person to hit on me today. Remember that guy, Finn? He said the same to me today, and then hinted that he wanted to take me out. But, I deflected, you know, with my usual cool banter...hey. What's wrong?" Gale put her menu down and leaned forward a bit, concern in her eyes.

"You always know what my mood is. I love that about you," Laura said wistfully.

"Yeah…and…you're in a funky mood. What's up?" Gale reached forward and held her hand. Laura grasped it instinctively and squeezed it, hard.

"Hey. I have something I need to tell you. You know how things have been so hectic at the office, and I told you I couldn't really say much?" She waited for Gale's nod. "Well, I can tell you, finally. The whole Darbear situation, it worked itself out."

"That's great news! What happened?" Gale exclaimed excitedly. Laura felt sad inside, seeing how happy Gale was, knowing that she would be crushed here in a second.

"Well, I got the video tape evidence of him. You know, the one I told you about?" Gale's smile froze, and then slipped away. She felt Gale's hand pull away from hers, and all she felt now, was the tablecloth.

"The tape with him confessing to the rape?" Gale whispered. "You didn't give it to the police, did you? You leveraged it to turn him onto your side, is that it?"

Laura took a deep breath. "Yes. I did that. And I'm going to be honest here. I did it because I'm selfish. Because I'm tired of playing by the rules, working hard, trying to move up in the world, but barely advancing. I did it because I wanted to win, at all costs. And I did it. I beat them at their game, see?"

Gale's eyebrows were furrowed together, and she saw something that would haunt her for eternity. Disappointment.

"How could you do that, Laura? I mean, seriously. You blackmailed someone, to get to the top. So what? What about the poor girl who was raped? What about her justice, her feelings, her game? You're going to let this rapist get away scot free. Answer me!" Laura blinked several times, and saw the heat, and the anger in Gale's face. She had never seen her so angry. It hurt her.

"It was the only way I could win," she said quietly. "Turning it over to the police…I would have been ousted anyways, no matter what happened to Darbear. This way, I can move up, and I can do better things. You'll see. When I win the Senate seat-"

"I don't give a fuck about your Senate seat!" shouted Gale. Several diners turned to stare at them, and Laura made a calming motion with her hands, pleading with Gale to tone it down.

"You let a rapist go free, Laura. How dare you!" said Gale, at a normal conversation level of loudness.

"I know you can't understand, and I know you will never forgive me-" she started to say.

"You're damn right! I am so shocked and disappointed in you. I just…I just can't even bring up the words to say how disappointed I am right now."

"I know. I knew this would happen." Laura stood up. She wanted to caress Gale's cheek, one last time, but she didn't think Gale would let her, so she didn't try. "Goodbye, Gale. I love you. I'll always love you." She turned but felt Gale's hand grasp her wrist.

"I'm going to come after this story, Laura. I'm going to investigate it and make sure the truth comes out," said Gale, her eyes cold.

"Do what you must. You won't find anything," she promised somberly. She pulled her wrist free, and turned away, closing one chapter of her life.

26

Daughter of Queens

One year later...

"How does it look? Is the pin on straight or crooked?" Laura asked, as she bent her neck downwards to try and peer at the United States flag pin that was pinned to her dress. It was positioned just above her heart, and she could make it out, but couldn't tell if it was straight or not.

"Fuck's sake, Laura. Stop fidgeting. It's straight, for the umpteenth time," mumbled Stacy with annoyance. She was using a lint roller to pick up any last-minute stray specks of dandruff or hair from her dark blue dress. The dress was modest, with a high neckline, and long hem that went to just below her knees. It was custom made, with long sleeves that had just a touch of white lace at the wrists, and large black buttons that ran up the front, single file. She tried to peer over Stacy's shoulder at the wall mirror to catch a glimpse of herself, but couldn't see much, and so she just sighed and stopped fidgeting, as instructed.

"What's the schedule again?" she asked absentmindedly, although she already knew it by heart. Hearing it from Stacy though, would ease her mind.

"Rally at five p.m., so that's in thirty minutes. We're ahead in the polls, by a fairly wide margin, so we're expecting a call from Senator Thorpe, by six p.m. or so, announcing that he is acknowledging defeat and congratulating you on your victory. Either way, we have a call with Fox News at five thirty, followed by a call with CNBC news at six p.m. That call has to end by six fifteen sharp, as we are having drinks and appetizers with constituents at the gantries over by the LIC library. That's being catered by your business friend, Jonas Friedman, so make sure you spend some time chatting with him, as he specifically asked to speak to you about a private matter, and this was the only way he could get on your calendar," said Stacy with a smirk. She tilted Laura's head up, pressing one finger under her chin, then tilted her head left and right to check for makeup smudges.

"That's because Jonas is a chauvinistic jerk, and I refused to meet with him unless he organized a fundraiser and then host tonight's mixer," she said wryly, but with no real anger. He *was* a jerk, but an ambitious one who played a dirty game. She knew how to deal with him, and Stacy knew just how much she disliked him.

"Right. So, drinks go on til eight p.m., and we should be in victory mode by then. We have calls setup with the Mayor of New York, and the Governor. Assuming we've won by that point, we're going to head to the Jacobs Javits center to join the rest of the Democratic party over there, and you'll do a short speech from the podium there. That will be broadcast live, and we have your speech ready on notecards, the one from last night."

"Assuming we've won?" came a loud voice from behind her. She turned and saw her campaign manager, Mary, striding into the room. "I can read the tea leaves quite well, especially this far in. There's no need to assume at this point. My team and I have done the analysis, and there's no way he can catch up at this point. You're looking at the next Senator of New York," Mary said with a smile. She was dressed in a loose-fitting black pants, and light blue sweater. She had a pearl necklace on, but that was it. Her hair was straight and hung down to just below her ears, and the crow's feet around her eyes creased as she smiled at her.

"There. All set. Don't touch your face, and please, do not touch your hair. At. All. Got it?" asked Stacy sternly. Laura's hair had grown longer since the last year, and it now hung almost to the middle of her back. It was straight, and black, and pulled back by an elegant hair pin right around the back of her neck. There had been a heated debate last night on whether to pull it into a bun, to look older, or to keep it loose and down, to look younger and more modern. Modern had won out.

"Yes, yes. I got it. What else? Where's Greg?" she asked Mary.

"Greg is already at the gym," said Mary calmly. The rally was being held at the school gymnasium of P.S. 122, up in Astoria, just a short ride from Flushing. "He's looking dapper, and handsome as ever. He's mingling with the crowd, getting them excited for your arrival."

Laura gave a wan smile. Greg was good with people and had that effect of inspiring immediate trust when you spoke to him. He had grown up in Georgia, in a wealthy family, but despite that, poor people and immigrants gravitated to him and loved him, by all reports from Mary. She had done well in screening him and matching him up with Laura. He was ambitious too and recognized her rising star. He also loved Asian women, as Mary had noted, and so it wasn't that hard to kindle a romance with him. They had dated for about eight months, then got engaged. They planned to get married in the spring, after she had won the Senate seat. At first, her mom had been skeptical, as Greg was black and her mom just hadn't known many black people, but his charm and gentle manners quickly won her over.

"Alright. Town car is outside?" asked Mary.

"Yes. Gassed up, driver's ready, and knows where to take you. Mary and I will follow you in another vehicle, right behind you," said Stacy.

"Wait. Actually, can you ride with me, Stacy? I just need to pick your brain on a few things," Laura said confidently. But inside, she was nervous and antsy.

"Sure, no problem."

"Stacy? When you arrive at the school, let Laura get out first, and give her like twenty seconds before you exit the car. We want the cameras solely on Laura here, and no need for you or I cluttering the background," instructed Mary, as the trio gathered their coats, and walked out of the foyer of her house and onto the sidewalk. As promised, there were two black Lincoln town cars, with drivers standing outside waiting by the rear passenger door.

"Mom's already there?" she asked, but already knew the answer.

"Yup. Brought a couple of her friends, like you asked, and she'll be seated on the right side of the stage. Your notes for the rally speech are already on the podium too," said Stacy as she got into the first town car and shuffled over to the far side, grunting slightly with the effort.

"Ok, I knew you'd be on top of it. Mary? See you there,"

Laura said as she waved to Mary, who was standing, waiting for Laura to get in.

"See you there, Senator," Mary said with a grin, and Laura couldn't help by smile back.

When the door shut, she heaved a sigh of relief, and turned to her right to stare out the window. The driver got in and started the car, and they were off. Fifteen minutes to the rally. Fifteen minutes to glory, the way she saw it.

After a minute she heard Stacy put her phone away and address her.

"Ok, Laura. What's up? What did you want to go over?" she asked.

Rather than answering her right away, Laura stared out the window. It was dark, being early November, and the blocks rushed by quickly as they turned onto the Grand Central Parkway. These streets were familiar to her, as she had grown up here in Flushing. Picked food out of the dumpsters here, clawed and fought her way through the tough streets, and rose out of the depths to make something of herself. And her plan was slowly falling into place. She was one step closer to her dreams, of being in the highest office of power, where no one could tell her what to do, and she held all the control. Power, and control. That was what she craved the most. More than money, more than love. She cringed, as she thought of the text, she had received from Gale today.

You sided with a rapist, Senator.

That was it. In the end, she had decided not to respond, and simply deleted the message. She was no longer that person from a year ago, who was foolishly in love.

"What good is love? It will only abandon you, eventually," she thought bitterly. She wasn't in love with Greg, but it was a good

partnership. A means to an end. She didn't dare think about what it made her, but rather, focused on where it would get her.

"Laura?"

She turned to look at her old boss. Stacy looked much older than when she had first met her. Time had not aged her well, and although she still had that fierce, proud look on her sharp and angular face, there was a tiredness underneath her steely visage. One that only Laura could sense.

"Can you believe it?" she asked softly. "Can you believe that we're here now? On the cusp of the Senate seat. Then, I'll forge alliances and belly up to the table, make a name for myself, and make a run for the Presidency. Can you believe it? Just a poor girl from Queens," she said thoughtfully.

Stacy gave a genuine smile and nodded slowly. "It is hard to believe. But, at the same time, you're the right person. You had the grit, the determination, the intellect, the hunger and drive... you had what it takes, and you played the game well. Remember when I interviewed you all those years ago?" She waited for Laura's nod of assent. "Well, there had been no one else."

Laura raised an eyebrow in confusion. "What do you mean?"

"I told you that I had interviewed many others, with stellar pedigrees, but that was a lie. I had watched you from afar. I asked around about you, found out that you had grown up poor, hungry, and smart. That was what I was looking for. I had Larry investigate you, and from his background checks, and my careful snooping around the company with people you worked with, I was confident that you would make a great Chief of Staff someday. I chose you before you walked into the room that day."

Laura gave an appreciative groan. "So that's how Geoff had my business cards, compensation package, and everything already printed and in the folder. I always wondered about that, but he would never give in and tell me the back story."

Stacy gave a short bark of a laugh. "Ha! Always loyal, to a fault, that Geoff. Tell him I miss him."

"Tell him yourself. He'll be at the rally tonight."

Stacy smiled. "I know. Two steps ahead of you." There was a silence, and Laura turned to look back out the window. They were almost there now.

"Did you ever hear back from Larry?" asked Stacy softly. She had heard the story but had stayed out of the details.

"No. He vanished. Not sure where he is, and Samuel always asks me now and then if I want to track him down, but I always say no. Better to let sleeping dogs lie."

"How is he, this, Samuel? Can you trust him?" Stacy asked carefully. He hadn't been around during Stacy's time.

"Yes, I do. He's an extremely cautious man. I promoted him up to Larry's spot, and he's running the team now. I've expanded it too. It's a ten-man team now, instead of five. With what I made as CEO, plus other income streams, I can fund the team for quite some time. Long enough to take me to the end." Stacy nodded her approval, and her phone buzzed, so she pulled it out and checked on the text message, typing back a note immediately.

Laura continued to look out the window, the darkness flying by, and in the streetlights that shone in furtively, she could see the reflection of her face in the glass. When she saw herself in the reflection, for a moment, she wanted to drop her eyes and look away, but she couldn't. Instead, she just stared at herself, and she felt sad.

www.ingramcontent.com/pod-product-compliance
Lightning Source LLC
Chambersburg PA
CBHW030604180626
46816CB00005B/1671